MARK OF THE VOID

I0587864

AMNIE ◆ YOUNG

THE STARCHASER CHRONICLES
Volume 1

Mark
of the
Void

AMNIE ✦ YOUNG

This is a work of fiction. Names, characters, places, and incidents are a product of the author's imagination. Any similarities to people, places, or events are purely coincidental.

For permissions and inquiries, please contact the copyright owner at storiesndreams.amnie@gmail.com

eBook ISBN: 978-1-7364351-0-6

Paperback ISBN: 978-1-7364351-1-3

Hardcover ISBN: 978-1-7364351-2-0

Second edition: October 2023

Thank you to everyone who helped me achieve this dream.

CONTENTS

The air thickened. She turned to look about as her strawberry blonde bangs danced upon her eyelashes. An explosive concussion hit, throwing her aside and shattering the structures around the courtyard. Then all fell silent... everything slowed. Stillness set in, darkness crept up, and the world became hot.

Chapter 1

Last & First

"When the monsters came, she ascended through the death and devastation to save us."
~*Bhelnir colony survivor*

Her head throbbed as she became aware of her surroundings again. Pushing away a slab that had fallen on her, she raised her eyes and blinked. Everything was hazy and spinning. Her fingers skittered across her skin until she found wetness. She pulled her hand away and tried to focus on it. Blood, *damn*, she thought as she coughed away some of the dust and debris in front of her face. *Gotta get up, gotta find someone, anyone....* She began to wiggle and crawl out from under the wall that had come crashing down during... *wait, what happened?!* The dizziness began to fade and she realized her hearing was also starting to come back. More explosions, gunfire, screaming, ...there had been a fight, and it was still going on.

She stumbled on the rubble, shook her head, then took a deep breath. Closing her eyes, she focused on a word and it came out as a whisper, "Ivanigis." A burst of glittering black light erupted from her body. It coursed around her like shimmering waves. She was slender but athletic. The curves of her figure lent a gentle grace to her rich plum uniform top. The sleeves stopped just below the elbow, at which point they flared slightly to allow for maximum mobility. The bodice cut straight across her collarbone and up into a point above the left shoulder. The front panel overlapped like a double-breasted jacket and sloped downward into crisscrossed tails on the right side, held together with the Psilic Crest pin. Her matte charcoal slacks tucked into the top of her knee-high black patent leather boots. The energy churned and flowed through the maze of bands and nodes that made up the control clasp embedded into her right forearm. An armored ebony bracer wrapped around her opposite arm, enclosed by a series of metal latches on the backside.

She opened her now clear sea-green eyes. They shimmered with violet flecks of energy. She caught a glimpse of a group of strange silhouettes in the distance, towering over a huddled mass of civilians. They stood twelve... wait, no... fifteen feet tall, she estimated, hovering close to the ground like imminent death. Their metal bodies were comprised of several razor points. A central apex reached toward the sky. On either side protruded spikes, the end of which curved sharply downward, creating stationary wings. Between the wings and main crest, were smaller points. The largest of these extended out into spidery arms. The smallest points formed mace-like heads atop flexible metal tentacles. At the base of the creatures, three pointed legs formed a tripod with hinged feet. The terrified crowd huddled in the corner of a shambled building.

She broke into a run, flying over the uneven terrain with fluid grace, her steps barely disturbing the ground beneath them. As she approached a rise behind the alien attackers, she gathered the iridescent glow around her right hand and forearm. She vaulted into the air and came down upon the creature with ground shaking force. It let out a mechanical scream. The other monstrosities turned on her. She pivoted to her left and sliced upward, her arm still glimmering with power. A blade of energy flew off her fingertips and carved through the next closest one.

Continuing her turn, she loosed her firearm from its holster on her left leg and in one smooth motion, brought it to bear on another approaching to flank her. She squeezed the trigger and felt the pulse of the plasma chamber releasing a round. Bull's-eye. The shot ripped through the core of the mechanical terror, causing it to erupt in arcing electricity and showers of sparks. It fell to the ground and toppled over lifelessly.

Closing her eyes, she brought her charged hand down in front of her, curling it into a fist. She let it swing downward like the arm of a pendulum. On the rise of her fist, she abruptly stopped at shoulder height. Her eyes and hand flew opened, "Volgihr!" A thundering shock wave pushed back the forces advancing on her right. All of her focus lingered for a moment on the result of her ability. Her openness was made apparent as an enemy's beam weapon struck her left side. Her gun flew from her hand, and she faltered from the hit.

She fell to one knee and looked at the colonists behind her. The human faces all stared at her, their every hope of surviving this encounter rested on her. The seconds felt like hours. She took a deep breath in and drew upon all of her power. The shimmering energy coursed over her whole body again. Even as pain surged through her arm and shoulder, she held up her hands. The energy coursed out her palms into a partial dome around herself and the civilians. Stray tears began to form in her eyes. "Raga ami velgihr!" She screamed out. The barrier rose up like a tidal wave, expanding in all directions. The earth shook as it washed away from them, clearing the area. She released the power and collapsed. Some of the forward civilians rushed to her side to help her up. "The Psilyria saved us." She heard from the crowd. A small boy ran up to her, holding her sidearm in both hands. He held it out for her to claim. She accepted the gun and re-holstered it, giving him a grateful smile.

"Thank you," she mustered her remaining strength to steady herself. Looking to the adults, she told them, "We're not out of this yet. I need everyone to make a run for the bunker. We will need to create a defensible position before those things come back. Hurry, we don't have much time." Everyone hustled toward the settlement's central square, picking up stragglers as they moved. One of the older gentlemen in the crowd offered to assist her, but she waved him off. "I'm fine, just need a little recharge."

As the group approached the bunker, the Psilyria spotted the remnants of her squad, a ragged trio of Adepts finishing off one of the machines. She turned to the closest man and pointed at the shelter entrance. "Get everyone inside. Anyone who can shoot a firearm guards the inside of that door. Everyone else goes to the back. Create cover with any tables or crates you can move."

The man nodded, "Yes, ma'am!"

She approached the squad. The young female Adept staggered toward her to salute. "Psilyria Frost!" The Psilyria placed a hand on the girl's shoulder for a moment to stabilize her.

"Save your strength, Lena. You have all done so well. I'm very proud of you!" She hesitated, "Unfortunately, we're not out of the woods yet...."

"We can still fight, ma'am!" the taller of the two young men affirmed. The other nodded in agreement despite the fatigue showing on his face.

"I appreciate your enthusiasm, Kean," she smiled softly, "but we will need to be careful. Everyone works together. We don't know when help will come..."

The other young man interrupted, "We sent out a distress call!" Then he looked back at the ground behind them. An emergency relay lay in shambles, "We just don't know if anyone got it...," his voice trailed off as he talked.

She placed her hand on his shoulder. "Aaron, ...*good job.*" She reiterated, "The relay should have triggered the colony's broadcast system." Hope stirred in the group again. "Now, our job is gonna be simple but challenging." She looked back at the emergency bunker's door as the last few colonists shuffled through it. "We set up outside that door. Nothing gets through. Dig in and let's show them no one messes with Psicorp!" The Adepts cheered. Behind her gentle smile, doubt and fear mounted. She had never felt so empty. All of her energy had gone into that last barrier and the recharge was slow like a leaking faucet, trickling back into a reservoir.

They took up positions around the door. Psilyria Frost stepped into the bunker to examine the defenses. She spied the colonist she had given instructions to before and waved him over. He approached, rifle in hand. She spoke in a hushed tone, "When I walk out this door, you seal and barricade it. No matter what you hear, do not open this bunker for *anyone*. We will defend it as long as we can, but you have to be ready for a breach. No heroics. You hold out as long as possible. Use internal systems only. Help is on the way."

The colonist gave her a worried look and glanced at the Psicorp Adepts outside, "But...."

She stared resolutely at him. "No matter what, you keep this door sealed!" A harsh mechanical chord rang through the air. "No matter what!" She darted back out the door and listened for the seal. A wall of the machines crested the horizon beyond the colony bounds. A shadowy female figure stood in the center of the horde like a general about to lead a charge. Even from this great distance the Psilyria felt the chill of the woman's gaze crawl down her spine. The mechanical monstrosities descended into the settlement, blasting anything in their way.

"Ivanigis," the faint glow of energy returned to her body. "Now we give'em hell."

Explosions rocked the ground beneath their feet. Lena closed her eyes and drew a deep breath. The maze of nodes and wires on her shoulders began to hum. A glittering blue light flickered across her collarbones and around the core of her body. She exhaled, her breath danced into a cloud before her. She shaped the nebulous form into a large flat shield and hit it with her palms, solidifying it. The first pieces of concrete and dirt began to rain down. She directed the shield to block the projectiles.

Only a few steps away, Aaron dug his feet into the ground. His essence coursed up his legs, through his control clasp on his left thigh, up his torso and into his arms. A slab of wall arced toward the group. Aaron reached into the air and shifted his weight in a circular motion, redirecting the piece in midair before it could impact Lena's shield. Kean shaped a channel of dark green energy into a long blade extending from his right hand where his control clasp was.

The mechanical army closed in around the open area in front of the bunker. The dance began as though they had practiced it a thousand times. Lena shielding against the small debris with her shimmering blue shield, Aaron imposing his shifts in momentum on the airborne boulders and rubble, Kean's blade slicing through enemies lit up the area up with fantastical sprays of sparks and flames. The Psilyria held her energy close, creating personal body armor. She covered the area with small bursts of precision shots from her sidearm. They moved harmoniously to and fro across the battlefield. Moments slipped away from them.

The Psilyria's doubts began to fade. *Maybe we'll pull through this after all....* Just then, she glanced back toward Kean. He had opened the distance between himself and the group, creating a vulnerability. The machines encircled him before she could utter her warning. "Kean! Retreat!" She cried out, loosing a rain of shots at his attackers. He turned to see that he was surrounded. A dark shadow fell over him and two sharp legs pierced his neck between them. Blood poured from his jugular. He dropped his psionic blade, and it hit the ground, dissipating into dust before fading away. She looked away, trying to choke back tears.

"Stay close, stay focused!" She shouted to Lena and Aaron. "Tactical retreat. I want us back against the bunker. Solidify and defend." At orders, Lena began to slowly back toward the nearby wall. Another monstrosity skirted the group. As it moved to flank Lena, its clawed tentacles spun up like drill heads. An explosion showered the group in a hail of concrete fragments. Lena focused on her shield, struggling to expand it to block the projectiles. The minion behind her took advantage of her distraction and shot its spinning heads toward her torso. Aaron and Psilyria Frost flinched at the sudden spray of blood. Lena's hands dropped to her sides as she staggered in place. She stared at the drill heads in disbelief. It jerked the tentacles back, and she folded to the ground.

Aaron roared in anger. The Psilyria snapped around toward him to stop his blind reaction but before she could act a large boulder, unmitigated by his power, flew forward, crushing him beneath it. It seemed surreal to her. In the blink of an eye, she was alone. Her three charges had died like candles in the wind. She walked backward until she could not find a good footing. The towering machines began to close in on her. She trembled, and slowly looked around at Kean's empty visage, Lena's crumpled form, and the seeping red pool that was forming at the base of Aaron's boulder.

Like waves gathering strength in the storm the Psilyria's emotions churned and quaked. Loss. Fear. Rage. Doubt. Suddenly, like the rise of a tsunami, her fury broke. This wasn't supposed to happen here, not now, not ever in this sleepy little colony. She screamed, tears streaming down her face, and activated her full power. Her control clasp hummed. A piece of razor sharp scrap metal sliced through the outside of her lower right thigh, but still she did not falter. She reached over to her clasp with her left hand. The virtual interface activated, creating a holographic covering into which she sunk her fingers. She grabbed a hold and ripped. The hologram's plasma splashed on the ground in front of her, sizzling as it cooled rapidly on the rocks and dirt. The remaining interface sparked and flickered out.

7

Tears seared her face as she held up both hands to summon forth every ounce of psionic energy in her body. She pulled on every tendril of power she could sense. The very ground trembled ever so slightly at her will. Closing her eyes, she reached further and further beyond herself until she felt something strange, like tugging on fine silk. The sensation passed through her fingers. She opened her eyes in time to see her tears fall into blackness, then ripple across the glassy dark surface upon which she found herself. Her gaze wandered. She stood on the surface of a pristine black endless sea, the whole of the universe stretched out across the sky like sparkling diamonds.

"What are you doing here?" a strange resonant voice asked her. She spun around, trying to find the source. Sitting across the watery surface sat a cat-like creature staring back at her. Its body flickered through shades of dark violet and indigo. His feline form was unusual in its sharpness. His legs ended in dagger like points. His tail, ears and whiskers extended out to elegant tips. Light glowed from the narrow slits that served as his eyes.

She stared at him bewildered. "*What* are you? And where exactly is *here*?" she glanced around, keeping him in the corner of her vision.

He thought for a moment, "In your terms, I am the Nexus, the conduit through which all the psionic power in the universe flows. I am pure energy in living bonds and this is my home, the calm beyond the veil. Now," he paused, "What are you doing here?"

She looked down at her hands. "Am I dead?"

"No. In fact," he tilted his head in thought, "you are the first of your kind to have ever passed beyond the veil... intact. Peculiar." He studied her stunned contemplation. "It seems you have a strong desire for power, but not for yourself. It is a strange trait among beings of such abbreviated mortality. And such an unyielding will. Why then? Why do you crave such tremendous sums of energy?"

"I'm a failure. If I cannot protect innocents in a place of peace, then what good am I? If I cannot hold on to the precious lives left in my care, then why am I given any gifts at all? What is the point?" silent tears streamed down her face. "I don't want to be famous or all mighty, I just want to be worthwhile." Silence filled the air between them for what felt like ages.

"I am intrigued by you. I will accompany you for a time and lend you that which you seek." The Nexus's eyes flashed. The Psilyria felt heat gathering between her shoulder blades. "You may want to put your hands up again...," he suggested, "and brace yourself." She looked at him quizzically but still raised her hands. Suddenly she felt pressure against her palms. There was no time for confusion. An unseen force slammed against her hands. She felt the hum of a barrier tingling down her forearms. The force slammed against her hands again. She winced.

In that flicker of a moment, she was back. The machine before her thrashed against her barrier. That same resonant voice echoed in her mind, "I grant you... everything." The heat between her shoulder blades flared into an inferno, burning across her back. Then the tide came. Power flowed up through her like an overfilled cup. It bled off her like a delicate fog. She had never felt so full before; the barrier was effortless now. She stood upright and turned her hands back toward herself to look at them. The barrier remained strong and unwavering. She smiled and glittering purple tears streamed down her face and drifted away.

Her resolve renewed. She flicked her right wrist out, and the surrounding monstrosities flew backward with ease. "You will not harm another living being here again!" Her eyes narrowed to a glare. She reached out to the sides with both hands, gathering the very air. Her fingers swept in circles. As she raised her palms, massive vortices rose across the battlefield, drawing in all the mechanical monsters. Brilliant violet lightning sprung forth from her, arching vortex to vortex. In her left hand formed an elegant long sword. She cast her barrier back upon the shelter, encasing it completely. She brought her hands together on the hilt and waited as the first stragglers broke free of their windy shackles and advanced upon her.

She danced for an eternity, her psiblade flickering through the shattering metal visages and showers of sparks. Time drifted away from her. She began to feel the pull. Fatigue was setting in. The power coursing through her body, while not waning, was far beyond anything she had conducted before.

Suddenly, the clouds broke around the familiar silhouettes of several large ships. They descended and let loose a rain of fiery barrages all around the central shelter. The machines began to retreat. The Psilyria looked up at the chariots of her salvation and she sighed with relief. Her psiblade vanished from her hand as she let her focus go. Her eyelids grew heavy, and she collapsed. *We did it. We saved them*, she thought as she drifted out of consciousness. *We... saved... them.*

Chapter 2

Psilyria

"Despite her injuries, the patient seems to be quite resilient,
a trait that may yet bring her through to recovery.
Observation continues."
~ Patient file Psi000641

The hum of the infirmary equipment was the first sound to register in her ears. Then came the soft rustling of a person moving about. Her eyelids were still so heavy. She fought to wake up. The person in the room moved to her bedside and stood for a moment, then moved a few steps away. The Psilyria turned her head and tried to open her eyes. The figure was blurry at best.

"Captain, our guest is beginning to come around." The medic's voice was stern, yet gentle. There was a pause. Slowly, the figure came into focus as she turned away from the comm screen. The woman had a shapely silhouette and mousy brown hair, streaked with silver, that curled just below her jawline. Her fairly plain gray uniform was more functional than stylish, over which she wore a classic white lab coat. She approached the bedside again. "How are we feeling today?" She held up a small light and moved it back and forth, watching her patient's reaction.

Psilyria Frost groaned as she tried to sit up. "Light headed, ugh, ...throbbing headache. Where am I?" The doctor placed a hand on her upper chest to keep her from overexerting herself. Tapping on the adjacent monitor, the upper portion of the bed

11

raised into a slightly reclined sitting position. The room spun and wobbled. She closed her eyes and raised her hands toward her temples. Shooting pain seared through her left shoulder, giving her a moment of pause. She let her left arm drop back down to the bed.

"Take it easy. I'm Doctor Wynn Tyronis. You've been in my medbay for the last two days." The doctor rounded the end of the bed. "You were found outside the colony shelter, a little worse for wear. It seems you went through quite the ordeal." The doctor took a hold of her right elbow and held a scanner against the skin of her exposed upper arm.

Only then did the Psilyria take inventory of her appearance. She was dressed in a capped sleeve tee and loose fitting scrub-like pants. Her right leg was secured to the bed by an electronic metal cuff just above the knee. A heavy bandage covered her right forearm control clasp, but she still had her armored bracer on. She felt a sliver of relief, seeing it still buckled securely. The doctor watched. Without so much as a glance toward the bracer, she remarked, "Quite the accessory you have there. Not many people bother to have security locks on their armor."

Psilyria Frost hesitated. "It was a gift... one I dare not lose." The doctor did not reply, letting the matter drop as she turned her attention to the leg cuff. "Doc, ...if I may ask, what *is* that?" the psilyria pointed to the cuff.

"It's a nanite repair cuff. You suffered some shrapnel damage during your encounter. It required nanites to extract the debris and repair the tissue damage. The cuff keeps you from exacerbating the issue while it keeps the nanites from dispersing in your bloodstream and becoming ineffectual." Dr. Tyronis smiled. "Everyone behaves and you get better in the end." She tapped on cuff's interface. It chirped in response to her touch. Setting aside the scanner, she reached into her lab coat pocket, pulling an oval palm sized clip out. She separated the two halves, extending it into a small holographic datapad upon which she double checked the readings.

"How badly was I injured?" the psilyria tried to sit up further.

The doctor moved back to the bedside monitor to enter some adjustments, "Plasma burns on arms, shrapnel in your leg, beam lanced shoulder, some bruised bones, and extensive superficial contusions. I'd say with whatever happened down there, you're lucky to be alive. Most of it has been treated, but the more major injuries will still take some time and will remain sore for a while." She slid a small tab out of a dispenser along the wall. A thin backing on the tab peeled away, and she gently pressed it to the lower left side of her patient's neck. "That should help with the shoulder pain."

A few stray strawberry blonde hairs escaped the clip, holding her bangs from her face. She reached up to brush them back when her fingers discovered something. A coarse metal band connecting a maze of fine metal wires and nodes was fastened tightly above her temple. It curled from the right side of her forehead back into her hairline.

"That's a neural inhibitor." She closed her holopad back up and tucked it neatly in her pocket. "You were experiencing a phenomenon commonly referred to as 'running hot,' your brain activity was off the charts, dangerously so. You were at risk of burnout, so I was required to take drastic steps to bring you back into acceptable levels before any permanent damage was done. As such, you will be required to wear the inhibitor and check in with me regularly until we can establish that whatever caused this is no longer an issue. Again, you are one lucky girl."

The whoosh of the medical bay door opening interrupted them. Through it strode a tall woman flawlessly clad in the trappings of a ship captain's uniform. The olive green material was trimmed with satiny black lines and dramatically offset by her fiery red hair that swept up into a careful tangle of twists. Her fierce brown eyes exuded confidence.

At her heel followed a man of equally powerful presence. Even as tall as she was, he seemed to tower over his commanding officer. His facial features were chiseled and strong to match his muscular build. He had intense bright blue eyes and messy charcoal hair that sharply contrasted with his crisp uniformed attire. Commander stripes marked him as a man of distinction.

The Psilyria took note of the nameplate above his left breast pocket, J. Gabel. "So what happened?" she looked back to the doctor.

"We were hoping that you could tell us that." The Captain stood at attention, her feet shoulder width apart and her hands folded together behind her back. Her gaze intently fixed on the patient, "I am Captain Alex Hadarian of the ESFV Themiscyra, and this is my executive officer, Commander Jackson Gabel." She briefly gestured toward him. "You are aboard my ship. We responded to an automated distress signal from your colony, but when we arrived, we encountered a... baffling situation. We detected hostile fire and sealed bunker protocols in place so we laid down defensive bombardment, but when we landed, we found no hostile forces, a bunker filled with terrified colonists and you as the only survivor outside of the shelter. All we can get from witnesses are wild stories of monsters and magic. What can you tell us, Miss...?" Jackson folded his arms across his chest and leaned back against the wall, watching, waiting.

"Psilyria First Class Kensington Frost, Psionic Security Investigation Corp," she nodded respectfully at the captain. She thought back on the events. "Everything was normal, quiet. I remember feeling a charge in the air like a storm was coming, but before I could respond, there was an explosion. It knocked me out for... I don't know how long. When I came to, there were these machines...," she closed her eyes, trying to construct them in her mind. The neural inhibitor buzzed, and she winced.

Doctor Tyronis grabbed her scanner again and took a reading over the inhibitor. "Easy now, take your time." She stepped back and clipped the scanner to the side of the monitor, turning it away from the others in the room as she analyzed the data.

"I'd never seen them before. They're hard to describe. They were herding people together. I fought off what I could. When it was clear enough, we made a break for the shelter. The civilians went inside. I rallied what was left of my unit. We tried to hold the ground outside the bunker, but...." Tears welled up in her eyes as she pictured Kean, Aaron and Lena dying in front of her all over again.

Jackson glanced between his unwavering captain and the doctor busily tapping away on the console. He unfolded his arms and stepped forward to grab her a tissue from a nearby shelf. His eyes remained fixed on her expression as he handed it to her. She took a deep breath, fighting to remain composed. Then it came back to her, the starry black abyss, the strange talking cat and the flood of power. She paused. *Was that real? Do I tell them? No, I can't! They'll think I'm fricken' nuts.*

Captain Hadarian tilted her head slightly to the side. "What happened next?"

Kensington hesitated, "I... can't remember. It's all a blur. There was so much fighting...." She quietly prayed that the subject would not get pushed further.

"I see...," The captain paused, "Psicorp has already been contacted. Given the loss of the facilities and personnel, a re-evaluation of the local operation is in order. As of now, you have been temporarily reassigned to the Themiscyra under my command, until such a time as a proper inquiry can be conducted. Doctor, how soon can Psilyria Frost be ready for duty?"

"If she feels up to it there is no reason she shouldn't be on her feet within the next day or two. But she will be available for light duty only for the next week, *at least*. No psionics until her neural stability is re-established. I will require regular check-ins, twice a day to be safe." The doctor pushed her monitor toward the wall. "I can fit her with a mobile nanite cuff if you need her sooner."

"Get her on her feet. Commander, you will provide escort to her new quarters and have her belongings delivered. I want to see you both on the bridge in two hours. We are resuming course and mission." The captain turned on her heel and strode out of the room.

Jackson turned to the doctor. "I'll wait outside while you work. I have calls to make." Then he too, slipped out the medbay door.

Doctor Tyronis nodded to him as he left. "Well, let's get you going." She tapped a keypad to unlock a nearby drawer. It slid open, and she pulled out an elaborate metal ring. She circled back around the bed to address the fixed cuff. Again, it chirped as the doctor's thin fingers danced across the interface. Kensington shivered as a tingle spread through her leg. Doctor Tyronis directed the nanites back to a single location and commanded them to lock together. When she was done the nanite cuff released and drew back into the bed, releasing her patient. She opened the ring and slid it under Kensington's thigh, buckling it into place. The new interface hummed to life. "This is going to feel strange again." The ring cinched down on her leg and the tingle spread through it again. "Now, let's try having you stand, Miss Frost."

"Please, just call me Kensy," she swung her feet off the edge of the bed. The room spun a little. She took a deep breath and regained her bearings, then slid slowly off the edge. Her bare feet contacted the cold floor, causing her to grimace. She took inventory of how she felt. "I'm good, right leg has a little numbness, oh... that feels weird."

Doctor Tyronis smiled. "That will probably feel a bit strange as long as the nanites are working, but not to worry. I have one more thing for you." She returned to the drawer and pulled out a small folded bundle. "I want you to wear this sling until your shoulder feels better. Take it easy and I will see you later." She handed the bundle to Kensy, and they moved to the door. At the threshold, the doctor turned to Jackson, "She may still experience some dizziness, and may need your assistance. Take it slow."

Jackson nodded respectfully, "Yes Ma'am." He turned back toward Kensy. "The elevator isn't far." His expression was stoic, cold. She gestured for him to lead on and they began a silent walk to the lift. In the elevator, she leaned against one of the walls and rubbed her feet together to warm them. He glanced down and saw she had no shoes. "Your belongings and new uniforms have been sent to the quarters Captain Hadarian set aside for you. I had to go off your records, so let me know if there is a problem with any of it and I'll put in a revised requisition order."

She fidgeted, "Thanks." Silence filled the space between them. The elevator door opened, and they stepped out. The hallway was short but clearly more thoughtfully adorned than the lower floor they had come from. As they walked, she felt a moment of dizziness and stumbled, grabbing on to the back of his sleeve. She stood up and quickly let go. Her heartbeat quickened as she took a deep breath. He stopped to look down at her. "Everything okay?"

She nodded in embarrassment. "Yeah, sorry about that." The room door slid open. The room had a small sitting area in front, toward the rear a bedroom was formed by a decorative folding shade dividing the room. Off to the right, an opening indicated a private bath.

"All the crew quarters were taken and seeing as you are not a regular crewman, the Captain assigned you to the diplomatic quarters." He hesitated. "I'll just wait outside while you get

17

ready." He turned on his heel and proceeded outside. The door closed behind him. She looked around the room. Neatly folded on the end of the bed was a pile of clothes. Along the right wall was a line of crates labeled for transfer with her name scrawled across them. She opened the crate closest to her. It was clothes. She dug through it for the items she needed, then snatching the uniform off the end of the bed, she entered the bathroom.

She laid her armful across the long vanity counter top. She looked in the mirror. She was definitely a little ragged looking. Her hair laid flat against her head. She was free of the dirt and debris of the battlefield, but black and blue splotches of color peeked out from the edges of her bandages and medbay clothing. A flicker of indigo in her peripheral vision startled her, but when she turned to look, it was gone. She shook her head. *I must be losing it.*

She carefully pulled her shirt over her head, trying not to aggravate her wounded shoulder. She turned to one side in the mirror to inspect the extent of her injuries. Something appeared off. She turned further and looked back over her shoulder. A shimmer passed over the skin on her shoulder blades and then faded, revealing a sprawling pattern on her skin in an inky black. She furrowed her brow, studying it, then the realization came to her and her eyes grew wide. *It's the mark of the void. I touched the veil! It was all real!* She shuttered at the implication. *I can't... I have to get cleaned up. I don't have time for this!* She drove the thought back and focused on getting ready.

Chapter 3

Neira

*"Have you seen that badass merc we've got onboard!?!
The rumors around her are insane!! Wonder if any of them
are true..."*
~ *Crewman T. Holloway*

Commander Jackson Gabel leaned against the hallway wall, waiting. Carefully, he scraped under each of his fingernails with his knife. They weren't really dirty, but he was bored. Here he was stuck waiting for this strange new girl, woman, whatever, that he had been assigned to escort. Something ugly had happened down at the colony, but she was hiding it for any number of reasons. Not that he cared to pry, but if she was gonna keep intel from those who needed to know, that could be dangerous. He scoffed and shook his head. With his luck, he'd get stuck babysitting her.

The door whooshed open. Kensy stepped out. Her soft strawberry blonde hair was pulled up into an off-center ponytail. The simple navy blue uniform fell loosely over her figure. She had rolled up and clipped the long sleeves so that her armored bracer and control clasp bandages showed. Her left arm rested in the sling the doctor had given her. She fidgeted with the black belt that wrapped around her waist. The pants of her uniform were relaxed and slipped over the top of her boots easily. "I believe I'm ready to go. Thank you for waiting, Commander, ...Sir?" She avoided making eye contact with him. "I... uh, couldn't find my holster and sidearm in my belongings...."

He stood up straight. "They probably went to the armory for inspection. If the need arises, we'll get them back for you. The Captain is expecting us shortly." He turned to walk down the hall, glancing back over his shoulder. She looked a great deal different now. She was no longer bloodied and broken as he had found her on the battlefield or as frail and sickly looking as she had been in the medbay. Still, she held a great sadness in her eyes, even as a soft smile curled over her lips. They stopped in front of the elevator.

"I have a question," she watched the elevator panel. He turned to look at her. "How many people made it? No one ever said."

The elevator door opened. He held out his arm to allow her in first. "At last count, I believe the figures put about sixty-one percent dead or missing." He watched her reaction carefully. Water began to well up in her eyes, but she quickly blinked it away.

She gave a slight nod. "Well, I guess, at least, it wasn't more. Has anyone been able to analyze the debris from the machines I destroyed for clues as to who attacked us?" She kept her eyes on the door as the elevator moved.

"No," he said curtly.

"No?!" She looked up at him in shock. Their gazes locked for a moment, then she turned back to staring at the door. "Why, may I ask, was that not pursued?"

The elevator stopped, and the door slid open. Again, he held out his arm to allow her to disembark first. "Because there was nothing to analyze. We didn't even know the nature of the attackers until you told us. They, evidently, picked up after themselves in retreat... or disintegrated. Take your pick. We found rubble, bodies, crazed colonists and *you.*" He folded his hands behind him and walked down the bustling hall of the main deck. "Follow me. The bridge is this way."

She had to jog a few steps before she could match his long stride. The hall opened into a large open area lined with technicians busily working on their individual consoles, like a colony of bees. Kensy examined everything she could as they proceeded briskly through the room. The walls were covered in monitors, flowing with massive amounts of data streaming over them. Some showed maps, while others buzzed with equations and diagrams. On the other side of the room, they turned down another hall. Several conference rooms of varying designs lined the passage.

Ahead of them, Kensy spied a familiar figure. She was a picture of extremes; her reddish-purple hair fell past her chin in front and rose in the back. The ends flipped out into spiky layers. Runic tattoos cascaded down the left side of her face, interrupted only by a cybernetic patch covering her eye. Her lips were black as night. Her remaining amber eye was heavily lined with dark makeup. Her armor was equally as identifiable. A circular buckle sat in the middle of her chest, out from which numerous leather bands spread across her body like the tendrils of a spider's web. The bodice underneath was a vibrant yellowish orange to match her eye. It hugged her figure tightly, complimenting every curve, even under the hardened plates that covered her midsection. Crisscrossed belts hung low on her hips and sleek tight pants followed her legs down into her tall armor-plated boots. A bracer matching Kensy's wrapped around her right forearm, complimented by a fingerless glove covering her left arm up to the elbow. She stood, hands on hips, in the middle of the hallway.

She glared at Jackson, "Move along, Commander Broody. The little princess and I need to have some words."

"Cross, I've had more than enough of your BS attitude. As I said back when you first stepped on this ship, you will show me and all aboard this vessel the proper respect or so help me—." Jackson snapped at her but was stopped by Kensy gently wrapping her fingers around the crook of his elbow. Startled by

21

the touch, he looked back at her, confused. The look on her face was soft and knowing.

"If it's alright, I *would* like to talk to her." She tilted her head slightly and looked up at him.

Jackson straightened his posture; grabbing the clip on his belt, he acquiesced, "I suppose we still have a little time, but make it quick. We will not keep the Captain waiting."

The woman moved to Kensy's side and placed a hand on the small of her back, giving her a push toward the nearest conference room. The two women entered the room. Cross quickly closed the door. Tapping the adjacent control pad, she shuttered the glassy wall paneling. As she turned around, she gazed with concern at Kensy, who in turn looked down and traced the tip of her right index finger across the table top. "Hi, Neira."

"Don't 'Hi Neira' me! What's this?!" She pointed at the bandages and sling. "I don't see you for a while and you go all tragic hero on me?! You know better. What were you thinking, defending a *fortified* bunker from the *outside*? They have bunkers for that very reason, so the building protects *you*!" As Neira lectured, Kensy just returned a soft smile.

"I missed you too."

Neira gave a frustrated sigh. "Yeah, whatever.... Why do I even try? Not like you ever did listen to me." Neira put her hands back on her hips and shook her head. "Don't even try to duck me here. I'm gonna be keeping an eye on you."

Kensy snickered quietly then gave her friend a quizzical expression. "Why are you here? I thought you left the army ages ago."

"Oh, no you don't.... This is not about me," she paused. "I freelance now. I go where I want. I do what I want. We are gonna talk more about this later. Better get you to the bridge before the boy scout, out there, has a cardiac." Neira opened the door and stepped back to let Kensy pass, then followed her out of the room.

Jackson unfolded his arms and stood up from slouching against the wall. "Done?" Kensy nodded, and the trio proceeded down the hall toward the bridge. There was an awkward silence between them. Kensy could feel the electric tension between Jackson and Neira. *They must have butted heads before,* she smirked to herself. *They seem so alike. A fact, I imagine, both would contest. Better not say anything. That would be an ugly crossfire.*

They entered the bridge from the left side. Massive virtual windows covered all the forward facing walls. A sloped platform rose up in the center of the room at the apex of which the captain stood, leaning on a sterling railing overlooking her crew. Each station was surrounded by colorful panels and monitors dancing with light. The floor was a rich navy tweed carpet that softened the sound of their footfalls. Silver accents dressed the functionally stark command center with a hint of formality. A technician walked up and handed the captain a datapad before returning to his post. The captain glanced back at the trio as they entered the room.

She looked down toward the helmsman in the center of the lower level, "Mr. Threaux, the bridge is yours. Maintain course. I will be in the strategy room if you need me." She turned and proceeded toward a door in the middle rear of the bridge. Pausing before it, she passed her hand over the control panel. The door slid open, and the captain waved in the group. One by one, they filed in, circling a large table in the center of the room. Captain Hadarian activated the table, causing it to light up. A three-dimensional representation of the system they were on course to popped up.

"We are headed here," she zoomed the view in on one of the planets, "This is Morwhex Four. Three days ago, the colony went black. No comms, no distress signals, no traffic. In light of the recent attack on Bhelnir," she glanced toward Kensy, "We believe that it may have suffered a similar attack. Morwhex is primarily a mining colony with no military presence to speak of. If they were attacked, it is likely they did not fare well."

Neira's gaze narrowed as she analyzed the projection, "What exactly were they mining?"

"Daecellyon. Highly unstable, very difficult to extract, extremely complex to process and invaluable to the space flight industry for propulsion tech." The captain zoomed the map in on the colony. "The colony is located in a difficult area. As such, the Themiscyra will remain in atmosphere, airborne above the site in the event that defensive bombardment is needed as it was on Bhelnir. Gabel, you will be in charge of the landing teams. We will be sending five shuttles down so you will have enough manpower to conduct a thorough search of the area. Ms. Frost, you will accompany Commander Gabel to the surface. You will be serving as a consultant. Inform the Commander of anything you find that can confirm or deny our theory of attack by the enemy you encountered on Bhelnir. You are not to engage in combat under any circumstance."

The captain looked back to Neira. "Miss Cross, considering your presence in this room, I assume you wish to join the landing party. I suppose that is your prerogative, given our continued agreement, but on the ground you will follow any and all orders from Commander Gabel. Is that understood?!"

"As long as it does not interfere with my own investigation." Neira crossed her arms.

Captain Hadarian looked between them. "You two *will* work this out. I will not have anyone's attitude jeopardizing my operations again." Both Neira and Jackson looked for a moment as if their elementary school principal was scolding them. "This mission is dangerous enough as it is, walking in blind to a potential powder keg. Get your heads on straight or I will personally lock you both in the brig." Awkward silence filled the room as Captain Hadarian drilled them both with her icy gaze.

"Ma'am," Kensy piped up softly, "will I be allowed a firearm?"

The captain returned to her businesslike demeanor, "No, Commander Gabel will assign you a protection detail on the ground. If combat ensues, you will retreat to one of the landing crafts. You are a non-combatant until Doctor Tyronis clears you otherwise." Turning her attention back to the map once again, she highlighted the landing route. "The colony is built around a spire between these two crags. There should be an access elevator here. If, for some reason, the elevator is inaccessible, schematics show an alternative route through this cavern, but we have reports that the area recently sustained some damage from seismic activity. The condition of this entrance is unknown. Even if it is clear, the stability could be suspect."

"Permission to take Kellar down with the ground team for seismic analysis?" Gabel inquired.

"Permission granted. Any further concerns?" she looked at each of them. "No? Then I suggest you all ready yourselves. We will be arriving shortly. Dismissed."

Chapter 4

Alpha Team

"Whatever you've heard about Alpha, believe it, right down to the bubble gum."
~ *Crewman B. Benson*

Kensy fidgeted uneasily in her seat on the shuttle. She felt powerless, helpless going on this mission without her psionic abilities or firearms. It was not an idea that sat well with her, especially if this mission went as expected. She shuddered at the thought of facing the machines that had killed her squad back on Bhelnir, unarmed and unarmored. Her Psicorp armor, while light, was lined with reflexive fibers to protect the wearer without inhibiting their abilities. The uniform they had her wearing now was little more than standard issue clothing. The only protection she still had was the metal bracer that covered her left forearm.

"Breathe," a deep voice interrupted her contemplation. She looked up, startled, and was met with a warm smirk and deep brown eyes. He moved past her and slipped into the pilot's seat. "Focusing that hard on your anxiety isn't good for anyone." He began to check his instruments. He paused and looked back around the edge of his seat. "Why don't you come up here? You can be my co-pilot."

Kensy sheepishly shuffled into the adjacent forward facing seat, "It's just—."

"That you're not used to going into a potential combat zone as a civy?" he interrupted. "I got the brief. I'm sure it'll be fine. Gabel's a good man. He'll make sure you're safe. And if things do get hairy, you just race back to the shuttle. I'll be here." He leaned toward her and whispered, "and I have a small armory stashed in here." Kensy giggled. "That's more like it. Gabel said you had a pretty smile."

Kensy blushed, "He said what?"

"Well, I suppose his exact words were 'She's not so bad if she smiles.' Which, believe me, is high praise coming from him." The pilot winked at her. Kensy felt her cheeks flush even more red. "By the way, my name's Daniel Bryden, shuttle and fighter pilot extraordinaire." He held his right hand out for her to shake. She took his hand. His grip was firm but not crushing.

"Kensy Frost, temporarily broken Psicorp officer," she tapped the inhibitor gently.

He made a grimacing face. "Oh, that's brutal. Don't worry, you'll be back to psyching everyone out in no time," he jested. Kensy relaxed in her seat, her anxiety melted away. Slowly, soldiers in their combat gear shambled into the transport and took seats lining the sides of the small craft, hushed murmurs passing between them.

Suddenly, all went silent as Commander Gabel entered the shuttle. His steps were heavy from the weight of his combat exosuit. He walked straight to the front of the craft and placed a hand on each pilot's seat. He leaned forward, glancing at Kensy before turning to Daniel. "Ready us for launch." Kensy stared at her hands to avoid looking at him. He stood and turned around. "Rasken. Shane. Reily. Hensley. You are on protection detail, guarding our *guest*." He nodded toward Kensy.

"Yes, Mr. Boss-man," a gruff woman's voice spoke up, followed by the pop of bubblegum. He shook his head.

Neira slipped between the shuttle doors as they slid closed. "Leaving without me?!" She glared at Jackson. Her outfit was much the same as before, with the addition of armored shoulder guards, a plated skirt and a partial visor that covered her good eye and wrapped back around her right ear. Clipped to her shoulders, two long, ornately carved blades curved in overlapping arcs down her spine stretching almost to the back of her knees.

"You're late, you get left behind," he snapped back.

"Doesn't count if you're early," she retorted. Kensy shook her head and looked at Daniel. He rolled his eyes in a mocking gesture without saying a word.

The shuttle bay doors began to open. Daniel fired up the engines, and the transport jarred as it left the docking clamp. Below them stretched a rocky red expanse. They glided through the air with ease. Jackson activated his communicator, "Shuttles two though five head down and establish a perimeter at the landing site. Bryden, do a quick once around. I want a survey of the area."

"Yes, sir!" Daniel deftly navigated the shuttle around the outcroppings and central spire of the colony base. Aside from the high winds sweeping dust across the peaks, there was no movement. "Not reading any energy emissions from the main facility. Only thing I'm getting is way down there and really faint... a drilling rig, maybe?"

"That's good. Take us in." Jackson directed. Daniel gently guided the shuttle into formation with the others. The doors slid open, and they were hit with a wall of dust. The soldiers closed their helmet visors and disembarked. Daniel leaned forward, opening a small console in the dash. He pulled out a pair of protective glasses and tossed them in Kensy's lap. She unfolded the stems and slipped them over her face as she rose out of her seat. The wind was hotter than she had imagined.

Much to her surprise, as she moved away from the shuttle, her guard detail took up formation around her. Jackson's voice came over the comm again. She cupped her hands over her ears so she could hear her ear piece better, "This mission is strictly reconnaissance. We go in, find out why they went dark and go from there. Teams Delta and Echo maintain perimeter, eyes up for hostiles. Charlie, I want you right here at the shuttles. Kellar, take Bravo to the secondary entrance and get on those surveys. Alpha, you're with me. We head for the facility core. Once we get power up, Charlie and Echo teams will join us for full sweep."

Kensy watched as the teams each dispersed into their designated directions. Jackson waved her and the rest of Alpha toward the elevator. Neira walked off to the side of the company, scanning the landscape suspiciously. Kensy noticed her stretching and flexing her fingers uneasily, readying herself to draw her blades at a moment's notice. As they neared the entrance, Rasken rushed forward to examine the control panel. She carefully pried the front of the panel off and began fussing with the wires.

Neira moved near Jackson and yelled over the howling wind, "I don't like this. Way too open." She turned away without waiting for validation.

He looked down at Rasken. "You got it or are we going the long way in?"

She slid her visor open and pulled out her chewing gum, "Don't get your panties in a twist, ...sir!" She wrapped two of the wires together and smashed the gum around them. Before closing the panel, she flipped open a port in her suit's arm and touched another exposed wire to it. Sparks flew as the panel came to life. She shoved it back into the housing and hit the open command, sliding the doors to the large elevator wide. "All aboard," she bowed.

Jackson, seeing the size of the elevator car's interior, turned toward the soldiers, not of Kensy's protection detail, "Go join Charlie for now. We'll regroup later. The rest of you load up." They entered the lift, and the doors closed behind them. Reily and Hensley opened their visors. Rasken popped another piece of gum in her mouth. Jackson glanced between Kensy and his helmet's heads-up display. Subtly, he scrolled through the programs on his suit's computer until at last he found it. A passive tracking protocol perfect for keeping tabs on his mysterious new charge. The roar of wind grew muffled as the elevator slowly crawled down below the cliff face. The rig groaned around them.

Hensley prodded at Rasken. "You sure we ain't gonna get stuck in this rat trap?"

She punched his shoulder, "Hey I just hot-wired a freaking elevator with *my gum*. Show some respect, Private! It'll get us down...," her voice trailed off, "...one way or another." She smirked as Hensley punched back.

Shane opened his visor. "Knock it off, you guys. You're gonna jinx—." Before he could finish his sentence, the elevator shuddered and shifted to one side. The emergency brakes squealed as they jarred the car to a stop. Kensy slipped and fell against the wall, striking her head on the safety railing. Neira grabbed the railing with one hand and braced herself against the low side wall as not to fall on Kensy.

Jackson reached back with his rifle, clipping it to the dorsal plating of his armor. He grabbed for the doors and began to pry them apart. "Hensley, help me get these doors open!" he barked over his shoulder. Hensley struggled to pull himself up to the opposite side of the door. Once in position, he activated the magnetic clamps on his boots to keep him from sliding. He clutched the panel opposite Jackson and they pulled with all their strength. Slowly, the doors groaned as they gave way. Jackson leaned out and looked around.

Hensley snickered, "Hey LT. I think you're gonna need more gum to fix this."

Jackson ignored the comedy commentary, slowly inching himself out the door. He looked back at Hensley. "I'm gonna jump. You got the door?" Hensley repositioned himself in the doorway, bracing the opening with his body, and nodded. Jackson took a deep breath and leapt, disappearing out of sight. There was a thud below them. "Looks like it's about ten feet down." Jackson yelled back up at the car. "You're gonna have to jump down one at a time."

Shane moved to one side of the doorway. "Ladies first."

Hensley grunted, "Why you lookin' at Rasken? That ain't no lady, it's a bubblegum addict."

Rasken ducked under Hensley's arms and snapped a bubble at him before jumping down. Reily carefully shuffled through the opening and followed suit. The elevator creaked and shifted further. Shane held out his hand for Neira. "Come on, you're next."

Neira shook her head. "No, take Princess next," she said, nodding at Kensy. "She knocked her head. Might need some help." Shane slid over next to her. He grabbed Kensy's right arm and hoisted her to her feet. Slowly, they pushed toward Hensley. The car jarred again.

"Hurry up!" Jackson shouted.

Shane looked at Kensy. "You're gonna have to get out there and jump." She nodded and worked her way under Hensley's arms. She stood on the edge of the car and looked down. She could see Jackson, Rasken and Reily below, waiting expectantly.

Suddenly, everything began to spin again. She wobbled and fell from the car with a shriek. Jackson lunged forward, snatching Kensy out of the air. They teetered on the edge of the shaft for a brief moment. Rasken and Reily each caught one of his armor's hip plates and jerked the pair backward. Kensy landed on top of Jackson, bewildered. She scrambled to get off of him as Neira dove from the ledge, cartwheeling to her feet gracefully. Shane dropped down behind her and extended a hand to help Jackson up. Neira moved up just behind Jackson and whispered, "Not bad. Just know that if you had dropped her, I'da killed ya."

Hensley reached out for one of the support beams and fussed to get a good hold on it. He deactivated the hold on his boots and swung out the door. Clumsily, his grip gave way, bringing him crashing to the ground. He stood up and dusted himself off. Reily shook her head, "Graceful, really graceful there, Hensley."

The last of the elevator's cables snapped. It made a hideous clamor as it cantered the rest of the way off its railings. The car tumbled and crashed into darkness below. Jackson turned on his comm, "This is Alpha team, the elevator is a no-go. Repeat main entrance is not an option. All teams stand by for further instructions."

Daniel's familiar voice echoed back over the comm, "Roger that, Commander. Standing by."

Jackson flipped on his helmet lights and pulled his rifle from its clip. "Now that that's out of the way, let's check this place out and get the hell outta Dodge." Each soldier flipped on their suit lights to survey the area. The group found themselves on a service platform above the main colony level.

Neira pulled her blades off her back. She firmly gripped the handles near the lower ends of the weapons. They curved up her arms like beautiful razor wings. She approached a nearby staircase and cautiously began down the steps. Reily followed close behind. "Are those authentic Ausk-Chelkai?" she inquired as she scanned the area down the sights of her rifle. "It's rare to see a real pair, rarer still to see someone who knows how to wield them."

"Well, keep your eyes open. This is gonna be a big day for you," Neira snidely responded.

Kensy headed down the stairs at Jackson's heel, flanked by Shane and Hensley. She grasped at the railing. Jackson glanced back at her, but she held up her hand to stop him from speaking. "I'm fine. Just a little dizzy, that's all." He grimaced and turned back to the path ahead. Lieutenant Rasken brought up the rear, keeping a close watch on the area behind them.

The various structures of the colony were as still as a ghost town. Together, the crew crept warily through the passages between buildings. The closer they came to the colony center, the more signs of distress were evident. The edges of scorched cuts crumbled like seeping wounds, dark red sprays spattered the walls and walkways, mining drills and picks lay sundered into pieces across the ground. Kensy stopped and knelt down by one of the doorways. Jackson turned toward her, "What do you got?"

She stood and held out her hand. A small pile of dark green dust covered her palm. "What do you suppose this is?" She pointed to the area around them. "It only seems to be in pockets in the most devastated areas. I didn't see any of it where we came in." She rubbed it between her fingers, letting it fall back to the ground. "Feels like sand."

Jackson waved at Rasken, Shane and Hensley, "Spread out. Look for more of this stuff. Grab samples. We'll take them back to the ship for analysis." The three soldiers dispersed. Kensy trailed behind the commander as they pushed further into the colony. The ground grew uneven and treacherous to walk across.

"They must have set something off in here, like back on Bhelnir. I remember the ground was like this outside the bunker." Kensy knelt down to study the ground again. She glanced down at her left pant leg. Something was wrong. She tugged at it gently and the fabric began to tear. Some of the green dust had gotten on her. She tried to brush it away, but it seemed to move on its own. She pinched some of it between her fingers to examine it more closely. A tingle began in her fingertips. "No, no! Get it off me!" She began to panic.

Jackson stopped moving and pivoted back to face her. "What's the issue?"

She gave him a frightened look. "The dust... it's nanites! They're reacting to the cuff. Somehow, it activated them!" She raked at her clothing, trying to get it off. Jackson quickly stowed his rifle and flipped out his pocketknife. He glanced up at her before sliding the blade under the cloth and ripping. He severed the pant leg just above the cuff. The two of them wrenched on the cuff, but it would not let go. Frustrated, he stood back up and contemplated his options.

"Well, don't just stand there! How do we get that thing off her?!" Neira lashed out.

Jackson reached for his pistol. He looked Kensy straight in the eyes. "Look away." She turned her head to the side, and he fired. The cuff fell to the ground, flickered, and shut down. They all breathed a sigh of relief as the dust nanites fell away, dormant again. A slow trail of blood began to run down the outside of her leg. He knelt down again, this time to inspect the injury. "I nicked you. That thing was on tighter than I thought, and it doesn't look like your shrapnel wounds are closed up all the way yet."

Neira sheathed her blades and stepped forward, holding out a hand to each of them. "Gabel, gimme your knife. Kensy, shirt now!" she snapped her fingers, "Come on, you two, make it snappy!" A crash startled the group.

Reily held up her hand. "Don't worry about it. I'll go check it out." She gave Jackson a nod, then stalked off to find the source of the noise. Neira snapped her fingers again impatiently. Jackson flipped the knife over, catching it by the blade for Neira to take a hold of the handle. Kensy slipped her sling off and quietly unbuttoned her shirt, revealing the square necked black tank-top she wore underneath. She slipped one arm off at a time, being careful of her still tender shoulder. Keeping her back to the wall, she handed the shirt to Neira, who proceeded to slice through it, removing the bottom several inches of material in strips. She tossed the remainder of the shirt back at Kensy. She handed the scraps and knife back to Jackson.

He tied the pieces end to end and went to work, carefully bandaging Kensy's injured leg. She gingerly slipped the remnant of her shirt back on, knotting the jagged sides together like a vest. Jackson grabbed her sling off the ground where it had fallen and stood to help her with it. She placed her hand on the sling to take it from him. Their fingers touched. "Thank you," she whispered. He let go of the sling and turned away, pulling his rifle again. She folded the sling and tucked it in her belt. Neira gave her a disapproving scowl. "Don't give me that look. I'm already handicapped enough down here. I'll deal with the pain... lets go."

Kensy took a step and paused. The rubble at her feet began to jitter and rumble. The ground split below the soles of her boots. She felt herself begin to fall. She reached toward the light as it disappeared above her. The thundering darkness swallowed everything as she closed her eyes.

Chapter 5
Dust

"Environments can add a number of complications to shuttle operations. Be sure to take these variables into account when operating the vehicle under potentially hazardous or hostile conditions."
~ ATC209 Field Maintenance Manual

Daniel reclined in his pilot's seat, boots on the dash, intently watching the scanner sweeps on his monitor. It had been a while since Commander Gabel had called up to the landing teams to tell them of the elevator malfunction. Radio silence on a mission like this always made him uneasy. But he kept a calm smile on his face. He hummed some of his favorite songs to break the silence. Gently, he tapped on the combat medals that adorned his console in time with the tunes. There was a quick shuffle outside the shuttle's open door. Kellar stumbled up to one of the soldiers. "This is wrong. It's all wrong."

A hushed snicker passed through some of the other troops milling about as Kellar juggled his holopads and sensor modules. The soldier sighed and rolled his eyes. "What's the problem, Kellar?"

"The instruments are all reading erratically, like we're in the middle of a seismic event right now!" Kellar tried holding up a pertinent datapad, only to scatter other parts and pieces across the ground. He fumbled and shuffled and fumbled some more.

"Did you make sure they worked before you dragged all this crap down from the ship?" The soldier brushed him off and walked away. The company grew uneasy as more time slipped by without feedback from Alpha Team. Tensions grew as the rust-colored dust swirled around them, carried on the furious Morwhexian wind.

Daniel looked back at his console, his attention drawn by a low rattling sound. The medallions began to skitter against the shuttle dashboard. Daniel stopped humming and put his feet down. He adjusted the sensor settings and activated another sweep. The data fed back alarming results. He shouted toward his open door, "Everyone load up NOW!" Kellar and the closest soldiers shoved his gear in overhand and climbed in. Daniel turned on his communicator, "This is Lieutenant Bryden, ordering emergency evac of all landing crews. Repeat, immediate evacuation of all ground units! Landing zone has gone hot. ESFV Themiscyra, this is Shore Party, requesting hangar protocol three-seven-nine." Daniel fired up the shuttle's engines. He looked out to make sure all personnel were readying for departure.

A voice came over the comm. "This is Themiscyra. Doors are open and waiting, Shore Party."

Kellar scrambled to secure his equipment in the shuttle's cargo racks. The ground began to shake noticeably. Daniel looked back to his passengers. "Everyone on board?" He glanced once more outside. Shuttle Three's engines were not lit up and several soldiers muddled about trying to work on it. Daniel called over to their pilot, "Shuttle Three, why are your men not on board?" There was no response. He called again, "Shuttle Three, collect your crew and launch immediately." Daniel turned up his thrusters, pushing off the quaking ground. His hands danced across the controls as he brought the shuttle to a hovering position.

Shuttle Five launched toward the Themiscyra without issue. Shuttle Two's thrusters sputtered, but she rose cautiously off the ground and began to climb, leaving Three and Four still ground side. The pilot of Shuttle Four called to Daniel, "Lieutenant, we're stalled out. This dust storm has killed my intake converters. Requesting assistance." Daniel maneuvered Shuttle One into position to launch tow cables at the stalled out transport.

He called back to Four, "Positioning for tow assist. Four, can you see the problem with Three from your position?"

"It appears, sir, that he's having the same problem. I think they're trying to fix it." She paused, "Still trying to fire engines, sir. Ready for tow anytime...," The ground beneath the dead shuttles began to crack and rumble. Daniel launched the cables. One of the magnetic clamps bounced off the shuttle's housing and began to whip wildly in the wind. "Confirming only one tow cable lock on, sir."

"Dammit," he cursed at the console. "Can you launch a counter tow?"

There was a brief pause as she assessed the situation. "No sir, the wind's too strong. Can't send anyone out to secure the line either. It's too dangerous." The peak that had served as their landing platform began to crumble away. There was another pause. "Cut us loose, sir," she calmly replied.

"I can't do that, pilot." He fought against the controls, trying to lift the shuttle off the ridge. Shuttle Three sputtered to life and began to ascend as the ground beneath it disappeared. As it passed Daniel's shuttle, the engine's lights flickered and died. The transport tumbled and wobbled downward, pitching its passengers out the open side door as it plummeted into the black sinkhole.

One of Daniel's passenger soldiers dug out a cable catch hook from one of the utility compartments. "I think I can secure the other cable, Sir! I'm going out there." Before Daniel could protest, the soldier opened the hatch, dropped a line and began to lower himself toward the other shuttle. He reached out with his hook, desperately struggling to capture the loose tow cable. The tethered shuttles lurched violently as the final remnants of their landing platform deteriorated. Shuttle Four began to sway and twist in the weather. Daniel began to steer toward another rise, slowly limping along. "I'm gonna try to set you down safely and we'll get that cable hooked on. Just hang in there."

The pilot of Shuttle Four looked up at the cable, keeping them from falling. "Call your man back now! The cable's—," A deafening pop pierced the air. Daniel's shuttle jerked sharply upward as the tow cable surrendered to the weight of the crippled transport. Screams filled the comm for a moment, then only static. He regained control of his craft and shook his head in frustration.

"Lieutenant, report," the captain's voice called over the comm.

Daniel grimaced, "Shuttle One reporting in, Captain. Landing zone is gone. Casualties include Transports Three, Four, and all crew therein." The comm was still as everyone listening waited for the response.

Finally, the captain came back on, "Understood, Lieutenant. Return to Themiscyra for debrief and situational assessment immediately." The soldiers in the shuttle watched breathlessly. Without a word, he turned the shuttle to climb toward the open hangar doors above them. The shuttle slipped in, tightly butted up alongside the hangar floor. Daniel turned in his chair, "Everyone out now!" The soldiers began to bail out of the shuttle.

As Kellar shuffled toward the door, he stopped and looked at Daniel, his arms still heavily laden with equipment, "Why didn't you dock? What are you going to do?" His glasses slid awkwardly down his nose, adding to his blundering turmoil.

Daniel turned back to his console. "I'm going back for Alpha Team." He punched in new scanning parameters and readied the shuttle systems for another departure.

"But there's no way...," Kellar tried to reason. Alpha Team was likely underground when the quake hit and without a word from them, their inevitable fate presented a bleak prognosis. Returning for them seemed a fool's errand, even for a pilot as skilled as Daniel. The environment had already claimed so many with the malfunctions.

"Get out now!" Daniel yelled back at him.

Kellar, startled by his pilot's bitter retaliation, scrambled to disembark. "But the captain—," he pleaded from the hangar floor.

"...can take it up with her XO when I bring him back!" Daniel interjected. He activated the shuttle door, sealing it in Kellar's face. The shuttle pulled away from the hangar and dove toward the colony site. The winds lashed against the metallic hull with unbridled fury. He adjusted the drive output to compensate. The shuttle glided deftly below what was left of the cliff face. He danced her to and fro through the crags and shifting rocks. He set his comm to block any calls that might divert his attention from the new mission at hand. The scanners hummed as they searched the site for any signs of life.

Daniel had repeatedly seen Commander Gabel pull teams out of the fire before. There was no reason in his mind to believe that this situation should be any different. He knew one thing for sure: he was not going to be the one to leave anyone behind. Whenever Alpha Team was ready for pick up, he'd be there waiting....

Chapter 6

One More Step

"Themiscyra to Alpha Team,
*please respond Alpha... *static*..."*
~ Communications Officer P. Sagan

Kensy rolled her head to one side and blinked away the haziness that loomed over her. She looked around warily. The quake had dropped her into a large cavernous hall. She had ended up draped over the crest of a large rocky outcropping, her back slightly arched along the curve of the stone. It was dark save for the blueish-green bolts of glowing ore that streaked the walls and ceiling. She laid there for a moment, taking mental inventory of her condition. Her body was stiff and soreness radiated from her left shoulder and bandaged leg. Slowly, she crawled to her feet. She was a little wobbly for the first few steps as she moved toward the cave-in. The way down had sealed itself with rubble and boulders. She wasn't going to be getting out the same way she had arrived.

A gleam in the corner of her vision distracted her. She caught sight of Neira's blades glinting back at her from over a rocky drift. "Neira!" forgetting her own pain, Kensy ran toward her friend. Neira lay on her side, unconscious, her legs partially buried in the dirt and rocks. Kensy began digging her boots out with nothing but bare hands. Dust filled her lungs, making her cough as she worked to free Neira. When enough had been scrapped aside, she grabbed Neira under the arms and pulled with all the strength she could muster.

The sensation of being dragged began to rouse Neira. As she came around, she clumsily grabbed at Kensy's arms in recognition. Kensy stopped, kneeling down to support her. Neira winced and pressed her palms against her throbbing forehead. "Ugh! What happened?"

Kensy shook her head. "Cave in, quake... something." She pointed up at the rock slide. Neira tapped and flicked the side of her visor, trying to get it working again. The holographic overlay on it blinked to life. "We're gonna need another way out," Kensy sighed. Suddenly it occurred to her, Jackson had only been a few meters ahead of her when the tremors began. He should be close by as well. She stood up and scanned the area.

Neira glanced up at her. "What's wrong?"

"Jackson... uh, Commander Gabel... he should have fallen down with us!" Kensy headed back to where she had awoken. Neira got up and slowly followed, using her visor to scan the area. They came to a small drop-off. There, about four feet below, sprawled out facedown, was a motionless armored figure still clutching his rifle with one hand. Kensy jumped down and rushed to his side. She pried the gun from his fingers and rolled him on to his back. The visor of his helmet had shattered, covering his face in numerous small bloody cuts. She searched for a way to unclasp his helmet, but to no avail.

Neira made her way down a nearby incline. "Well, scanner says he's still breathing," she crouched down and removed his helmet. "Check his armor's chest and leg compartments for anything we can use to clean him up. We'll probably have to use the remainder of your over shirt."

Kensy hesitated for a moment, contemplating the mark on her back. So far, she had managed to keep from revealing it to anyone, but that would be impossible with only the tank-top to cover it. She nodded, "Yeah, okay." Kensy stared at his face for a long moment, then began searching through his armor. She came across an old-fashioned flask tucked in his right side outer leg pocket. The top unscrewed, and she held it up to her nose.

"Alcohol?" Neira inquired.

Kensy shook her head. "No, odorless. Probably water."

Neira shrugged, "It'll do." She snatched the flask and held her hand out for the shirt. Kensy unknotted the bottom of it and slipped it off. She moved closer to his head and propped him up on her lap. Very gently, she began to pluck the shards of glass from his skin, tossing them aside. Neira turned the shirt inside out and wetted it with water from the flask. She set it on his chest plate to clean his face with. Neira stood. "I'm gonna scout around while you get him cleaned up, ...see if I can find us a way out." She turned and walked back up the incline.

Kensy looked at her dirty hands and reached for the flask resting on the ground beside him. She held her hands away from him and tried to clean them with as little of the water as she could. When the worst of it was gone, she grabbed the shirt. Wadding it into a ball, she carefully wiped the blood and remaining shards away. Every so often, she moved to another portion of the cloth when one spot would become too saturated. "Come on, wake up," she whispered. He did not respond. Looking up to the glowing rivers of light in the rocks, she let her thoughts drift. *How did I get here? My life has got to be the greatest cosmic joke of all time. I can shape energy with my mind, but I can't escape this chaos.* She shook her head and ran the damp shirt across his brow again. He groaned. Her eyes widened, "Commander?" She sighed with relief as he opened his eyes. "Oh, thank the stars! Are you okay?" She helped him sit up.

Jackson tilted his head to one side, popping the joints in his neck as he stretched. "Yeah, I think so...," His gaze fell on the pile of bloodied glass shards beside his smashed visor. He picked the helmet to examine the damage. "Great...." He pulled the comm piece from the inside, pitched the rest aside, and rose to his feet. Furrowing his brow, he scanned the surroundings.

Glancing back down at Kensy, he realized her fingers were streaked with blood from the rag in her hands. He turned back toward her and knelt down. He took the rag from her and discarded it. Grabbing his flask from the ground beside her, he sprinkled the last of the water over her hands and wiped them clean with a handkerchief from another compartment in his armor. He slipped the flask back where it belonged and helped her to her feet. She felt her face flush red. He lifted her chin to look at him. "Thank you." He withdrew his hand and gave her a gracious nod. They stood there in the glistening cavern, only silence between them.

Kensy looked away first. "Neira is somewhere around here. She said she was gonna scout for a way out." Her eyes searched for a diversion to diffuse the tension between them.

"Here, hold on to this just in case." Jackson grabbed her left elbow so he could tie the handkerchief around her arm above the bracer. He picked up his rifle and took a deep breath. "Now let's find Cross and get out of here." He slipped the helmet's communicator in his ear. "This is Commander Gabel. Is anyone on this frequency?"

Neira slid down a rocky slope on the other side of the cavern. "Don't bother. My scanner's picking up all kinds of metals in the walls. The signals are just getting bounced." She sauntered up to the pair. Kensy took a step back, making sure her back was facing away from the others. The knowledge of the mark haunted her thoughts. She would have to be very careful if she wanted to keep it her little secret.

"Find anything useful?" Jackson examined their surroundings.

Neira shook her head, "Not this way, it's all dead ends and collapsed tunnels. I think that's the next path to check." She pointed down the hall. The walls sloped inward, creating a narrow passage. "I'll take point since you're down a helmet." Jackson gave her an approving nod.

He turned to allow Kensy to walk ahead of him, but she refused. "Oh, no. You're the one with the gun. If we run into something down here, you're better equipped to deal with it. By all means, go right on ahead." She waved him on. He paused in contemplation. Pulling his pistol from its holster, he offered it to her. "Thanks," she accepted the firearm, and they began a cautious march down the tunnel.

"Their operations must not have gotten this far down. There is a ton of this stuff in these tunnels." Neira gestured toward the glowing veins of ore. "Considering the volatility of this stuff and the concentrations we're seeing down here, I'm surprised that quake wasn't any worse." They crept through the passage, one foot in front of the other, analyzing every crack and fissure.

"You mean that's daecellyon ore? It's prettier than I had imagined." Kensy replied in awe. They approached a fork in the tunnel. Neira held up a closed fist to signal the others to stop. She activated her visor's holographic interface projection. Her hands danced through the data as she evaluated the readings.

Jackson stepped up next to her. "Two directions. What kind of choice are we looking at here?"

Neira brought up her terrain scan and overlaid the relevant information. "To the right, we have more of this: winding cave with lots of ore lighting it up. Nominal sound readings and no apparent life forms detected. The left side, however, is giving me some trouble." A perplexed look washed over her face as she tried to translate the readings. "The ore concentration is much lower, so less light, but getting intermittent bursts of some kind of sonic disturbance. Nothing constant, like a working rig, but definitely something there. And getting something else... of indeterminate origins. Not life signs, or at least not any life form I've ever seen. Can't pinpoint it. The metals in the cave are still wreaking havoc on my sensors. Would have to be a lot closer to get a better analysis." She collapsed the interface down.

"This just might be what we came here to find, but we're not exactly at full squad strength." Jackson debated, "That could be dangerous," he sighed, "It could also be our best chance to get out of here." Neira and Jackson stood quietly, contemplating the options.

Kensy watched their faces for a moment. *They both know which way we need to go, but they're hesitant to go that way... because of me. They must think I'm a liability. Of course, I'm a liability, a psionic with no powers, but we have to get out of here. If that's the way out, we have to take it!* She looked down at the pistol in her hand. Steeling her resolve, she ejected the clip to check her ammunition count. Her guardians looked back at her as she tapped the clip back into the gun with the palm of her opposite hand. "So, left it is. Let's go." She gave them a determined stare.

Neira rolled her eye and pulled her blades from her back. "Visiri activate." The fine mesh of lines that covered her patch began to glow, casting a golden light wherever she looked. She began down the left tunnel. Jackson shook his head and moved to follow Neira. Kensy again brought up the rear, smiling to herself. *They really are so alike.* The tunnel floor steepened as they trudged along. They were climbing, hopefully, toward the surface.

Suddenly the group was hit by a wall of wicked stench. Kensy gagged. "Holy hell, what is that?!" She stopped in her tracks, overwhelmed by the smell.

Jackson swiveled around to face her. "Cover your nose and mouth with the handkerchief. It might help. And stay close." She unknotted the cloth and held it up to her face. It was still damp from Jackson cleaning her hands off, and it still smelled like him. She took slight comfort in his scent. He raised his rifle to look down the sights. He and Neira exchanged glances.

They both recognized that gut-wrenching odor as the unmistakable reek of death. As the tunnel broke into another cavern, they moved up side-by-side to cover the room.

Kensy gasped at the sight before her. Dropping the pistol, she clamped her hands tightly over her own mouth to stifle a scream. Tears welled up as she stared at the atrocity before them, unable to avert her eyes. The bodies hung limply from mechanical collars scattered across the ceiling. Energy sporadically leapt out of the bodies along the wires and tubes toward a central point. Their eyeless visages leered hauntingly at nothingness.

Kensy staggered backward and her feet slipped out from underneath her, breaking her gaze. Jackson reached out and clutched her left arm. He hoisted her to her feet. Pain seared through her shoulder, but her attention was stolen away again. She tried to shrink away from him, but his grip held firm. "Frost! Get a hold of yourself!" He whispered a yell at her. She raised a shaky finger toward the perimeter of the room. He followed the line of her focus.

Against the rock face, clawed into the walls, hung the barbed silhouettes of the Subjugators, looming over the demise of the Morwhex colonists and miners. "Bhelnir?" She silently nodded in affirmation, casting her eyes downward. Neira dimmed the glow of her eye patch. The mechanical monstrosities remained motionless. Jackson clenched his jaw, surveying the landscape of the room. Neira waved at him to redirect his attention. She gestured to a ramp on the opposite wall. It climbed toward a hole in the ceiling. They nodded in agreement. He pulled Kensy close and whispered in her ear. "We're gonna very quietly cross the middle of the cave. There's a ramp there. We're gonna go up it and try to climb out of the room from there. Do you think you can do that?" She nodded again, *yes,* and reached for the fallen handgun.

Neira slowly sheathed her blades to free her hands. Carefully, she pulled two sets of hardened rings from her belt.

She slid the knuckle weapons over her fingers as she stepped cautiously away from the doorway, ducking under the dangling feet of the colonists. She searched for any sign of movement, but none came. Glancing back to the others, she gave the okay. Jackson gave Kensy a push and turned to face behind them. He kept his eyes on the machines, moving slowly backward as he scanned back and forth across the rear of the room.

Kensy held her arms close, pistol in one hand, handkerchief in the other. Chills ran rampant through her body as she moved. She stared at the ground as she crept across the room, trying to block out the surrounding horrors. Kean, Aaron, and Lena's faces flashed through her mind. Tears poured silently from her eyes despite her best efforts to focus on the march across the room. *One more step, just one more step,* she repeated over and over. She tried to force all other thoughts and images from her mind. The only thing that mattered right now was taking that next step. For her, the ramp up on the other side couldn't be close enough soon enough. *One more step....*

As they cleared the field of bodies, Kensy closed her eyes and took a deep breath through the balled up cloth in her hand. Neira gave her an understanding glance. For the first time in ages, Kensy saw the flicker of fear behind her friend's eye, though her demeanor did not betray her to such feelings. The three of them moved quickly and quietly up to the opening at the top of the ramp.

Neira removed her knuckle knives and nested her fingers together to grant Jackson a boost up into the opening. He lifted himself up and disappeared out of sight for a moment. Kensy turned her eyes back to the center of the room, taking in the devastation one last time. Jackson laid down beside the opening and reached down for Neira's hand. She climbed over the edge with his aid, then it was Kensy's turn. She reached up with her right arm, wrapping her fingers around his arm. He gripped her forearm just above the bandage and lifted. As

Kensy's shoulders cleared the opening, Neira too, stepped into help.

Finally, they were out of that horrid room. Kensy shivered one last time, then pushed aside the feeling. It had never occurred to her before why those machines would want to herd the colonists together. She had just assumed it was to kill them more efficiently, but this? ...what was this? Nothing was making sense anymore. "Lets get out of here," she whispered. A warm breeze whipped past them as if beckoning them onward.

Chapter 7

Reunion

"We're gonna die on this rock.... fucking Morwhex."
~ Ensign Kaitlyn "Kait" Reily

Relief washed over the group as they caught sight of the metal framed stairway leading up in front of them. "I don't think I have ever been so glad to see stairs in my entire life," Neira jested. Jackson cracked a hint of a smile and nodded in agreement. Kensy chuckled weakly as she slumped down on the bottom step and leaned backward on her elbows. The walls of the caverns they were in now were spotted with work lights tethered together with twists of cables and chords.

Jackson glanced down at her. "How are the injuries?"

She shrugged, then winced. "Still there, still not going to hold us up. Just needed to sit for a sec." She stood and dusted some of the dirt from her clothes. She stepped to the side. "I'm good now. Lead on, Commander." She looked away, unconsciously rubbing her bandaged shoulder.

"You really should put your sling back on." He gave her a disapproving look.

Realizing that she was fussing with the injury, she stuffed her right hand in her pocket. "You can lock me in the damn medbay when we get back to the ship. I'm not putting it back on." She fidgeted uncomfortably as her mind raced through a million subjects at once. Lingering amongst the myriad of fleeting thoughts was the mark on her back. Neira and Jackson still hadn't seen it. *Would they even know what it was? Neira knows I would never get a tattoo, but Jackson...* her internal inquiry was abruptly interrupted.

"Are you two done flirting yet?" Neira glared at the both of them.

"We are not—!" Kensy took a deep breath to choke back the embarrassment. "Look, we've been down here for hours at least. Everyone's tired. Let's just keep moving. The sooner we are back in the air, the better. For all of us...," she let her voice trail off. Neira walked between them and up the stairs.

Kensy motioned for Jackson to go next. He gave her an odd look. "Maybe you should—."

She stopped him, "No! Just...." She searched for an excuse. "Listen, I just feel better being in the back. So just go." She stared at the ground to avoid looking at him. He shook his head at her and began up the stairs.

At the top, they came to a suspended walkway that disappeared into one of the walls. Neira stepped aside to let Jackson take the lead. She spun around to face Kensy, "What's with you—?" A noise ahead of them stopped everyone in their tracks. Jackson held a finger up to his lips to motion for the girls to stay quiet. Slowly, he brought his rifle up to his shoulder and looked down the sights as he approached a bend in the path. He counted to three silently, then snapped around the corner to face the intruder. There, in a mirrored pose, stood Lieutenant Rasken.

"Commander? Geez, I almost shot your head off!" She dropped her gun to her side. Jackson relaxed his stance and motioned for Neira and Kensy to approach. "I heard a ruckus and came to check it out. No offense, but we pretty much assumed you were toast in that cave-in." Rasken slumped against the side railing, obviously relieved. Her armor was badly scraped up and dinged. A large gash extended across her left side, caked with the dark red tinge of dried blood, and like Jackson, she was missing her helmet. Several of the plates showed stress fractures through the dirt and smudges.

"Rasken, you look like shit. What happened?" the commander pointed at the gash.

She lifted her arm to look at it. "Oh, that... rough landing. When the quake hit, my fall was broken by a mining drill." She shrugged it off. "Come on, I'll take you to the others." She reluctantly stood back up and started down the tunnel.

"The others?" Neira questioned.

"Reily, Shane and Hensley. We managed to find each other, but... well, it'll be easier to explain things back at the group," she explained over her shoulder. Rasken led the party through the tunnels back to a maze of ladders and scaffolding until, at long last, they arrived at the remnants of the colony. Only pieces of half a dozen structures remained standing. Above, they could see where the colony had originally stood. Rebar and twisted beams protruded from the crumbling edges. Metal walkways drooped from their anchorings. The crags of the canyon walls had fallen in, closing off the sky. The work lights on the walls flickered.

As they approached the rest of Alpha, one thing was apparent: the past few hours had been a trial for everyone. Reily perched on one of the broken walls, rifle in hand. She nodded to the group as they approached, but did not lower her gun as she scanned the area for trouble. Her unarmored figure looked almost fragile with how snugly her tank top and leggings hugged her wiry frame. They ducked under a partially collapsed door frame. Inside, Shane sat holding his right arm tight against his body, the skin around his shoulder and upper arm was blackened by injury. Beside him lay Hensley, staring at the ceiling, clenching his teeth. Hensley gave a weak salutation. "Hey, Boss-man."

Jackson jogged over to them to assess their conditions. He found one of Hensley's legs smashed between two sizable boulders that had evidently come through the wall. Rasken walked up behind him. "We're pretty sure his leg's broken, but since we don't have a working scanner among us, we can't tell if it's safe to extract him. We decided to set up around him and wait for help, but comms aren't picking up anything. Themiscyra probably thinks we're all dead. Kinda surprised we're not...." She slumped down on the ground beside Shane.

"I'll take a look. Just give me a few minutes to take some readings," Neira said as she moved up close to Hensley. With a wave of her hands, the scanner in her visor hummed to life again. Hensley writhed in pain. She glared at him. "Hold still, unless you'd rather I just field amputate it. Hey Gabel, got any sedatives on you?"

"How'd you and Reily end up without armor?" Jackson shot a look at Shane as he searched his armor for any supplies that could help.

Shane fidgeted. "I got caught between some mining equipment and the rocks. LT and Reily found me, but we couldn't get my armor unstuck. I had to shed it to get free. Even then, it was... a challenge to break loose." Kensy gazed down at her folded up sling in contemplation.

Reily leapt down from her perch, "I had to abandon my armor cause it got infested with that nanite dust stuff you found. Didn't know it until they ate through one of the energy cells and killed my suit's sensor system." She watched Neira and Jackson for a moment. "There's something else you need to see, sir." Rasken nodded and moved to the watch post. Jackson pulled a small zippered case from one of his suit's compartments and handed it to Neira.

Standing back up, he looked over his shoulder at Reily. "What is it?" She beckoned for him to follow. Kensy pulled the sling from her belt and handed it to Shane with a forced smile. He unfolded it and looked up at her questioningly.

"You need it more than I do." She knelt down to help him slide his arm into the sleeve. He flinched as she pulled the shoulder strap over his head. "Sorry." Her fingers fussed with the adjustment buckle as she watched Jackson and Reily slip through a gap in the rocks out of the corner of her vision.

When she was sufficiently satisfied that Shane's arm was secured, she took a deep breath and inched her way back from the group. While everyone else was distracted, she ducked into the crevasse to follow Jackson. The path descended slightly as it left the colony grounds. Her curiosity tugged at the back of her mind. What did they find? They were too high up to have run into the captured colonists.

A bright light illuminated the far end of the passage. She hastened her steps. A massive chasm lay open before her at the end of the passage. Jackson shot a quick glance her way. There stood a massive open reactor. Energy oozed off it, arching into brilliant prominences. The air held an intense charge that tingled over Kensy's skin. "It feels just like...."

"Bhelnir." Jackson finished her sentence.

"I got some readings on it before I lost my suit. It's building up a charge. I estimated we only had an hour, maybe two at best. Certainly a whole lot less now." Reily shifted all her weight to one foot as she leaned back against the wall.

"Before what?" Kensy gave her a confused look.

"Before it detonates." Reily stared at the core, mesmerized by its brilliant light show.

The walls of the chasm began to crackle in response. The walls here were streaked more intensely with the daecellyon ore than anything they had seen before. "We have to get everyone out of here! What are we waiting for?!" Kensy turned to Jackson.

He simply shook his head, "Impossible. We'll never outrun it. Between the size of that thing, and the volume of ore in here.... this thing could nuke the entire region. If the Themiscyra is still in atmo, she won't even be safe." Frustration and anger burned in his eyes. Kensy looked back at the bomb, her thoughts racing again. Suddenly she darted back into the passage and rushed back toward the group. "Frost!" Jackson yelled after her.

She burst out of the opening and staggered to a stop in front of the others. The sense of defeat was visible in Rasken, Shane, and Hensley's faces. She recognized that now. They had all resigned themselves to this bleak end. Neira looked up at her questioningly. Jackson and Reily emerged behind her. Kensy turned back around to face him. "I'm not giving up yet! There has to be a way!" She gave him a pleading gaze.

"What's going on?" Neira stepped toward them, confused by the exchange.

"There's a massive bomb down there that's about to go off. I'm not going to just lie down and die! I didn't survive hell and back for *this*!" Kensy ranted at Jackson.

Neira watched for a moment, observing the stalemate between Kensy and Jackson. "Well, how about instead of a stare down, someone helps me dislodge Hensley from the rocks?! *Then* we can worry about the next course of action." Reily and Jackson looked to her skeptically. "Jackson, help me shift this boulder, then Reily yards his dumb-ass out from underneath." They hesitated. "Come on! Snap to! We're on the clock here." She snapped her fingers at them. Jackson shook his head as he moved to the far side of Hensley. "One, two, three...."

Reily sat Hensley up and crouched behind him so she could wrap her arms around his ribs. The rock slowly gave in to the force behind Neira and Jackson's push. Reily pulled as hard as she could muster; then, with an abrupt lurch, she and Hensley flew backward on to the rubble behind her. Hensley cried out in pain for a moment. The adrenaline sped the medicine Neira had administered to him through his system, and he settled back down.

Static buzzed over the communicators. A faint voice could be made out through the crackling. Jackson pressed his comm piece to his ear. "This is Commander Gabel. Do you read? Please respond!" He paced back and forth. The static fuzzed out and all was quiet again. Jackson grimaced and punched a nearby rock in dismay. A thunderous boom rang out above them. Dirt began to rain down. Kensy raised her arm to shield her face as she looked up. Sky peaked through the dirt as an opening formed overhead. Two more blasts widened the hole.

The hum of a shuttle's thrusters resonated through the air as Daniel's voice came over the comm. "This is Shuttle One calling Alpha Team." The transport descended and scanned the area for movement.

"This is Alpha Team. It's about damn time Bryden. What took you so long?" Jackson cracked the slightest hint of a smile. He turned back to his team. "Pack it up! We're getting out of here." Hope stirred again amongst the group, save for Reily. She looked back at the crack in the wall, fear still filling her cold gray eyes. Daniel brought the shuttle down near the rubble and opened the side door. Reily and Jackson helped Hensley to his feet. Slowly, everyone loaded on to the shuttle.

Neira could see tumultuous thoughts stirring in Kensy's contemplative expression. "Move along, Princess. We have a shuttle to catch." Kensy turned her eyes toward her friend and nodded. Quietly, she waited for Neira to board the shuttle. Thoughts still churned over and over in her mind as she stood before the open shuttle door. *We'll never outrun it.* Jackson's words echoed in her ears. *I grant you... everything.* She recalled the resonant voice of the Nexus and the flickering figure that had been at the edge of her vision in her quarters on the ship. She took a slow, deep breath. "Kensy?" Jackson's attention was drawn by the concern in Neira's voice. Kensy wrapped her fingers tips around the neural inhibitor and ripped. "What are you doing?" Neira shouted at her.

Kensy raised a barrier across the open door to stop her. "Daniel, I need a favor... protect them." She turned off her comm and enveloped the shuttle in her barrier. "Nexus, I need your help," she called out. Jackson and Neira beat against the barrier in protest. The vibrant, feline figure appeared next to her.

"I'm here," he replied calmly, looking up at her. "I have been here the whole time."

She smiled at him. "I have to save them, all of them."

Nexus peered into her thoughts, reviewing the situation. "I see, then we have our work cut out for us." He leapt up to her shoulder like a bolt of lightning. "We can't shield the bomb from exploding, but we may be able to deflect the brunt of the blast with barriers." Behind them in the cavern, a crackling sound arose. Charged air erupted from the passage. "We'll need a better vantage point." The mark on her back began to gather heat. Tendrils of psionic power sprung out of her back, searing through the tank top and bandages.

"Ivanigis!" she breathed. The wrap on her control clasp disintegrated as the violet-black glow coursed over her body. She crouched. Power filled her, bolstering her will. She pushed off the ground, gracefully flying through the air like a brilliant comet. Arching through the air and out of the cavern, she stood and scanned the horizon for the Themiscyra. It wasn't far away. The shuttle rocketed out of the hole and came alongside her. Jackson beckoned at her through the barrier covered door way.

She turned her comm back on for a moment. "Everything will be all right. Return to the ship." She gave him a disarming smile. He acquiesced and talked back over his shoulder at his pilot. The shuttle climbed skyward and vanished into the hangar bay.

Kensy looked to Nexus. "Shall we hitch a lift?" She bolted for the end of the rocky shelf and sprung off the end. The tendrils from her back formed into ethereal wings that lifted her into the sky. She reached up with one hand, extending a channel of power out to grab an edge on the main ship. She swung from it, arching over the prow to land on the top of the Themiscyra. "Can we use the ship's shield capacitors to extend the barrier?" she asked Nexus.

He leapt down. "Yes, I think that might do nicely."

Chapter 8

Determination

"While her talents are considerable, it is Psilyria Frost's unwavering compassion and drive to protect that truly set her apart."
~ note of commendation
Site Lead C. Pacey

As the shuttle cleared the hangar doors, the barrier dropped. Daniel swooped toward the hangar floor before heading to the docking clamp. As he neared the ground, Jackson leapt from the open door, followed by Neira. She tucked into a roll and sprung back up onto her feet. They both sprinted for the nearest lift. Kensy's voice echoed over the comm. "This is Psilyria Frost calling Themiscyra. Please activate your shields immediately."

"This is Captain Hadarian. What is going on? Explain yourself!" the captain barked back at her.

Jackson pressed his hand against the side of his ear. "Just do it! I'll explain later!" Neira impatiently tapped her foot as they waited for the elevator car. She spied an emergency ladder running up the outer wall and made a break for it. Jackson turned to look her direction. "Engineering, I need someone on schematics. Give me the fastest route topside!"

"I've got ya, Gabel. Searching routes from hangar bay to topside access hatch...." The lift doors opened. "Get on. I'll run an express bypass." Jackson stepped into the car. The doors closed, and he staggered as the elevator began rapidly ascending. The lights of the floors flashed by. "Okay, when the doors open, step out and head right. At the second branch, you'll see a short hallway to the left. At the end is a bulkhead to a maintenance tube. Should be a ladder in there that leads up to a repair station airlock." The elevator jarred to a stop, and the doors opened with a ding. Jackson sprinted down the right passage.

"Commander, report!" the captain ordered.

"No time, Ma'am. There is about to be a massive explosion ground-side. All hands, brace for impact!" He rounded the second corner. The bulkhead slid open as he approached. The emergency alarms blared overhead, accompanied by pulsing red lights. Jackson ducked into the access tunnel and began to climb. He crested the top of the ladder into the alcove that housed the repair drones and equipment. He grabbed a tether bundle and breather mask from a shelf. "Allen, open the airlock!" The outer door unsealed with a whoosh. Jackson wrapped the mask over his nose and mouth as he pushed against the released hatch.

The wind caught the door and jerked it out of his fingers. He clawed his way out against the bulldozing gusts. Neira called to him, "I can't get out there. The bulkhead won't open." She hesitated, "Bring her back, Gabel!"

"I intend to." He lifted an arm to protect his eyes from the wind. In the center of the ship she stood, her eyes closed, hands extended out with palms up. A purplish fog poured from her hands and trickled across the hull of the ship. It eddied around the shield capacitors before spreading out further across the ship. Kensy reached out with her senses, gradually pushing the barrier further out. Jackson activated his magnetic boots and trudged toward her.

"You shouldn't be out here," she responded without opening her eyes as he approached. "I have to focus." She cast a wave of energy rippling in all directions. The ship was larger than she had originally estimated. Her struggle showed on her

59

face as she concentrated on covering every inch without weakening the structure.

The ground below rumbled. "We have to get inside!" he yelled over the wind.

"I can't." She looked back at him. "You, yourself, said we'll never outrun it. I can do something about it! I can... no, I have to do this!" Her sea-green eyes glittered with flecks of violet energy. A beam of blueish-green energy erupted from the ground. It struck near the back edge of the ship, rocking it to the side. Kensy and Jackson stumbled apart but remained on their feet. He stepped toward her. She waved her hands through the air in sweeping motions as she reinforced the barrier near the impact site.

Jackson moved up behind her, locking his boots onto the plating. He wrapped the tether around them both and grabbed her waist firmly with both hands. She gave him a confused look. "If you're determined to do this, then I'm going to do my job. Focus on your hocus-pocus. I'll keep us from falling." He fortified the joints on his armor, effectively anchoring them both to the rocking ship. Kensy smiled to herself and turned her focus back to the barrier. The energy tendrils from her back weaved through his armor and into the nooks and crannies of the hull. Shock waves shook the ship violently, but they remained steadfast.

Rocks and dirt churned chaotically around the central beam of the bomb, pelting everything in their way. Kensy closed her eyes to help her focus. The air became unusually still for a moment. *The main blast must be about to happen,* she realized. "Ivani raga khiran!" Her words echoed through the barrier, infusing it with tremendous power. She pushed aside her fatigue and braced for the oncoming blast. It began as a low rumble, gathering strength as it grew. The very air around them trembled. Blinding light filled the sky as the energy of the explosion broke.

The barrier fluctuated under the stress of the blast. Periodic beams ruptured through the shields and tore into the ship. Kensy tried to choke the openings closed as she fought against the torrent. The explosion coursed through the web of subterranean caverns, sending debris flying as it ripped the earth open. Like the battle on Bhelnir, time began to slip away from Kensy. She focused on holding on to her barrier. The figures of her adepts flashed in her thoughts. "Lend me your strength," She whispered to the faces adrift in her memories.

"It is yours," her guardian whispered back. The ship shuddered beneath them, but her barrier did not waiver. She felt the wash of the final shock wave as it passed them. The pressure on the barrier lessened. The glow around her body faded, her hands trembled, and she let them fall to her sides, exhausted.

Jackson released the tether and locks on his armor, then scooped her up in his arms. She did not resist. He walked back to the open hatch. She wrapped her arms around his neck as he descended into the opening. Once inside, he slumped against one of the walls, Kensy leaning against him. "Allen, you still there? The outer hatch can now be secured." Jackson called over the radio.

"Roger that," the door slowly closed and sealed. Chatter ensued over their comms as damage reports began to pour in. Kensy pulled her ear piece out and nodded off in his arms. He looked down at her. *Who is this girl?* He brushed her bangs from her face. *What have I gotten myself into? Looking after her is no simple task but, ...there is something about her. Guess at least I won't be getting bored around her.* He shook his head and stared up at the ceiling, lost in thought.

Chapter 9

Brace for Impact

"Hell hath no fury like Captain Hadarian on a bad day."
~~I'm sure as hell not giving you my name~~
~ Anonymous Crewman

Kensy turned her head to the side and slowly opened her eyes. The light in the room was soft, like the bed beneath her. The muffled voices of two men and a woman echoed just beyond her view. She could hear the strain of forced tolerance in their voices as they spoke in turn. She smiled and listened for a few minutes, just lying there. As she tried to sit up, she was surprised by the wooziness and pain. An unsolicited groan escaped her lips. The voices stopped. A woman's footsteps approached. She swung her feet off the edge of the bed and composed herself.

Neira passed through the privacy field. Kensy looked up with a cheery expression, "Hey, I must have dosed off. Did I miss anything?" She gave a slight chuckle. "I guess I better get cleaned up," she looked down at her ragged, torn uniform, "Can't walk around the ship like this. Someone might mistake me for a homeless person."

"Everything okay?" Neira inquired suspiciously.

"Of course!" she nodded with a smile.

Neira gave her a skeptical sigh and turned her gaze in the direction of the sitting area. "Guess I'll leave you to it. When you are done getting ready, you have an audience lingering about out here."

"I'll be right out. Definitely gonna have to shower first." Kensy did not falter in her facade as she dismissed her friend. Neira passed back out of the field and struck up conversation anew with Kensy's guests. Kensy bit her lip as she stood. Glancing back at the bed, she noticed blood on the turned down sheets. She lightly touched her shoulder. The bandage was no longer providing the pressure or containment she needed. She wiped her fingers on her clothes, getting them as clean as she could, and pulled the covers up to make the bed over the stain. It would have to be dealt with later. She moved to her crates beside the bathroom door and pulled out an arm full of items.

She dumped them across the floor and countertop, looking for a solution. With the pieces she needed set aside, Kensy began carefully pulling her clothes from her wounds. She stripped down and turned on the shower. The warm water felt fantastic on her sore muscles but stung her shoulder like a thousand knives. Despite that, she closed her eyes and let it soak in for a few moments. She finished washing up and slipped out of the shower, wrapping herself in a nearby towel.

She wadded up a piece of cloth and held it tight against the front of her shoulder wound. With her opposite hand, she wrapped a stocking like a bandage around the area, keeping it tight. She tied off the ends and fussed until it was of a satisfactorily low profile that could be concealed under her shirt. Piece by piece she dressed, trying to keep from vocalizing the pain in her shoulder. *Doc will want to see me later. I'll talk to her about it then. No sense in worrying anyone else over this.*

She reached for a brush with her right hand. For the first time, she examined the unbandaged control clasp. Small dark burns spotted the skin between the nodes and bands. The back of her thumb had a light spray pattern extending from her wrist. It had never occurred to her what would happen as a consequence of ripping her clasp interface apart. *One more scar*, she thought, *one more reminder.* She sighed and grabbed the brush. Carefully, she swept up her hair, affixing it with a simple metal clip into her traditional off-center ponytail.

She gathered up her mess of clothes, discarding the bloodied uniform in a nearby trash receptacle. Everything else she tossed into her moving crate. As she stepped toward the sitting room, the privacy screen deactivated, opening up the room. Her guests stood to greet her. Jackson Gabel was once again in his stately officer's uniform. The cuts on his face were clean and mostly closed up. Only a few small, faint red lines remained on his left cheekbone. A small split extended down from his lower lip; however, he still was quite handsome, even with his usual broody expression.

Daniel gave her a soft smile and nod. It was the first time she had seen him outside of the pilot's seat. He stood a few inches shorter than Jackson, but still surpassed Neira's stature. He too was dressed in the officer's grab with slight variation. Pins and badges marked him as a seasoned combat pilot and lieutenant.

"I hope you are feeling better, Miss Frost," He cordially greeted her.

"Right as rain," she replied.

"Well, not to darken your happy little rain cloud, but we have a standing summons to meet with the Captain as soon as you are up to it." Daniel informed her. Playing cards lay strewn across the coffee table. Evidently, they had been here for a while, passing the time. *Etra Vas, Neira, must have goaded them into playing. She loves that game.*

She glanced down and gave an acknowledging nod. "I understand." *The Captain's gonna have questions. What if I can't answer them? I've probably gone and gotten everyone in trouble. What if someone got killed because I chose to barrier the ship instead of helping it escape?! Could I have tried harder?* She looked up toward Jackson with a gentle grin, "Shall we go then? Wouldn't want to keep her waiting."

Jackson and Daniel headed for the door, leaving Neira lingering behind. She began picking up the cards. "Not sure how I managed to fly under her radar, but I think I'll use this opportunity to make myself scarce." Kensy shook her head and waved as she followed her escort out of the room. The door whooshed shut behind the trio.

Kensy's mind raced with questions and scenario outcomes, but she remained quiet as they proceeded down the hall. Daniel matched his stride to Kensy's. "I heard things got pretty rough down there. Are you doing alright?" He seemed to pry ever so gently into Kensy's thoughts.

"I'm fine... really," she assured him as they stepped into the waiting elevator. He smirked knowingly. "What?" she glanced at him skeptically.

He shook his head, "Nothing. If you don't want to talk about it, that's fine. Just know that if you ever do want to talk about it, I'm sure you could find someone who wouldn't mind listening." He shot an incredulous look out of the corner of his eye at Jackson, who was actively ignoring the both of them. Daniel shrugged, dismissing the conversation.

The elevator dinged, the doors opened, and Jackson took point, walking with purpose down the corridors toward the bridge. Kensy struggled to keep pace with him. Daniel followed on her heels with little effort. *He probably could have easily matched Jackson's stride if he had wished,* she noted.

More people filled the command level than had last time. They buzzed up and down the halls, chattering about repairs and estimates. The atmosphere hummed chaotically. Tension could be felt in the air as technicians scurried about. There was no time for Kensy to take it all in.

A young looking female crewman accidentally walked into Jackson as she studied her datapad with a singular focus. "So sorry. Sir!" she collected herself and stepped aside so the trio could proceed. "On your way to see the captain?" She glanced questioningly toward her executive officer. He nodded to affirm as he stepped past her. She gave a nervous smile, "Brace for impact, Sir." She tilted her head down and walked expeditiously in the opposite direction. Confused by the comment, Kensy's eyes darted between her escorts.

Jackson drew a sharp breath and shook his head. Shooting a sideways glance toward Daniel and Kensy, he sarcastically commented. "This should be fun," he straightened his stance. "Captain's in a mood."

They stepped on to the bridge. The Captain shouted orders over the top of the bustle, directing her underlings with a curt confidence and clarity. She turned toward the trio, her piercing gaze shooting past everyone between them. She simply pointed at her strategy room at the rear of the bridge and they filed in silently. She entered the room, her posture rigid. The door closed sharply, causing Kensy to flinch slightly.

"What does the word INSUBORDINATION mean to you three? I would like an explanation of how each of you felt it so necessary to disobey direct commands, not once, but nearly continuously, for the duration of this mission!" The captain tossed a pair of datapads into the center of the table and slammed her hands down. "This was supposed to be a recon and potentially a rescue mission.

"Instead... I have a hotshot pilot who ignores protocol and dumps passengers out in a fury to go fly some rogue rescue *against my orders*. I have a XO who disappears, arms a non-combatant *against my orders*, and then promptly begins giving orders, and refuses to give his commander much needed information in a crisis situation. And last but not least, I have a non-combatant who all out *disregards* the explicit mandates given by both the medical officer and myself, engaging in direct combat and potentially endangering not only herself but the entire crew of the ship she has *just* been reassigned to.

"Never before have I had officers under my command engage in such blatantly foolish, reckless and utterly irrational behavior. The engineering team is tasked to capacity fixing hull breaches and critical systems. External sensors are fried, effectively blinding us to our surroundings. We are dead in the water, so to speak, in a potentially hostile environment. And the reports you two turned in...." She pointed to Jackson and Daniel, "...read more like fantasy novels than mission analyses. What am I supposed to do with this crap?!" She crossed her arms and stared them down.

Silence filled the room as no one dared speak against the captain. The seconds crept by. She sighed, "I suppose in light of the outcome of this whole ordeal, I could grant some leniency. But this kind of behavior will not be tolerated any further. Do I make myself *perfectly* clear?!" All three nodded in agreement. "Now, we still have a lot to deal with. Bryden, get down to the hangar with the loss of shuttles, I will need a complete re-assessment of our remaining vehicles, gear, and tactical capabilities." Daniel saluted the captain and ducked out of the room.

"Now, ...Miss Frost." The captain faced back toward Kensy. "You should know that your little stunt was *reasonably* effective. We suffered no further fatalities. However, the structural damage is significant and a large portion of the crew have reported injuries. The most severe of which have Doctor Tyronis and her staff fully occupied. You *will* be expected to report to her *immediately* when she summons you. Until then, you are to stay out of trouble and out of the way while we work on repairs." She waved Kensy away, leaving only Jackson to face her remaining reprisal. Kensy quietly hoped the tide of reprimands was subsiding for his sake as she walked out the door.

Chapter 10

Questions

"... and confessions."

Kensy leaned against the observation deck windowsill, staring out at the starry night sky. The rest of the crew bustled about the corridors and damaged areas of the ship, leaving this part of the ship unoccupied. She took a deep breath and soaked in the silence. Her thoughts drifted listlessly through memories of days past. She was so bemused that the soft footfalls behind her escaped notice. He watched her for a moment before clearing his throat to draw her attention. She turned, startled by the noise. "Sorry, didn't mean to scare you," he apologized. "Mind if I join you?"

A soft smile curled across her lips. "By all means, after all, it is your ship. I mean... well, ...you know what I mean." She fussed nervously with the hem of her loose fitting black shirt. "I hope I didn't get you into too much trouble back there with the captain," as she looked away.

"Nah," Jackson moved to the window beside her and leaned his left shoulder against it, staring out at the sky. "We did what we had to. The captain understands that." He hesitated. "Actually, I didn't come here because of that. I was looking for you. I... need to apologize."

Kensy gave him a confused look. "Why...?"

He held up a hand to stop her question. "When I found you on Bhelnir, I dismissed your survival as... a fluke. Then, when I met you in the medbay, I resented you for withholding potentially valuable intel. I thought you would jeopardize the mission. The thought even crossed my mind that you may have been at fault for at least part of the deaths back on Bhelnir. I realize now that none of that is true. After what we saw down there...."

Kensy cast her eyes down. "You're not as wrong as you think. I held my unit outside of the bunker on purpose. They died because I demanded that they stand and fight instead of retreating per regulation. It was so important at that moment, but now... it haunts me." Tears welled up in her eyes. "And then I did jeopardize everything when I let fear of those stupid things paralyze me in that cave. I should be the one apologizing, not you." She looked up at him with her glittering, sea-green eyes.

"How about we call it even and start over then?" He cracked a smile, secretly hoping it would help dry her eyes.

She nodded with a chuckle. "Yeah, I think I can handle that. In fact...." She used the cuff of her right sleeve to wipe her tears away. "I'd like that. So, what now, Commander?"

He grimaced. "Just call me Jack, or Jackson."

She smiled back at him, "Only if you call me Kensy instead of Miss Frost."

"Deal." He turned to lean his back against the window. "I have another admission to make. While you were out, I had some downtime, so I snooped through your file."

She stepped back from the window and held her hands behind her back. Slowly, she swayed in place. "Was there anything in there of interest to you?" Silently she braced for oncoming questions.

Again, he hesitated. "It said you were a ward of the state...."

"Ah, yes," she recalled a moment long past. Her gaze wandered toward the looming stars beyond the window. She drew in a slow, deep breath before replying, "I was rescued from a drifting pod by a passing freighter, along with one other girl, Ellise Neru." She fidgeted. "I don't even know how long we had been lost. The only thing we knew was that we were alone. They nursed us back to health and dropped us off at a nearby military station. We were just kids, about 10 years old I think, and no known parents so we became wards of the state. Since we both had... *talents*," she lifted her clasped arm, "they sent us to the Psicorp Academy as soon as we were able. It's been eons since I thought about that. Seems like forever ago." She scuffed the sole of her right boot across the floor.

Reflexively, he asked, "What happened to your families?" Her eyes grew cold and distant. "I don't know."

"I'm sorry. I shouldn't have pried." He bit at his lower lip, "If you don't mind... how did you meet Neira? You two seem to have quite the history." Her demeanor visibly relaxed as the subject changed and she let slip a modest laugh.

"Ellise and I met Neira on our first post-graduation assignment. We had been sentenced, sorry—stationed, to this tiny little research outpost in the boonies, Alpha Bael. We were supposed to be providing protection for the brain-trust they had there, but most of the time we just seemed to be in the way. Neira was the most energetic, mischievous army grunt we had ever met. She could always find new ways to get us all in trouble."

"We are talking about the same Neira Cross here, right?" he gave her a confused scowl.

Kensy chuckled. "Yes. Back then, she was incorrigible. We had so much fun! But unfortunately, that also meant that no one took us seriously when it counted." Her expression faded to sorrowful remembrance. "One day while we were out trekking beyond the outpost grounds, we stumbled onto a pirate base camp. We eavesdropped long enough to find out that they were planning an attack to seize the research. We beat feet back to the others to warn them, but no one listened. So we did the only thing we could think of.... We locked everyone we could inside and set an ambush for the pirates. They came ready for a war. We were *under* prepared."

"What happened?"

"At first, we tried to fight them all off. There were so few soldiers with us, we really didn't stand a chance. They surged past us, blasting in doors and gunning down anyone who tried to stop them. Ellise went after the grenades on one of the guys we had actually managed to take down. She said if we couldn't save the outpost, it would be better to keep them from getting it. She was never very good with barriers though, and they dropped her.

"I pulled her back to Neira and covered us with a deflection field, kinda like I did with the ship only on a whole lot smaller scale. Anyway, Neira managed to patch her up, but we were pinned down. Neira grabbed a couple of their guns and waded out into the open. She sprayed down everything that moved. I grabbed the grenades and bolted for the main lab. I set them on the main generator and ran like hell. The three of us took cover in a creek. I remember the blast was so intense I nearly lost my barrier. We were saved by a truck that rolled across the bank above us.

"We each spent the better part of a month, at least, in the hospital for that one. After that Ellise asked to be reassigned to a ship, anything to leave that place behind. I went back to the academy, to my own little safety net. Neira lost her eye... and her free spirit. She left the service and never looked back. Nothing was the same after that."

He shook his head. "That's rough. I didn't realize you two were in the Conflict of Alpha Bael. That's crazy. I remember when that hit the news, the worst pirate attack in nearly fifty years. The entire outpost wiped out...." He paused in contemplation. "Seems like you've seen your fair share of shit hitting the fan."

She shrugged, "It's not so bad. There were a lot of good memories too."

"Like getting the nickname Princess?" He raised an eyebrow. "It's a pretty absurd nickname, you must admit."

She snickered, "First time I met Neira, I introduced myself with my full name, Kensington Anastasia Gennavieve Frost. She gave me this awkward look. I'll never forget it. She said it was far too froufrou for her tastes and if I insisted on having such a ridiculously formal name that she would be forced to call me Princess instead. Needless to say, it stuck. She even had the outpost coordinator put it on my locker and bunk."

"I've one more question, then I promise no more interrogation." He stared straight into her eyes, "About the mark on your back...."

The smile dropped off her face as she contemplated the mounting question. She knew this would come up eventually. "You saw...."

"Yeah, I caught a pretty good look at it while I was playing anchor out there." He pointed toward the ceiling and folded his arms across his chest, waiting for an answer. "And that's not like any tattoo I've ever seen."

"Bhelnir. I acquired it on Bhelnir. I was tapped out before even getting the colonists to the bunker. I thought perhaps I could get by without power, but then when my adepts died I lost it... I didn't stop to think. I ripped out my clasp interface and tried to pour every last molecule of energy into lashing out. But something happened. I, somehow, managed to do the impossible. I touched the veil, passed it actually. And then it was like this unending spring of energy rose up and engulfed me. I don't quite know how to describe it. But I *knew* what I had to do, what I *could* do.

"The inhibitor Doctor Tyronis put on me seemed to cut me off from it. I couldn't sense anything. I thought for sure I had hallucinated it all. It wasn't until I was in my quarters getting cleaned up that first time that I even believed that it might have really happened. And then when we were on the ground after seeing that bomb, I just *knew* what I had to do." She squinted and shook her head as the room became blurry. "This is all so new...," she wavered in place.

"Kensy?" Jackson stepped forward and reached for her left shoulder to steady her. She collapsed into his arms as he jerked to catch her. He drew back his right hand, blood. "Kensy!"

She struggled to focus on his fingers. "Guess it was worse than I thought...."

She passed out of consciousness. *How long has she been hiding this?* He turned his comm on, "Code Blue! I need medical to B deck starboard observation hall!" he cradled her in his arms as he knelt down. "Come on Kensy, hang in there."

Chapter 11

Chimera

"Some monsters can can be fought. Some can be contained.
But more terrifying yet, are those that cannot be slain."
~ unknown Alpha Bael researcher

Jackson stepped out of the medical bay door with his hands in his pockets. Neira stormed toward him. Her amber eye reflected a fiery intensity. "What happened?" she demanded.

Jackson raised his hands to stop her. "Kensy and I were talking, and she collapsed. Evidently, she reopened an earlier injury in her shoulder. Doc's got it. We'll just be in the way if we linger in there. She'll let us know when we can come back." He positioned himself in front of the door.

"Talking? Talking about what?!" she glared at him suspiciously.

"If you really want to know, we talked about how you two met, ...among other things." He scowled back at her and crossed his arms.

Neira took a step back, and her expression turned to shock. "She talked to you about Alpha Bael? Wait... you said shoulder?" she hesitated, searching her thoughts. "Which shoulder?" She reached out and grabbed his arms. A dark smear extended down the inside of his left forearm and bled out from his left cuff where he had held her. He gave her a confused look and pulled away from her. "She was bleeding! Which shoulder was she bleeding from?"

"From her left shoulder. What does it matter?" he looked into her eye. The fury was gone, only worry remained. She tried to push past him. "Neira! I said you're not going in. There is nothing you can do that the doctor doesn't already have covered. Now, what does it matter which shoulder was bleeding?" He grabbed her shoulders to force her attention back to the question at hand.

Neira kept her face tilted down and her voice grew quiet. "Gabel, let go of me. I have to go in there, now!" She clenched her fists in a struggle to remain calm.

"Why?!" he shouted at her.

"Because she's dying!" she screamed back at him through stray tears. She shook her head and recomposed herself.

He let go of her and leaned back. Registering his proximity, the medbay doors slid open. Skepticism filled his mind. "What?" She pushed past him into the room. He turned to follow. "Explain yourself!"

Neira pushed past a tech and approached Kensy's left side. She grabbed her friend's arm and drew her index finger and thumb down either side of the buckles that held her bracer on. An interface lit up, and she began tapping the unlock codes into it. Without looking up she answered with a question, "Alpha Bael. How much did she tell you?" An eerie calmness echoed through her words.

Doctor Tyronis stood at her monitor and quietly observed with little more than a glance toward Jackson during the exchange. "She told me about your early career definition of guard duty, the pirate attack and blowing the base generator to protect the site from seizure. She said you and your friend were hospitalized with injuries for a month." He grabbed the railing at the end of the bed. "What does that have to do with anything? What difference does it make?"

Neira looked up at him. "Did she tell you what *her* injuries were?" The interface deactivated, and one by one Neira began to unbuckle the bracer.

He shook his head. "No, no, she didn't...." Neira flipped the last buckle apart. The sides of the bracer opened, exposing her inner arm. Jackson let go of the end of the bed and shuffled backward. "What is that?!" His eyes were fixated on the shifting orange, red and yellow streaks that spread over her arm like webs.

A small circular disk sat over the center of the markings. Very carefully, Neira released the disc from its fittings. She held up the disc and examined it. "That is Chimera. Doctor, we'll need your best engineer up here to fix this." She set the disc on the closest tray and turned to evaluate the shoulder wound. "Chimera was the research they were working on in the Alpha Bael labs, a living biological weapon. They wanted a programmable virus if you will. Something that could discern between friend and foe and adapt accordingly. But the only part they got right was the 'living weapon' part."

"You mean to tell me she has been carrying a biological weapon around with her, *in her*, for..., what, years?" Jackson paced, trying to wrap his head around the dizzying information. Questions flooded his mind: *Why was she on active duty? Who knows about this? How has she survived this THING for so long? What does it do? Is it contagious? Why wasn't she quarantined? Why didn't they try to get it out of her? Does she even know? She would HAVE to know. Why didn't she say anything?*

Doctor Tyronis placed a gentle hand on his arm. "Commander, you're going to wear a hole in my floor. Why don't you take a seat. We'll get this figured out." She turned away and paged down to the engineering department, "Allen, please report to medbay. I have a special task I need to ask of you."

"I'll be right there, Doc," a deep masculine voice called back over the comm.

"Thank you, Doctor." Neira pulled back the gauze on the shoulder wound. She blotted away the worst of the blood and pointed to the edges of two glowing veins in the wound track. "I'm guessing the weapon that did this partially cauterized the wound to start with." The doctor nodded in affirmation. "That makes it damn near impossible to catch if you don't know what you're looking at. The Chimera is actively blocking her body's ability to self repair. It probably broke down any initial scabbing. It's trying to make her bleed to death. Do you have any diklodemir on hand?"

Doc pointed to a panel behind Neira. "Fourth panel down, it should be on the third shelf, right side. I think it has a cream colored label." She pulled out a sterile syringe and set it on Kensy's abdomen. The compartment rolled smoothly open, revealing shelf after shelf of small glass vials. Neira snatched the chilled bottle from its resting place and slid the panel closed again. She opened the syringe and inserted it into the lid, drawing out just enough of the milky liquid.

Neira shook her head and looked down at Kensy. "I'm so glad you're out for this." She took a deep breath and stabbed the needle into the area just to the right of the wound. She pulled the empty syringe out and handed it to Doc to dispose of. "That should slow it down, buy us some time. If we're lucky it might even make it pull back down into her arm."

Jackson slumped down in a nearby chair and sat silently for a few moments. "What happens if it gets to her heart?" He rested his elbows on his knees.

Neira stepped back to allow a medical tech to attend the seeping wound. "Best-case scenario? Cardiac arrest." Just then, the medbay doors slid open. A short man strode through a silver tool case in his dark reddish tan hands. His build was solid and muscular. He had soft brown eyes behind frameless spectacles and rust-colored hair that pulled back into a relaxed ponytail. *Solson, he has to be...* Neira surmised.

"What can I do for you Doc?" he inquired.

"Allen, Miss Cross here is actually the one with a most important task," she gestured toward Neira. "Neira Cross, meet our Chief Engineer, Allen Petroski."

Neira picked up the disc and handed it to him. "I need you to fix this, and time is of the essence." She paused. "It's a micro stasis generator. It must have received some damage in combat. My expertise only extends as far as installation and extraction." She placed her hands on her hips and fidgeted nervously.

He squinted as he examined the tiny disc shaped machine. "Fascinating. I'm gonna guess this is for her? Some kinda of local containment system for that stuff on her arm." He nodded toward Kensy. "I'll need a place to work. Preferably with a magnifier lamp." He smiled, "I'll have it good as new in no time at all."

Doctor Tyronis stepped forward. "You can use my office. I'll show you." Allen followed her beyond the rows of examination beds and they disappeared into a room on the back wall. Neira accepted a damp towel from one of the techs and cleaned her hands. She slumped down in a chair beside Jackson and let out a weary sigh.

"How?" He looked down at his hands. "How was she exposed?"

Neira leaned back and stared up at the white ceiling. "When the generator blew, we took cover in a shallow creek that ran along one side of the camp. She tried to cover it with a barrier, but this transport truck rolled over us. It pinned her arm underneath. We waited until things died down and Ellise and I crawled out. We found some cables and tried to pull the truck off her, wedging debris under it as we lifted. But we were both in really bad shape. It took us hours to nudge it enough to get her out. When we did, we found that someone had filled a smuggling compartment with vials of the stuff.

"She fell into a coma for months. They spent so much time making that damn thing and no one had bothered to engineer a counter agent. Or, if they had, it went up in smoke with all the other notes and files on that stupid base. Hard to tell either way, but Kensy was exposed because some greedy bastard was trying to get a bigger piece of the take. I wanted to track down every last one of the scientists and beat the antidote out of them. But, as luck would have it, they all either died in the attack or from complications afterward." Neira folded her arms across her chest. "Then some brain-child lab-tech came up with this system. Crazy bastard actually managed to save her, at least temporarily."

Jackson attempted to reconcile the thoughts that raced through his mind. "Why didn't they just take the arm once it was contained?"

"If only it was that easy. The Chimera is actually spread through her whole system. They tried to biopsy part of it, the piece they believed was the core, and it changed. It came back stronger, started manipulating her primary and psionic nervous systems. They figured to kill the infection, they would have to kill the patient. I was not about to let that happen, so I... *negotiated*... for enough time to find a real solution." She tilted her head from side to side, audibly cracking the joints. "I gave her the bracer to protect the system until we can find a way to get that crap out of her. But it's been so long... I don't know. Sometimes I think she is just waiting for the day it wins."

Jackson stared at Kensy's motionless figure. "Unacceptable." Neira shot him a curious glance. "I hate this. Good people shouldn't have to suffer this kind of crap. Give me a freaking gun and I can stop an enemy charge, but this.... I can't fight this. It just pisses me off!" His knuckles turned white as he clenched his fists.

Neira leaned forward. "On that, you and I completely agree." A victorious cry emanated from the office. Engineer Petroski rushed out of the room, the activated disc in his tweezers. He gently set the humming disc in the palm of

Neira's hand. She jumped out of her chair and headed for Kensy's bedside. She clicked the disc back into the fittings. A pulse rippled through the Chimera. Slowly, the shifting colors began to fade into green and blue hues as the lines shrunk toward the central point. The lines continued to fade little by little. Neira looked up at Allen, relieved and bewildered. "It's never shrunk this much. What did you do to it?"

"I found room for improvement in the design. It should provide slightly better containment now. Give me the full specs and a little more time, I could probably even do better." A smirk curled around Allen's lips. Doctor Tyronis walked out, the engineer's case in hand. He graciously accepted it. "Let me know if you need anything else. I love a good challenge. Speaking of which, I gotta go get this bucket on the move before the captain makes me push it home." He chuckled and sauntered out of the room.

Doc smiled, "Now, you two.... I can take it from here. Go get some sleep. By my calculations, you're both running on fumes. Stress and sleep deprivation aren't going to help anyone. And we don't have any spare beds down here." She urged Neira and Jackson out the door. She could read their reluctance, "Doctor's orders. I don't want to see either of you out and about for the next eight hours or I'm ordering medical restriction." She put her hands in her white lab coat and watched as they each trudged off in their separate directions.

Chapter 12

Nightmare

*"Love. Fear. Concern. Hope. Sometimes these whispers
that slip past our lips are the truest expression we can
manage in a moment of distress."*

~ unknown

Kensy closed her eyes and stood in the warm wind, letting
it swirl around her. The tails of her Psicorp uniform flapped
gently against her leg. From the jagged marble floor beneath
the soles of her boots, small bits of rock crumbled away. She
stood surrounded by humming crystalline pillars that drifted
listlessly about her. At the edge of the world brewed a storm.
She could smell it and feel the charge of its building energies.
She took a deep breath.

"It's coming. You can feel it, can't you?" A wiry woman
with pale olive skin and silvery colored eyes walked up the
broken steps behind Kensy. She wore a flowing gown of
sapphire silk that danced in the breeze. Her ebony hair laid
loosely over her left shoulder, braided almost down to her
waist. She stared at the storm's edge. "Destiny... I guess we
didn't run far enough."

Kensy turned her head to look the woman in the eyes,
"Was I running? It feels more like I've been fighting the tide,
trying to hold back whole oceans. But what for?" She glanced
into the black abyss below. "It has been waiting for me for so
long.... How have I remained here without a future? And for as

81

terrible as your fate was supposed to be you managed to slip quietly into the abyss. It's just me now...."

The woman smiled softly. Her eyes glittered with a sisterly love, "Oh, you silly girl! You forget too much. It's never just you. Is Neira not doing her part? Do I have to scold you in your dreams instead? Now, there is even that handsome boy who would miss you too. Though, I don't think he knows it yet." She chuckled delicately and turned down the stairs.

"Elle, don't go!" Kensy suddenly shouted after her. The last ripple of Elle's blue dress disappeared behind a ruined wall on the platform below. Kensy jogged down the steps in a hurry. "Elle, please! I don't know where to go from here!" She grabbed the edge of the wall and swung around only to find a labyrinth of ancient marbled ruins sprawling out before her.

A chill crawled down her back as an ominous shadow crept up behind her and began to swallow the landscape. She broke into a run, darting through the obstacles calling for Elle until the sound of her own voice faded away. She stumbled to a stop and began to cry. No matter how she screamed, there was only the roar of the distant storm in her ears. She slumped down against a wall and curled up.

"Heading out?" A different voice whispered over the gusting winds. It sounded almost familiar but she could not place it. She put her head up and listened.

"Yeah, now that we're moving I should probably go get some sleep before the Captain needs me. I'll try to come back and check on things later but if anything changes let me know." Jackson's voice rang louder through the air. She scrambled to her feet. As she turned to run toward his voice she felt a pull on her left arm. Looking down she found it chained to the ground with an old iron manacle. She tugged and thrashed against it to no avail.

"Jack! Jackson!" she hollered into the void, her voice once again capable of sound.

"Will do, Commander. Seems you've taken quite an interest in Miss Frost. I hope you don't mind me saying but it's nice to see you showing an interest in something other than your work." Kensy recognized the other voice now. It was Doctor Tyronis.

"You misunderstand my interest in her. The captain has ordered that her welfare be a priority. There is no place for personal feelings in my assignment." Kensy stopped struggling against the chain and listened to his cold rationale. Had he been this removed during their talk on the observation deck?

Doc's gentle words rolled through the sky, "From what little I've observed you two have a natural chemistry. All I'm saying is that it might do you both some good to entertain the idea of a non-assignment related friendship. She seems to need your stability and you could use someone to make you smile once in a great while. You're human, not machine, despite the fact that sometimes I think you strive to make people believe otherwise."

Kensy looked back down at her shackled wrist. *They must be talking right now. I'm dreaming. I have to wake up!* She closed her eyes and tried to focus on waking up, "Wake up. Come on, wake up! Dammit! I have to wake up. I have to!" The intense feeling of foreboding came over her again.

She blinked and there was Elle again. This time her clothes were tattered and her hair an unruly dripping tangle. Dark shadows covered her eyes, "It's coming." She staggered in place. "You will need him before the end. Don't let go...." Elle's ragged form melted into the rising darkness.

Kensy began to tug on her chain again. Inch by inch the darkness seeped toward her. She felt a panic come over her and she renewed her fight against the chain. This time the tears on her face were cold and real. Fear stirred inside her. "Wake up!" she screamed at herself.

"I don't have time for...," Jackson glanced over to Kensy's bed. A glittering streak of water rolled down her cheek. "Doc!"

They rushed to opposite sides of the bed to check on her. Her breathing became irregular and she began to fuss as if struggling against some unseen force. Jackson grabbed her right hand with his and watched the pained expression on her face. She squeezed his hand tightly. "Doc? What's going on?"

Doctor Tyronis sifted through the graphs of data on her monitor. "Looks like she's dreaming but she's pushing redlines all over the place. Her new found abilities must be complicating things. I am reading the same energy flow as if she was actively creating a psionic manifestation. Whatever dream she's having, she has lost control of. If we don't wake her, she could burnout. I'll have to prep another inhibitor. Try waking her while I get that going." She took long swift strides toward her office and began shouting orders at her med techs.

Jackson brushed her hair from her face and wiped the tear away. "Come on, Kensy. You made it through the worst part. Don't let go now." He gently squeezed her hand, "I'm right here. Wake up!" More tears silently streaked down her face. "None of that is real, whatever you're seeing... I'm real. Right here, right now...," he bit his lip nervously. He leaned in and whispered to her, "Kensy, wake up. Come back to me." Her eyes opened suddenly and she gasped. She looked about feverishly as she tried to figure out where she was. "It's okay." He brushed her hair out of her face again and rested his hand on her head to calm her. "You're in medbay. Everything is going to be fine." He shouted toward the office, "Doc, she's awake."

Kensy breathed a sigh of relief as she regained her bearings. She relaxed and turned her gaze toward Jackson. She gave him a weak smile, "Thank you." She squeezed his hand gently, then let go. He straightened his posture and set her hand down on the bed beside her. She turned to look at Doctor Tyronis as she approached, "How long was I out, Doc?"

"Going on five days now. It's good to have you with us again. We were beginning to worry. But we were able to get some reconstruction done on that pesky shoulder wound of yours. I think aside from some stiffness, you'll find it almost as good as new." The doctor smiled, "Well, since you're back, I had better go put that new inhibitor away." She turned and left Jackson and Kensy alone again.

"Five days? Did I miss anything?" she folded her hands neatly on her lap.

Jackson stuffed his restless hands in his pockets, "Well, the ship is moving again. Engineering managed to patch it just well enough to get us back to the Sol system. We're on our way to Hades Station where the Themiscyra will be in dry dock for a while getting fixed. That's about it I guess...." He fidgeted uneasily, *Why did she thank me? Did she hear what I said? Would she even remember anything she heard before waking up?* An awkward silence filled their little corner of the room, interrupted only by the ambient sounds of infirmary equipment.

"Sorry about fainting on you. I remember we were talking.... It was irresponsible of me. I should have gotten Doc to repack the shoulder earlier. I must have overexerted myself. Shoulda worn the sling I guess." She gave a weak chuckle.

The muscles in his jaw flexed as he clenched his jaw trying to decide what to say. "I hardly think this is a laughing matter. You should have said something." She opened her mouth to apologize but he interrupted, "Did it not cross your mind to tell us about the Chimera? It could have killed you and no one here would have been any the wiser." Her eyes grew wide as she realized he knew about her arm.

"Did Neira...?" Her words seemed to stumble out through her gauntlet of racing thoughts.

"She saved your ass!" He paused pensively, "She told us how you got exposed. Why didn't you tell someone about your condition? Like, Doc! How can you expect anyone to give you an accurate treatment without that very important piece of information?"

Water welled up in her eyes, "Oh, I'll have to add it into my conversation starters. Hi, I'm Kensy Frost and I'm a walking time bomb. Keep an escape pod prepped, you may need to jettison me into empty space at a moments notice." She pulled back the blankets on her legs and began ripping the sensor nodes off her skin.

"What do you think you're doing?" He grabbed her right wrist to stop her, but she jerked away from him. She slid her legs off the far side of the bed and tried to stand up. Her legs were weaker than she anticipated, and she fell to her hands and knees on the cold floor.

Rushing around the bed, Jackson lifted Kensy to her feet, "Don't you get it? You nearly died. If Neira hadn't stepped in, you would have bled to death and no one could have stopped it." For a moment only their eyes spoke: hers whispered of fear and pain, while, his spoke of confusion and concern. Volumes were expressed in those few moments of stillness.

Kensy turned her gaze to look past him, "Doc, if its all right I would like to go back to my quarters." He stepped back to clear the path between doctor and patient. Doctor Tyronis quietly stepped forward and wrapped a sensor band around Kensy's right wrist.

"Wear that until I tell you otherwise. And no shooting this one," she glanced to Jackson. "It will continue to report your vitals back to me. I will also be assigning an observation detail to you so we don't repeat any unnecessary incidents. Commander, please escort Miss Frost back to her quarters. She seems to still be a little woozy." Jackson nodded to Doc and held out his left elbow for Kensy to wrap her arm around. Quietly, they walked out of the medbay one uneasy step at a time.

Chapter 13

Psionic Echoes

"The applications of psionic manifestations are greatly varied, and few come without some degree of risk. However, bearing witness to such a phenomenon can be both informative and awe-inspiring."
~ Psicorp Academy Instructor

The training room door slid open for the captain and company. They entered the large round room, passing one of the medical techs intently reading his holopad charts. In the center of the room stood Kensy, dressed in new uniform pants and a black tank top. She looked up from her meditation at her arriving audience. For a fleeting moment, she and Jackson locked gazes. She gave a subtle nod to Neira before addressing the captain. "Thank you for coming down here, Captain. It has come to my attention that I have been thus far unable to give an accurate or detailed assessment of the events on Bhelnir. So, I have decided to show you instead."

"Show me? How exactly do you intend to accomplish this?" the captain replied skeptically.

Kensy drew in a tenuous breath. "I will use my power to create a three-dimensional recreation of the events as I witnessed them." She ran the palms of her hands down the outer seams of her pants to wipe away the clamminess. "This will take some room, so if everyone could stay close to the outer wall, it would be appreciated."

Captain Hadarian took a step back and nodded to her, remaining at attention. "Proceed."

Kensy took a deep breath and exhaled slowly. A dark purple fog poured from her lips. She closed her eyes and began to shape the raw energy into a glittering representation of herself. As she waved her hands through the swirling nebulous haze the scene unfolded before them. They watched as she fought off the first wave of machines to protect the colonists. Everyone except the captain shuddered as the beam weapon ripped through her shoulder. The captain's attendants breathed audible sighs of relief as her barrier washed away the remaining machines. They continued to watch as she directed the colonists to the bunker.

Another measured breath renewed the scene at the bunker as she and the adepts took their last stand against the overwhelming tide of assailants. One by one they fell, every painful detail inscribed on the air. First Kean, Lena, then Aaron. Jackson turned his eyes toward Kensy as a few stray tears escaped her closed eyes. The room flashed and everyone found themselves in Kensy's vision of the beyond for a moment. She struggled to redirect the energy display back to the fight on Bhelnir. The vision of her last battle began to blur as she fought to maintain the scene. She staggered in place and the manifestation collapsed. She opened her eyes and straightened her stance.

The medical tech ran up to her to verify his readings, but she waved him off. Composing herself, she looked toward Captain Hadarian, "Sorry, it takes a great deal of focus to put so much detail into a projection. Is there anything I can clarify for you?" She placed her hands in her pockets to hide her shakiness.

"Gabel, are those the same machines you saw on Morwhex?" The captain asked over her shoulder.

"Yes Ma'am. Though the ones we encountered seemed to be dormant." He kept his eyes fixated on Kensy. She focused on the captain to avoid looking in his direction.

"Psilyria, are you capable of showing us one of those machines again? In as much detail as you can manage, please." Kensy nodded and drew on her power again. She concentrated on the size and shape to begin with. Her hands trembled as she tried to zero in on the details of its form. "Computer, scan projection and record," the captain ordered. A matrix of lasers traced the shape, creating a wire-form overlay. "That is enough, Psilyria."

Kensy tried to drop the manifestation, but a slip in her concentration caused a surge of feedback. A brilliant flash erupted toward her outstretched hands as the shape dissipated. She let out a pained cry, stumbled back against the wall, and clamped her hand down on her right forearm. Neira rushed over to her. "We need to check it." They both looked at the bracer and Kensy acquiesced. She held her arm out for Neira to open the bracer, allowing the med tech to attend to her without protest.

Jackson hesitated, unsure if he should move to assist her. In his indecision, he remained at the captain's side. The captain examined the virtual model. "There are no defining marks to denote origin. It is an exceptionally lethal design. The versatility is remarkable. Beam-based weapon capability, we would have to assume all of these smaller points are capable of extension and manipulation." She pointed to the small mace like heads that lined the internal body of the creature. "They each have three distinct ridges. They can probably open as well as spin, judging from the design. The long spidery arms would have to be exceptionally sharp to do the kind of damage we saw on that one young man. And they seem to be capable of rapid tactical adjustments on the battlefield. The question is: are they automated or directed?"

89

Captain Hadarian turned toward Kensy. "I accept this in place of your report. We will be arriving at Hades Station in a matter of hours. You and Commander Gabel will present before the Logistics Committee upon our arrival. They will decide what to do with you after that. I have been informed that a new Psicorp uniform will be awaiting you in dock so that you may be in accordance with regulation for the Committee tribunal."

"Tribunal? Captain...?" Jackson gave her a confused look.

"The losses of Morwhex and Bhelnir must be addressed, Commander." The captain gave him a stern gaze. "I will, of course, be submitting my recommendations, but this is beyond my authority. Unprovoked acts of aggression from an unknown enemy.... The implications of this could stir hostilities in already fragile relations on a galactic scale. I suggest you two ready yourselves." She strode past him and out of the room, followed by her attendants.

Neira looked to the tech, "I've got this. You are dismissed." He hesitated. "I'm sure you have patients in the medbay that need your *undivided* attention," she glared at him and he bustled out the door. Jackson gave a frustrated sigh and put his hands on his hips as he stared at the closing door. "Don't worry about it. Just give them the facts as you know them. I'll make sure none of this comes back on you two." She double checked Kensy's Chimera disc and began to close up the bracer again.

"And just how are you going to do that?!" Jackson shot her a sharp look.

She buckled the last of Kensy's bracer, "We all have our own talents and connections, Gabel. I personally happen to have a fair amount of pull with the Committee." Though her body language expressed a cold, calculated determination; she looked at him with the same fiery look in her eye that he had seen outside the medbay. "When we dock, I have to ask that you deliver Kensy's uniform to her and then escort her to the tribunal. I will meet you there." She turned back to Kensy, "Keep the pyrotechnics off-line for the time being. Now, if you will excuse me, I have some calls to make before we reach Hades." She walked out of the room, leaving Jackson and Kensy alone again.

Kensy quietly approached him. He held his arm out for her again. "Come on. I'll walk you upstairs." She smiled weakly and wrapped her fingers around the crook of his elbow. He paused and looked down at her. "Kensy... I'm so sorry. Even though you told me.... I didn't know how bad it was. If it is my power to do so... I will make sure that you never have to relive that again."

She leaned her head against his arm and whispered, "Thank you, Jack."

Chapter 14

Styx & Stones

*"Graven appearances are always shrouded in mystery and
rumor as surveillance and recording devices seem to cease
to function on their presence.
It's the damnedest thing."*
~ Hades Station Security Officer

Kensy's delicate fingers fastened her Psilic Crest pin to the
tails of her uniform. She stood straight and examined herself in
the mirror. It felt good to be back in uniform, but she couldn't
help but be nervous about what was coming next, the tribunal.
She smoothed her bangs into place with the tips of her fingers.
It was time. She walked out of the bath and nodded to Jackson.
"I'm ready."

His dress blue uniform was delicately trimmed in satiny
black and silver lines. He had slicked his hair back to keep it
from falling in his eyes. Untucking his hat from his arm, he
slipped it on, adjusting the brim appropriately. He pivoted to
face the door as it glided open. Kensy gave Jackson a nod, and
they exited her quarters without a word.

Awkward silence filled the air as they walked side-by-side
down the hall toward the elevator. It was only a momentary
wait before the lift arrived with its customary ding. The doors
slid open. Kensy stepped toward the back of the car so that
Jackson could access the control panel without issue. He
stared at the floor display as they began to descend. "You look
nice. The uniform suits you."

"Every Psicorp uniform is individually tailored so that the control clasp can be accommodated," she explained, holding up her clasped arm. She turned her wrist to examine the bands and nodes on her skin. The interface still needed rebuilt, rendering the clasp as little more than an elaborate metal tattoo.

"No, I mean...," he searched for the right words. "Psicorp suits you."

She folded her hands behind her back and looked down. "Thanks." A flicker of a smile crossed her lips, then faded away as she turned her thoughts back to more solemn topics. *They wouldn't convene for a simple debrief of encounters. They'd just pass along the reports. What are they really after with this trial?*

The doors opened to the main deck; the personnel hushed as they walked by. A murmur of whispers trailed behind them as they made their way through the main corridor to the primary airlock. The first door slid open, allowing them entry. The compartment closed behind them and the air pressure adjusted to station levels. Kensy felt herself begin to shake as the tension mounted in her shoulders. She took measured breaths, trying to calm herself.

Jackson glanced down at her. "You okay?"

She nodded, "Yeah." The subtle quiver of her lower lip betrayed her nervousness.

He held out his elbow for her. As her hand tucked around his arm, she felt him pull his elbow in tight. She could feel the tension in his muscles. He was nervous too. The outer door opened, and they stepped out onto the docking concourse. "Listen, whatever happens... just... don't worry. We'll get through this." Despite sensing his anxiety, she felt somewhat reassured.

The walk from the ship's docking concourse to the diplomatic plaza was not far. Jackson and Kensy traversed the distance fairly quickly, despite the bustle of the station crowds.

They passed through a large outer courtyard and into the halls of virtual tapestries and holographic landscaping until they arrived at last at the Committee audience chamber.

Massive doors opened for them. The oval-shaped room was crowned by several rows of elegantly carved desks of wood and stone. The main floor held numerous pews of onlookers. A nearby guard directed them to two elevated pedestals in front of the pews.

As they stepped into their respective positions, a booming voice came from the front of the room, "Psilyria Frost, Commander Gabel, we are glad you could join us. We have been reviewing the events in which you have been involved in these last few weeks. We find it disturbing that there is little evidence to support these claims aside from the fact that one colony is completely gone and another is not far behind. There are no bodies to examine or parts from these supposed machines to be analyzed. Why is that?"

In an attempt to take the pressure off Kensy, Jackson began explaining, "Sir, the enemy we faced on Bhelnir and Morw—."

"We? Commander, it was my understanding that only Psilyria Frost was involved in the events at Bhelnir." The spokesman's resounding voice curtly interrupted. Jackson shot an annoyed glance up at the central seat of the assembly. The muscles in his jaw flexed as he searched for a better phrasing to his statement.

Seeing his distress, Kensy quickly spoke up before Jackson could reply, "That is correct, sir." She took a deep breath to still her nerves. "I was the only one between the two of us that was involved in the confrontation on Bhelnir. After which I was temporarily reassigned to the ESFV Themiscyra under the command of Captain Hadarian and Commander Gabel."

"On Bhelnir, you violated protocol, getting your entire command killed, and obtained no evidence of your alleged attackers." The voice drilled at Kensy with staggering allegations. "What justifications do you have for this?" She could not see her accuser behind his raised bench, nor did she need to. His words were sharp enough for her.

Kensy stood silent for a moment, then in total calmness she replied, "None, Sir." A storm of whispers swept the room. "It was a dire situation, and I chose to prioritize the civilian lives. My squad understood the situation. They gave their lives to protect the citizens of Bhelnir." She blinked away the gathering water in her eyes. "In the face of uncertain battlefield conditions, I made the only call I could. To stand between an unknown enemy and non-combatants with the forces available to me. Everything I did, I did to protect the innocent," she affirmed to the committee.

"Does that include supposedly 'touching the veil' as it was later referred to by Commander Gabel?" Another flurry of whispers passed through the assembly. Kensy looked at Jackson for a moment. He met her gaze with apologetic eyes. "The 'veil' is a convenient myth to explain the limitations of psionic prowess. But you claim to have surpassed this. How do we know that this isn't some elaborate stunt intended to misdirect our attentions from more sinister motivations?"

She gave him a gentle smile and turned back to the committee spokesman. "I cannot explain what happened to me during the fight on Bhelnir; but, I have expressed the situation as best as I can, with honesty and integrity. And I will use any gifts bestowed upon me by my experience there to protect and to serve as I have always done." She stood tall, resolute in her promise.

"And what kind of service can we expect from you? From everything we have seen you have disobeyed orders and violated regulation. Not to mention that upon your introduction to the ESFV Themiscyra, the ship's executive officer seemingly adopted this recklessness. Commander Gabel, what possessed you to blatantly disregard the mission's parameters?" the voice redirected toward Jackson.

Jackson returned to attention. "Mission parameters changed, sir. My team and I were required to adapt to complete the underlying goals of the mission and return." His eyes scanned the lines of the committee chamber with intensity and determination.

"You were supposed to ascertain the nature of the colony's distress and provide aid. Instead, you dropped out of contact yourself, and did not aid or save a single colonist, nor did you provide evidence as to their demise," the spokesman sneered at the commander.

"As stated in my report, which you no doubt have in front of you," Jackson spurned the spokesman, "unstable geological conditions created unforeseen communications issues. We proceeded with reconnaissance, only to find that there was no one left to save. I determined under the circumstances any evidence retrieval would have jeopardized my secondary mission objective: to return Psilyria Frost safely to the Themiscyra." Jackson stood confidently and unwavering in the face of the pointed questions.

"You would have this committee take your word of a new and mysterious enemy based on vague accounts and wild speculation?!" the spokesman hissed back at him.

The chamber doors flew open with a boom. In the great archway of the main doors stood the cloaked figure of a Graven soldier. A hush fell over everyone in the hall. Not a single member of the assembly dared speak. A sense of awe and apprehension seeped through the crowd. A Graven making such a public appearance was a rare occurrence indeed. The Society of the Graven were infamous for being the shadows of the universe, a deadly and secretive force of galactic guardians that bowed to no one.

The figure strode up the central isle, "If you will not take their word, then you will take mine!" Kensy's eyes grew wide as she recognized the voice, Neira. She pushed her hood back and tossed a holodisc out into the center of the hall. It activated, projecting the scan of Kensy's manifestation and video of the colonists from Morwhex, "Your witch hunt ends here! The phantoms *are* real."

The assembly erupted into pandemonium. Neira held up a closed fist and silence fell over the room once again. "Under Graven Law, I hereby conscript Commander Jackson Dean Gabel and Psilyria Kensington Anastasia Gennavieve Frost to the order which they will serve for the greater good of all life in this galaxy." The chairman jumped up from his seat. Her icy stare pierced his throat, rendering him momentarily speechless. She smirked, "Oh, and one more thing, while you're up.... We demand immediate access to Legacy."

Chapter 15

Legacy

*** // Clearance Level Nova 1 Required \\ ***

Kensy sat quietly in one of the rear shuttle seats, her legs neatly crossed at the knees. She folded her hands one over the other in her lap and waited. The minutes ticked by painfully slow as anxiety gnawed at her. She played the tribunal over and over in her head, trying to make more sense of things. *Neira is a Graven? Why didn't she tell me? I thought she trusted me. And what's all this conscription business? Then there's Legacy... What is it and why is it so important?* She zoned out as she mulled through the rampant questions in her mind.

A group of hushed voices slowly approached the shuttle. "I still have no idea what the hell is going on. Hopefully this little field trip will be illuminating for all of us," Jackson spoke just above a whisper. "Let's just wait and see what happens. And... don't bother Kensy with questions either. I think she's even more confused than I am about this whole mess."

"Kensy, huh? First name basis now?" one of the other men spoke up.

Jackson glared at him. "Yes, do you have a problem with that, Morgan?" Jackson crossed his arms in front of him. "She's been through enough. Be nice or I'll let the captain know about your 'fine tuning' you tried to pull on the jump from Raxis that caused the mid-flight stall out."

"You wouldn't...," Morgan grimaced, "Fine. I'll play nice with the other kids this time." He rolled his eyes and muttered under his breath, "You have a talent for sucking the fun out of everything."

"Quit bitching and get on the damn shuttle," Daniel snickered at the exchange as he moved to the open shuttle door. He ducked inside and smiled at Kensy. "Are we feeling any better?" She jumped, startled by the sound of his voice.

"Sorry, I was a little too preoccupied. Didn't hear you coming. Yes, I am feeling better. Thank you." She smiled softly and brushed her bangs aside. Daniel gave her a nod and slipped into the pilot's seat. Behind him, Jackson stepped into the shuttle, moving to stand beside Kensy. He grabbed the ceiling rail with his left hand and the two of them exchanged silent looks.

An excessively charming man followed Jackson into the shuttle and glided into the seat opposite Kensy. He had long spiky blonde hair and dark, sultry olive green eyes. "Flight Lieutenant Morgan Threaux, and you are...?" He curled a flirty smile around his lips. "Well, aside from a radiant vision of a Psicorp officer...."

"Psilyria Kensington Frost." She looked down at her hands again, uncomfortable with Morgan's forward overtures. Subtly, she leaned toward the side where Jackson stood and redirected her eyes toward the front of the shuttle. "Any idea where we're going? Or what this Legacy thing is?"

"Not yet. Neira should have more information whenever she gets here. Only thing I could find out is that Legacy requires the highest levels of clearance I've ever seen." Jackson stuffed his right hand in his pocket as he looked down at her. "Doing okay?" She nodded in reply, *yes*.

The click of Neira's armored boots could be heard across the shuttle bay floor as she approached. She stepped into the waiting shuttle and glanced around. "Everyone's here, good." She moved toward the pilot's seat to speak with Daniel. "Let's get going. Head to these coordinates planet-side." She turned back to see Kensy, Jackson and Morgan all staring, waiting for an explanation.

Kensy spoke up first. "Neira, what's going on?"

"We're going to a secret project base. You told Gabel that you 'touched the veil,' right?" Kensy sheepishly nodded in affirmation. "Well, I have a theory about that. We're gonna go test it and if I'm right, we'll get our own ship. Then we can continue this investigation on our own terms." She slumped down into the seat to Kensy's left. "And later you can talk to me about why you told him and not me."

Kensy scowled at her. "Oh, like how you told me that you're a Graven?!"

Neira shook her head. "Point taken. Guess we both need to work on this sharing thing."

The shuttle jarred free of the docking clamp and glided through the air as it departed the Themiscyra. Daniel activated the virtual windows on the shuttle so everyone could see out as they left the Hades Station air space. Stars stretched out all around them, scattering from the dusty band of the Milky Way across the ebony sky. The sun glowed like a delicate pearl set against the endless expanse of space. Slowly the shuttle descended toward the jagged frozen peaks of Pluto's landscape. Charon loomed overhead like a sleeping giant.

A faint aurora-like flame flickered around the shuttle's hull as they slipped into Pluto's thin atmosphere. The planet's surface danced with sprays of frozen geysers and shifting ice flows. Daniel deftly navigated the shuttle toward the coordinates. He spied a plateau among the rocky outcroppings and glided them toward it. "I see a landing zone, but this place is a wasteland. You sure the coordinates are right?" He asked back over his shoulder.

Neira stood and stepped toward him. "Just take us down. It wouldn't be much of a secret base if just anyone could see it." Daniel shrugged and set the shuttle down. A force field activated over them, sealing the shuttle to the ground. Everything lurched to one side as the platform beneath them began to flip over, revealing a darkened tunnel that plunged into the planet's depths. Jackson placed a firm hand on Kensy's shoulder to keep her from falling out of her seat. Morgan braced himself in his seat and tried to look around.

The platform finished moving and locked into place with a thunderous boom. Daniel flipped on the external lights and glanced back at Neira. The force field dropped. She placed a hand on his shoulder. "Okay, now take us in nice and easy." He kicked the thrusters up and crept down the twists and turns of the corridor, guided by delicate path lights in the smooth walls. They turned one last corner and emerged in an enormous room, the far side of which could not be seen. Kensy and Morgan rose out of their seats and stared in wonder. Hundreds of ships, the likes of which they had never seen, sat in neat and tidy rows.

Jackson glanced at Neira. "What is this place? How long has this been here?"

She crossed her arms in front of her. "This is Legacy. The largest fleet in the known galaxy. We don't know how long it has been here. Who ever built this is long since gone. Several hundred years ago, before the Divergence, humanity found this place. We began studying everything we could about it. But still, we know very little, if anything, about it or those that built it. We do know that they studied early humans, and for whatever reason they altered Pluto's structure to leave this behind, perhaps for us to find.

"The technology behind this entire structure is beyond anything we have ever seen, even to this day. This was built by altering the fundamental structure of the planet without disrupting its ecosystem, gravitational identity, or atmospheric balance. Even an orbital scan can't detect it. It was only when we sent a ground team to the planet to explore that it was discovered, quite by accident, at that," she leaned against the back of Daniel's seat. "Every ship is spec'd to human needs internally. There is even evidence that over time they have adapted to the changes we as a people have experienced. There is nothing like it in the entire galaxy."

"But if it was made for us, why aren't we using these ships?" Kensy asked inquisitively.

Neira tilted her head to one side, "That's where you come in...." Jackson and Kensy both gave her an incredulous look. She waved them off. "Don't worry, you'll see." Neira gazed back over her shoulder as they approached the middle of the complex.

In the very center of everything sat an elegant, small cruiser-sized ship. She was different from the rest. The lines of her hull looked more akin to the graceful profile a bird. From the delicate point of the bow, the ship arched back into two small wings extending toward the rear. The body of the vessel curved outward into four larger wings that swept forward around the rest of the ship. The very aft section drew the lines of the hull back into a beautiful flowing tail that more than doubled the total length of the ship. Kensy took in the majesty of the form and gasped in awe. She felt drawn to it ever so slightly.

Jackson swept past Kensy toward Neira and spoke in a hushed voice, "Are you mad?! There's no way we all have the clearance for something like this!"

Neira looked him straight in the eyes. "You do now." She paused and looked at Morgan. "Well, he might not, but if he talks, we can just shove him out an airlock and make Bryden the pilot." She smirked. "Let's just see how this goes." She shrugged, "And who knows, I could be wrong and we will waltz out of here empty-handed." The shuttle jarred as Daniel docked it with the primary catwalk. Neira glanced back over her shoulder. "Keep the engines warm. We should know fairly quickly what direction this thing will go." She turned back to

Jackson and patted him on the shoulder as she moved toward the shuttle door, "Now, let's go meet us an admiral."

Neira disembarked, followed by Morgan and Jackson. Their boots clanked against the fine metal grating that made up the walkway. Slowly, Kensy stepped out of the shuttle, still taking in every detail. The air was breathable and fresh, unlike the recycled air typically found on ships and stations. The draw she had sensed before now felt like a full-blown tug at her very core. Something was calling to her beyond the confines of sound. She curled her fingers into a fist against her chest as she walked just a bit slower than the others.

A line appeared in the seamless hull, revealing a doorway. The party was met by a small entourage led by a very distinguished silver-haired man. Captain Hadarian approached from behind him, stepping off to one side. "Excellent. Admiral, I would like to introduce you to my first officer, Commander Jackson Gabel, the Themiscyra's helmsman Flight Lieutenant Morgan Threaux, the Graven Neira Cross. And in the back there is Psilyria Kensington Frost, the one we picked up on Bhelnir. Everyone, this is Sol System Defense Force Admiral Kristopher Khaivol." Jackson and Morgan saluted the admiral respectfully. Neira gave him a polite bow and Kensy graciously nodded toward him, distracted by the strange pull she felt.

"Welcome to the Legacy fleet's flagship, the Legacy One. I would also like to introduce my lead technician, Doctor Micah Hirayama. She oversees all the research and development of technology related to the Legacy Fleet. She can answer any questions about ship specifics that you may have." A small stature woman with smooth black hair and olive colored-eyes gave a slight bow at the admiral's introduction. The admiral turned toward Captain Hadarian, "Now shall we begin with the bridge?"

She nodded in agreement and gestured for him to lead the way. Everyone turned to proceed into the ship. Jackson and

Morgan fell in line promptly, following on the captain's heels. Neira took a few steps before pausing. Kensy had remained on the catwalk, entranced by something on the ship's exterior. Withdrawing from the group, Neira attempted to gain Kensy's attention. Snapping her fingers, she caused Kensy to flinch, startled by the sound. "Come on. You can daydream later. You're falling behind."

Kensy looked down and muttered softly, "Sorry. Guess I was distracted...." As she stepped over the threshold, she reached toward the doorjamb with her right hand. Her fingers and boot contacted the ship simultaneously. A shock wave cascaded through the air, rippling away from her. Lights and panels flickered to life as energy coursed across previously dormant channels throughout the ship. Everyone stopped in their tracks and turned to look at her.

Doctor Hirayama's holopad became flooded with information. "Fascinating!" She glanced up at Admiral Khaivol. "Subsystems all over the ship are coming online." She hesitated, stepping toward Kensy with a quizzical expression on her face, "...almost as if it's responding... to the psilyria!" She glanced back at the admiral before redirecting her attention to the holopad to sort through the readings.

Slowly, Kensy raised her eyes to meet Neira and Jackson's gazes. Neira was surprised, but pleased. An affectionate smile curled around her lips as she waved her friend in. Kensy cautiously stepped the rest of the way onto the ship. Jackson, on the other hand, mixed in confusion and concern with his usual scowl. Kensy cast her eyes downward again as she proceeded. The pull was still strong, but now she was painfully aware of everyone around her. What was she getting herself into?

The admiral led the way down the hall. As the path split in two, it circled around a sizable central column and emptied into a large, open room. The walk divided the room in two and disappeared on the other side into another hallway. On either side wide stairs descended toward a lower level of computer stations in tidy rows that curved along with the arc of the forward wings. As the group moved, Jackson slowed his pace, allowing Morgan and Neira to pass him by. He fell in step with Kensy without a word or a glance as the group marched onward.

They entered the short, forward hallway. Upon reaching the far end of the path, the walkway again split in two. This time it diverged around a glowing beam of light nearly six feet across and twenty feet from floor to ceiling. Twin curved stair cases wrapped around the beam to a teardrop shaped area with a single station facing into the forward point. Admiral Khaivol and Doctor Hirayama stepped down the left side stairs as Captain Hadarian, Neira, and Morgan took the right side. Jackson took two steps down the left side so he could survey the whole of the room.

Kensy stopped at the beam, entranced by its light. There was something here. She could feel it in her skin. It called to her at the very edge of her hearing, but she couldn't place the sound. Everything else seemed to drift away. Time felt obscure and inconsequential. There was only her and the beam. Nexus wrapped around her ankles. She felt the tingle of his energetic presence, but ignored him.

"This is the bridgehead. Helmsman, please take a look. Do you think you could pilot from this console?" Doctor Hirayama asked. Morgan stepped forward and began studying the panels. "I believe it will also be augmented by virtual consoles based on pilot preferences and the ship's natural adaptations." She explained as he poked about.

"Could you activate the virtual consoles?" Morgan glanced up at her. "I would like to make sure I have the options that are missing from the hard boards. I don't recognize a lot of these controls, but I could figure it out. Give me a little time and I can fly anything...." He straightened his stance and placed his hands on his hips.

Doctor Hirayama shook her head at him. "This ship is actually designed for two pilots from what we've been able to piece together. So some of the controls that you are looking for may not be available by default." Jackson and Morgan both gave her confused expressions.

"Where exactly is this second pilot going to sit, Doc? Not in my lap, I hope, ...unless she's really hot," Morgan jested.

She shook her head. "The second pilot doesn't sit. The second pilot is a psionic." She pointed at the beam. "Though we've had no luck getting it to respond to anyone so far. I am hoping that if Miss Frost truly did touch the veil that it would somehow make her... different." Everyone looked toward Kensy, who stood just before the beam. Her fingers slowly reached for it. "Miss Frost, if you could, please try to activate the beam," Doctor Hirayama directed. Kensy did not respond. She seemed completely unaware of the others. Jackson stepped over the top two stairs and moved up next to her. He grabbed her hand, bringing her back to reality.

She looked up at him, "I know what I have to do...." She gently withdrew her hand and whispered, "Ivanigis." The purple glow burst from her body and she focused it on the underside of her arms, boots, and wrapped it up her legs. She stepped forward into the light. Jackson instinctively lunged forward to catch her, but the force of the beam repulsed his touch. He reeled from the shock. Kensy's body began to fall before the beam whisked her up into the air. Her energy permeated the beam and flowed up into the ship. The main drives came online and primary systems began to start up. Everyone watched in awe.

Doctor Hirayama glanced down at her holopad. Something caught her eye, and she began tapping furiously on the pad. "What's wrong, Doctor?" The admiral inquired.

"It's the ship, Sir." She turned her eyes up toward him. "It's using her like a battery to jump start... everything."

The pleased expression dropped off Neira's face. "What? Stop it! Get her out of there!" She gripped the stairway railing with both hands. Her knuckles turned white. *Shit! What have I done? Why did I think this would be a good idea? Stupid, Neira! So damn stupid!*

"Shut-It-Down!" Jackson demanded.

"I'm trying!" The doctor shouted back at him. "It's not responding!"

Suddenly the all of the lights on the bridge turned to a brilliant purple, matching Kensy's power emissions. A feminine mechanical voice rang out over them. At first the sounds were foreign but as it spoke the words became familiar, "-anguage calibration complete. Acquiring local solar date. Processing.... Uploading relevant data banks, ...please stand by."

Admiral Khaivol turned toward the doctor, "Issue project kill command—."

"I'm sorry, but interruption of start up processes will greatly affect the accuracy and efficiency of the complexity engine in rendering crew assistance for upcoming missions." The computer spoke up.

Neira walked up the stairs, a fire in her eye. "I don't give a damn about your complexity crap. I won't have a computer risking her life!" She pointed at Kensy.

"Psilyria Frost is in no danger of harm from this vessel," the computer retorted.

"You are aware of who the personnel on board are?" Captain Hadarian folded her arms across her chest and looked up at Kensy's motionless, floating form.

"Indeed, Captain. It was relevant information," it said matter-of-factly.

"How can you be draining her power and not be harming her?" Jackson's right forearm tingled from the beam's shock. He held his arm, flexing his fingers to get the sensation to pass.

"To be clear, the energy that I am drawing upon to activate my systems is not that of Psilyria Frost's. She is merely acting a conduit or doorway to the void. She was informed of the risk. Her consent was given." There was an awkward pause amongst the group. "Start-up process finalizing. Releasing beam control. Attention: Psilyria Frost may experience fatigue from interaction. Please feel free to utilize the officer's quarters on the upper deck."

Kensy's body floated backward out of the beam, where Neira and Jackson caught and cradled her between them. She looked up at them, exhaustion visible in her eyes. "Did it work?" She asked in little more than a whisper.

Neira nodded, "Yeah, it worked...." Kensy smiled as her eyelids grew heavy and her body relaxed into her friends' arms.

Chapter 16

Trust, Faith & Orders

"Sometimes unconventional problems require
unconventional solutions."
~ *Admiral Kristopher Khaivol,*
Sol System Defense Force

"Arriving at Central Command Deck. Commander Gabel is presently within the Strategic Operations Center." The mechanical voice of the computer announced as the lift arrived at the main floor. The doors slid open and Kensy stepped out, cautiously eyeing the elevator's control panel. She turned to look back at the large column that contained the lift. After taking several clumsy side steps, she halted her movement and looked around, managing to stop just shy of the stairs to the left of the walkway.

A short distance away, Jackson sat quietly, cleaning out from under his fingernails with his pocketknife. He paused for a moment and patted the stair beside him before returning to his task at hand. Kensy walked down the first few steps and quietly sat down beside him. "Feeling better?" he inquired.

"Yeah." She watched him meticulously but gently scrape at the underside of his nails. She tucked her hands under her thighs and tapped her boot heels against the edge of the stair they rested on.

They sat there in quiet contemplation for a few minutes before he finally broke the silence. "You know...," he hesitated, "...we need to have a talk about a certain bad habit of yours."

He flipped his knife closed with one hand and tucked it into a small pouch on the back right side of his uniform belt. He took a deep breath. "Somehow you have a knack for finding the craziest, most fantastical means of pushing yourself so far beyond your own limits that you end up passing out in my arms."

"Only cause you're so good at catching me...," Kensy blurted out before her brain caught up. She turned her head away and made a face at herself. *You colossal idiot! You just said that OUT LOUD! Holy freaking hell, he must think I'm totally mental.* She shook her head, "I mean... I don't mean to... it's just...." She fumbled over her thoughts. Her eyes traced the lines in the floor, searching for the right words to cover her embarrassment.

He lifted her face to look him in the eyes. "I just wanted to say, be careful." He withdrew his hand and broke eye contact. "I'm a soldier. The mission has to take priority. That's my duty, first and foremost. I can't be your parachute. You shouldn't rely on there always being someone close at hand that has your best interests in mind. It's dangerous."

Kensy shrugged, "Tell you what... next time we have to wake up a creepy alien ship, I'll let you be the living energy conduit," she cautiously jested with a gently smile. He glanced back at her incredulously. He surrendered, letting slip an amused sigh as he shook his head. She nudged him with her shoulder. "So, where is everyone, anyway?" She surveyed the Ops Center. It seemed as if they were the only two people on the ship.

"Oh, they're around. I think the doctor lady and Morgan are down the hall on the bridgehead arguing about control schemes and other technical crap. Neira found some poor tech to do her bidding, and they wandered off down one of the rear corridors. The Captain and Admiral Khaivol said they had *things to discuss.* And they vanished into one of the conference rooms." Jackson glanced around. "Oh, and I think someone made Bryden the unofficial errand boy. He's been in and out of here a bunch. He actually passed through just before you came down."

Kensy tilted her head toward the front of the ship as the clamor of footsteps became audible. "Sounds like he's on his way back," she leaned back on the upper step to look at him as he walked into the Ops Center, "...and with company."

Daniel smiled as he glimpsed the ruddy blonde of Kensy's hair. Morgan strode up beside him. Daniel guided his salutation toward Jackson, "I've been told to round everyone up. Sounds like the brass has something to say to the lot of us." Daniel extended his right hand to help Kensy up. She placed her hand in his, rising to her feet. "I hope this hasn't been too terrible of an experience for you."

She dismissed it with a wave of her hand. "One more day, one more mess. I wouldn't know what to do with an uneventful life, as mine has been anything but." She gave a light chuckle and glanced back at Jackson, who had risen to stand beside her.

"Well, this mess should be over soon. Then, hopefully, you can have a well-earned respite. Tell you what, drinks are on me after this." Daniel beckoned them on, "Come on, let's go get this meeting over with."

Jackson gently placed his hand on the small of her back to urge her to follow Daniel. Her heart fluttered, but she kept her eyes forward. As they rounded the column toward the conference hall wing of the main deck, Kensy's steps didn't quite keep pace with the surrounding company. It occurred to her that all three men were career military, driven and disciplined. Psicorp was significantly more varied by nature and probably seemed lax in comparison to the rigid structure of naval life. Her thoughts drifted until she felt the gentle press of Jackson's fingertips against the curve of her lower spine. She jogged a few quick steps to close the distance again.

The passage opened into a small foyer with a holographic centerpiece of exotic flowers atop an elegant pillar. On the far side, one of the conference room doors sat ajar. Daniel lead the way, opening and holding the door for everyone to pass through. Inside, Neira sat quietly waiting alongside Captain Hadarian. The Admiral stood beyond the head of the table, staring out the window, his hands folded neatly behind his back. Daniel gave the captain a slight bow. "That's everyone Ma'am, I'll be waiting just outside if you need me."

"Take a seat, Lieutenant," the admiral spoke up. He turned to survey the group. "Please. If everyone could take your seats, we can begin." He stepped up to his chair and placed a hand on the backrest.

Daniel hesitated but moved to the next available seat. When everyone had sat down, the captain straightened her posture and leaned her elbows on the table. She laced her fingers together as she spoke. "As you well know, several of our colonies have come under attack from an unknown enemy. This has led to certain... unique circumstances, including the overly public conscription of Commander Gabel and Psilyria Frost to the Graven Order." Neira shrugged off the pointed statement, all the while keeping a close eye on the admiral.

The admiral asserted himself, "In light of this, it has been decided that you will be given operational autonomy under the condition that you continue to pursue the investigation of the events that led us here." He stared directly at Jackson and Kensy. "You are still bound to your contracts of service to the Navy and Psicorp, respectively, but it behooves both Graven and Military alike to create a specialized task force to address this issue." He pushed his chair aside and reached for the tabletop. His fingers tapped across the glossy surface, activating a central holographic display. "What you don't know is that Bhelnir was not the beginning." The light coalesced into the form of the Milky Way. Brightly colored call-outs appeared throughout the display. "Given what we now know, these points of interest are all of the unsolved reports that have been flagged as potentially related. They are everything from blackened colonies, missing persons, attacks by mechanical constructs to urban legends and suspicious sightings. You will have to determine relevance on a case-by-case basis."

Jackson leaned on the right arm of his chair, deep in thought. After a moment of staring at the map, he turned toward the admiral. "Sir, who will be leading the task force? Are we going to be reassigned to another ship?" The captain raised an eyebrow at Jackson and shifted her gaze to her superior.

The admiral cracked a smile and pressed the fingertips of both his hands to the tabletop. He nodded. "Yes, you will be reassigned. If fact, you will *all* be reassigned... to this ship."

"Sir...?" Jackson hesitated.

The admiral held up his hand to halt the impending question. "Considering that this is a very special ship with need of two pilots and that the mission at hand is of the utmost importance we found it only suitable that she will have two captains, one specialized in tactical and strategic planning and one more suited toward diplomatic endeavors. Both have extensive military training and combat experience."

Jackson glanced across the table. "Captain?"

She shook her head. "Nope, my ship is the Themiscyra. But she will be in dry dock for some time, so in order to make the most of the resources at hand her remaining active crew will be transferred to this ship. You know the personnel." She shot a fleeting glance at Kensy. "Take care of the crew and they will serve you well, I have no doubt."

Admiral Khaivol interjected, "Your crew will be complimented by a number of my technicians who are already familiar with the ship for the best possible transition. This will bring the approximate head count to two-hundred and fifty souls stationed aboard this ship; a light crew to be sure, but it should be sufficient given the technology aboard. Now, under normal circumstances, a new captain would be given the freedom to review personnel selections, but time is unfortunately against us and you two will have your hands full with the investigation. An experienced and familiar crew is really the best option."

"Wait! What?!" Kensy blurted out. She and Jackson exchanged confused looks. "Sir," she hesitated, "You mean that *we* are going to co-captain this ship?" She folded her hands together in her lap and wrung them nervously.

The admiral raised an eyebrow at her. "Is that a problem, Psilyria Frost?"

"No, sir! It's just that...," she took a deep breath, "Speaking for myself, are you sure I'm qualified for a command of this... magnitude?" She glanced toward Neira. Her friend smirked and nodded in affirmation.

Jackson straightened his posture. "I think what Psilyria Frost means is that this is an honor, but it does seem abrupt. Neither of us have completed the officers' training program to that level."

The admiral nodded. "As we said before, circumstances surrounding these events are unique. To be sure, any resources you require regarding training will be at your disposal, but we have confidence that you will have little need of them. You have both demonstrated exceptional leadership skills and a willingness to see the mission through."

"And what of me, Admiral?" Neira leaned forward and rested her forearms on the table. "Where do I fit into the command structure?" She tilted her head in his direction.

"In matters regarding the Graven, you are the senior officer, but in all other matters, including the command of this vessel, you will defer to Commander Gabel and Psilyria Frost. You may advise as they see fit, but this is still a military vessel." The admiral looked around the table. "Any other questions?" No one responded. "No? Well then, I think it's time to undock this bird and take her up to the station for personnel and equipment transfers. In preparation, we have already ordered the station optics systems to undergo intensive diagnostics calibration. No one will have eyes on the ship's exterior for the duration of the transfers. This way we can maintain operational security for everyone involved. Now, Psilyria Frost, Lieutenant Threaux, would you please take her out?"

Slowly, everyone swiveled out of their chairs and began to shuffle toward the door.

Kensy waited for a moment, steeped in contemplation. "DeCadejra." They all turned to look at her. She lifted her eyes to meet the admiral's. "The ship's name... I remember hearing it when I was in the beam. She's the DeCadejra."

He smiled. "I think we can do something about that." She returned a satisfied smile and headed for the exit.

Chapter 17

Brave First Steps

"In our line of work, the first step isn't inevitably the hardest. It's just the point at which you pick a direction."
~ Captain Alexandria Hadarian

Kensy flexed her fingers anxiously as she stared at the command beam. "Please to proceed into the psionic submersion interface, Psilyria Frost," the computerized voice requested.

Neira stood slouched against the right wall, glaring up at the beam from her place at the base of the bridgehead stairs. "This won't be a repeat of last time?" She crossed her arms and tapped her fingers against the upper portion of her arm.

The mechanical chords responded accordingly. "I assure you all systems are fully functional and require no further draw to sustain them. Psilyria Frost's experience will differ drastically from the previous encounter. She will retain all cognitive abilities and will be capable of controlling ship operations with ease. Please proceed."

Jackson glided up next to Kensy. "You got this?"

She blinked a couple times and breathed in deeply. "You do realize I know nothing of ships or piloting?!" She exhaled nervously. "What if I screw this up?" she whispered.

He tilted his head to one side and cocked an eyebrow at her. Leaning in close, he spoke in a hushed tone. "Then the rest of us will know you're human just like us." He turned away and began down the left side steps. With a brief glance back in her

116

direction, he reached the base of the beam, and took up a strong stance adjacent to Morgan's chair.

Kensy rolled her eyes in exasperation. He was being no help at all. She shook her head, "Well, here goes nothing...." She closed her eyes and stepped into the light. It felt more solid this time, lifting her without the aid of her psionic abilities. Her eyelids slowly opened. The view was breathtaking. Rivers of energy coursed around her and the ship. She focused on her companions on the bridge and they became illuminated by the interface. With only a thought, she could see vital statistics and entire files of information on each one. She pushed that aside and focused on the ship. The scale of her vision changed, and she saw everything as if though she were the ship. Astrogation data and volumes of stellar cartography were overlaid, giving her endless seas of information. Awe filled her voice, "Holy stars...."

"Doing alright?" Neira's voice rang clearly, as if she stood only inches away.

Kensy nodded. "Yeah, you wouldn't believe this even if you could see it."

Jackson folded his hands together neatly at the small of his back. "Take us out, Lieutenant."

Morgan's hands danced across the layers of holographic and hard panels, gracefully and quickly. "Engines on standby. System idle looks good. Disengaging magnetic docking arms. Now, any idea which way is the garage door?" Morgan jested.

"I know the way." Without a second thought, Kensy tried to hand the data readout to Morgan. The screen disappeared from her interface and popped up in front of him.

He blinked in surprise. "Nifty trick. Now I'll drive if you think you can manage to open the door." The ship slowly began to drift forward. Two holographically projected gyroscopes appeared in front of Morgan's hands. He grabbed the core of each one and felt a tingle spread up his arms. "Oh yeah! This is more like it." He smirked as the ship began to move under his direction. He followed the plotted course toward the exit.

"Now for that door...," Kensy focused on it. She reached out with her fingers and her thoughts. Once it felt the touch of her mind, the colossal locks began to tumble and twist away. As the way opened, she stared in disbelief, "No way...."

Neira pushed away from the wall, "Oh, do share...."

Kensy cupped her hands in front of her, palms facing outward. She drew them apart in an arc. The entire bridgehead seemed to disappear as the walls became virtual windows. What they beheld defied all reason. They gazed into the underside of one of Pluto's frigid seas, but even with the open doors, not a single drop escaped inward. Everyone stared in astonishment.

Jackson placed a hand on Morgan's shoulder, "Take us out nice and slow."

"You got it, boss." Morgan pressed the controls ahead gradually. The forward wings pierced the fluid barrier, sending ripples cascading across the opening. Jackson began to pace behind the pilot's seat, watching as the ship pushed forward.

A chill ran through Kensy's body as the bridgehead became submerged. She shivered and her breath became visible inside the beam. "You think you can pick up the pace a little there? That is awfully cold." She wrapped her arms close in an attempt to warm up.

Neira stepped forward. "You heard her, fly-boy. Punch it." Morgan looked up to his commander. Jackson nodded in affirmation, *do it*. He then turned his eyes toward her floating figure.

Morgan tilted his head from side to side, causing the joints in his neck to pop audibly. He flexed his fingers. "Now, let's see what this baby can do." He slammed the control gyros forward, and the ship rocketed forward. She burst out of the sea and up through the atmosphere. In moments, they were sailing effortlessly in the vacuum of space.

Kensy relaxed as the chill passed from her. She caught a glimpse of Jackson turning his attention away. Smiling to herself, she lifted her chin to examine the lay of the stars above them. So beautiful and so full of wonder.

From back in the hallway, the admiral and captain observed quietly. "I must admit," the admiral spoke up, "I had my reservations about this, but I think you're right, Alex. Those kids will do just fine. It isn't going to be easy on them, though. There's a whole galaxy of things that will want to kill or manipulate them, and we need them to solve the mystery of the needle in a haystack. Where is it and why is it there?" He let out a heavy sigh.

"They're good kids, Kris. They'll figure it out." The captain chuckled and shook her head. "Oh, listen to us talk about them like children. We're getting too old to chase down the secrets of the galaxy. Before long, it's going to show."

"Only if you stop getting your hair treated," he jested.

"Tell anyone I'm going gray and they'll have to court martial me for murder." She straightened her posture as she heard Jackson approaching from the bridgehead. "Commander, how are we doing?"

Jackson stood to attention. "Lieutenant Threaux is bringing us into dock at Hades Station as we speak. We will be ready to begin the transfer of crew and supplies immediately."

"Very good, Commander. Maintenance crews will take it from here. It will take a little time to fully stock her. You and your crew will have enough to do starting tomorrow. Take some time tonight for yourselves. We can't have our new task force burning out before their very first mission. Dismissed."

Jackson nodded to her, "Thank you, Captain. I will inform the others immediately." He pivoted on his heel and returned to the bridgehead. Kensy began to descend toward the beam entrance like drifting through a cloud. She held her hands out to reach for the railing, but Jackson intercepted one, taking it firmly in his and guiding her on to the walkway. Her boot touched down on the metal grating and she stepped out of the light and into the artificial gravity environment once again. "Our duties begin tomorrow." He glanced back over his shoulder. "It has been recommended to me that we all take some shore leave tonight."

Morgan swiveled his chair around with a conniving smile wrapped around his lips. "Didn't Bryden mention something about drinks being on him? I think it's time to get this party started!" He clapped his hands together and sprung out of his chair.

Neira placed her hands on her hips and gave him an icy glare. "Oh, you think you know how to party, fly-boy?"

"That sounds like a challenge...," Morgan began.

"Aht," Jackson put up a hand to interrupt their banter. "Just don't party too hard. I want you on the bridge ready to work at o'seven hundred. We need to get this ship in order asap."

Morgan shrugged. "There you go again. Do you want me to bring your morning coffee too?"

Jackson cracked a smirked, "Well, if you're offering...." He turned and walked away from the bridgehead without another word.

Chapter 18

The Eve

"Mistakes were made ...."
~ by several people

Laughter and hollering filled the bar's vintage Earthen atmosphere with a warmth. Morgan slouched back in one of the side booths, beer in hand and silver tongue in motion as he flirted shamelessly with a young lady whom he had charmed into sitting with him. Jackson rolled his eyes and turned back to his conversation with Daniel and Allen at one of the elevated tables in the front center of the bar's open loft. "I don't know what they see in a charlatan like him." He shook his head and took a sip from the tall frosted glass in his hand.

Daniel laughed, "Probably the same thing he sees in them, sex, and a complete lack of obligation. He ships out tomorrow and she gets bragging rights to her girlfriends with no chance of fact checking regardless, of the outcome." He leaned forward onto the table. "Now, what I'd pay to see is the woman he can't resist who wants nothing to do with him. The sheer torture of that would be hilarious." He took a swig from the mug in his hand. Movement outside the bar's ground-floor windows caught his eye, and he smirked. "And I think I know the best prospect for that...."

Allen glanced down and to his left. "Really?! Prospects aside, I think something far more interesting than Morgan's inevitable rebuke is en route." He gave a knowing nod to Daniel, who immediately understood the innuendo.

"Enough with your theories. I have the night off and would rather not spend it thinking of him." Jackson missed the implied turn of subject. "And no tech talk either. I'd rather like to actually be able to participate in the conversation." Jackson rested his elbow on the back of an adjacent chair, his back to the front door.

Daniel raised his glass, "Perhaps then you would rather discuss a vision far more fair and enchanting...." He nodded toward the door as it opened. The delicate ring of the overhead bell was barely discernible over the sound of the crowd. Confused, Jackson slowly looked back over his shoulder and down into the crowd.

Neira stepped through the entrance, satin black clutch in hand. Her top was cut like the rays of a crimson sun, wrapping up around her neck, out across her arms and down her torso. The sleeve of her right arm stopped just above her bracer while the other extended to only a few inches shy of her left wrist, on which she wore a wide band silver bracelet. Two plain black belts crisscrossed her hips over the cranberry straight cut skirt that matched her top. She hollered to the barkeep as she stepped away from the doorjamb.

Then his eyes fell on Kensy. Soft strawberry blonde curls cascaded down the right side of her face from the top of her delicately twisted up-do. Her wispy periwinkle dress flowed like water around her as she moved. The lines of the dress were far less dramatic than Neira's, but conveyed an unmatched elegance. It scooped from the outer crest of her shoulders across her chest, just below the collarbone. Her shoulder injury was nearly indistinguishable now. She shyly swept to the side of the door. The crystalline accents of her dress and jewelry glittered in the low lights. Even her skin seemed to shimmer as if kissed with stardust. Jackson stood enraptured and speechless.

Neira turned her attention to Kensy. They spoke too softly to be heard over the other patrons, but the expression on

Kensy's face was clear enough to decipher from across the room. She fidgeted and pleaded with Neira. They argued as Neira worked to persuade her. Kensy shook her head in defeat. She caught a glimpse of Jackson staring at her. Her face flushed red, and she looked down. Even in his casual attire, he was handsome. The khaki cargo pants, flat black dress shirt and sharp leather jacket that he wore, while simple, gave him a dapper presence.

"...isn't that right, Gabel?" Allen directed at him.

Jackson snapped back to the others. "Huh?" He tried to act casually oblivious as he kept Kensy in the corner of his vision. "Sorry, I didn't catch that over the ruckus." He took another drink. "It's almost too loud to think in here," he feigned to dismiss his inattentiveness.

"Sorry bud, can't blame the volume for your inability to think this time," Daniel jested.

Jackson turned toward him with a scowl. "What's that supposed to mean?!"

Daniel shrugged, "I'm just saying, any red-blooded man with a pulse has got to find *that* more than a little distracting, well, for those of you that are into women." He smiled and kept eyes on Kensy, "You know, you two are going to be working pretty closely on this mission—."

"No! Don't even start—," Jackson began.

"Are we interrupting?" Neira asked as she crested the wrought iron stair behind Jackson. He turned, startled. "Where does a girl go for fun around here? This can't be it." She circled around behind Allen and took up a seat between him and Daniel. She snapped her fingers at a passing waitress, "A reaper on the rocks for me and...," she looked at Kensy.

Kensy politely nodded to the woman. "A stardust sparkle, please." The waitress nodded and danced her way past the shifting crowd between them and the back bar. Jackson flipped the chair he was leaning on around to face their table and offered it to Kensy. She hooked her heel on the foot bar and lifted herself gracefully into the seat. "Thank you." She set her purse in her lap, letting the strap fall over her left leg. He stood tall and clenched his jaw as he tried to focus on other things. Kensy directed her attention to Allen, holding out a hand to him, "I don't believe I've had the pleasure...."

He gently shook her hand, being mindful of her delicate fingers. "Lieutenant Allen Petroski, engineer."

She smiled warmly. "Then I owe you more than an introduction. Psilyria Kensy Frost, glad to make your acquaintance and thank you for your assistance." She subtly waved her armored left arm. "I owe you a great deal."

He leaned back in his seat and chuckled, "Nonsense. The pleasure was mine. I always love a good challenge!" The waitress appeared beside Kensy with her precariously balanced drink tray. She handed Kensy a tall stemmed glass of glittering white wine, then spun around through the maze of chairs to pass off Neira's blackish tinted drink in its stout and rounded glass. She proceeded to disappear into the crowd as she pocketed the tip card Neira had slid her.

The sound of giggling reached Neira's ears, causing her to spin her chair around to investigate. "Hey fly-boy! Is that you trying to play fastball with the jail bait?" she sneered at him.

Without so much as a sideways glance, he responded, "Oh Bethany, here is no jail bait. She is so much woman that it's almost criminal." She giggled again as he whispered in her ear.

Neira held up her right hand and examined her perfectly manicured nails. "Hmm. Too bad you're so preoccupied. Guess it's better this way. I'd hate to embarrass you in front of your little girlfriend there when I drink you under the table." Her mocking tone elicited a glare from him.

Allen let out a hearty laugh. "Ooohh! Them's fighting words! You gonna let that slide Threaux?" Everyone at the table waited for the reprisal.

"Fine," he retorted. "Let's see how little girls handle their liquor."

Neira hopped out of her seat and stepped toward him with a conniving grin. "You're on!"

A jovial spirit filled the air, subtly putting everyone at ease. Neira and Morgan took turns egging each other on between drinks as Kensy sipped her wine and listened to Daniel and Allen regale her with tales of mishaps and mayhem aboard the Themiscyra prior to her arrival. Jackson stepped in to correct his friends on the occasion that the facts became too exaggerated by drink and enthusiasm. They shared laughs as the night crawled by.

As the competition between Neira and Morgan drew more attention Kensy found cause to excuse herself from the table. She slipped out onto a small balcony overlooking the street below. She took a deep breath and relaxed in the crisp open air. The sounds of the bustling bar grew muffled as the door swung shut. She leaned on the railing, gazing up at the virtual windows that covered the city-station.

"You ... uh, doin' okay?" Jackson hesitated.

She smiled and looked down at the wineglass in her hands. "Yeah." She snickered, "Needed a little fresh air. Things are getting a little too rowdy for me in there." Turning around, she leaned backward on the railing and watched through the window as Neira downed another drink and taunted Morgan.

Jackson stuffed his hands in his pockets and peeked back at the others. "Seems like some pretty wicked stuff she's getting the bartender to pour." He leaned his left shoulder against the wall.

Kensy drew in a breath trying to remember, "I think she told me once that is actually three drinks in one: a dark space slide, the mad minion and death by cosmos, ...I think. Poor Morgan has no idea what he's gotten himself into." She shook her head in pity.

Jackson gave her a questioning glance. "You really think she'll out drink him?"

"Oh, yes. He doesn't have a prayer. Thing is...," Kensy rocked back and forth on the rail, "after Alpha Bael Neira hunted down every potential cure or concoction she could find from immuno-boosters to cybernetics. Many were experimental at best. And none of them worked; but, in order to test the waters, so to say, she had them done to herself first. The last one I knew about was some kind of metabolic anti-toxin implant. It identifies toxins in her system and creates counter agents to breakdown and neutralize them, even alcohol. Ten minutes after she's done drinking, she's as sober as a kraydian priest."

Jackson shook his head. "Well, she better not make him drink himself to death. We have a lot to do tomorrow without losing our pilot to alcohol poisoning."

Kensy stepped up to the window beside him. "No worries. Watch the bartender when he pours this next drink." They watched intently for a moment. and then he saw it. "She started having him progressively water down Morgan's drinks about half an hour ago."

Jackson looked down at her with a gentle smile. "You noticed that?"

"Pretty easy to spot when you've seen it before." She sighed and blinked slowly. "I must be getting tired. I don't even want to know what hour it is."

He pushed off the wall with his shoulder. "Yeah, you're probably right. It is getting late. Tell you what, I'll walk back to the ship with you. I've had about as much of the festivities as I can stand." He grabbed the doorknob and opened it for her. She sleepily nodded. Quietly they slipped through the crowd and down the stair. As they approached the door, Daniel spied them leaving together and smirked.

Outside, Jackson offered her his elbow to hold. She curled her fingers around his arm and they began to walk. "I've always loved nighttime. No matter where I've traveled, I've always found it to be a little more peaceful, a little bit slower," she mused. "Sometimes it feels like we just get swept away by the bustle of everyday. That's when I miss the quiet." She leaned her head on his arm as they walked.

They turned off the main street and headed through the park. A chill ran down her back and she shivered. Jackson paused in his tracks. "You cold?"

"Yeah, sorry." She drew back from him, embarrassed, "Guess the station's a little chillier than I anticipated. Prolly shoulda brought a shawl or something." He pulled his jacket open, letting it slide down his arms. He caught the collar on his fingertips and flipped it around. Stepping toward her, he draped it over her shoulders. "Thank you but are you sure? You won't be cold?"

"Nah," he held out his elbow for her to take, "You need it more than I do right now. 'Sides it's not that far of a walk back to the ship." She smiled softly.

They continued along the path at a leisurely pace, taking in the night. She looked up at the starscape displayed across the station's ceiling. "You know, if anyone had asked me a month ago where I'd be now, this is about the last thing I would have guessed. Sitting on the outskirts of the Sol system, on the eve of taking up a joint command on an alien ship... I could not have even imagined this." She looked down at the cobbled path passing underfoot. "Not sure I deserve a command... not after what happened."

"And why not?" He gazed down at her with concern.

"My last command ended with me getting them killed," she replied in a self-scorning tone as her thoughts wandered.

"B.S." he stopped and turned her to face him. "Listen to me. You saved lives. Everything I've seen you do, you do to keep saving lives. Yeah, sometimes we lose people in order to save others, but it's what we do. And it bites, big time! Every single person in the service, no matter what branch, knows... we do this to save lives. You saved a colony from being wiped out, hell, you saved the entire crew, myself included, back on

Morwhex. Don't sell yourself short. You've earned this." Her heart fluttered as she stared up him, his hands firmly holding her shoulders between them. The perfection of the moment was interrupted by an abrupt snap.

She tried to look past him. "Did you hear that?"

Jackson let go of her as he spun around. He pushed her back with one hand and moved to investigate the noise. Suddenly, a shadowy figure sprung from the foliage and brought a blunt implement down across his skull. He staggered backwards. The blow was disorienting, dropping him to his knees. He squinted, trying to refocus his vision. Kensy instinctively rushed to help him up, but the assailant interceded. "Not so fast there, Blondie." He jabbed a dingy plasma pistol in her direction. In his off-hand he waved a bloodied length of steel pipe. From the looks of it they had not been his first victims, only the most recent. "Fork over the goods, purse, wallet, jewels, and maybe I don't put holes in the both of ya."

Jackson struggled to stand. He gave a snicker. "Oh man, you picked a bad one tonight." Jackson maneuvered himself between Kensy and the gunman. "This girl's a psionic, one of the most powerful. She's wiped out whole platoons single-handedly. I've personally seen her deflect the blast of a nuke, and you want to mug her?!" She watched them, confused and concerned. What was he doing? She felt a tingle in her fingers as she tried to decide what to do. Did he really think he could intimidate this guy into leaving without a fight based on her reputation? Jackson wavered and stumbled toward the guy. "You have some kinda crap luck picking this one."

The mugger sneered at him, "Oh, yeah? If she's so bad-ass, why are *you* protecting *her*?"

Jackson's eyes became clear and determined. In a flash, he knocked the gun away, locking his arm around the shooter's. With a fluid step, he swept around behind the man, jamming his elbow into the kidney area. He slipped his arm under the assailant's and threw him through the air with tremendous force, swiping the gun and pipe from his attacker's grasps mid flight. The man landed with a thud, writhing in pain. Jackson stood over him with a piercing glare. "Because I'm *more* dangerous than she is." The mugger whimpered and scrambled away as fast as he could, disappearing from sight.

Jackson winced, tossing the weapons aside. He tried to shake the lingering haziness. She stood in stunned amazement for a moment, processing what she had just seen. It was all an act, an attempt to gain the positioning he needed without arousing suspicion. He had struck like a viper, turning the tables in an instant. She ran up beside him and grabbed at his shirt. "Are you okay? That was... amazing." She delicately drew her fingers across his forehead. "You're bleeding!"

He pulled away from her touch. "It's nothing."

She tilted her head and raised an eyebrow at him. "Oh, who's the one pushing too hard now?" He stopped resisting as she pulled a familiar handkerchief from her purse. It was the one he had tied around her arm on Morwhex. She gave a slight laugh. "I've been meaning to give this back. Just, ...not like this. Guess it's my turn to take *you* to medbay," she jested. She dabbed gently at the scrape and searched for the right words. He sensed her hesitation, but remained silent. Finally, her lips parted as she found her voice again. "Why *did* you protect me? You're no longer under orders to do so. You don't have to answer to anyone about my well-being. So why? Why put yourself in harm's way for me?"

The question struck him off guard. He reached up and cupped her hand in his. "Why shouldn't I?"

Chapter 19

Settling In

*"Sometimes it's important to take the little moments...
or you'll never get unpacked."*
~ DeCadejra Quartermaster

The dark ambiance of the enormous war room was augmented by the brilliant glow of the massive central table's holographic display. Numerous charts, maps, and articles littered the air. The room buzzed with the warm hum of monitors and consoles that encircled the outer reaches of the chamber. An aura of intensity filled the open space and wrapped around Kensy as she circled the domed table, checking various pieces and packets of data against one another. She shuffled the stacks of datapads strewn about before her, hoping the answers she sought would illuminate themselves. She took a deep breath and leaned on the lip of the table. The tap of her nails against the glassy surface alerted Neira to her frustration. Neira circled the far side of the table, tracing the curve with her right index finger as she examined the console. "So, it seems your evening was a bit more interesting than I had anticipated...."

Kensy shook her head. "There is nothing to tell."

Neira stopped and gave her an incredulous look. "Oh, now we're skipping to bold face lies, ...or is it denial?" Kensy glared at her. "Oh, this is good...," Neira placed both palms flat on the table and leaned forward, "...you like him, he plays hero and nothing happened? You're either dumber than I thought or we need to have a serious talk about your ridiculous adherence to regulations."

Kensy shook her head in exasperation. "I have work to do, if you don't mind. And so do you if I'm not mistaken. Besides, I thought you hated him." Kensy's voice became absent of interest as a revelation came to her. She began re-sifting through the datapads.

"Well, I don't think there's any accounting for your taste in men but it doesn't really matter what I think, does it?!" Neira leaned her hip on the edge of the table and folded her arms neatly across her chest. "Don't think you're going to get out of talking about this. Bryden told me he saw you two leave *together* last night and then I hear from the gossip trail that a gang of bloodthirsty thugs descends on you two in *the park.* And he heroically beats them all down with the attackers' own weapons. Then you two show up together in medbay. The good doctor treats him for a concussion and you walk out together again. Where'd you go from there? Back to his quarters, perhaps?"

"You are incorrigible!" Kensy rolled her eyes. "Yes, we left the bar at the same time. It was late and there was a lot of work to be done. And oh yeah, we're living on the same ship, so yes, we walked together. We made small talk, took a shortcut because it was late and on the way, a rather sad excuse for a mugger attempted to hold us up. Jackson was hit in the head, but disarmed the guy, and we reported it, then went to Doctor Tyronis to make sure he was okay. After which we went our separate ways. End of story." Kensy refused to look up at Neira as she described the evening's events in cold detail. "Now, if you're done writing me a fictional love life, how about we actually try doing our jobs?"

Neira turned her gaze away and stood in silence for a moment. "Listen, I didn't mean to push your buttons so hard." Her voice was softer this time, concerned. "Just promise me something. If there is something that makes you happy, don't throw it away for rules that don't mean anything. Allow yourself some semblance of normalcy. You deserve to be happy." Kensy contemplated her words for a moment, then nodded.

The war room door slid open with a whoosh. Jackson strode in, head down, lost in thought. He looked up and paused. "Already working on the data correlation?"

Kensy squinted at her star charts, "Yeah, been in here working for a while. I didn't have anything better to do, so I thought I'd try to find a pattern or solid lead in all this." She gestured to the scattered tablets and displays. "I thought I had something, but I can't remember where it was it now. Someone came in here on a rant and distracted me." She shot a glance to Neira, who waved it off.

Jackson approached the table. "Didn't you want to get your stuff moved over and settled?"

Kensy shrugged. "I never unpacked after Bhelnir. It took like half an hour to get my things transferred. I figured I'll have plenty of time later to settle in. There are more pressing matters."

"Wait, have you been in here all morning? Have you even eaten today?" He glanced between the two women.

"Not hungry," she stated.

"Kensy!" Neira protested.

"Later," a sudden recollection stirred Kensy's thought process once again, and she began frantically searching through the datapads.

"I know the mess hall is still getting set up but go get something to eat." Jackson scowled at her. "That's an order."

Kensy seized the pad she had been searching for. "I said later." She scrolled through the contents as she walked around him, pausing for a moment to whisper, "By the way, you can't pull rank on me, co-captain." She reached for one of the virtual interfaces and began to type. Neira and Jackson exchanged hopeless expressions. Kensy's eyes widened, "That's it... has to be."

Her cohorts closed in on her from both sides, eager to see what she had discovered. "What is *it*?"

"It's our first lead." She transferred the articles from the datapad with a flick of her fingers. Reaching up to the hologram, she arranged her findings. "I was looking at timelines and patterns, trying to backtrack the attacks. I was hoping to find a point of origin through data extrapolation, but given the unreliable nature of some of our information, the computer couldn't pinpoint an area of interest, which is also why no one else has been able to either. So I thought perhaps what we have is a crisis of too many variables. I simplified and found this:

"More than fifty years ago, a colony named Rosealleon had not one but dozens of different reports of mysterious attacks from settlements across the planet. Several people described the machinery coming to life and hunting their co-workers down. Yet others mention metal coils coming out of the walls and enveloping anyone nearby. More than a hundred and fifty colonists vanished within a six month time span. Local authorities blamed a mining operation malfunction for releasing hallucinogenic compounds and causing numerous fatalities. They followed up with a claim that the continued investigation was inciting panic in the population and the cases were closed."

"And nothing abnormal since?" Neira moved to another console and began her own search.

"The colony remained intact, but they declared the incident to be the result of corporate and military conspiracies aimed at exploiting their community. The colony seceded from the Terra Ascension Core, closing off all official channels. Ascension forces were pressed out of the system, and soon after, all of the major corporate entities were expelled or voluntarily withdrew, citing growing hostilities from the populace. They only deal with 'independent' parties now. With no oversight, the place must be a hotbed of criminal activity. But it's our best lead." Kensy pleaded to Jackson with determination in her eyes.

He shook his head. "I don't like it. An entire colony hell bent on keeping us out. This could go south real fast. How do you suppose we get in there without them shooting us on sight?" The muscles in his jaw flexed as he contemplated the next course of action.

"No, this is good." Neira stood tall. "This is perfect. This ship is not of any known make. We go in plain clothes. Convince them that we're underground, scouting new trade partners for private investors. That gives us plenty of excuse to hit the ground and do some digging."

Kensy looked to her, "But what will we say we're trading that won't immediately flag us as frauds? They probably won't take to a blind negotiation of general goods."

Neira smiled. "So we bring them a taste of something not strictly legal. I have just the thing, Nordux Crystals." Her conniving expression did nothing to settle Jackson's apprehensions. "No way they'll paint us if we're trading those."

"That's because they'll just think we're nuts, walking around with something that unstable! It's restricted for a reason. How do you think we're gonna get a hold of something like that even if it is just for show?!" He paused and shook his head, "No. Wait. I don't want to know, do I?!"

Neira looked him straight in the eyes. "No, you really don't. Just make sure you have something less conspicuous to wear." She strutted out of the room, leaving Jackson and Kensy alone in the confines of the war room.

Kensy turned back to her datapads and began searching for the next tidbit or kernel of knowledge. Jackson watched her silently for a few moments. She delved through the charts and reports with singular focus. He stuffed his hands in his pockets, "You said she came in here on a rant. Mind if I ask what about?" He turned around and sat on the edge of the table, crossing his legs at the ankle.

"Last night," she curtly replied.

"What'd you tell her?" He asked with cautious interest.

"I told her that we have work to do, just like I'm about to tell you." Kensy reached up to the holographic display, her fingers delicately tracing the lines of information. "If we're going to figure out who is attacking our colonies and why, then it will take more than just me sifting through all these reports."

He gave her a sideways glance. "Did I do something wrong?"

Kensy withdrew her hands hesitantly. Casting her eyes down to the side, she inhaled slowly and deeply, searching for the right words. Her thoughts raced. She couldn't tell him how her heart felt as if though would burst at his very touch. She couldn't make him understand her hesitations. The haunting recollection of her medbay dream stirred long buried memories of her impending fate. What happiness could she dare to hope for with such an ominous destiny awaiting her? "No." She pressed her palms against the tabletop and leaned forward on them. "You've done nothing wrong. I promise." She shook her head. "It's me. I'm just... conflicted. Confused. Overwhelmed. I don't know where to go from here. I don't know what to do. I don't even know where to begin."

He reached out and placed his left hand atop her shoulder. He gently squeezed it, "You know, you're not alone. You don't have to do this all by yourself. We have our first lead and we haven't even gotten the ship fully loaded yet. There will be time. We'll figure it out *together*." He stood up, pivoting to face her. "Now, you are going to start by getting something to eat from the mess, then head back to your quarters and unpack. Take some time for yourself. You won't do anyone any good if you burnout before we even leave space dock." He ushered her out of the room before she could mount a protest.

"But...," she looked up at him with pleading eyes.

"Go. The universe isn't going to end while you take the afternoon to get settled." Reluctantly, she turned and meandered toward the nearest lift. He stuffed his hands back in his pockets and watched as she disappeared down the corridor. He shook his head and shuffled back into the war room, letting the doors glide closed behind him.

Chapter 20

Requisitions

"If sexy was a mode of transportation, this is what it would look like."
~ CS675 Gavinine Ultra Bike user manual

Kensy pulled her strawberry bangs off to the sides and tucked them behind her ears as she stopped to look around at her progress. The rooms were definitely starting to feel more like home as she distributed her belongings across the shelves, drawers, and closets. A heavy sigh escaped her lips as she surveyed the spacious living quarters and assessed what remained of her unpacking. Only two boxes left. She shook her head, *How did I accumulate so much stuff? Had I really been on Bhelnir so long?* She lifted the next crate on to her bed and pressed the lid releases. The seal broke on the box with a whoosh. She slid the top aside and paused. She stared for a long moment. Then with trembling fingers she reached in and lifted the topmost picture frame from its resting place.

She slumped down on the bed beside the crate. Her eyes welled up as she traced the edges with her fingers. She stared at the faces, lost in memories, until the chirp of the communication system brought her back. "Psilyria Frost. Your presence is requested in the Hangar Two cargo bay at your earliest convenience," the mechanical voice informed her.

Kensy straightened her posture and wiped her eyes, "Who is asking for me?"

"The request was made by Lieutenant Daniel Bryden."

Kensy nodded in acknowledgment, "Thank you, Computer. Please inform him that I will be on my way momentarily." She dropped the frame back into the box and slid the lid shut.

"If I may, my proper designation is Magthaeleon. I am the DeCadejra's advanced complexity engine and tactical assistant. Addressing this unit by the correct designation may be vital for future operations to avoid any potential confusion."

Kensy paused in thought, "Umm, ...you have... a name? And it's not the same as the ship's?"

"That is correct." Magthaeleon replied, "The ship was constructed and space-worthy long before my implementation. I was commissioned as a separate entity and installed when it was determined that my services might be required in the event of a deferred alien activation."

"Well, someone called that one dead on." Kensy set the crate back against the wall and pondered her reply carefully, "As you may have noticed, we humans like to abbreviate names for ease of use in casual conversation and your name is like mine, a little too... formal. Would you accept me giving you a nickname? Say, Maggie perhaps?" Kensy waited for a response, as she contemplated the oddities of this conversation.

"Maggie. This designation would be sufficient... and agreeable," there almost seemed to be a note of satisfaction in Maggie's words.

Kensy smiled, "Well, thank you, Maggie. It's good to have a name to put with the voice." She bowed slightly and turned toward the door. "I should be heading down to meet, Daniel."

"Of course. Please proceed to the waiting elevator car."

As Kensy moved across the room, the loose airy material of her peridot colored shirt swirled and danced around her arms and torso. She fussed with the zipper of her high-waisted black vest. Why would Daniel need her assistance in the hangar? Had he asked for Jackson's aid as well? The purpose of the summons eluded her. Perhaps this was the beginning of her command duties, answering questions and making decisions. Was she really ready for this? Doubts and questions tumbled turbulently through her thoughts. Quietly, she stepped out of her quarters and headed toward the lift. The soft tap of her patent leather boots was muffled by the tightly knit hallway carpeting. She sauntered into the car and slouched against the rear wall rail. "Hangar Deck please," she requested.

She rode down in silence, listening only to the questions and theories in the back of her mind. A pleasant melody registered in her ears, drawing her attention. She looked around, "Is that... elevator music?" she asked, realizing that the sound was new.

"Yes, my research into human culture revealed a number of short comings in my original programming. I am in the process of rectifying these deficiencies," Maggie dutifully replied.

"And you felt that the lack of elevator music was a deficiency?"

"Indeed. It seemed obligatory for this mode of transportation." There was a pause, "Is this analysis erroneous?"

Kensy chuckled, "I don't know about obligatory, but it is nice." Her musings about the conversation at hand were interrupted by the ding of the opening doors. She stood to exit the lift and nearly stumbled into Jackson. Lifting her eyes, she met his brooding gaze, "Good. You're here. I was going to come looking for you. Evidently, a shipment came in that requires your inspection. Bryden has it set aside for you." He doubled back into the hallway, heading toward the rear port side hangar.

"My inspection?" Her mind harkened back to the reason for her venture into the lower decks. She puzzled over the possibilities.

He glanced back over his shoulder at her as they walked, "You'll understand when you see it."

They rounded the final corner and slipped through the inner vestibule. Small prototype fighter pods hung from racks above them. Dozens of crew members buzzed around the open hangar, shuffling cargo containers and loading a handful of different ground vehicles. Jackson led her toward a secluded subsection off the aft portion of the bay. As they cleared a wall of crates, Kensy finally spied Daniel standing beside an oversized container, reading his manifest charts. He glanced up with a smile, "Ah, there you are. I hope I wasn't interrupting anything, calling you down here. Gabel said you were still getting moved in, but I thought you might like to see this."

Kensy waved her hand dismissively, "It's fine. What was so important that *I* inspect it? A shipment from Psicorp? I wasn't expecting anything."

Daniel gave a nod to Jackson, "You wanna give me a hand?" The two men stood at either end of the container and set the locks to release. The middle seam popped open with a burst of air. They placed their fingers in the seam, forcing it further open. Kensy paced back and forth, trying to glimpse the contents, but to no avail. "On three...." They nodded in agreement. "One, two, three!" With one forceful push, they managed to drop the sides to the ground, revealing the contents. Kensy's eyes grew wide as she beheld the flowing black lines of the chassis.

"Is that...?" she slowly walked toward the bike, hand outstretched.

Jackson stepped onto the now flattened container, "It's not your original bike. It unfortunately did not survive Bhelnir. It took some finagling, but since you had it covered under your service contract, we managed to get it replaced. She's all yours."

They watched as Kensy gently ran her fingertips over the graceful lines of the body. Daniel smiled, "I even finagled you a reserved parking space for it." He leaned his elbow on the crate beside him. "She sure is a sweet ride: a Stellar Industries

CS675 Gravinine Ultra Bike complete with GSX Microflex-plate tires and the super cool self-sustaining clash core power module. I gotta hand it to ya; you have great taste in bikes."

Kensy threw one leg over the bike and straddled it. She ran her fingers up the seat cover and onto the orb of the clash core. It hummed and danced like a ball of lightning. She could feel the tingle of its energy against her skin. She smiled and let slip a sliver of laughter. "Thank you. I hadn't even thought about replacing it. This means a lot. It must have been near impossible to get a hold of. They didn't make very many."

Jackson moved up beside her, his hands in his pockets, "Actually, Bryden managed to smooth talk requisitions out of more than one. We have... what, five more coming?" He glanced to Daniel for confirmation.

"Six, plus parts," he shrugged, "I managed to convince them that our mission warranted special equipment for all those unforeseen circumstances. We have lots of other cool toys coming too," he smirked, his well-earned sense of achievement oozing off him.

Jackson turned his attention to Kensy, "Actually, I have one other matter I'd like to run by you." She gestured for him to continue. "While this ship does have two captains, I still believe she needs a first officer. Someone we both trust and who is a skilled leader."

Kensy nodded, "I couldn't agree more."

"I was hoping that you would concur. I have already submitted the request for promotion." They both turned their attention to Daniel. "Congratulations, Lieutenant Commander Bryden." Daniel straightened his posture, saluting his commanders respectfully and they in turn. "Now, if I'm not mistaken, I think it's about dinner time and the three of us should have a meal waiting in the officer's dining hall. There are other departmental appointments and a number of ship business topics to discuss. Not to mention this upcoming mission."

Kensy drew in a deep breath in an attempt to contain her excitement. She pressed both hands against the seat and pushed to lift herself enough to dismount the bike. An infectious smile emerged despite her best attempts to keep a serious expression on her face. She stepped backward and took in the elegant profile of the cycle again. Slowly, she circled around to meet Daniel and Jackson at the wall of the crates leading out to the main cargo floor. Daniel leaned toward her with a smile, "It's okay to be excited."

She chuckled delicately. Jackson and Daniel exchanged a quick glance as she took one last look at the bike. For the first time since they had met her, she seemed genuinely happy. She had surrendered her mask in the moment, revealing a glimpse of her guarded heart. The lightness of her demeanor was refreshing. Then, as subtly as the façade had faded, it returned. She straightened her posture and folded her fingers together behind her back, "Shall we get going?" They followed her lead out of the hangar bay and back toward the elevator. The doors slid open as she reached for the call button. Kensy paused, "... uh, thank you, Maggie?" She looked upward questioningly.

"You are welcome, Psilyria Frost. Please proceed into the elevator car. Your destination has already been set," Maggie informed them.

Daniel furrowed his brow in confusion, "Maggie?" He stared at Kensy in anticipation of an explanation.

"My formal designation is Magthaeleon. Psilyria Frost has informed me that a more concise designation would be desirable. Thus, Maggie was deemed appropriate," the mechanical voice informed him.

The doors closed behind them, and the elevator began to climb swiftly and smoothly. Kensy sheepishly glanced up at Daniel and Jackson as she slouched against the back wall. "There could be worse scenarios than an intelligent ship anticipating our every need," she jested.

"Speaking of which, if I may...," the lift doors slid open far too early to have reached the officer's deck. "I would like to draw your attention to the fifth lab on the right. Please proceed down the hall. A complete briefing will occur once you have arrived."

Jackson led the way out of the elevator, his expression stoic and rigid. Daniel held back to allow Kensy to disembark next. Then he followed closely on her heels. They counted the doors in the hall in apprehension. Only four doors lined the right side wall. Jackson doubled back and checked again, only four doors. He approached Daniel and began to talk.

Kensy stared off at the wall, distracted by a sound at the edge of her hearing. She hesitated before stepping away from her fellow officers. She placed her palms against the wall, waiting for something. Slowly, she inched away from them. Her hands softly caressing the material of the wall. She paused and closed her eyes to focus on her sense of touch. Abruptly, she opened her eyes and pulled back. The material of the wall began to fall in on itself, creating a door-frame where there had been none before. Jackson and Daniel jogged to close the distance she had opened between them. The doors slid smoothly open, and they cautiously peered inside.

Kensy warily advanced into the newly revealed laboratory. A number of consoles bordered the right forward side of the room. A large testing chamber took up the remaining area on that wall. Three exam chairs and their accompanying mobile workstations crowned the center of the room under brilliant lights. On the left side of the lab, they beheld a light beam similar to the bridgehead one and an arcing row of suspension tanks. Kensy recognized much of the equipment as she stared in awe at the complex setup.

Jackson scowled, "I don't get it. What are we looking at here, Maggie?"

"During my activation, a diagnostic of Psilyria Frost's person was completed." Daniel and Jackson looked at Kensy with concern. "At that time, a number of issues were identified with her person as well as the ship's accommodations. Her control clasp has been sundered, resulting in non-functionality. Her power flow balance has been offset by a recent increase in psionic capabilities. At that time, I deemed that any prolonged endeavors would require appropriate facilities for repair and maintenance of the Psilyria's systems. Construction of this specialized laboratory began and is nearing eighty percent. Projections place completion of facilities and full lab functionality in sixty-four hours, twenty-seven minutes from now. It is highly recommended that the control clasp interface be reconstructed and tested prior to the upcoming mission for the best probability of success."

Kensy looked down at her control clasp. Gently, she ran the fingers of her left hand over the bands and wires up to her wrist. She felt the mottling of the plasma burn scars that traveled up the heel of her hand and thumb. She remembered the sensations of her fingers in the interface as she ripped it apart. The emotions of that moment lingered over her like a heavily laden storm cloud. She nodded in affirmation, "I will have to see to it." She felt a tightness in her chest. Without another word, she turned out of the room and made an expeditious retreat for the elevator.

"Kensy!" Jackson's voice stopped her in her tracks. She took a deep breath and stared at the ceiling in front of her. He came up on her left and looked down with the same concerned gaze he had given her in the war room earlier this morning. "What's going on?"

She glanced off to the right as Daniel approached. He could see the water gathering at the edges of her eyes. "I can still feel it." Her knuckles whitened as she squeezed her clasp arm, "I can still feel everything about that moment, when I sunk my fingers into the plasma and ripped it to pieces. Every searing drop, every tear, every... everything. I thought that... I dunno. I've put weeks and several star systems between me

144

and that moment, and it hasn't been enough." She shook her head, "I can't lead if I can't get my head out of that experience."

Daniel placed a reassuring hand on her shoulder, "No one expects you to be over that. You're only human, just do your best. It will be more than enough. Don't worry about a thing. The rest of us will pick up the slack." He smiled, "And if anyone gives you grief, I'll put them on inventory duty for a month." She snickered at the thought. For the first time, it really sunk in: they were in this together for the long haul. Come hell or high water, this was her new home.

Jackson looked over Kensy toward Daniel, "Now, I believe we have a dinner to get to." He subtly ran his hand down the back of her arm, then gently urged her forward with a soft push.

Chapter 21

DeCadejra

"We are the Legacy Flagship DeCadejra."

Kensy fastened the upper left corner of her jacket as she stared into the reflection. Slowly and deliberately, she smoothed the waves and lines her uniform into a perfect profile. Her boots were shined to a glassy finish, her pins and buttons all properly faced, her makeup subtly accenting her soft features, and her hair pulled cleanly into her traditional ponytail. Her eyes wandered across the mirrored wall and fell upon the two unpacked crates that lingered against the wall behind her. She drew a deep breath and lifted her chin.

The ship was loaded, the cargo stowed, the personnel moved in, and the first destination set. It was time. She pivoted on one heel, heading for the hall. With every ounce of confidence she could muster, she strode out of her quarters and approached the neighboring door in the elegant lobby of the captain's deck. Curling her fingers into a loose fist, she knocked gently on the smooth finish of the entryway. It slid open, and she proceeded in as beckoned.

"Come on in," Jackson glanced her way as he clicked the buckle of his metal uniform belt into place. She gave a modest wave as her eyes fell on his handsomely uniformed figure, butterflies filled her stomach. "I'm almost ready. Bryden just called up. Everything is in order and the crew is standing by," he reached up to a small shelf beside his dressing mirror and snatched up a palm sized clip of leather and metal. He slipped it onto the right side of his belt. Only when he turned to face her, did Kensy realize it wasn't a part of his regulation uniform. She thought back on all the times since they had met. It had always been on him from what she could recall, but never once had it drawn her attention before. She leaned against the couch beside his entry way, lost in thought. "Kensy? Everything alright?" He paused to fasten his cuffs.

She shook her head, "Of course, just nerves. For all of my training and powers of speech, I have no idea what to say to the crew. I keep thinking of those *things*...." She cast her eyes down to her fidgety finger tips. "Feels like I'm asking them to stare down monsters. How do you ask someone to do that?" she sighed heavily, "I've been really hoping you have this better figured out."

He paced over to his desk, "Don't worry about it. This is more ceremony than anything. Everyone has been briefed accordingly. You're not asking them to do anything they haven't already signed on for." He pulled his top desk drawer open and stared down at a satiny black case sitting neatly beside his folded handkerchief. He reached into the drawer when Maggie's mechanical voice rang out over the comm, derailing his train of thought.

"Please pardon me. Commander. Psilyria."

"Yes, Maggie, what is it?" Kensy crossed her arms and lifted her eyes in acknowledgment of the disembodied voice.

"I have been reviewing our communications capabilities and have discovered an area in which significant improvement can be made." A panel in the wall beside Jackson's desk opened, revealing two small devices. He reached up and pulled them out. The compartment slid closed, vanishing into the seamless wall again. "Those are nahdvi, compact communication devices that can maintain long range up-links. They monitor and transmit wearer's vital statistics as well as limited environmental telemetry and can provide limited emergency assistance in the form of distress signals, synaptic pain control and black box transcription. These devices would be an advisable replacement of the traditional and rudimentary communicators with which the crew is currently outfitted. With your permissions, I would like to distribute the nahdvi ship-wide."

Kensy stood and walked toward Jackson. He nudged the drawer closed with his knee as he held the devices out for her inspection. "Are these some kind of experimental tech?" Kensy asked, plucking one from Jackson's hand to examine.

"Only in the respect that I have modified the original design to suit human physiology. These were standard issue to the original crew and creators of the Legacy Fleet," Maggie informed them. "Nahdvi is the closest approximation to the original term that my linguistics matrix could devise, considering that no equivalent word exists in your language."

"Just how invasive are these devices to collect and transmit this extensive volume of information?" Jackson turned it over in his fingers, examining the tech with a scrutinizing eye.

"Not at all invasive," Maggie informed them. "The device sits behind the ear. It creates a synthetic bio-fusion with the wearer. For additional communications clarity, a small tendril will extend into the ear canal. The unit should overall be very comfortable and even over time become less noticeable to the wearer as it synchronizes to them biologically."

Kensy shrugged and reached up just behind her ear, gently holding the nahdvi to the skin. A subtle tingle passed down the side of her neck. She shivered involuntarily as the tendril wrapped into her ear. The sensation passed quickly. She glanced up to Jackson who looked at her suspiciously, "Once it's on, it's not bad. I actually expected it to be heavier, or at least more awkward." She turned her gaze away to address Maggie, "If we want it off...?" The tendril snapped back into the main piece and tumbled from her ear, bouncing from her shoulder back into her hand. They both stared at the device in surprise.

"As you can see, the nahdvi is telepathically responsive. It will also attempt to auto synchronize with the ship, allowing access to my systems for field reference and analysis. Once bio-fusion is complete the unit will retain an extremely complex biometric encryption matrix making the device utterly unaccessible to anyone other than the intended user." Maggie paused. "Are there any other inquiries I may process at this time?"

"I don't think so," Kensy said as she reattached the earpiece to her skin.

"According to my calculations, the crew will experience a small period of adjustment to the wear and use of the devices. I, therefore, suggest immediate distribution ship-wide prior to any mission-critical encounters." Jackson placed his nahdvi on as Maggie spoke.

He made a disgusted face as the tendril worked its way into his ear. "Fine. But I expect regular reports on the function of these devices. I want to know immediately if there are any problems or complications caused by their use or wear." He shook his head in surrender. Something about a telepathically linked and biologically fused communicator did not sit well with him.

"As you say, Commander," Maggie promptly replied.

Kensy looked up at him, "Shall we head down together?"

"After you," Jackson nodded in affirmation. He gave a quick glance back to the closed desk drawer. It would have to wait for now. He turned to follow her from quarters into the lobby.

Neira stepped out the door directly opposite Kensy's and met them at the elevator. She wore a neatly trimmed burgundy tunic style top with a high collar and long, loose sleeves. Tight black pants covered her legs and tucked neatly into her heavy black combat boots. Bound around her upper left arm was a black braided chord with a burnished copper emblem of the Graven order. She gave a salutatory nod toward the duo. Jackson responded in kind. Kensy tilted her head to one side and smiled nervously.

The elevator arrived and slid its doors open for the anxiously waiting passengers to file in one by one. They rode down in silence. As the doors opened on the command deck, Kensy heard a voice call out over the bustling crew, "Captains on deck!" Stillness settled over the strategic operations center as Jackson and Kensy stepped out on to the main walk. She glanced around at all the men and women standing at attention. She kept in step with Jackson as they strode toward the bridgehead with confidence and purpose. This was not the place for apprehension, so she tucked it away tightly in the back of her mind.

Neira stayed at the heels of the two newly appointed captains. This was their moment. *Despite her doubts, this command really does suit her perfectly*, Neira thought as she looked upon her dear friend with pride and satisfaction. *It's about time.*

As they entered the bridgehead, Kensy and Jackson nodded to one another in unison before moving to their positions. Neira shuffled off to the side of the stairs, crossed her arms and slouched against the wall to observe inconspicuously. Kensy closed her eyes and plunged into the beam. She let her hands dance through the light, pulling in the ship's data that she would need. She opened her eyes and tapped a single point on her display with the tip of her index finger. Ripples cascaded through the ship as every station lit up, ready for the coming captain's address. She grabbed the virtual control node and set it spinning down to Morgan's console with a flick of her right hand.

Morgan looked up to his commander, "The comm is yours."

"This is Commander Gabel. Today we embark on a new path. This mission isn't one we sought out. It's not one we would have picked for ourselves. We face an unknown enemy. We set out on a strange new ship with many new faces and without many of the old ones we knew well. But make no mistake we will still succeed. We will work together to overcome any obstacle in our way. We are now the men and women of the Legacy Flagship DeCadejra and we will distinguish ourselves through the honor and integrity with which we have always served. We will become a force to be reckoned with. Countless innocent lives hang in the balance. Failure is not an option. The enemy has already struck. We will hunt them down. We will bring a reckoning for all those we have lost. And we will stop them, whoever they may be." Kensy watched as cheers erupted throughout the ship from the crew, new and old. She smiled. Jackson glanced up at her as she linked the sound of cheering to his nahdvi. She mouthed the words 'thank you.' He smirked at her and turned back to Morgan. "Confirm departure clearance and take us out, Lieutenant."

Morgan's hand skittered across the panels of his station, "This is Legacy Flagship DeCadejra, requesting final departure clearance."

Admiral Khaivol's voice came over the comm, "You are cleared for departure, DeCadejra. Safe sailing." The ship subtly shifted as the station's docking clamps released the outer hull.

"Roger that." Morgan activated the holographic gyro controls and gently drew them back, easing the ship from her docking bay. They glided effortlessly around the curve of the station and out into open space. "Course laid for Rosealleon Colony on your command, sir."

"Open her up," Jackson paced quietly behind the pilot's seat.

"Yes, sir!" Morgan enthusiastically replied. Kensy opened her hands, palms up, and created a fan of psionic energy between them. Tiny sliver-like openings formed in the smooth hull and spread until a maze of runic channels became exposed from the DeCadejra's tail to the tips of her four grand forward sweeping wings. Light coursed through the channels as the engine output increased. A shimmering wake trailed behind them as they glided effortlessly into the vast black sea of stars.

Chapter 22

Stormy Memories

"Head first isn't always the best direction to go, sometimes its the only direction to go."
~ Commander Jackson Gabel

With a heavy sigh, Kensy slumped down on her bed. She cast her eyes out the overhead window. The stars migrated across the glass and out of view, dancing in the shimmer of the ship's shields. Every moment was one step closer to the unknown. *How do I always find myself here, wandering through space like a vagabond?* She closed her eyes, and the answer escaped her lips as little more than a whisper, "... because I am." She took a deep breath and raised her gaze to the two solitary crates along the far wall. The picture frame and all the details of the memory held within were crisp in her mind. She let her eyes drift aside, *So many light years crossed and I'm still at the beginning.* A few stray tears slipped from her tired eyes.

She pushed the covers back further and slipped her feet into the folds. She fussed with the hem of her nightgown, smoothing out bunches in the satin. Then, like a tidal wave, the fatigue of the day overcame her. Her eyelids became unbearably heavy. She ran her fingertips across her forehead, trying to regain her fleeting thoughts, *What was I...?*

Movement caught her attention briefly. She tried to look at the source of her distraction, but the image blurred and shifted. Kensy felt herself falling upon the pillow as if in slow motion. The bed cradled her like a cloud. She felt almost as if the billowing form would engulf her entirely. Rolling her head to the side, she glimpsed the figure of a woman with long ebony hair and a blue flowing dress walking toward the bedside. A red crackle of energy leapt from the woman's hand toward Kensy as sleep conquered the whole of her being. The slumber enshrouded her in the darkness of the room.

Slowly, sinister visions crept into her mind and began warping the landscape of her dreams. Kensy tossed and turned in her bed, struggling against the tumult of her nightmare. She raised her left arm to shield her eyes from the searing rain and piercing wind. Everything was so disorienting. She could hear her name being called faintly amidst the storm, but from where? She curled the fingers of her right hand into a tight fist and lit it up with psionic energy. The glow illuminated the dense forest surrounding her just enough to cast a menagerie of imposing and distorted silhouettes. A flicker of movement caught the corner of her eye once more.

She trudged, one step after another, toward the flitting figure. A loud crack broke over her. One of the towering trees began to twist and fall. Instinctively, Kensy released the energy from her fist into the air with explosive force to either destroy or divert the tumbling timber. Desperate hands seized her arm, catching her off-guard. Her head snapped around to face the figure.

Elle clung desperately to her arm with pleading eyes, "What are you doing here? You shouldn't be here!" she screamed over the storm. Her uniform was tattered and dirty. Stray hairs escaped her ebony braid. Kensy looked at her friend with stunned amazement. "You have to leave! I'm already gone. I flew too close to the sun! You have to leave me behind! There's nothing left here! You have to leave now!" Elle looked back over her shoulder, leery of the shadows that lurked around them. Her silvery eyes flashed with panic as lightning struck ever closer to them.

She stood tall and shoved Kensy to the ground. Her expression became cold and calculating. She raised both hands over Kensy, her fingers spread wide. Kensy felt paralyzed in fear and disbelief. Red energy crackled like a halo around the clasp embedded across Elle's forehead and down her neck. It danced up her arms and sprung forth from her fingertips. Kensy cowered before the incoming attack. A flurry of lighting bolts struck all around her, shattering the ground like glass. Kensy began to plunge into darkness with the glassy shards of the world. They bit at her as they dropped. Even her screams were eaten up by the emptiness that lay beneath her.

A thunderous clamor emanated from Kensy's room, shaking the walls and surging through the floor. Her chamber door opened abruptly as Jackson and Neira barreled through in their pajamas, only to be stopped in their tracks by the brilliant violet psionic storm that churned around the bedroom. "Shit," slipped from Neira's lips. She snatched a decorative pillow from the nearby lounge and tossed it into the chaos with a snap of her wrist. The pillow spun lithely through the air for the first few feet. It reached the perimeter of the storm and was struck in to a cloud of ash and seared fabric.

Kensy let out a strained shriek, unable to break free from her nightmare. Jackson shook his head and clenched his jaw. This was gonna hurt. Neira glanced up at him in passing, then paused for a double take, recognizing his determination. "No! You can't be serious! That is raw psionic energy. Controlled, that is some crazy shit, but you're *actually* thinking of walking into it in its base form in nothing but pajama pants! It could kill you!"

"If you have a better idea, spit it out! I'm all ears! But we don't have time to debate this, if she's lost complete control, this could rip through the ship!" he gestured toward the swirling tempest.

"I have diverted the main shield core to project around the psilyria's chambers. It should increase the amount of time before hull structure reaches critical levels. We have approximately two minutes and forty-seven seconds at current projections," Maggie interjected.

Neira glared at the disembodied voice in spite. She shook her head and tilted it to one side, "She's never gonna forgive herself for this. You know that, right?!" She placed her hands on her hips and shrugged. Just then, Daniel burst through the door in lounge pants and a tee-shirt, holding out a small metal device in his outstretched hand. They looked at him, confused.

"Maggie notified Doc. Doc said wear that to dampen effects. Should protect one person's nervous system long enough to wake her up. She regains consciousness, shit stops," Daniel rattled off in rapid succession. Jackson nodded, taking the inhibitor without hesitation, and fastening it to his temple as he had seen on Kensy when they first met. "Hopefully," Daniel muttered under his breath. Neira shot him an incredulous stare from the corner of her eye. He shrugged dismissively.

Jackson approached the edge of the field, breathing in deeply as he plunged into the raw chaos. He tightened his muscles as the storm fought him for every step. Bolts of lightning seared into his back and arms. Neira and Daniel watched helplessly from the sidelines with breathless anticipation. Blood began to slowly seep from his burns as he reached Kensy's bedside. Tears stained the pained expression on her face. He placed one knee on the edge of the bed. As he leaned over her, he slipped his left hand behind her neck. Gently, he lifted her head and reached for her trashing clasped arm.

Holding her hand tightly, he called out to her, "Kensy! Wake up!" She gasped as she snapped back to reality. The crackling energy dissipated into a haze, then nothing. Delirious and exhausted, she slumped against his bare chest and sobbed. He wrapped his arms around her and nodded to the others that all was clear. Neira and Daniel sighed in relief.

"I'll go let Doc know she'll be having two guests for the night," Daniel excused himself and slipped from the room.

Neira cautiously approached the end of the bed, keeping her gaze on Kensy. Words seemed too intrusive for the tension in the air. After long moments, she cautiously spoke up, "We should get you two down to medbay. Doc will want to check you both out after that." She crossed her arms. For a moment, no one moved, and the room was still. Jackson nodded his head and swept Kensy's thin frame up into his arms. Neira watched as he carefully carried her broken friend out of the room. She took a step to follow, then hesitated. Two crates lay in shambles along the far wall, contents scattered about the floor. She stooped down and scooped up a shattered picture frame. Delicately, she pulled the image from amongst the pieces.

She looked back up at the empty doorway. *I didn't know she still had this. Could this have been the cause? Is this what she was dreaming about?* Neira cast her eye down in sorrow. *Some wounds never heal.* She sauntered toward the door, depositing the broken frame into a receptacle beside the threshold. Ducking into her own room, she tossed the photo in, and released it above the desk, letting the picture flit down to the desktop like a tumbling leaf.

She lingered there, entrenched in her own calculating thoughts. Something was amiss. "Maggie, please collate all of the sensor logs for Psilyria Frost's chambers for two hours preceding my entry through now. I will also need security footage and her personal biometrics." Neira began to pace as she folded her arms together across her chest.

"Please state authorization for requested data."

"My authorization is granted under the Gamirhan Accord, Statute 613, Graven authority supersedes the local command structure in order to prevent or resolve an imminent crisis." She narrowed her stare, but did not miss a beat. "And if that's not enough, I'm her best friend and I reserve the right to watch after her well-being." Annoyance filled her voice as she responded to the challenging of her authority.

"Understood. Data collation underway," Maggie promptly replied. "Shall I notify you when the request is available for review?"

"No. I will check back with you shortly. You are under no circumstances to inform *anyone* else of this query until I say so." Neira paused, glancing back at the resting photo. "Scan and isolate any psionic disturbances prior to the core event." She bit at her lower lip nervously. "Also, pull everything you can on Psicorp Academy Incident 0797426-38b...," she unfolded her arms and murmured, "and pray that my intuition is wrong." With the snap of her fingers, the lights in the room turned off, and she departed for the medbay. The last rays of light from the lobby faded on the surface of the picture as the door closed behind her, leaving the memories to rest in silence.

Chapter 23

Fallout

"When I said the captains should get a room,
I didn't mean the medbay."
~ Anonymous Medtech

Kensy curled up in a ball on her medical bed, trying to make herself as small as possible. She clutched the bedding tightly in her fists and stared off into nothingness. She had stopped sobbing, but the tears still soaked her reddened face. Not a single word had passed her lips. What could she possibly say to make this better? She hadn't manifested in her sleep since childhood and even then; it was nothing close to this magnitude. The smell of Jackson's psionically seared flesh lingered in her nose and it was her fault. She held herself in contempt. She had forced him to endanger himself. Silently, she reassured herself that he must despise her equally as much. This was inexcusable.

Jackson sat on the edge of his bed as one of the techs cleaned and bandaged his burns. He stared quietly at Kensy's back, pondering. *What could have pushed her out of control?* The tech touched a fresh rag to his left side ribs. There was a sizzle as it cooled the skin and he winced. She finished cleaning the burn and firmly pressed the flexible metallic bandage to his rib cage. There was a faint flash of light around the edges as it sealed to his body, "There. All done." She picked up her tray and briskly walked away, leaving Jackson to his thoughts. He rested his elbows on his knees and sat in quiet contemplation.

The medical bay doors whisked open for Neira. Kensy remained still, diverting only her eyes to acknowledge the movement at the corner of her vision. The flash of her eyes was enough to convey the raging thoughts within. Neira could see the anger and frustration burning through Kensy's stone-faced expression. She cautiously approached the bedside and in a hushed tone tried to calm her troubled friend, "It's okay. None of this is your fault...."

Kensy dropped her stoic façade and sat up. "Bullshit! Bull-fucking-shit!" she erupted. Jackson straightened his posture, startled by the outburst. "The only person's fault this *can be* is mine! Don't give me some crap platitude, just cause you want me to let this go!" Kensy pulled her knees up and wrapped her arms around them. She stared off into nothingness, "I lost control. I had a fucking nightmare, and I lost control!" Neira reached out to reassure her but Kensy pulled away, "Don't touch me right now... you might lose a hand."

Neira hesitated, unsure of what to do next. "Well, ...you're in good hands, so I'll... just... I'm gonna head out. Night." She fidgeted before pivoting to leave. The doors parted for her again. She paused. A sad and broken expression slipped through her otherwise composed veneer as she glanced back at Kensy and Jackson. She vanished around the corner without another word. Only time was going to soothe this stinging reprisal. Kensy took a deep breath and hung her head. It wasn't her intent to take her frustrations out on Neira. *Just one more thing I'm screwing up...,* she thought as she let slip another heavy sigh.

"I wouldn't believe it if I hadn't seen it, but I think Neira took that personally. Next time we should probably have Doc lock the doors and you can use me as a verbal punching bag instead." Jackson shrugged casually. Kensy lifted her head and gave him an incredulous look. He raised an eyebrow, "Feel any better now that you've blown off some steam? 'Cause I can take it if you need to keep yelling at someone. Can't be any worse than the nurse with the sandpaper rag taking the skin off my ribs." He jested to lighten the mood in the room.

The medical bay was empty save for the two of them. Doctor Tyronis had retired for the night after examining her patients and passing along comprehensive instructions for the graveyard-shift medical technician who was probably off in one of the rear rooms cleaning instruments and filing her documentation. The DeCadejra's medical bay was easily twice the size of the Themiscyra's. The main room was a sterile white with light blue panels and silver trimmings. Toward the rear of the bay were side rooms for more intensive treatment needs like surgery and critical care situations. The floor had a soft marbled gray matte finish that differentiated it from the rest of the room.

Kensy shook her head, "I'm sorry. None of this would have happened if I had just kept a reign on my mental state. I can't believe I lost control like this." She brushed her hair back and tucked it behind her ear with a sweep of her fingertips.

"I think it's pretty crazy to think that anyone can keep control of their powers in their sleep." He shook his head, "This is all way out of my league." He glanced back over his shoulder to make sure the tech wasn't present. "Listen. I know this is probably a little personal, but if something caused you to have this nightmare, we could talk about it. Or you could talk about it...." Kensy turned to look at him and her expression softened. *There he goes again, offering to be my knight in shining armor. I wonder if he knows....* Her thoughts wandered. "I understand if you don't want to share. I just wanted you to know we're in this together... if you have any concerns, we could work them out."

Kensy took another beep breath, "It's not even really about the nightmares. As a psionic, I have trained since childhood to maintain absolute control at all times. It's like learning a combat maneuver. You practice until the muscle memory makes it second nature. And I have, somehow, let that automatic response slip. It doesn't make sense, I do my control exercises every single day as part of my routine." Kensy crossed her ankles and slipped them under her legs, letting her knees fall into a cross-legged position. A shiver passed over her.

Jackson stood and began looking through the wall cabinets. "Maybe you've been spending too much time in the beam. Since we left space dock three days ago, you've spent almost every waking moment in that thing." He pulled down two blankets from a high shelf and closed the cabinet door.

Unfurling one of the blankets, Jackson gave it a strong shake and wrapped it around Kensy's shoulders. "Thanks," she nodded to him. As she reached up to pull it tighter around herself, their fingertips came together. There was a moment of pause as they both realized they were touching.

Jackson cleared his throat and stepped back to his medical bed. He wrapped the other blanket around himself and sat down. "I think we've got things pretty well settled up there, you probably don't need to be on the bridgehead so much. Maggie can notify us when you are needed."

Kensy tilted her head to one side, "Yeah, you're probably right." She gave a nervous chuckle, "I wouldn't mind the nightmares going away in any case. Ever since I touched the veil, they have been... painful."

Jackson furrowed his brow, "Nightmares? You've had more than one?"

"Yeah," she smiled softly. "You saved me from one of them back on the Themiscyra, too." The memory came back to him. He remembered Doctor Tyronis talking in the background as he stared at Kensy's tear-stained face. He could feel the soft wisp of her hair that he had brushed from her face and the smoothness of her hand that he held as he called out to her in a whisper. ...*I'm real. Right here, right now.... Come back to me.* There was the look of recognition as he recalled every nerve-racking moment. The sound of her voice brought him back to the moment, "Everything okay?" She gazed at him with those gentle sea-green eyes.

"Yeah, sorry. You were saying about the nightmares...," he redirected the subject back to her.

She fidgeted anxiously with her fingertips, "You remember me telling you about Alpha Bael? ...about *before* Alpha Bael? The other girl I was with... Ellise, Elle, I've been dreaming about her. I thought I had let go but...."

"Why? What happened?" he inquired.

"Elle wanted to get as far away from colonial life as she could. There were a lot of very bad memories there. She asked to be stationed on a ship. Maybe it was her way of running away. I never got to ask her about it. We didn't keep in contact very well after Alpha Bael. Then about four years ago, the ship she was on was destroyed, the Icarus. I don't think a cause was ever found, just a massive field of wreckage, all hands lost." Water began to collect in the corners of her eyes, "We had survived so much together and then she was just... gone. For the longest time I thought maybe if we had stuck together—."

"Something nasty enough to reduce a ship to rubble in space... You can't blame yourself for it. Even for all of your talents, you can't save everyone." Jackson slid back further on his bed until his feet no longer touched the cold floor.

"It took me a long time to accept that. Playing by the odds has never really been my thing," she mused, "but I did get there eventually, or so I thought." She flopped back on her bed and stared up at the ceiling. "In the whole of our lives, I never once feared her. She was my oldest and closest friend. But in these dreams I see her and it's like nothing I've ever seen before. She's haunting and terrifying. She comes to me as a friend, then some unseen force overtakes everything and she turns on me." Kensy ran her fingers back though her hair. "This must sound like nonsense to you," she scoffed at herself.

"Meh," he shrugged. "I think the people who say they have dreams that make sense are usually the crazy ones." They both chucked. "The brain does some weird shit to work things out. If I understood, I'd find someone to pay me a lot of money for it." Jackson leaned forward, resting his elbows on his thighs. The lights in the room dimmed slightly. He glanced back just in time to see the tech's hand slip silently out of view.

Kensy rolled on to her side, pressing her palms together as she tucked her hands under her head on the pillow, "Thank you." Jackson turned back to face her. "You always listen to my sob stories without complaint." She gave a half-hearted smile, "I kinda wish I'd met you sooner. There are things in my life that could have been... different... better, with a friend like you at my side."

He drew a slow breath as he stared into the sadness in her eyes. He lifted an eyebrow and averted his gaze, "Don't give me that. You've had Neira and this Elle person. Everyone who's spent time with you adores you. You can't tell me in all that not one person listened to you, not one person had a shoulder for you to lean on before me."

She thought for a moment, *...adores me? No, he couldn't...,* "Neira has always been in one of two modes: either moving too fast for me to catch or more interested in saving my body than healing my soul. Soft stuff really isn't her cup of tea. Elle, well let's just say, she knew my every dark secret. And we both worked very hard to bury the shadows rather than talk about them. There really hasn't been anyone else I would consider a close friend, someone I could spill to." She shrugged, "You're easy to talk to, its nice." Her mind wandered as she fought back her tired eyelids, "You listen to my ramblings, always about me, my life, my past. You never talk about yourself. I would listen if you wanted to do the rambling instead."

He glanced at her, "I'll pass. You should get some sleep." He sensed her hesitation. "You catch a couple hours, I'll stay up, keep watch. I got some decent sleep earlier after the department heads' meeting."

"I suppose. If you insist...," her voice trailed off.

"I do. Go to sleep," he replied sternly. She let her eyelids slowly fall. She inhaled slowly, forcing her body to relax. As her breath released, her mind slipped into the eagerly awaiting slumber. Her body rolled lazily backward.

Jackson rose to his feet one last time. He cautiously approached her bedside as not to disturb her sleep. Tenderly, he picked up her hands and laid them on her stomach so that she would be more comfortable. He gently slipped his hand behind her neck and pulled the blanket from beneath her shoulders. She murmured but did not wake as he eased her back down onto the pillow. He straightened the blanket and covered her with it, lingering over her for a moment. Brushing a hair from her face, he studied the serene expression of her peaceful sleep. He scoffed at himself and rolled his eyes, *You're a sentimental fool. Everyone who's spent time with you adores you?! Riiight.... At least she glazed right over that one. Dodged a bullet there.*

Chapter 24

Unsettling Parallels

"Sometimes the hardest part of a putting a puzzle together is finding all of the pieces."
~ Neira Cross, Graven Mercenary

Neira let herself fall back against the wall outside the medical bay. She tilted her head back and stared at the lines of the overhead lights. *None of this is your fault?! You dim witted moron. What kind of dumb consolation is that supposed to be?! No wonder she railed against you! You're an emotional clod.* She balled her fists up in her hair, her frustration palatable, "Arg!"

Slowly, she unfurled her hands and drew her fingers over the tattoos that cascaded down the side of her face. Her fingertips followed every groove and rise of the Visiri eye-patch and surrounding scars. She let out a mournful breath as her frustration melted into sorrow. *Things were better back then. I was better then. Is this it? Doomed to fail at the one thing I've sworn to see through no matter what? I can't protect her any better now than before.*

Her hands fell to her sides as she pushed off the wall and began to wander down the corridor back toward the lift. *Quit moping. You have work to get done! And you're not gonna wimp out now!* She steeled her resolve and raised her chin. Determination flashed in her eyes. She stepped into the lift and took a deep breath as the doors closed, "Captains' deck!" The seconds crawled by as the elevator silently climbed toward its

166

destination. She anxiously tapped her nails against the soft linen of her pajama pants as she contemplated what Maggie may have found during her data collection. The system dinged and the doors swept aside for Neira to disembark. She rounded the corner of the door and headed for her quarters, "Maggie, report status of earlier inquiry."

"All data correlation complete and awaiting analysis," the mechanical voice informed her.

She waved her left hand to the side triggering the door of her quarters to open. She strode in with purpose, pausing for nary a moment as she turned toward a large wall screen, "Begin playback of security footage at four times speed and summarize sensor log events for me chronologically."

"As you wish, Miss Cross," Maggie chimed back as she initiated the data log playback. Several charts streamed information alongside the security feed detailing various factors. "No anomalies detected before Psilyria Frost entered quarters at zero-two-fourteen-hundred hours this morning. She proceeded to disrobe, re-dress into sleep apparel and attend to a nightly hygiene regimen for the next twenty-seven minutes, at which point she moved to the bedroom area. She exhibited signs of an internal conflict for several minutes—,"

"Clarify," Neira interrupted as she narrowed her focus on the visual before her.

"She spoke as if to answer a question that had not been—," Maggie began to explain.

"STOP!" Neira shouted abruptly. "Stop playback and go back to ...there!" She pointed at the screen. "Play from that point at half speed." The video slowly began to crawl forward. Strange flashes appeared in the frames, flickering from one point to another. "Freeze frame," Neira breathlessly ordered. There in the still she beheld a ghostly image that hovered over Kensy's bedside. She gasped as she searched every pixel for answers to no avail. "It's not possible." She turned away. Confusion overcame her. Should she be scared? Angry? What did this mean? *Think it through! There has to be a logical explanation. Find it. Find the answers.* She coached herself back into a focused state. "Have you retrieved the Psicorp incident report and related data?"

"Requested information has been acquired."

"Compare psionic sensor logs between the original event and this point." Neira began to pace, "I want a baseline comparison of the psionic profiles and manifestation signatures."

"Running analysis." Maggie displayed the relevant graphs on the screen first side by side then over lapping. The lines danced around one another and then together. "Analysis complete. The psionic profiles correlate on all primary levels. One may conclude that the events are of a similar nature."

"Okay, but how... why did she do it this time?" Neira mulled over the findings, "the circumstances don't match...."

"There is a discrepancy of note." Neira paused to listen. "The signatures of the two events bear distinct variations. Conclusion: The event was triggered by an external source. Error: Signature matched to closed records. Reason: Personnel classified as deceased Earth-date: 715-02-03." Neira shot a glance to the photo still resting upon her desk, her thoughts weighing heavily on her mind.

"You are *absolutely* sure of the signature match? There is no possibility whatsoever that this could be the work of any other psion?!" She began to pace again.

"Accounting for corrupted segments within the signature there is a one in two-million nine-hundred eighty-six-thousand one-hundred-fifty-three chance of being conjured by an undocumented psion. Further analysis also dictates that the psionic event in speculation has only been documented to have ever been accomplished by three individuals in human history." Maggie reported.

Neira crossed her arms, "Yeah, I get the picture." She tapped her finger tips against her upper arms as she cogitated on the results. An unsettling quiet filled the room. After several long minutes Neira raised her gaze again. "Collect all files and send to a clean datapad. Set encryption level to Codex Seven. Password: OCM4XR12." She continued to pace, "Report on the status of the Psionics Lab."

"Lab was completed eighty-nine hours and four minutes ago. Psilyria Frost has not attended the completed facility as of yet." A panel in the wall beside the screen opened up allowing a small mechanical arm to extend a new datapad set up to Neira's specifications. She retrieved the pad and proceeded to enter the pass code. Carefully she pored over the contents, verifying the information and conclusions. "Is it to your satisfaction?"

"Indeed." Neira paused, "I believe it has become imperative that the Psilyria has her clasp repaired as soon as possible. Clear her schedule for tomorrow morning and early afternoon. As soon as she has some rest she will be addressing that issue." Neira turned toward her bed and knelt down. Reaching under the edge she pulled on a heavy case that reluctantly conceded to her draw. Her fingers danced across the lock interface. The latches popped open and she flipped the lid up. Her Ausk-Chelkai laid elegantly in the satiny lined grooves carved for them. She swept open a small compartment between the blades and tucked the datapad neatly inside.

Closing everything tightly she slid the case back into its hiding spot. "This inquiry and all related information is now classified under Graven authority." Neira turned and slid onto her bed. She pulled her knees up and rested her heels on the edge of the frame. She leaned back on the heels of her hands entrenched in her thoughts. With the impossible becoming more like the everyday the next few weeks... hell, this whole mission was certainly going to be ...interesting.

Chapter 25

Ghosts

Cross and Gabel get along like caesium and water and that's not a room I want to be in."

~ *Crewman T. Coyote*

Neira lurked at the edge of a blind corner, peering cautiously down the hall waiting for the medical bay doors to open. Her breath was eerily quiet as she silently laid in wait for her opening. It was rather early and the halls remained empty thus far but Neira knew that her waiting was soon to end. Kensy never could sleep in when there was something to be done and there was *always* something to be done, especially with last night's schedule changes. Her patience paid off. She drew back as the doors whooshed open. She waited only moments as the voices moved away.

She rounded the corner catching a momentary glimpse of Kensy and Doctor Tyronis before they slipped from view. Cautiously she headed for the medbay. Her foot falls were barely audible as she approached the doors. One more glance behind to make sure the coast was clear ... good. She stepped backward through the opening and pivoted on one foot, redirecting her attention toward her target.

His back was to her as she approached. The morning med tech finished resealing the last of his bandages and snatched her tray. Jackson turned his head just far enough to see Neira in the edge of his vision. "Kensy's not here. She just headed up to the psionics lab with Doc to work on her clasp." He turned away again.

"We need to talk," she tossed a bundle toward the foot of his bed. The clothes tumbled apart beside him. "Get dressed. You're gonna want to hear this." She crossed her arms wearing a cold and calculating expression on her face.

Jackson sighed and gathered up his belongings. Slowly he stood up from the medical bed. "What's this about, Cross?" He meandered toward an empty side room to change. Leaving the door open he placed his things on a side counter within and began to ready himself.

Neira moved to the wall outside the door and leaned her back against it, "It's about last night's pyrotechnics. I did some digging, but what I found...," She brushed a stray hair from her face. "We are going to need to keep this under wraps. At least for a bit. Until we know more, this is strictly between you and me."

Jackson tucked in his shirt and clicked his belt buckle closed. "If this information is so damn sensitive why trust me with it? Why not keep it between you and Kensy?" He balled up his pajama pants and moved to exit the side room.

Neira snapped around the corner, pointing a finger in his face. In a hushed yell she railed against him, "Not a single word to her! You hear me? Not so much as a snivel or a peep in her direction!" She glared at him with a gaze that would have pierced the darkest reaches of space.

He threw his hands up in surrender, "Fine!"

"If I could keep tabs on everything at once, I wouldn't share with you. But against my better judgment, she has developed a fondness for you. And given your new partnership it might be easier for you to keep tabs on certain *aspects* of this investigation." The medical bay doors whisked open allowing one of the lower deck crewmen to enter. The medic peeked out from the office on the opposite wall and waved her new patient in. "We can't talk about it any more here," Neira whispered,

"Meet me in the war room in ten." She scoffed loudly and threw her right hand up, "Whatever. You can take your damn regulations and stuff them." The medic and crewman turned to look as Neira stormed out in feigned anger.

Jackson rolled his eyes. He waved a hand in the direction of the onlookers, "Carry on." With a subtle shake of his head he sauntered toward the door, muttering curses under his breath. His mind wandered as he made his way toward the lift. *What's her problem now?! I don't have time for this cloak and dagger shit.* He paused.

In the past twelve hours he had seen new sides of Neira. She had become paralyzed with apprehension during the psionic storm in Kensy's room and visibly wounded by her friend's verbal retaliation in the medical bay. His thoughts turned to contemplation. What could have possibly driven her to ask for *his* help? Even as she ran to Kensy's aid when the Chimera was active he had been little more than a speed bump to her. Was she desperate? Scared?

"Gabel, sir?" The voice stirred him from his deliberation. Jackson stopped to respond. The ship's corridors intersected about four feet behind him at the corner of which Daniel stood in his stately officer's uniform. "I was hoping to catch you... is everything okay?" Daniel cautiously stepped forward.

"Yeah, just... what did you need?" Jackson redirected.

Daniel shook his head and looked down to the datapad in his hand, "We'll be leaving Ascension space soon. We should be nearing the Rosealleon system in a couple days. Given current events I was wondering if you thought it prudent to maybe hang back a little until things are settled.... We could easily divert a day or two off course. Might help with repairs and recovery and give the Psilyria some time to take advantage of that new lab."

"She's already working on that. ...headed down with Doc to get things rolling on the clasp repair a while ago. Still...," Jackson pondered, "probably wouldn't be a bad idea. Have

Threaux slow us down. I have some checking to do on another matter. I'll update you when I have some things figured out better. Until then let's just cool our heels."

"Yes, Sir." Daniel turned to leave.

"Wait!" Jackson's thoughts turned back to the analysis of Rosealleon's political climate. "One more thing. Send a reminder notice, plain clothes only after we leave Ascension space and personal comm blackout. If we're want them to think we're not Ascension affiliated we might want to look the part before we arrive. Just in case." Daniel nodded in acknowledgment and gracefully bowed out of the conversation.

Jackson took the last few steps toward the lift when Maggie chimed in, "Sir, would you like me to deliver your personal effects to your quarters while you attend to your meeting?" He paused and gave a scrutinizing glare toward the disembodied voice. A line appeared in the wall beside him and he watched as it traced its way into the shape of a small door. The compartment opened revealing a round capsule. "Please place any contents you wish delivered to your quarters into the container. They will be waiting for you at your leisure." Jackson shook his head, *I'm never going to get used to this crazy ship.* Drawing the container from its resting place, he opened it and stuffed in his night clothes.

He tucked the capsule back into the compartment. His hands now free he paused. Neira had retrieved a full set of attire for him but still his outfit was incomplete. He hand fell to the right side of his belt. The clip that he wore there was missing. *I suppose at least she didn't dig that much through my stuff but its strange not having it on me. I'll just have to pick it up after we have our little talk.* He stepped over the threshold of the elevator, trying to shake the uncomfortable feeling in his skin. "Strategic Command Deck," He folded his arms and leaned back against the rear wall as the lift doors closed. "and next time don't allow her in my quarters."

"Yes, Sir," Maggie replied.

He watched the lights of the intermittent floors pass swiftly by. In only a few short moments the elevator car had traversed the four decks between his point of origin and requested destination. The doors opened allowing him to depart the car and turn down the hall toward the war room. Jackson stuffed his hands in his pockets as he tried not to fixate on the missing belt clip. *Neira sure is acting weird. What could she have possibly found that warrants keeping crap from Kensy? Not that I should be surprised I suppose. It's not like they tell each other everything ... found that out with the whole Graven thing.* He sighed. *But, why do I have to be in the middle?*

The war room doors slid apart as he approached. The room was darker than he anticipated. The only light in the room emanated from the projection table at the very center. He took a few steps in and down to the recessed central area. The doors slid closed causing him to glance behind. *Where is she?* He drew his hands from his pockets and rested them on his hips. From the shadows in the far corner of the room emerged a figure. She approached the projection table and placed her hands against it, leaning forward, "What I'm about to share with you stays strictly between us. No exceptions."

"Enough with the dramatics, just get on with it." He retorted.

She stood up straight and began to circle the table toward him. "First things first. You need to know a little bit about our illustrious psilyria." An archival news video began to play in the air above the projection table. "She is one of two. Some twenty years ago she was discovered along with another child floating in a piece of space debris. After they were rescued they were sent to Psicorp Academy. Both showed incredible innate talent for psionics. But Kensy was a class above. From the very beginning she was capable of master level manipulations. She was a prodigy like they had never seen before and without a control clasp." Jackson watched the old footage as it followed the sensational recovery of two young girls. One with dark tangled braids, one with fair rumpled curls, and their transition into Psicorp custody.

"And this has what to do with now?" He prodded impatiently.

Neira shot him a sharp glare and continued with her story, "Shortly after receiving their clasp implants and the first stages of training the dark haired girl, Ellise Neru, experienced something similar to what happened last night. A complete loss of control, violent and powerful." Neira played back the Psicorp incident footage. "Now this is where it gets really interesting...."

As Jackson narrowed his gaze to analyze the footage it appeared. The ghostly image of a young girl walked into frame, she passed through the storm and placed a hand over Ellise. Slowly the storm died down and the image of the girl faded. "What was that?!"

Neira crossed her arms and leaned her hip against the table, "*That* is Kensy. Or rather a part of her." She put up the next night's footage. Again the storm began and again the ghost appeared to stop the destruction, but this time a second feed streamed an image of Kensy fast asleep in her own bed, in her own room. "It's an ability referred to as a psi-walk. It is a rare and difficult feat to perform. The psionic projects a representation of themselves. Most of the time it can be only be used to observe things within a limited range from another perspective. However, Kensy Frost managed something else entirely. She not only created the projection but was able to interact with Ellise from a significant distance away and all while she was soundly sleeping.

"The powers-that-be ended up putting Ellise in isolation until her abilities stopped 'possessing' her. And every night Kensy psi-walked to her to stop the storms. After it was all said and done Kensy had walked every night for twenty-one days in a row. No one could figure our how she did it, nor did she remember. And it never happened again according to records ...until last night." Neira played back the logs and recordings of Kensy's room.

Jackson rubbed at his eyes with his right thumb and forefinger as he tried to process what he was seeing, "Wait. This doesn't make any sense. Is it even possible for someone to help themselves like that? And why would she walk *before* there was an issue? That flicker is what you're talking about right?!" He moved closer for a better look.

She put a finger up toward him, "Just a sec. Let me slow it down for you...." She tapped the console beside her. The frames chugged by until at long last they stopped on the still image of the ghost beside her bed. "Take a real good look. The walker isn't Kensy."

"Wait, is that...?" He pointed at the unknown woman.

Neira brought up one of the candid images of the rescued girls beside the still. The same dark hair and wiry voidir build was visible, "Ellise Neru. I think the walker is none other."

Jackson turned toward Neira, "How is that possible? Kensy said she was dead. Killed in some kind of shipwreck." He leaned forward placing his hands flat against the outer rim of the table.

Neira stared at the faces in the projection, "I don't know how. But I believe there is a bigger picture here we're not seeing. I think there is something sinister at work and I suspect that Kensy's loss of control was no accident. Until we know more I hope that you can see why we need to keep this under wraps. This would be devastating to Kensy. She already blames herself for not saving Elle, no need to complicate things."

Jackson stood up and folded his arms across his chest, "Okay. So you suspect some crazy weird psionic shit is messing with her. What do you want from me? This is all over my head." He shot an incredulous glare in Neira's direction.

"A lot goes over your head. That's beside the point." She shut down the projections and pulled her datapad from the table interface, "What I need from you is another set of eyes. Someone to keep watch in case things get weird around her. Any anomalies, any incidents. If this..., whatever it is, tries to affect her again we need to be on top of things. The more we know, the faster we can track this thing down and eliminate it."

Jackson raised an eyebrow, "Even if this is really your dead friend somehow? You still going to eliminate her?"

Neira strode past Jackson and toward the door, pausing for a moment to look back over her shoulder. "Make no mistake. Anything or anyone tries to harm her and I will end them regardless," She turned away. Determination filled her every step as she left the war room. There was no room for hesitation.

Jackson shook his head and stared at the deactivated table his thoughts racing. *Vacuum will harm you if you're not prepared. No matter how good you are, you can't end everything.* He sighed, *Better go see Allen. See if he can setup some precautions....*

Chapter 26

Safe Guards

"Whoever designed this ship was as much
an artist as an engineer."
~ Crewman Theodore Ivey

Jackson fastened his belt clip securely into place as he stepped off the elevator on the engineering deck. The hallway was a bustle. Crewmen and women passed by with little more than a nod toward their captain as they made their ways to and fro between the auxiliary systems and engineering laboratories engrossed in conversations with their peers. The hum of the lower decks made the ship feel alive. He cracked a sliver of a smile for a moment as he watched, absorbing the ambiance of the crew filled ship. The upper decks were much quieter and sparsely populated at this stage of their journey. "Do you need something, sir?" a mousy young crewman asked.

"Chief Engineer Petroski," Jackson responded.

The young man pointed down the largest corridor from their position, "He's in Main Engineering, sir, working on system tests." Jackson nodded in appreciation and headed toward the heart of the ship. He moved deftly in and out of the flow of people as he navigated his way toward the large bulkhead that heralded the entrance to the reactor core room. The chamber was enormous. Data consoles and stations dotted the outer walls. Pathways and catwalks weaved through the pillar-like tubes that fed into the outlying systems. Situated at the center of it all was the ship's main reactor core. Encased in a glittering globe of web, was a ball of brilliant blue-violet light. From the base of the sphere, rich greenish prominences flared up to a fantastic spectacle. The bloom of light resembled an enchanted lotus flower. The energy it generated coursed up the encasing web and out along sweeping coils that fed into the walls and ceiling. Below the globe, a collection of crystalline columns created an elegant base upon which the entire assembly rested. It was a sight to behold.

Jackson found himself drawn toward the glow of the reactor. No ship he had ever served on had an engine that looked anything like this. He kept a stoic facade as he admired the grace of it all. For all of its complexity, the design was clean and fascinating. There was a harmony amongst the components, like a symphony in perfect time. The chief engineer grabbed one of the thinner poles connecting the catwalk to the ground level. He wrapped his knees around it and slid down, landing behind Jackson. As he walked up beside his old friend, he placed his hands on his hips, "Sure is something, isn't she?!" A smile curled around his lips.

Jackson looked at his stocky companion, "How do you make heads or tails of this?"

Allen pushed up the bridge of his glasses, "You'd be surprised how similar things actually are. Evidently, most modern star-drives are actually reverse engineered off of this very ship. The R&D techs that the admiral had given us help quite a bit, but once you get key pieces down, it all makes a certain kinda sense," he beamed with a sense of accomplishment. "Now, I doubt you came all the way down here for a lecture on alien engine systems. What can I do for you, Commander?"

"I know you're still getting things figured down here, but I was hoping we could discuss some upper deck modifications." Jackson looked around them at the crowd of technicians and engineers, "Is there someplace we could talk?"

"Of course, of course! Follow me." Allen waved Jackson to follow, then turned to one of his underlings, "Ivey, go get Grave and Coyote and get those crisis simulations we started wrapped up."

"Sure thing, boss!" The tall dark-haired man with thin rimmed glasses replied as he saluted toward the chief and commander. Allen and Jackson made their way to a curved staircase on the outer edge of the room and began to climb. At the crest was a door that led to a large, spacious office overlooking the main reactor. Allen turned his head to one side as he headed for the planning table along the center of the rear wall, "Now, where were you thinking of having some work done? Are we talking deck-wide or just a few rooms?"

The office door slid closed behind Jackson, making the room surprisingly quiet. "Just one room, actually. Psilyria Frost's quarters. I was wondering if you could install a psionic dampening field." Jackson approached the end of the table as Allen punched up the ship's schematics.

"Ah, yes. I heard there was an issue last night. Word travels fast in closed circles." Allen zoomed in on the captain's deck, within the three-dimensional representation of the ship. "The entire ship has a kind of noise-canceling system for psionics, but it's nowhere near strong enough to affect an intentional manifestation."

Jackson rubbed at the bandage on his ribs, "Well, it wasn't so much intentional as out-of-control." He rested his hands on the edge of the table. "I was thinking of something she could control. Turn on and off when needed, if that's possible."

Allen flipped through different views, examining the hardware built into the specified area. "Oh, I think it is more than possible. A few strategically placed capacitors and modifications to these environmental banks.... We could probably even allow control by degrees, from light dampening to total suppression," he pointed out the changes.

"Fantastic! How fast can you get this in place? The psilyria is currently down in the psionics lab working on her clasp and I'd like it to be as low impact as possible on her." Jackson stood up straight and crossed his arms across his chest.

Allen smiled, "Oh, ...a few hours at most if I do the work myself."

Jackson nodded, "Please do. I'd like this done asap."

"Consider it done," Allen reached for his silver tool case. "I'll get started right now."

Jackson walked toward the door, then paused. "Thanks." They exchanged a knowing glance. There was so much riding on this. While the precautions were meant to protect Kensy as much as to protect the ship, there was a challenge in the implications that rode alongside it. What will she think? How will she react to the modifications? He pushed his apprehensions to the back of his mind. He would have to figure out how to tell her later. The two men nodded and departed the quiet confines of the office.

Chapter 27

Veil-born

"Collating relevant information. Analysis complete.
Calibrating new psionic profile.
Pending implementation...."
~ a.c.e.t.a. designation "Maggie"

"Excellent timing, Commander," Jackson turned his head toward the voice addressing him. He made eye contact with her soft chestnut colored eyes framed elegantly by the loose curls of her brown and silver hair, "I had to send my assistant back to medbay to deal with another issue and it's just about time to pull her out. I would greatly appreciate some assistance."

"Anything you say, Doc. Just tell me what to do." He redirected his attention toward the row of suspension tanks that lined the left wall. Kensy delicately floated within the pale blue liquid that filled the end most tank. A breathing mask covered her lower face while a tangle of bands and wires wrapped around her body to monitor her vital statistics. A set of tubes fastened to the control clasp nodes on her right arm. He watched as the last of the new plasma flowed into the projection cells in her arm.

"I'll need you up top," Doctor Tyronis pointed to a steep set of metal stairs alongside the tanks. "When I initiate the release, you'll need to help pull her out."

He tipped his head, waving with two fingers as he jogged toward the stair, "Got it." Grabbing the railings, he hoisted himself up, skipping past the bottom few steps. He swiftly crested the rise and moved down the walkway just above the tanks. Once in position, he crouched down on one knee, wrapping his fingers around the edge of the platform. He nodded to the doctor.

She looked down to the control panel in front of her and began busily typing away at it. There was a sound of rushing air, then the top hatch of the suspension chamber popped up and rotated away from the opening. The tubing connecting to Kensy's clasp unclipped, floating freely away from her. Next, the belts folded back on themselves and her body began to rise toward the surface. She reached up, looking for the rim of the tank. Jackson grabbed her wrist. As she pulled against him, her face broke the surface.

He lifted her enough to get an arm under hers and hoisted her up onto the walkway. Carefully, he began detaching the sensors from her arms. Kensy pulled the breathing mask from her face and looked over her shoulder at her assistant. "I coulda sworn the medic that was supposed to be here was decidedly shorter... and blonde," she cracked a smile for a brief moment. Her fingers swept from her ear around the back of her head and into a twist as she tried to wring the excess fluid from her hair.

"Well then, I am sorry to disappoint. Guess I'll just have to work on being shorter... and blonde." Kensy struggled to stifle her snicker. Jackson gently removed the last sensor from her forehead. He grabbed her hand, helping her to her feet.

"Oh, that's quite alright. Sometimes changing up peoples' expectations is a good thing." She rested her palms on her hips, "But careful, Commander, I might get the impression that you're following me." She slipped past him and down the stairs. Doctor Tyronis waited patiently with towel in hand beside the crown of chairs in the center of the room. Kensy graciously accepted the towel and began blotting away the remaining water.

Jackson jogged to catch up, "I was actually coming to see how things were progressing down here." He stuffed his hands in his pockets and moved into a comfortable stance, his feet shoulder width apart. Kensy gave him a soft smile and turned to grab a loose-fitting pair of pants from a nearby tray. She slipped them over her skin tight body suit then continued to fuss at her hair with the towel.

"The plasma injections typically take the longest portion of time in a clasp rebuild and now that we have that part done, the rest will hopefully move right along," Doctor Tyronis looked back toward Kensy, "How is it feeling?"

She flexed her clasp arm and fingers as she analyzed the sensations, "Still pretty warm, but the weight is there. Didn't realize how much I had become accustomed to it."

Doc nodded, "Good, good. Now we'll have to reload your control scheme. I had Psicorp forward your profile, but we'll have to make adjustments for your...."

"If I may...," Maggie interjected. Everyone paused and looked up toward the disembodied voice. "After analyzing the data from the Psionic Security Investigation Corp in conjunction with the biological data received during the beam scan of the psilyria's system, a new profile has been compiled. Adjustments were made for increased power draw, fatigue capacity, and projection efficiency. If you wish to implement this schematic, please select 'Veil-born' from the list of profiles."

The doctor and Kensy exchanged glances. Kensy shrugged and hopped up onto the edge of the nearest chair, "Why not? Let's give it a shot." She laid back, placing her arm on the extended armrest.

Doctor Tyronis slipped the interface sleeve over Kensy's arm, "You're sure you want to try this new profile?"

Kensy nodded, "Either it will work and we save a ton of time on tweaking calibrations or it won't and we reload my old profile and work on it. So far Maggie has been helpful even if she's a little stranger than we're used to. I'm willing to at least give her calculations a shot."

"Alright. Uploading 'Veil-born' to your clasp controller." Doctor Tyronis tapped on the screen to launch the data transfer. Jackson stared at the console as the progress bar crawled across it. Kensy clenched her jaw and braced for the jolt of energy that passed into her arm as the signal calibrated her clasp. The pain was more intense than she had remembered, and she let a pained cry slip past her lips. As Jackson instinctively lurched to move to her aid, she held up her free hand to stop him. She clamped down on the upper portion of her arm as if to stop the pain from reaching the rest of her body.

"Doc! Something's wrong. What's it doing to her?!" he asked with angst clearly audible in his voice. Doctor Tyronis focused on the readings, searching for an answer.

"Don't... I can..." Kensy struggled to choke out the words on her mind, "...almost... done." The transfer completed on the screen, and Kensy relaxed back into the chair. She blinked away the water in her eyes. "Told you," she let out a sigh of relief. Doctor Tyronis shook her head and began to remove the interface sleeve. She gasped as her eyes fell on the newly reprogrammed clasp. Kensy and Jackson both turned their attention toward it.

The last of a red glow faded from the bands of her clasp, leaving behind an elegant etching across the metal. Kensy picked up her arm and turned her wrist as she examined it. The fine wires had been etched into tiny rope like structures and the wider pieces sported flowing and unfamiliar writings and designs. Even the edges of her skin, previously scarred by the initial implantation of the clasp, were changed and smoothed out as if they had never been scarred in the first place. "Beautiful," she murmured under her breath.

Kensy leapt from the chair and jogged to the testing floor along the right side of the room. A force field popped up behind her. She held her arm up, focusing on her well of energy. The faint glow of violet energy began to coalesce around the maze of nodes and wires in her arm. It was effortless and natural. "Ivanigis," she called out. The glow burst forth from her whole body and settled in against her skin. She stood there for a moment, savoring the sensation of being wrapped in energy.

Jackson watched in silent wonder as she tested the functionality of her clasp. The light that danced over her skin glittered beautifully. He thought back to the sight of her standing on the hull of the Themiscyra, pouring massive amounts of energy from the palms of her hands and the subtle dance of her body as she directed its ebb and flow. Then there was the terrifying storm of energy just the night before that seethed with destructive energy. But this was different from both of those. There was a grace to the tightly controlled manifestations that she now called upon. Even when she had used her powers to activate the ship, the energy had seemed more chaotic within its tightly held form. Now it appeared to flow without turbulence around her.

She cast one hand out, flicking her fingers open, "Volgihr." A pulse burst from her palm and broke against the rear wall. She scooped at the air with both hands, raising a domed barrier in front of her, "Raga ami velgihr." The tiles of the testing floor rumbled as the barrier pushed toward the far end. As the energy subsided, the floor tiles righted themselves and waited for the next blast. She cupped her hands together and formed her psionic long sword between them. Drawing her right hand away, she flicked her wrist and excess energy flew from the blade like water, leaving only the sharp profile of the blade. She waved and danced with the blade as if it were an extension of herself. She turned back toward Doctor Tyronis and Jackson, "This is fantastic! I don't think I've ever had this fine of control before and it feels effortless, smooth." She admired the sword in her hand. The hilt and blade were sharper than before and more detailed. She smiled, "I think this will work quite well. I'm not getting any feedback or resistance strain."

Doc nodded, "It does seem to be working, but I would like to keep an eye on your vitals just in case there are any unknown instabilities within the new control structure." Kensy nodded absently as she released her manifestations and stepped from the training floor in admiration of her new clasp. "Well, since that is taken care of, I will be returning to medbay. Let me know if you have need of anything further." Doctor Tyronis gathered a few items and departed the room.

"Ready to save the galaxy now?" Jackson jested.

Kensy placed her hands on her hips, "I think I just might be able to." They shared a light laugh and Kensy began to walk toward the door.

"Wait," Jackson anxiously called out. As she directed her attention back toward him, the words seemed to stall on his lips. He forced them out slowly and deliberately, "There was something I was hoping to talk to you about." She gazed over her shoulder at him. His nervousness was palpable as he tightened his jaw and became rigid in his stance. Slowly, she turned and stepped back toward him. Reaching out with her left hand, she touched his arm in reassurance. "I, uh, didn't know how this whole clasp thing was gonna work out, so I asked Allen to do some work on your quarters...." She gazed up at him with her soft sea-green eyes. "I had him make some changes to the environmental systems so you can enable a dampening system if you need it, so you don't have to worry about a repeat of last night." He cleared his throat, "I know how much it was bothering you...."

Kensy gave him a weak smile and lowered her eyes. She slid her fingers toward the area on his ribs where she had seen the medic place a bandage, gently running her fingers across it, "I'm so sorry it came to that. But I understand." She withdrew and tilted her head to the side, "Thank you." Pivoting on one foot, she headed for the door again, disappearing beyond his view. He let out a frustrated sigh and shook his head, *Brilliant, just brilliant....*

Chapter 28

Comparing Notes

"Many hands can make the work light, a few conspiratorial hands can make the work disappear."
~ Crewman K. Morrison

Saltwater and particulates filled the air as the wrappings of her left hand met with the synthetic surface of the heavy bag, followed swiftly by her right. The flurry continued while she focused on the precision of her movements. She flowed like water, spinning into a kick, then closing in to continue punching. Sweat wept slowly from her pores, making her skin glisten in the lights. She bounced back out of range and stayed lightly on her toes while using her forearm to wipe her brow.

Nexus observed from the side of the room, "Fascinating, do all of your kind engage in this primitive expression of aggression?" Kensy chuckled.

She shook her head and resumed her workout. "It is a common means of honing both our physical bodies and mental acumen." She pulled away from the bag and glanced toward him. "I can work on improving my stamina, which in turn allows me to maintain manifestations for longer. And practicing precision helps concentration, which may otherwise falter...," she tilted her head down and mumbled, "...like it did last night." She threw another few punches.

Nexus ignored her mumbling and turned his gaze toward her, "And here I assumed you were using it as an avoidance technique."

She paused again, taken aback by his comment, "Wait, can't you read my mind?!"

He smiled in his peculiar way, "I see a fair amount."

She bristled at the implication, "I am not avoiding anything!" Her hands landed on her hips as she stood defiantly before her otherworldly companion.

Nexus tilted his head to one side, "You mean you're *not* avoiding returning to your quarters while the modifications are being made?" He grunted in disbelief, "I suppose I will need to work on my interpretations of your neurological patterns some more." He began grooming himself, smoothing stray streaks of energy into his form as a domestic cat would attend to rumpled fur.

Kensy looked aside, entrenched in thought. She sighed in resignation and slumped down on the floor beside him, folding her legs together. "Maybe you're right... or maybe," she posited, "I just don't want to be in the way. They have important work to get done, protecting the rest of the ship from *me*." She threw her hands up in the air. "And what do I have on the agenda? Nothing! Because a certain meddlesome friend of mine had a point to make about my priorities."

Nexus narrowed his eyes to tiny scrutinizing slits, "Now, now. Do you really believe that?!"

She hung her head, "Some days I don't know what to believe. Every time I think I have a good handle on things, the universe banks hard right." Nexus stood and rubbed his body across the fronts of her knees like a real feline before settling down in front of her. "Neira. Jackson. The crew. I know they're just concerned about me, about everything... but they wouldn't have to be if I wasn't so damn toxic to be around. If I didn't know better, I'd swear I was cursed." She gave a strained laugh. *I suppose this is my price for defying destiny*. They sat there for a long moment, lost in Kensy's thoughts. Time crept slowly by when at last she let out another sigh. "I suppose I should head out and see how the work is progressing." She rose to her feet again, and Nexus followed at her side.

They strolled down the corridor toward the main elevator. As they passed by several crewmen engaged in a doorway conversation, Nexus snaked through their ankles. Neither man acknowledged the energetic apparition, and a thought stirred in Kensy's mind. As they rounded the next corner, she looked down at Nexus. *No one else can see you, can they?!* she mentally inquired.

Nexus bolted up to her shoulder before replying, "It *would* be possible for someone with gifts like yours to see me, but alas, you are the only one among the human crew who has been awakened."

Kensy approached the elevator and waited briefly as the car arrived. She stepped in, "Captains' Quarters," and gave Nexus a perplexed scowl, "What do you mean human crew? The entire crew is human."

Nexus shook his head, "I didn't mean anything by it. Perhaps it was a poor choice of words, I will have to attend to that. Now, I believe you will not be needing me for a while, so I will retire for a little recharge."

Kensy smiled and nodded, "Of course, talk to you later." The elevator doors opened with a ding. Nexus leapt down from Kensy's shoulder, vanishing as he neared the floor. Kensy shook her head and stepped from the elevator car into the vestibule outside her quarters.

The door was open. Cautiously, she approached the entryway, peering around the doorjamb. Chief Engineer Petroski glanced up from the panel at which he knelt and gave her a quick smile before turning back to his work. "Just wrapping up here. I'll be out of your hair in a few minutes."

Kensy hesitated, "If you need more time, I can come back later."

Allen tilted his head back to look through the lower portion of his spectacles, "Nonsense, these are your quarters.

New and improved even!" He tucked the wires and tubes with which he had been fussing back into the open slots of his work panel. "All ready for the patch up!" he informed Maggie. A new square of flooring slid into place and melded with the existing structure, leaving it seamless and blemish free.

He rose and approached Kensy at the door. His fingers directed her attention to a small control panel alongside the entry way. "This here is your new dampening system. The slider allows you to pick your poison. Up is your basic noise control, nothing more. As you pull it down, the environmental systems will bring the dampeners online. And this here...," he pointed to a glassy black toggle, "is your panic button. Press that, and this room becomes a psionic dead zone, complete suppression. Maggie will also notify medical, command, and engineering as needed." Allen packed up his tool bag, "Just a little peace of mind for you. And if there is anything else you need, don't hesitate to call, boss."

Kensy cordially bowed to him, "Thank you, Chief." She watched as he finished collecting himself and departed. Slowly, she walked to the center of the room, examining her surroundings. Most of the damage from the storm was gone. A few dark edges were still visible on her personal items that adorned the room. As she glanced at the settee, she realized that one of the decorative pillows was missing. Turning her attention to the other side of the room, she noticed a sizable trunk where her last two crates had rested the day before.

She furrowed her brow, approaching the trunk for inspection. Dangling over the main lock pad was a small sheet of flexiglass with a note:

The storm trashed your crates. Made the boys clean it up while I tucked any sensitive items away from prying eyes. This baby should weather better and thought you might like a little more personal security.

~ Neira

P.S. Temp combo is your AB locker number. Feel free to reset it.

Kensy set the note down and ran her fingers over the top of the trunk lid. She smiled softly. Drawing a deep breath, she looked at the clock beside her bed. *Hmm, so late already? Guess I better get cleaned up for dinner. Still a lot to get done tonight.* She showered and dressed for the evening in an unarmored version of her Psicorp uniform. The top was made of light but durable material that hung more loosely on her figure, accompanied by full length charcoal slacks and black dress flats.

On her way out the door, she scooped up her primary holographic datapad. She flipped through the pages of reports and requests that had collected throughout the day. Her attention was so wrapped up in her work that she failed to notice as Jackson strolled up beside her in the foyer. He cleared his throat to announce himself. Startled, she nearly dropped her pad. "Sorry," he promptly apologized, "was just headed down to dinner, you?"

She smiled softly, "Yeah, and having a bit of tunnel vision along the way. Evidently, I took too long to get things squared away. I've got a mountain of stuff to go through just from today." She sighed and stared at the lists some more.

"I swear the paperwork multiplies when you're not looking." He waved his holopad in acknowledgment. "Although I may be able to knock out some of that work list for you, since we get copied on all memos. And I already addressed a bunch of them earlier." He cautiously segued toward a question, "Would you like to join me for dinner and we can compare notes?"

The tension between them from earlier melted away as she turned her eyes up toward him, a gently grin curving around her soft lips. "I would like that... comparing notes," she quickly added with a self-conscious stammer. The elevator arrived, and they stepped inside. Kensy tilted her head down and bit at her bottom lip as she fought the butterflies in her stomach. *Get a hold of yourself. You're acting like a crushing school girl,* she chastised herself. *He probably thinks you're just about as moody too with how you acted earlier.* She coughed at the thought, "I'm... sorry about earlier." She glanced up at him with and apprehensive grimace, "Sometimes I don't know how to react to things. It was a thoughtful gesture, getting that system installed. And I know you didn't mean anything bad...." She began to ramble nervously.

Jackson chuckled as he paused her mid-rant, "It's okay, I kinda botched the whole conversation too." He thought for a moment before continuing, "How about we take a blank slate on today? Just pretend the whole awkward mess didn't happen. Deal?"

"Deal," she nodded.

As the elevator passed the officer's deck, it paused to let another passenger embark toward the central levels. Daniel smiled as he saw Kensy and Jackson politely keep their distance within the confines of the car. "We're headed down to the mess. You?" Jackson informed him.

"Likewise," Daniel replied, "Thought I would grab a bite before turning in for the evening."

Kensy smiled and cautiously shuffled toward Jackson as she made room for Daniel to step in, "You're welcome to join us if you don't mind talking shop. I evidently have some catching up to do with the day's reports."

Daniel slipped in next to her, "Sounds good. I have some items to go over myself." The doors closed, and they continued their descent. When at last they reached their destination, only moments later the level was buzzing with traffic. The trio navigated through the rivers of crewmen and women, arriving at the large open hall that served as the mess.

A mix of table and booth seating made for a comfortable atmosphere. They circled around to the large cases of prepared meals, each grabbing something suited to their particular tastes. Jackson hung back, surveying the room for a place where they could sit down and work. Kensy lithely ducked in front of him and headed for the far wall, where a series of raised booths lined the great virtual windows looking out onto the passing stars. She slid into one of the empty seats and paused for a moment to admire the glittering dark curtain of lights. Jackson sat down beside her, allowing Daniel the opposite side to himself. Kensy sighed, "I know the window isn't real, but the view is still so breathtaking, so... stunning."

"Yeah, a pretty amazing sight," Jackson glanced at Kensy for a moment as he spoke, then back to the stars. Daniel smirked. Jackson redirected his attention to the dinner table, "I suppose we should get started on something productive here or we'll never get through everything." Kensy took a bite of her dinner as she began tapping away at her datapad. "While you were busy, I went over the duty rosters from the department heads. Seems like everyone is settling into their new stations fairly well. A few of the admiral's techs had initially slipped between the cracks, so I had Doctor Hirayama add them to her team."

Kensy nodded, "Sounds good. You know... if you have things settled already on any of this, I'm more than happy to defer to your judgment. No sense in us overlapping on the menial things. Just flag it for me if there is something special I need to look at."

"In that case...," Jackson synced the reports lists, clearing the majority of items.

Kensy laughed, "Wow. You're going to make my job just too easy."

"I had Maggie do some streamlining of our reports system earlier. Figured we have enough on our plates without worrying about the condition of every light fixture on the ship. There are enough redundancies to make sure the everyday stuff gets done." Jackson explained as he fussed with his sandwich. "And we'll be notified if any problems come up."

"Guess then it's my turn to filter away even more of those pesky reports for you," Daniel spoke up. "We had some squabbles on the crew deck earlier. Nothing I couldn't handle with a few stern words and a little shuffling of the living quarter assignments." He played with his spaghetti absently. "I'll keep an eye on the trouble makers all the same and make sure no further issues arise. I figure it's just stress of a new mission, a new environment. Everything will work itself out given a little time."

Kensy turned her spoon over and over in the rice pilaf on her plate, "Did you two leave *anything* for me to take care of?" she snickered and took another bite.

The two men glanced at each other and shook their heads as Jackson replied, "Nope. Nothing that I can think of." His expression was cool and collected. He had known all along that everything was well in hand.

Kensy gave him a scrutinizing glance. *Why didn't he say something sooner? Did he just want me to feel like I was contributing?* She adjusted her focus past him to the figure approaching the table. Hensley diligently tried to walk as normally as possible, but his body betrayed him. Each step was slightly uneven, even despite his best attempts to mask his limp. Kensy tilted her head to the side, "Hey Sergeant. How is the leg feeling?"

A fiercely serious expression soured his face as he saluted his superiors, "Sirs, that's what I was hoping to speak with you about. I know we're on our way to a potentially hostile colony for this mission. I want to be on the ground team."

Kensy peeked back over her shoulder and spied the rest of Alpha Team watching and whispering at the end of the row of tables. Daniel leaned back, throwing an arm over the back of the booth casually, "I don't believe you have been cleared for regular duty yet, Sergeant. I believe the last report I received from medical had you on light duty with regular check-ins for another two weeks."

"I'm good to go, sir!" He grunted, "I didn't stay on the mission just to warm the bench."

Jackson spoke up, "We know that, Sergeant. You stayed on the mission because you are a good soldier and you know what must be done. But this mission is too important for false bravado. There will be other battles. What you *will* do is follow all directions given to you by our good doctor so that you are ready for the next battle and the one after that. Do you understand, soldier?" He stared at Hensley with an intensity that exuded his unswaying conviction. Kensy silently admired how he wore the mantle of authority so naturally.

Hensley snapped to attention and saluted, "Yes, sir!" Jackson dismissed him, and Kensy watched as Hensley shuffled back toward his group of peers. Though their words were too soft to be heard across the bustling room, Kensy studied their movements. Shane and Reily offered gestures of condolence to their dejected compatriot as Rasken prodded him for a laugh.

Kensy shook her head and returned to her dinner, "I understand his frustrations."

"We all do," Jackson nodded, "But we won't get very far if we let everyone go around recklessly pushing their limits. And at least he listens when I pull rank, unlike some." He cracked a sarcastic smile in Kensy's direction. She rolled her eyes at him.

Daniel mused at the exchange, "Ah, such a shining example of camaraderie—." The conversation was interrupted by a cacophonous chorus of notifications.

Kensy grabbed her pad and began reading. She sighed deeply, "Mine's from Neira. She wants a meeting in the morning. O' seven hundred. Hangar Two. Something mission critical."

Daniel pulled a clip from his belt and activated its virtual interface. "Mine too," he scowled, "Doesn't have any other specifics included." He deactivated the interface and slipped it back onto his belt with a shrug.

"What does she want now?" Jackson scoffed at his tablet and cast it aside.

Placing her elbows on the table, Kensy folded her fingers together and leaned her head on them. "I guess we'll find out bright and shining early in the morning." She looked between her companions curiously.

Chapter 29

Stars & Shadows

"Stars guide my sleep that I might find
serenity instead of storms."
~ *an Audrumirwan prayer*

The bristles of her hairbrush gently parted the soft strawberry blonde strands into order as she paced around the room, lost in thought. The soft hum of the ship around her and the cozy warmth of her quarters were almost hypnotic. She paused and shot a glance toward her new control panel beside the doorframe. Restless contemplation overcame her for a long moment. She inhaled deeply before her legs would allow her to move toward it.

Gently, she rested the tips of her fingers upon the slider. Cautiously, she drew the control down until she could feel a slight pressure in the atmosphere, as if someone had wrapped her in a heavy blanket. She turned away and closed her eyes, analyzing the sensation, getting familiar with it. She took measured breaths, counting the moments. Opening her eyes, she drifted toward the bedside and set her hairbrush down.

Slowly, Kensy lowered herself into the softness of the bedding. She raised her eyes toward the virtual window above her bed and wrapped her arms around her knees. Her words passed her lips as little more than a whisper, "Stars guide my sleep, that I might find serenity instead of storms." As she closed her eyes, her thoughts drifted toward Jackson.

Butterflies filled her stomach as she recalled that one moment when he had wrapped the medical blanket over her shoulders. And then it happened... their fingertips overlapped. His strong, warm hands rested against hers. Her heart raced. In that split second, she felt secure, as if nothing in the universe could touch her. She glanced back toward the door. Her right hand slid up to her left shoulder, and she rested her cheek against it, savoring the memory. A sweet smile curled around her lips.

Kensy stretched and yawned. She held onto her smile as she sunk into the waiting sheets, allowing herself to relax. *Perhaps tonight my dreams will be sweeter*, she mused as she pulled the blankets tight around her and slipped into peaceful slumber.

Under the dimmed lights of the room, a faint shadow formed, one hand outstretched, reaching for her. Its form was unstable, flickering in and out. The shadow touched her temple for a brief moment, then faded into nothing. Red lightning bolted across her forehead before being dissipated by the suppression system. She furrowed her brow and attempted to withdraw further into the protective grasp of the blankets. Her fingers clenched the crest of her shoulder as she fought to resist the subversion of her dream.

Kensy lifted her head and glanced around. Strings of beads and jewels jangled delicately against her skin as she moved. Her hair fell in elegant curls from the twists that ran up the back of her head. The breathtaking view from her balcony brought a torrent of tears to her eyes. She fought against the storm of emotions that overwhelmed her. Waves of rosy pink gossamer fabric fluttered around her figure as she turned into the room, trying to escape. Shadows of two young girls danced around the chamber, giggling and stirring more turbulent thoughts. She ran for the entry, throwing the door open with a thunderous clamor.

Her footsteps quickened until at last she broke into an all-out run. The palatial residence seemed to go on forever. Frantically, she searched for the exit, only to find more halls, more rooms. *I can't be here! I shouldn't be here! Why am I here? I don't belong....* She stumbled to her knees and sobbed. *Not now. I have somewhere to be. I have something I have to do.*

She raised her tear-stained face again and beheld a grand vestibule. Two massive staircases curved together and down to a lower floor. Elegantly flourished stonework framed the towering front aperture. She crawled to her feet and carefully made her way down the steps. She mustered enough strength to jog toward the doors. As she reached out for them she paused. She drew close and rested her forehead against the smooth, enameled surface.

It's just a reflection of a memory. Nothing here is real. Maybe it never was.... She wobbled her head back and forth and looked down at her hands pressing against the doors. She noted the jewelry and gown that she was wearing and with a slight chuckle thought; *I mean really, I never did look like this, did I?!* She let slip a gentle sigh. Allowing herself a long moment, she began to calm down. *It's just another dream. No matter how real it feels, it's all in my imagination. I can control this. Focus.* She closed her eyes.

Something scuffed across the marbled flooring behind her. Slowly, Kensy turned to inspect the sound. There stood Elle, battered and broken. She hunched over as she fought to approach her friend. Elle's figure seemed to blink and shutter as she tried to move. "Kensy... it's so hard... to be here now," she choked out, "...something I have to tell you." She let out an agonized cry and collapsed on to her hands and knees.

"Elle!" Kensy lunged toward her friend, only to be stopped.

Elle looked up at her with pleading eyes, "No! You're flying... toward the storm... must... nothing left to save... turn around before... too late." Elle screamed in pain. "Go! The shadow will consume... please, go!"

Kensy knelt down in front of her, "I don't understand. What is going on? Elle, please, I already lost you once. Help me understand." Kensy tentatively reached for her, "Why am I seeing you? What do I need to know?"

A shock wave burst forth from Elle's body, knocking Kensy back. With the aftershock, she became more tangible. Terrified, she attempted to stand as she looked at Kensy. "You have to go, NOW! The shadows are coming! I can't hold them back. Get out of the dream. Find the exit. Wake up!" She fell back to her knees. A pool of darkness formed under her spreading in slithering tendrils. Elle fought against the tide, but to no avail.

Kensy clamored to retreat from her friend when a figure at the edge of her vision caught her attention. She glimpsed only a sliver of his image, but it was familiar. She scrambled to her feet. Giving a wide berth to the growing darkness, she darted back up the grand staircase after the mysterious figure. With one last glance over her shoulder, Kensy watched the last tendril pull Elle into the abyssal dark. In her stead rose the sinister figure of a woman wreathed in blackness and red lightning.

Kensy broke into a run. The click of her heels against the floor was muffled by the soft carpet that ran down the center of the upper corridor. Frantically, she looked for the stranger, passing room after room. Whispers rang in her ears as she approached another stair. Her mystery man vanished over the top step. *Dark hair, uniform, could it be...?* "Jackson!" She cried out for him, but the stranger did not respond. The ground behind her shook and cracked as the dark entity gradually began to close the distance between them.

Kensy raced up the staircase. The stranger disappeared onto the grand balcony and Kensy followed in kind. As she emerged from the doors, he stepped off the railing. Running to the edge, she stopped herself abruptly, catching sight of the drop before her. But there he was, walking away from the pool below her. Kensy crawled up on the railing, her balance wavering. She took a deep breath. "This is your dream. You're in control," she reassured herself. She took a step and plummeted toward the ground. She landed in a crouch, but none worse for the wear. The water around her rose up in glistening curtains of droplets. She looked up and the droplets slowly began to rain back down one-by-one. She sprang forward into a sprint, time bending to her presence, as she chased after the stranger.

She crossed through an enormous pavilion and down to the main courtyard steps. Hundreds of faint figures filled the courtyard, unmoving as they stared toward a capsule standing at its very heart. The sight of it created a knot in Kensy's stomach. She hesitated. The stranger moved through the crowd and up to the construct. He opened the side hatch and stood back. Kensy cautiously stepped forward. The sea of ghosts parted before her. She clenched her fists as she walked toward the instrument of her fate. The stranger faded as she approached. Kensy looked back one last time to see the darkening horizon behind her. She placed one hand on the edge of the door. "And so you deliver me once again...," she shook her head and stepped into the capsule. A blinding light overwhelmed her senses.

She snapped awake as she sat upright and startled. The room was still. Slowly, she unclenched the blankets. She exhaled her held breath and looked around. Kensy reached up to her left shoulder again, trying to bring back that moment of peace. Water filled her eyes as she slumped back down into the covers. Her focus dissolved away as she stared at the wall blankly, *Stars forgive me, I can't seem to let the dead rest.*

Chapter 30

Subterfuge

"Hot damn! Did you see what the captains are wearing?
Whatever mission that is, sign me up."
~ *Crewman M. Xander*

Leaning against a large cargo container, Neira, dressed in her usual amber and black armor, ankles crossed, tapping the toe of her right boot against the floor, waited impatiently for her audience. "Did you deliver the packages?" Neira inquired, studying her datapad intently.

"Indeed. The subjects are en route and should arrive shortly," Maggie promptly replied.

Neira glanced at the current time stamp and sighed, "They certainly are taking long enough."

"If you are going to complain, maybe you should reconsider the mandatory change of wardrobe." Jackson sauntered into the room. The legs of his heavy ballistic fabric cargo pants fell over the top of his boots. A snug black shirt hugged his chest and abdomen, showing the definition of his muscles, over which he wore a bulky combat jacket lined with articulated armor plates. "What's with the special get-up, anyway?" He held up one of his hands, showing the spiked fingerless gloves she had included.

Daniel slipped through the cargo bay door behind him, Morgan in tow, "Just what I was thinking." Both adorned in similar but equally unique fashion.

Neira shook a finger at them, "Now, now. That would be telling, and we still have one more member yet to arrive to this little party." She shot a sideways glance toward the men. "I should have known it would take her the longest to get dressed for the occasion."

"I could take longer, if you'd like." Kensy's voice rang out behind the group. "I feel ridiculous. You couldn't come up with something better than *this*?" Everyone turned to look at her and suddenly Kensy felt self-conscious as their eyes fell on her. A small tank-top accented her lithe figure, letting skin peak out from her waist between the hem and the top of her hip-hugging navy pants. A metal-studded belt wrapped around the top of the pants, coordinating with the bands that ran down the outside of the legs and disappeared into the top of her knee-high chunky-heeled boots. On top of it all, she wore a loose fishnet shirt and a ballistic mini-vest with studded metal shoulder guards.

"Good," Neira strutted up to Kensy. "Gotta lose the ponytail, though." She reached up, pulling Kensy's hair tie out and tousling her hair into loose waves. She turned back to Jackson, Morgan, and Daniel. "I *almost* believe. I have talked to Doc. She will be helping you with some fun tech tattoos. Once you have your full disguises, you will look the part, but we need to talk about the attitude, the story. We are going into this place as a private merc force." Neira paced back to the crate on which she had leaned earlier. She tapped the control pad with the side of her fist. The front panel released and slid away. Inside, racks of weapons and various containers spotted the shelves and mounting racks. "I took the liberty of having your custom gear manufactured, so you look a little less Ascension and a little more black market badass. And a contact of mine supplied the toys, including...."

Neira removed the very center container gingerly. The cylinder glowed and pulsed with the crystal that floated inside the complex containment matrix. Jackson scowled, "Tell me you didn't bring an actual, live Nordux Crystal on board the ship." He crossed his arms, fighting the urge to take another look toward his co-captain. His thoughts danced between Kensy and the crystal in a mental tug of war, tucked carefully under his stoic façade.

Neira placed the container back in its resting place. "Of course I did. Our cover could easily be blown by a fake. This gives us credibility as well as being a potential resource. If we need to demonstrate, we have the capability and if we need to blast our way out, we have our very own custom wrecking ball."

"Or a means to blow ourselves sky-high. None of us are trained to handle a material that volatile," Daniel moved in closer to examine the container in detail.

"That's not *entirely* true...," Kensy piped up as she wrapped her arms around her lower ribs uneasily. Jackson casually turned his attention back toward her, being careful not to gawk at how the lines of her clothes hugged the graceful curves of her body. "I had a post ages ago at a research outpost. Granted, they were more focused on contamination than combustion, but the container looks familiar enough. A modified GC-L48, if I'm not mistaken?" Neira nodded in affirmation. Kensy's fingertip gently smoothed a few stray strands into place behind her right ear. "A pretty stable unit, if I remember correctly. Should be reasonably safe as long as we don't drop a truck on it." Kensy shot a glance toward Jackson. Immediately, he understood her reference, Alpha Bael and Chimera.

Jackson snapped back to Neira, "So you two can safely manage the cylinder.... That still doesn't address the issue of material handling if they want a demonstration." He paused, "Unless you have that covered too...." Neira raised an eyebrow toward him and flashed a smirk. "You do. Of course you do. I don't know why I even bother...," he shook his head.

"Don't strain yourself thinking about it," she snidely retorted. "Now I have had some contacts laying the groundwork for us. Whispers in the right corners and such. By the time we arrive, word will have reached the right ears for us to waltz in and demand an audience for a lucrative business arrangement. We go in armed to the teeth, an elite strike team of a larger shadow organization." Neira set her hands on the crest of her hips, "Now here's the hard part... I need you to forget your military conduct. The moment we hit the ground, I will be acting as your boss. Whatever I say goes. No ifs, ands, or buts. No ranks or titles. Last names only. In fact no talking to anyone outside the crew if you can help it. I can sell quiet disdain."

"Who died and made you in charge?" Morgan snapped dismissively.

The soft rustling of her metal and leather belts drew his attentions as Neira closed the distance between them. Her eye narrowed to a sharp, icy glare, "Even your dumb-ass reeks of career military service. You open your yap and this mission will be over before it begins." Neira crossed her arms over her chest and shifted her hips to one side, "I, on the other hand, have been posing as a shadow op merc for the better part of a decade. Who do you think they will believe more?"

"Okay, I know you have all these details lined up with the outfits, the equipment, the rumor-mill... but won't our cover be blown the second someone runs facial recognition on any one of us?" Kensy apprehensively asked.

"That is where the tattoos come in." Neira pulled out a hand-held holoprojector, bringing up the image of a generic human head, "These tats aren't your run-of-the-mill archaic ink. These are an incredibly advanced new tech, still in the experimental stages. The tattoos scramble visual scans and feed pre-programmed information to virtual sources. It won't fool the human eye. You will still look like you, only with ink. But I have carefully crafted cover identities for each of you.

Each will be embedded in the tattoo data Doctor Tyronis will imprint on your skin. I have also forwarded each of you dossiers to study up on the new you." The hologram ran through a demonstration of tattoo features as she spoke. "The downside here is that the tech has a limited lifetime. It will begin to break down after several hours. So we get in, find what we need and get out as fast as we can."

Jackson furrowed his brow in contemplation. Kensy slipped toward him, sliding up behind his left arm. She glanced up at him, "Something wrong?" He turned his eyes to meet her and looked back toward Neira and the others.

"Hmm maybe." He folded his arms together. "Cross. I have another point of concern."

She raised an eyebrow toward him, "Of course you do."

"You don't expect that we are all going ground-side, do you? I'm not sure that's a terribly wise course of action," he scowled at her.

Neira smirked, "No, I'm not planning on leaving the ship leaderless. Smart-ass over here will stay on board and filter communications from the bridgehead," she thumbed toward Morgan. "I figured Bryden will shuttle us down, then return to take the bridge. We can relay any last-minute info before the drop-off. And by keeping the shuttle out of reach, we reduce the risk of exposure. Between us and Alpha team we should be equipped well enough to handle most situations. We can call for pickup when we either find what we need or our cover gets blown. At which point we won't need to tip-toe anymore."

"Fine." Jackson shrugged, "Are we done here?"

Neira eyed him suspiciously, "Go ahead. Run away. Just know that Doctor Tyronis is expecting you... both." She smugly tilted her head and pivoted away from the captains toward Daniel.

Jackson rolled his eyes and nodded for Kensy to follow him out of the cargo bay. As they cleared the doorway, he took a deep breath. "I want your honest opinion. You think this op is gonna work?" His eyes fell on Kensy's loosely flowing locks.

She stayed quiet for a long moment as they proceeded down the hallway, her head down as she thought through the plan. "I do." She looked up into his eyes with a soft stare. She blinked and shook her head, trying to rethink her choice of words. "I mean, ...yes, I think it's at least worth a go. This really is more her cup of tea than ours." Absent-mindedly, she reached up and wrapped her fingers around the crook of his elbow. "She is an excellent strategist and thinks well on her feet."

Jackson flashed a quick smile as he felt the subtle pressure of her gentle touch on the arm of his jacket, "Well, I suppose at least her taste in disguises isn't a total loss. You look good."

Kensy's face flushed red as she became aware of her appearance again. She angled her head down to let her hair fall over her face. A giddy smile curled around her lips, "You don't look so bad yourself, Commander."

Chapter 31

Be Mercenary

*"I don't know what that means, but given its coming from
Cross, I'm not going to ask."*
~ *Crewman H. Andraphel*

The imprinting laser danced in her hands as Doctor
Tyronis carefully executed the predetermined pattern on
Kensy's skin. Slowly, three black triangles developed over her
lips like perfect icicles. The doctor then moved up toward her
left eye, encircling the orbit and cheekbone in an elaborate
crescent shape. Kensy fought the urge to fidget as her technical
tattoo was being drawn. The clothes Neira had devised for her
cover identity still felt uncomfortable even after being
weathered and washed repeatedly over the course of the last
few days.

Instead, Kensy tried to focus on the mission. They were
nearing Rosealleon. The lead she had dug up felt thin at best,
but it was all she had. Whoever this new enemy was, they had
covered their tracks well. Would they even find anything here?
Unlike Bhelnir and Morwhex Four, this colony hadn't been
destroyed, but something dramatic had happened, forcing
them to cut Ascension ties. She puzzled over the possibilities.

Jackson dabbed a towel at his freshly washed face. He
traced the lines of his tattoo with his eyes. A series of bars,
blocks, and lines passed from the right side of his nose over his
cheekbone and back toward his ear in a sharp geometric
design. He averted his gaze in the nearby mirror, redirecting it

toward Kensy and Doctor Tyronis. He could see the wheels turning in Kensy's thoughts. Before he could say anything, Morgan's voice came booming over the intercom, "Captains, please report to the bridge immediately."

Jackson tapped on his nahdvi, "What is it, Threaux?"

"Sir, we have several bogeys on sensors. Looks like they plan to intercept us before we reach the planet." Morgan reported.

Jackson pivoted around toward Kensy, "Call Miss Cross too. We'll be there shortly."

Kensy looked toward Doctor Tyronis, who was wrapping up her procedure with a verification scan. The results beeped back favorably, "All done. You are free to go." Kensy hopped out of the chair and, together with her co-captain, headed toward the bridge at a brisk pace. As they entered the bridgehead, Kensy dove into the beam without breaking stride. Neira stood behind Morgan, watching the closing ships.

Jackson descended the last few steps and approached the helm, "Report."

"We have two known pirate ships followed by a salvage vessel heading to intercept and we just received a communication from the colony asking our intent and threatening to blast us with orbital defenses." Morgan summarized. Neira crossed her arms and glanced toward Jackson.

"This is your show. Get us down there," Jackson nodded to the mercenary, "preferably without incident...," his voice trailed off.

Neira smirked and placed her hands on her hips. "Princess, get me a targeting lock on the pirates' central drive power cells. Fly-boy, get me a line, I want open broadcast to all ships and the colony." Morgan tapped away at his consoles for a moment before nodding to her. "This is the DeCadejra, flagship of the Black Ion. We have potentially lucrative business to discuss, but I will not tolerate acts of aggression against my ship or any member of my crew. You will stand down or we will open fire."

Silence filled the bridge as they waited for a response. At long last, Kensy broke the silence, "Planetary defense grid is going to standby." She turned her focus back to the pirates. "No change with the others."

"Charge weapons," Neira ordered over her shoulder. Turning back, she redressed the adversaries before her. "I will not repeat myself. You can choose to profit or burn. I am happy to oblige either way." The ships slowly began to turn away, allowing passage to the nearby planet. She looked down at Morgan, "Keep an eye on our friends. If they try anything... be mercenary." Neira made an about-face and strode confidently toward the main elevator.

"Threaux, you have the comm until Bryden gets back from the drop off. Keep her in one piece and try not to scratch the paint." Jackson crested the steps and held out a hand for Kensy. She grabbed his fingertips and descended from the beam. They followed Neira. He tapped his ear to signal the beginning of a transmission, "All hands, Code Yellow. Alpha Team, prepare to deploy."

"Alpha standing by," Lieutenant Rasken's voice called back.

They stopped at the doors to lift as they waited for it to return from delivering Neira before them. Kensy glanced over the wings of crewmen busily working away at their stations. She watched as they coordinated information with an almost symphonic rhythm. The elevator door opened, disrupting her train of thought. Jackson waved her in ahead of himself. As she slumped against the rear wall, he glanced toward her, "You ready for this? You seem distracted."

She mused, "It's nothing. I was just taking a moment to soak everything in. I know if I don't seize the chance when I can, sometimes the details of life can just get lost." She tilted her head to one side. "What about you? Are you ready?"

"I guess we're about to find out." He placed his right hand on his left shoulder as he rotated his elbow in a circle to stretch. After tilting his head side-to-side, he repeated the motion with his other arm. Inhaling deeply, he stood a little straighter and taller. Kensy watched the routine silently. Jackson let a slight snicker escape his lips, "I suppose it's not necessary to prepare the same, not wearing the exosuit this time. Old habits die hard, I guess." In the corner of his mind, he contemplated a small, neatly folded handkerchief stowed securely in his pocket. The token within had lain patiently in the confines of its satiny black box for nearly two weeks now.

Kensy shrugged and turned her eyes toward the control panel, "Meh, probably doesn't hurt either. Who knows, we could be walking into a war zone." The doors opened on the hangar deck. As Kensy moved past Jackson, he caught her arm in his hand. She paused, a look of confusion on her face.

"When we're down there... just be careful." He let her arm go and nodded for her to proceed. There was an uneasiness in his eyes. She nodded back and continued down the hall. He followed close on her heels. *What was that about?* She pondered, *Is he concerned this will be like Morwhex? I have my powers back. Maybe he thinks I'm going to fall apart again.* She took a deep, measured breath. *Not this time. I can do better. I will do better.* She flexed the fingers on her clasp arm. A faint violet flicker danced between her fingers. She raised her chin and extended her stride as they entered the cargo bay.

Alpha team stood around the weapons container checking and loading their gear. The air was filled with a chorus of mechanical clicks and the subtle whine of battery packs. Rasken looked right at home with her black leather and canvas covert armor. She blew a bubble until it popped and pulled it back into her mouth. "Alpha team load up!" she shouted. As they filed onto the transport Neira had procured, Rasken turned toward her captains, "Alpha locked and loading, sirs!"

"Understood. Prepare for departure, Rasken." Jackson nodded toward her as he approached the weapons cache. Rasken pivoted and followed the rest of her team. Jackson turned back toward Kensy. His fingers were wrapped around the barrel of a pistol not unlike her standard issue one.

She took hold of the grip. It was heavier than she was used to. She turned away and checked the sights. Tilting it in her hands she ejected the plasma core to examine it. Two cylinders released from the chamber and dropped into her palm. *Modified for increased capacity, that explains the weight.* She slammed the cores back into the gun and holstered it.

Jackson stowed a small arsenal of weaponry into the sheaths and holster throughout his gear. He looked to the center of the container; the crystal was gone. Neira must have already loaded it. He reached for his last piece, a heavy assault rifle. He checked the weapon over. His eyes traced the lines of the gun, briefly familiarizing himself with the details. It was time. He looked over his shoulder. Their eyes met for a second. Kensy broke the stare first. Her long eyelashes flitted closed for a moment as she averted her gaze.

She strode into the transport. Neira stood amidst the soldiers holding out a long swatch of material for Kensy, "For your clasp. Had Maggie make it special. Shouldn't interfere with your voodoo or burn up." Kensy accepted it. She slid in onto her arm. The cloth formed a sleeve that extended from just shy of her elbow to the back of her knuckles, leaving her fingers and thumb exposed in a kind of pseudo fingerless glove.

Jackson entered the transport and headed for the co-pilot's seat. Neira caught his arm as he passed her. She whispered, "When we find the boss, I'm gonna let your rank slip. Just play along. Gonna test the waters about these people's anti-ascension attitude and try to dispel any reservations they have about us."

Jackson gave her a discrete nod. As he sat down, Daniel flipped some switches and the rear door began to close. "Strike Team Transport Scythe, preparing for departure. All doors secured. All systems green." The engines fired up.

"Roger that Scythe. You are go for launch. Fly safe." Morgan called back over the comm. The transport lifted off the deck, and they gracefully slipped out of the hangar toward the planet's surface.

Chapter 32

Aggressive Negotiations

"Oh, this looks like a friendly place ...."
~ Crewman Anthony Daily

"Keep everyone on their toes. There is no telling how this is going to go down. We will keep in contact." Jackson checked his rifle again as they neared the ground in the transport.

"We'll stay frosty," Daniel replied. "I'll keep a shuttle on standby in case you need a fast extraction." Jackson nodded and glanced over his shoulder at Kensy and the rest of the team. Neira spoke to her in a low tone as they reviewed the cover story. Kensy fussed with the glove Neira had given her to cover her clasp. "Nearing the LZ," Daniel called out over the rustle of his passengers.

Neira turned her gaze toward him, "Don't fully touch down. I don't want to even give them the illusion of getting their mitts on this thing. Just bring us down to a foot or two and we can jump."

"I'll try to keep her steady." Daniel remotely opened the rear hatch for disembarking. Wind and the roar of the engines blasted in their ears for a moment as the nahdvi compensated for the noise. Jackson tilted his head in approval, *maybe these silly contraptions aren't so bad,* he thought. He turned as he rose from the co-pilot's seat. Bringing his rifle up, he clutched the fore portion of the weapon solidly with his left hand. His right index finger rested against the trigger guard, ready to slip back onto the trigger at a moment's notice. His boots hit the ground, stirring up a little bit more dust. The shuttle hatch closed behind him as it pulled away.

He strode through the members of Alpha Team toward the leader of their charade. Everyone was on high alert, watching the movement of every onlooker and guard surrounding them. Neira motioned to the rest of the group to follow as she approached the closest authority figure with a cool determination, "You are going to take me to the man in charge. We have business to discuss." The armed man examined the entourage for a moment. "Is there a problem?" She placed her hands on her hips defiantly.

Without a word, the man turned and headed away. The party cautiously followed. As they neared one of the more prominent structures, he pointed to a well-weathered door. Neira led the others up a few shallow steps. The door burst open and the stocky silhouette of a man stared them down, "You can't bring those weapons in here!" he shouted at Neira.

She leaned down to match his height. Her eye narrowed to a glare. In a hushed tone she hissed at him, "Either you allow us to pass as we are or you can explain to your boss that these negotiations will happen out here in plain view of your populous, and it will not be pleasant. Now I know that your own guards are armed *at least* as much as we are, so consider us starting on an even footing." She straightened her posture, staring at the doorman menacingly. He grumbled and disappeared for a moment.

As he popped back into the doorway, he sneered at her, "Then you come in alone. The rest stay out here."

She raised an eyebrow, "These two come with me. It's not negotiable." She gestured over her shoulders to Kensy and Jackson.

The little man examined them intently for a moment. He glanced back up at Neira. "Fine," he curtly conceded, "but you had better not cause any trouble."

Neira shoved past him, "Wouldn't dream of it." She smirked, connivingly. Kensy followed her into the building. Jackson paused to signal Rasken to stay put before joining Kensy and Neira inside. They shuffled down a long hallway adorned in dilapidated finery. A mustiness filled the air. The doorman skittered past the group toward a heavy wooden door at the far end. He slipped inside, closing it behind him. Muffled voices argued briefly before the door lurched open again.

One after another, they filed into the office. Dark wooden bookshelves climbed the walls like imposing giants. Most of the books listed in varying directions, as though shoved into their resting places haphazardly. Behind the central desk sat another stout man, immortalized in a larger-than-life painting of himself that hung above him on the rear wall. Across a tarnished placard on the base of the frame, the title MAYOR was emblazoned in large letters. The wall sconces and desk lamp shed a sickly yellow light that failed to reach all corners of the seemingly cramped room. Four guards sulked at the perimeter of the room. Jackson kept his eyes on as many of them as he could.

The stout man leaned onto his desk, leering at the company before him, "What brings the Black Ion to *my* doorstep?"

"Money," Neira rubbed her fingertips together.

"Yours or mine?" he replied skeptically.

She crossed her arms over her chest, "If you did you homework, you know that my employer prefers to work outside the stranglehold of the Ascension. It is rare to find such a well-established community with the qualities we are looking for." She unfolded her arms, leaning down, her fingers pressed against the scarred surface of his desk. "Now, are you interested in making lots of money or not?"

He folded his hands together. "What is it that you are looking for, exactly?"

"We are looking for enterprising communities outside Ascension control where we can establish distribution hubs. We provide premium goods to private concerns." She glanced back toward Kensy.

"What kind of goods?" he pried.

Kensy stepped forward, container in hand. She set it on the front of his desk and turned the handle, making the chamber transparent. Neira leaned back, one hand on her hip, "Nordux Crystals, for example... are just one of the many items we provide." The guards and stout man lurched backward from the container sharply. "We require an adequate location on which to establish facilities and will in turn provide a portion of profits or products to be negotiated *after* an inspection of potential sites."

The little man scooted back up to his desk, keeping an eye on the container. "We will have to verify...," Neira gestured for them to go ahead. Kensy ejected the containment chamber for scanning. One of the guards stepped forward and took readings on the crystal. He handed the scanner to his boss. "You brought a *live* crystal in here?!" The stout man's anxiety became apparent as he began to perspire. Kensy slipped the containment chamber back into the canister and locked it down. "You are crazy!"

Neira smirked and leaned over his desk, "I'm also dead serious."

"Perhaps we can work something out," he nervously managed.

"Good. Now my people and I will need some time to examine potential sites." Neira gestured for Kensy to step back with the container. "I also want to know if the community is capable of supporting our interests."

Kensy kept eyes on the stout man. His focus turned from the crystal as Neira spoke, but his anxiety only grew. "You can look around to the southwest, but don't wander far. We had an incident in one of our mines some years ago. Much of the outlying terrain is still contaminated with various chemicals."

"I'll keep that in mind." Neira pivoted toward Jackson, "Commander...," as the word escaped her lips, she awaited the reaction. Her mind raced through her plans to reason it away. The boss directed one of his guards to block the doorway. "Do we have a problem?" Neira looked back over her shoulder without breaking her façade.

He glared at her, "Commander?" He sneered. "How do we know this isn't some Ascension plot to subvert our little community? You come flying in here on that weird-ass ship and spin this ridiculous story that we're supposed to just swallow whole?"

Neira gradually turned back toward him, "My command structure is none of your business. You need only concern yourself with whether you are going to reap the benefits of this arrangement or if I'm leaving you a sliver of my disdain on the way out. Behave yourself and the genie stays in bottle. Piss me off and no amount of sweat will save your hide."

He shook an accusatory finger in her direction, "You could be bluffing!"

Neira grabbed his clammy finger and pulled it to just shy of its breaking point, "Don't push me, I will end you." She shoved him backward into his chair. "You really want to know?! Many of my crew are X-ers. I take my enemy's soldiers and bring them to a better understanding. And for every one I turn I gain an asset. No one knows their way around the Ascension patrols and security like their own people. Besides...," Neira pulled a sidearm from her hip holster and primed it, "keeping familiar ranks eliminates confusion when I spontaneously promote someone." She stared at her gun with a devious gaze.

"You talk like you're at war with them," he questioned.

"Life is a war. Anyone who thinks differently is either naïve or stupid. Which are you?" She brought her pistol up to her shoulder and waited for his response.

The mayor waved a shaky finger at Jackson, "You there, why'd you leave the Ascension?"

Without flinching, Jackson flatly replied, "Got thrown to the wolves so a politician could pad his ego, fuck the Ascension."

Nervously, the mayor's attention darted between the figures standing before him. He met Neira's piercing amber-eyed glare and waved the guard off. They began to file out of the room. Neira deactivated her gun and slipped it back into its holster. "Wise man," she sauntered out of the office.

Chapter 33

Suspicions

"Which creepy door do you want to knock on first?
*Eeny, meeny, miny, ..." **knock***
~ Specialist Tomas Malek

Neira stopped in her tracks and surveyed her surroundings. They had room enough to confer without being overhead. What bystanders there were hugged close to the buildings and gazed suspiciously at the entourage. Neira turned into the group, her eyes still scanning the perimeter. In a hushed tone, she spoke, "All right. We have some room to maneuver now. I want everyone to split up and gather whatever information you can, maps, gossip whatever. Grab a partner and don't let them out of your sight. I still don't trust these colonial scrubs. They're all a little too twitchy for my tastes." She tipped her head toward Kensy, "Princess, you're with me. We all meet at these coordinates in two hours... and lose the tails. We're being watched." Neira forwarded the navigational point to the group's nahdvi.

As they began to divide up, Jackson brushed past Kensy. Their eyes met for a moment as he slipped his tightly folded handkerchief into her hand on the sly. He circled behind her, "Wright, let's head out to those hills, find a good survey vantage point." Tapping one of the Alpha team soldiers with his knuckle, he began to walk away. He cast a fleeting glance back at Kensy.

What was that about? She looked down at her hands for a moment. *Why did he...? Hmm, there's something wrapped in it. But—.* "You ready?" Neira interrupted her thought process, "I want to do a lap through the side streets, see what kind of shadows this place has." Kensy affirmed with a nod and followed closely behind. She fussed with a button on the right rear portion of her pants, as she walked, slipping the tightly folded bundle into the safety of her back pocket. She smoothed the closure flat with her hand and turned her gaze to the surrounding environment. "Eyes up. This place is... off."

Kensy matched her stride, "You really think we'll find what we need here?" She carefully chose her words in case of listening ears. The cover had held up so far, but it would all be for naught if they were discovered now because of a careless word. And it was even more dangerous with the team split up, however temporarily.

Neira shrugged, "You picked this place out of a pile of possibilities. I think the prospects are promising. Your instincts are usually right on point." The two women meticulously crafted the conversation as they wove through the dilapidated side streets. Both kept eyes on the citizenry that shuffled in and out of the city's nooks and crannies. Corners of buildings flaked and chipped, paint peeled from nearly every surface, and rust accented the fittings and fastening throughout. Accompanied by a dark smokey haze that hung above the rooftops, the air was filled with a choking despair.

They maintained the veiled small talk for several city blocks before Kensy paused. "Hmm." She muttered as they turned beyond one of the small stalls. Neira glanced her way. "I think I must have a burr in my boot. Mind if we step out of the traffic so I can attend to it?" She feigned discomfort, shaking her left ankle. "Should only take a minute if I can find a spot to sit."

Neira raised an eyebrow, "Of course. Just make it fast." They jaunted down a nearby alleyway. Kensy approached a

223

small pile of crates and took a seat. She set the crystal container at her side as she unzipped the top of her boot. Neira slumped against the wall beside her. "What did you see?"

Kensy pretended to fight with her footwear. "It's what I don't see. Not a single kid. In fact, I don't know that we've passed anyone under sixty besides the guards."

Neira drummed her fingers impatiently as one of the guards casually paced across the mouth of the alley, "Yeah, noticed that too, did ya?"

"Also noticed they all have a little something more in common." Kensy zipped her boot up and began brushing the dust from it. "They all have a little black... I dunno, plate? On the back of their necks. Weird shaped. like a Y or a W mashed together with a little line across the middle." Kensy stood, turning side-to-side to inspect her boots. "And they don't seem to want us to see it. They pull up their collars or scarves whenever we get close."

"And you managed to catch a good look at it?" Neira questioned. Kensy turned her gaze toward her friend, faintly shimmering flecks of violet dancing in her sea-green eyes. "Well done, but knock that off," Neira scowled. "They catch wind of your powers and we kiss our stealth approach goodbye. Pretty sure the provincials will come unglued." Neira pushed off the wall with her foot. "Now grab that crystal and let's bug out. Just about time to head for the rendezvous and I've had about all I can stand of these people. Any more time around them and I might just start twitching myself." She rolled her head from side-to-side popping the joints in her neck as she stretched. "Now, I think we've strung this poor man along long enough. Time for us to lose the tail," she smirked. Kensy firmly grabbed the handle of the container and returned the conniving smile as the guard drifted past again. Neira cracked the knuckles of both hands, "Now it gets real."

As the guard patrolled back into view again, Neira whistled at him. He stopped in his tracks and eyed them suspiciously.

Neira beckoned him forth with the curl of one finger. Cautiously, he approached. Slowly and deliberately, she swung her hips from one side to another. "Hey there, handsome. As you probably already know, we're new in town. My boss wants us to set up shop here. But there's just a little something that's bugging me." She closed the distance between them. She drew a finger down the center line of his jacket. "If I'm gonna get stuck manning an outpost on a backwater dump like this one, where would a girl like me go to get a good ride from a stud like you?" She brushed against him as she began to circle her prey.

He watched as she slipped out of his peripheral vision, her hand firmly sliding across his body as she moved. He looked back toward Kensy. She playfully bit her lower lip. Slivers of porcelain skin peeked out as she toyed with the hem of her tank-top and fishnet overlay. She moved her hand to her belt buckle and slid her thumb along the top of her belt. With his attention wrapped up in Kensy's flirtations, Neira silently drew her pistol from its holster. Kensy winked. Thpt! The muffled sound of a shot echoed within the confines of the alleyway. The guard wavered in place and dropped.

"I was wondering how long you were going to take," Kensy jested. "We've really got to find another routine besides seduction. Always make me feel like I need a shower afterward."

"Aww, but it works so well," Neira teased. "Though he didn't drop as quickly as I anticipated. Point blank that should have done a number on him even with thumpers loaded." She holstered her weapon and pulled the back of his collar down. At the nape of his neck sat a metallic object, just as Kensy had described. Three bold points fanned out across the top, flowing down into one narrow spike. From the center of the object, two pin like legs branched out and sunk into the man's scarred flesh. An arc of electricity danced across it, startling both women. He groaned. "That's our cue!" Neira grabbed Kensy's wrist, and they bolted from the alley.

Their boots pounded across the dried ground as they headed for the outskirts of town. Neira counted her breaths, calculating her distance by their cadence and tempo. The buildings began to thin out and the encroaching foliage loomed beyond. The tall grasses and brambles whipped about their bodies as they pushed into the woods.

Gradually, they lost momentum. Neira leaned over and placed her hands on her knees. Kensy stood tall, watching and listening for movement behind them. Neira spied Kensy's white knuckles, still tightly wrapped around the canister handle. She reached toward the container, "I'll take it." Kensy looked down at her hand, only then did she feel the ache and tension in her muscles. She pried her fingers apart and passed the canister to Neira.

"Even if we were followed, I don't think the locals are super eager to run through the overgrowth. I don't hear or see anything." Kensy surveyed the terrain again, her eyes glittering with power.

Neira stood up straight, "I thought I told you to knock it off." Kensy shrugged in resignation and allowed her power to fade. "We should be able to weave around the town to the rendezvous point without drawing any more attention. Visiri activate." The eye-patch lit up, casting a warm glow over the immediate area. "Hostile territory navigation mode." The glow shifted and warped, displaying discreet markers on the ground in front of Neira's feet, "Let's move."

Kensy followed quietly as Neira led the way through the rugged terrain. Her thoughts drifted from one moment to the next. She reached for her back pocket. It was still there, the tightly folded handkerchief that Jackson had so discreetly passed to her before they parted. She unfastened the pocket with her fingertips and slipped the bundle from its hiding place. Gingerly, she turned the package over and over in her hands. A faint crinkle emanated from it as she bent one corner slightly. Paper? Puzzled, she began to unfurl the cloth. One layer at a time, she revealed a small folded note and a glittering champagne colored chain.

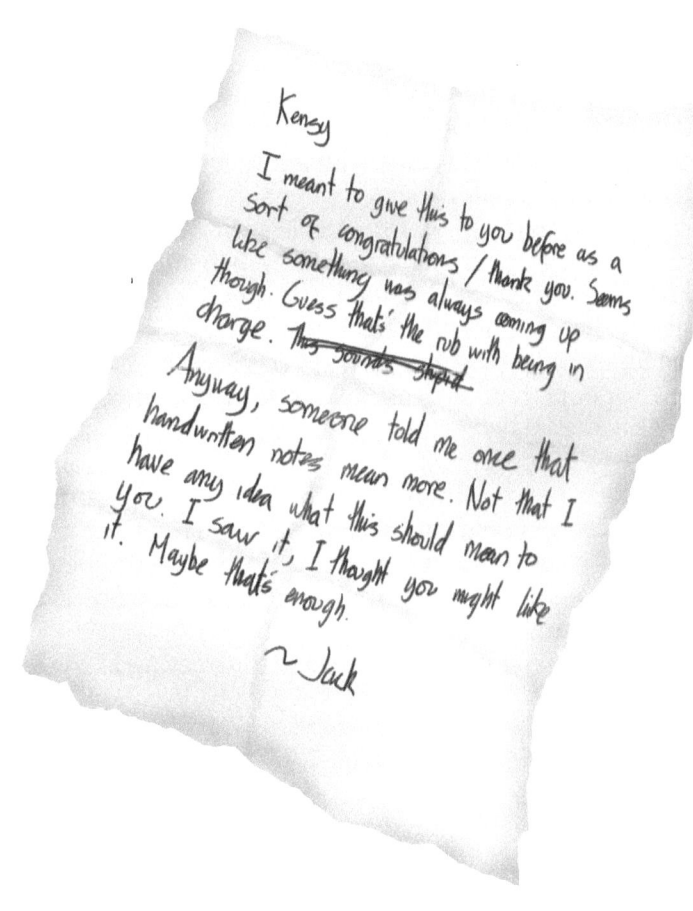

She smiled as she stared at the elegantly crafted pendant in her fingers. Light danced across a star-shaped jewel as it slid along the chain. Intricately curling flourishes formed a dazzling tail. She slipped the note and cloth back into her pocket. Glancing toward Neira, she released the necklace's catch and slipped it on. Delicately, she tucked it under the edge of her shirt, letting her fingers rest on it for several seconds.

Reaching into her back pocket once again, she grabbed the note and wrappings. She rolled the note into a tight spiral and slipped it between her pant leg and boot. Looking at the handkerchief in her hand, unsure of what to do with it, she brought it up close to her face with a sweet smile. She recalled the soft brush of the fabric against her skin as he tied it around her arm, "...just in case." Her memories drifted to their moonlit stroll through the park. There they were beneath the stars. She nervously dabbed at his forehead with the handkerchief. Then he grabbed her hand and gazed into her eyes, confused and concerned.

Neira stepped up to the next rise and glanced back at Kensy. "Really? Daydreaming in a combat zone?" she asked incredulously. Kensy snapped back to reality. Neira rolled her eye and shook her head in disbelief. "You might want to clear the starry-eyed expression off your face. We're about to reach the others." Kensy ignored her friend's prodding as she caught up. Neira leaned toward her and whispered, "Try not to make googly eyes at him during the mission."

"Neira!" Kensy retorted in outrage. Correcting her volume, she hissed back, "I do not make googly eyes! Of all the ridiculous...."

Neira snickered and sauntered toward the group, "Everyone here yet?"

Shane looked back over his shoulder as Neira and Kensy approached, "Almost. Though we haven't seen any sign of Daily and Malek for some time. We were just discussing it."

Neira crossed her arms, "When was the last contact?"

Reily stood with her hands on her hips in a fairly casual stance, "Maybe an hour and a half ago. Daily thought maybe he could chat up some of the locals. Get a little history on this place. Last I saw, he and Malek got invited into someone's house, but neither are responding to nahdvi pings."

Jackson sauntered up to the conversation, "I'm thinking they may have gotten in some trouble, but I had Rasken and Kyo swing past the place on their way here and it was cleared out." He casually shifted his gaze toward Kensy. Her fingers curled around his balled up handkerchief and a slip of the chain peeked out from under the edge of her shirts and vest. "I was just about to call up to the ship, see if they could find their signals. Unless you'd rather."

Neira affirmed, "Sounds like a plan." She activated her link to the ship, "Ground to DeCadejra, come in DeCadejra." The comm cracked in her ears.

Kensy took a few meandering steps away from the group. She cupped her hands together behind her and swayed back and forth as her focus wandered. Jackson shuffled toward her, watching the perimeter. As he closed in, she fought the urge to grin like a giddy school girl, "Thank you. It's quite lovely." She held the handkerchief for him to take. He nodded in acknowledgment and reached for it. His fingertips swept across her palm as he drew the cloth from her hand. She turned her thoughts toward more somber concerns, "You think Daily and Malek are okay?"

He grunted, "Let's just say this is one of those times I would love to be wrong."

She turned her eyes up toward him. There was a tension in his expression, "You know them well? Are they good soldiers?" she tentatively pried.

"Daily likes to talk... a lot. Always figured it would get him in trouble one day. Malek is an ass, but a good fighter." Jackson watched his lieutenant out of the corner of his eye. "Rasken knows them better than I do. She requested them to replace some of the guys we lost on Morwhex. If they *are* in over their heads, she'll be hardest on herself, but...."

"Decadejra to ground," Daniel's voice broke up as his signal finally cut through the interference. "We have techs working to compensate for the spotty connection, but it's touch and go. What's your status?"

Kensy and Jackson pivoted back toward the group. "We are missing two members, Daily and Malek. We were hoping you could track their signals," Neira informed him.

"One second," the connection buzzed in the absence of sound. Everyone listened eagerly. "All right, we are receiving telemetry from them, but the signal is scattered. It generally seems to be coming from an area north of your current position." Daniel spoke in a muffled tone with someone else on his end before returning to the conversation, "One more thing. It looks like whatever is causing this interference is in the same area. Any closer to it and we'll lose you."

Jackson spoke up, "Well, like it or not, it looks like we're gonna have to head in and check this place out."

"Understood. Forwarding our data to you. We'll continue to passively scan the surface. I'll keep Scythe on standby for extraction. Shut down that interference if you can. DeCadejra out." Daniel signed off.

"Has anyone managed to get eyes on this northern area?" Jackson scanned their faces.

"No, but I did get this." Reily raised a large rolled sheet in hand. Together they unfurled it, revealing an oversized holographic map upon the flexible synthetic surface. "Bought it in town from a nasty little man with no desire to actually sell anything in his shop." The group examined the projected map in silence for a moment. "Looks like we're here," she touched a spot, creating a way point. "And if we overlay the data the ship sent us...," she tampered with the controls embedded in the corner of the map. "Looks like they are in here," the dots of scattered readings overlaid within the center of an ominously marked area, the Cruxias Hazard Zone.

"Hmm, looks like our options are limited." Neira analyzed all the pieces together. "There's what I'm assuming is a well-guarded front gate here. And a rise that crests the containment wall here." She contemplated the complications before looking up at the others. I think this time we split into two groups. I'll take Shane and Reily to investigate this front gate, the rest of you head for the rise."

Rasken raised an eyebrow toward her, "You want to knock on the front door and see what happens?" She crossed her arms and popped her bubblegum.

Neira smirked, "Oh hell yeah."

Rasken looked to her subordinates. Reily and Shane both nodded in agreement. "Fine," she conceded, "Just don't get my people killed." Rasken turned and stormed off toward the ridge, Kyo and Wright falling in line behind her. Jackson jogged to catch up.

Reily rolled up the map and handed it to Kensy, "Hey, take care." Reily glanced toward her superiors. "If it gets too hairy, call for that evac."

Kensy surveyed the faces staring at her, "Yeah, you too." She hastened to join the rest of her group. *Stars, please let them be okay.*

Chapter 34

Illusive

"Note to self: exploring an antique precariously perched on the edge of cliff, definitely a bad idea."
~ Specialist Nathan Wright

Kensy ducked beneath a branch that hung in her way. Her delicate fingers waved it aside as she passed the tangled leaves. A glint of something beyond view beckoned toward her, driving her forward. She reached out with her other hand brushed the undergrowth from its resting place. The surface was smooth and hard, once a small piece of something greater. Gingerly, she pried the piece from its resting place. As she cleared the hard metallic surface of debris, an etching became visible.

Jackson crouched under the low hanging limbs as he drew near Kensy. "What have you got there?" He peered over her shoulder. The words were worn but unmistakeably a ship's name and embarkation date, The Illusive emb. 547-06-11.

"It's a piece of a ship." She looked up, scanning the foliage for more clues. "Hang on to this for me." She thrust the plate and map into his hands. Cautiously, she walked forward. The ground rose sharply before them. She studied the surroundings for a moment before leaping to a nearby rock. With a carefully calculated jump, she landed on the rise. Her boots thumped against the semi-hollow sounding ground. She and Jackson exchanged wide-eyed glances.

With a sharp whistle, he beckoned the rest of the group to him. Kensy stooped down, running her fingers through the dirt. The layer was thin and lightly caked to the hull plating. She turned her eyes toward the treetops. From the higher vantage, she could see the swath of younger trees that followed what must have been the crash trajectory.

The crackle of twigs and fallen leaves announced Rasken, Wright, and Kyo's less than stealthy approach. Jackson waved them toward the rise, "We may have found something... a crashed ship. Look for a way inside, maybe we can find something of use."

Cautiously, Kensy crept down the hull, away from the group. She analyzed the form of the ship trying to deduce its general structure from above. As she reached the nose of the vessel, she gasped. The hillside dropped away sharply, creating a dramatic cliff face. The view over the zone before her was astounding. A large pit sat in the center of the zone like a black hole. The remnant of mining rigs and cranes littered the jagged surface.

The sound of tumbling pebbles drew her attention back to the immediate surroundings. Slowly, she backed up. More rocks tumbled down the cliff. The wreck was not as stable as it had seemed. She headed toward the aft. Jackson waited patiently for her, holding out a hand to help her down. "Come on. We got a cargo hatch open."

"We need to be really careful. The front of this thing is on the edge of a cliff over the zone." Jackson thought about Kensy's warning for a moment.

He nodded in affirmation, "Let's give it a quick once over, then we'll hunt for a safe way down." He stepped around an uprooted bush and into the ship. Kensy followed closely on his heels. The others were already inside snooping through compartments and containers. "Looks like we might have a climb in our near future. Grab any equipment that we could make use of," he called out to the team.

Wright approached with a satchel and scroll case in hand, "Could stick whatever we find in these. Make it a little easier to carry."

Kensy accepted the scroll case with one hand as she reached toward Jackson with the other, "Map?" He passed it back to her. She popped the cap on the tube open and shoved the roll inside.

He held up the etched plate, "And what would you like to do with this?"

"Trade ya." She held out the case for him. Wright intercepted the tube with a smile and slung it over his shoulder. Kensy nodded to him, "Alright, that works too." She snagged the satchel instead, slipping the strap over her head and across her body. Being aware of the twisted edges, Kensy tucked it into the bag, "I want to do some research on this thing when we get back. Maybe figure out how a hundred-and-seventy-something-year-old ship ended up here."

"Hey, boss," Rasken called out toward them. "Got a crate here with some gear we might want to go through. Wanna help us get this thing outside so we can have a little more room to maneuver?" Jackson moved toward her, surveying the find. Kensy glanced through the nooks and crannies as she slowly ambled through the ship, listening for any signs of shifting.

As she passed through the front end doorway, she beheld the cracked and mangled windshield. A dark, dried stain covered much of the controls and seats. *Hmm, the pilot probably died on impact*, she surmised, but no body was to be found. Drag marks ran beneath her feet and into the main compartment behind her, *but someone survived*. Just then a thought occurred to her, the flight recorder. With that she could potentially determine how this wreck happened. "Hey, Wright," she called out to her closest compatriot, "where would the black box be on a ship like this?"

"Umm, somewhere protected in the event of a crash, toward the back of the cockpit. Maybe under the seats," he guessed with a shrug. She pried the pilot's seat forward, running her fingers over the base plates for a seam. There was a lip that caught her attention. Bit by bit she worked at it until at last she worked her fingers between the pieces. The crash must have tweaked the frame just enough that it refused to surrender to her persuasion. With all the effort she could muster, she jerked against the small gap, wrenching the panel from its fittings. She tossed the warped cover aside.

Briefly, the sound of rocks tumbling against the hull gave her pause. The sound died down, allowing her exhale in relief. One at a time, she gently removed the fastenings and wires from the small box within. Delicately, she lifted it from its resting place and slipped it into her satchel alongside the name plate.

Her fingertips wrapped her loose hair behind her right ear. Apprehensively, she stood and gave one last look around the cockpit. The console lights flickered and buzzed to life. She looked toward the others. Wright popped his head in, "Did that do anything?" He leaned his shoulder against the doorjamb, grasping it with both hands. "I hooked up a backup power cell. Didn't look like it was in great condition, but figured it would give us a few minutes of juice."

Kensy smiled, "Then let us used this time wisely." She stepped up to the main console and began tapping away at the sketchy interface. "Do you have a link drive or datapad on you?" she asked back over her shoulder.

Wright pulled a palm-sized datapad from his pocket, "Try this...." A chilling screech echoed through the wreck as it jarred everyone. Silence fell over the crew as everyone waited for more. The air was still as they all held position. Kensy looked down at Wright's outstretched hand. Gradually, she reached for the pad. She coaxed it from his grip, turning back to the console in slow motion. There was a click as she sunk it into the receptacle on the dash.

"All right, people. Let's clear the ship. I want everyone out now!" Jackson called out. Kensy ignored him as she began downloading files.

Wright shuffled back a few steps. He glanced between the two ends of the ship with hesitation, "Psilyria, ma'am...." At the far end of the ship, Jackson, Kyo, and Rasken nudged the heavy crate ever closer to the cargo ramp.

"It's fine. Just go, I'll be right behind you," she absently replied.

Nervously he protested, "Ma'am, I don't think it's worth —." The piercing crack of breaking metal interrupted him.

Jackson looked to the side as one of the cargo hatch torsion bars snapped. He seized Rasken's wrist, yanking her out of the ship. "GO!" Kensy yelled at Wright. She looked back to the progress bar on the display. She braced herself against the console as the ship lurched forward. The wreck heaved again.

Kyo scrambled for the opening, flailing for Jackson's hand. They locked wrists together. Jackson fell against the remnants of the gate with a grunt. His eyes widened as he watched the rest of the ship fall away, with Wright and Kensy still on board. He took a deep breath. Clenching his teeth, he strained to lift his dangling crewman toward safety.

Kensy turned around just in time to see Jackson disappear from view as the wreckage tipped into a dive down the cliff face. She took a deep breath. In one motion, she snatched the datapad and shoved off the console with her foot. Wright helplessly fell toward her. She wrapped her arms around his torso and closed her eyes, "Ivanigis ahri." Her power wrapped around the both of them and black tendril wings sprung from her back. The tendrils shot into the air above them, sinking into the rock face as the ship fell away from them. The nose of the wreck pierced through the surface and sunk into the earth below in a billowing cloud of dust and dirt.

Kensy and Wright swung toward the rocks. She slammed into the jagged terrain shoulder first, letting a pained cried slip upon impact. Bewildered, Wright gazed in amazement at his rescuer. "Grab...," she fought to get the words out, "the rocks. I can't...." The wings burned under the added weight. Frantically, Wright searched for a sturdy hand hold.

Kensy furrowed her brow and focused on drawing more power through her clasp. It coursed over her, bolstering her will and strength. She gazed upward. They had fallen too far to climb back up, even with her powers. "Our only way is down," she focused on Wright's concerned stare. "I can get us down, but the landing may be a little rough." Wright nodded, *okay*. "All right. When I say go, let go of the rocks and hold on to me. I'm going to push off the wall and try to slow us on the way down. This is energy I'm playing with here so... it may get hot." Wright nodded again.

"Okay, one... two... now!" She shoved against the rocks with her boots. They rocketed toward the ground like a blazing psionic comet. Kensy channeled her power into a field of dense fog, increasing the air resistance against them. They slowed slightly in the haze before tumbling across the hazard zone floor at a still considerable speed. She allowed her power to wane as they came to a stop. Wright groaned as he struggled to his hands and knees. *Good, he's okay*, she thought as she blacked out.

Jackson and the others watched from the cliff top as Wright and Kensy fell to the ground. He kept his eyes on her as the purple-ish fog dissipated. Kensy remained still. A ruckus rose behind Jackson. Rasken overhanded items left and right out of the crate. Jackson stared at her quizzically. She glanced up at him, "Well, don't just stand there. Give me a hand." She furiously chomped at her gum.

"What are you doing?" He questioned.

"Help me empty this thing. Then we can wedge it behind that tree and anchor one of these cables to it." She thumbed toward a sturdy forked tree firmly planted aside the crash site. "Unless you think you can free climb *that*." She placed her hands on her hips.

He acquiesced, "Yeah, I suppose that could work. Good plan."

"Of course it will work, it's *my* plan," she sassily replied.

Jackson began helping her, and Kyo empty the container. "Thank you, Lindsay," he quietly muttered. Kyo stepped away, separating the bundles of cables as his commanders spoke in hushed tones.

Rasken paused. A fierce determination flashed in her eyes, "I'm not losing anyone else today."

Chapter 35

Knock, Knock

"What's the point of knocking if no one hears it?"
~ Neira Cross, Graven Mercenary

Neira drew in a silent breath as she pressed her back to the coarse tree trunk, her Ausk-Chelkai at the ready. The crystal containment cylinder tapped softly against the top of her armored boot and the edges of her plated skirt. Subtly, she rolled one shoulder backward in a gentle stretch. Another measured breath escaped her lips as she steeled herself. She glanced left. She glanced right. With a nod, she signaled her partners, *now*. With a catlike grace, she swept around the tree and into the open before the main gate. Her eye darted over the surroundings. Stillness.

Shane surveyed the tree line and overgrown roadway, his assault rifle tucked securely against his shoulder. Reily swung her sniper rifle back over her shoulder as she turned toward Neira, "So much for the welcoming committee." Sprawling before them, a tangled pile of barricades and broken reinforcements crawled up the towering gate. Heavy chains wove through the debris like an iron serpent. Neira scanned the heap.

Shane slowly backed up alongside Neira. "Doesn't look like they've used this entrance in a long-ass time. They certainly did a thorough job of barricading the site," he said as he kept his eyes on the road.

She pressed her boot against a concrete slab at the front of the pile, "Yeah, but were they keeping people out or in?" She leaned forward.

Reily shook her head dismissively, "Regardless, there has to be another way in. The locals are way too twitchy about us getting close to this." She kicked at a clump of tall grass in frustration.

Neira pivoted away from the gate, "There is that possibility. Could take us hours to find the alternative route without direction. On the other hand, ...we could just knock a little louder." She clipped one of her blades to her shoulder and lifted the containment canister from its place on her hip. She balanced the handle on the tip of her index finger, allowing it to sway slightly. Shane and Reily glanced between the canister and each other.

Shane scowled at Neira, "Do you have any idea the kind of ruckus that is going to cause?!"

She smirked, "Oh yeah. I have a *very* good idea. What's the point of knocking if no one hears it?" The mischievous look that crossed her face unsettled him even further.

"I'm in!" Reily piped up. "How do we set the charge?" Determination flashed in her eyes.

Neira set the canister on the dirt and began tinkering with it. "You two head up a ways. Find cover and sit tight. I'll set the shard. One of you will have to shoot it to set it off. Then we stroll in like we've been invited." She hooked the other Ausk-Chelkai to her shoulder.

"I got this," with an unfaltering confidence Reily pulled her sniper rifle from its resting place, firmly gripping it in both hands. She jabbed at Shane lightly and pointed toward a fallen tree up the hill from their current position. Slowly, the swish of their footsteps faded from Neira as she extracted the crystal from its resting place. Her fingertips gingerly cradled the sharp base of its angular structure. Gently, she drew a laser knife from the canister housing. She inhaled and held her breath as the knife carved off a thin sliver of material that slid smoothly into her palm.

Turning the knife off she snapped it back into the canister housing. With surgical precision, she lifted the main crystal from her fingers and returned it to the open containment field. The canister accepted the volatile crystal, drawing it inward, and sealing tightly once again. She exhaled.

"You ready, Reily?" Neira shouted up the hillside.

Kneeling down behind one of the large fallen trees, Reily adjusted her sights. The gun's bipod rested uneasily on the splintered bark. She nudged the positioning of her rifle ever so slightly to settle it into a more stable position. "Good to go on your signal," she hollered back.

Neira began to scale the debris before the gate, "After I set this, give me twenty feet before you blow it." One of the slabs shifted under her weight. Her heart raced as she made sure not to drop the shard from her carefully curled hand. She reevaluated her next step fastidiously. Reaching out with her free hand, she pulled herself to the next point. Her cybernetic eye patch analyzed the heap, overlaying the information with her vision. She brushed dust from a crack within the largest piece of the barricade. "You'll do." She whispered. Warily, she slid the sliver into place and backed down the pile.

Reily gazed intently down the scope, measuring each breath carefully. She trained her gaze on the shard as she listened for her cue. As Neira reached the ground, she scooped up the waiting canister. Her eye turned toward Shane and Reily for but a split second. A massive wave of force blasted past her. She cascaded into the roadway face first; the canister escaping from her hold. "Reily! What the hell?! Are you trying to kill her?" Shane chastised his partner. Reily shot him a piercing glare as she unprimed her rifle.

Concrete, wood, and metal shards showered the area. Neira's ears rung from the concussion. She shook her head as she crawled to her hands and knees. Two hands reached through the haze to help her up. Reily and Shane stood, one on each side, staring at her wide-eyed.

"I thought I told you twenty feet," Neira shouted, unaware of her own volume.

Reily leaned in and spoke loudly, "I didn't take the shot." Neira pressed the heels of her hands to her temples as she tried to shake off the effects of the blast. A startled realization came over Neira. Her scanner sparked to life once again. The readouts echoed a faint tremor within the ground as a roiling clatter reached their ears. She stared at the coordinates of the rise the other team had been headed towards. Slowly, she turned to the now gaping hole before them. Stepping toward the debris, she nudged aside a rock and planted her armored boot firmly in the dirt. Her second step compacted dust and shale with a crunch. She widened her next step beyond a twisted piece of metal jutting from the mangled remnants of the barricade.

One step at a time, she traversed the rugged path into the Cruxias Hazard Zone. A cloud of dust settled across the far wall of the valley, revealing a comet of dark purple energy streaking toward the ground and breaking on the rocks like a tide. She clenched her jaw and her fists.

Reily's hand wrapped over Neira's shoulder firmly. She snapped a sharp look at Reily for a moment before the hardness of the sniper's expression sunk in. While worry and rage churned within Neira, Reily held to a firmness and resolution. The distance between the groups was great and treacherous. Without positive confirmation of distress, few options were available to them. Neira reluctantly cast her eye down in contemplation. The mission was everything now, there was no room for rampant emotion.

"Hey," Shane stood, holding out the canister for Neira, "The best thing we can do for them now is shut down that communications jammer. Then we can all figure out what's going on here." He paused, "They'll be fine. Now, let's go find out what these ass-holes are hiding." Neira nodded to him and took the container from his grasp. She secured it to her side once again.

Her mischievous smirk curled over her lips again. She tilted her head to either side in turn, the cracking of her joints filling the air. "Let's do this," she pulled her blades from her shoulders. With a renewed confidence, she strolled down the access road as it descended into the ground. Reily and Shane flanked her with rifles at the ready and eyes on the perimeter.

Chapter 36

Let Go

"In case of emergency, break glass."
~ Illusive owner's manual

Wright lifted his head to the nearby sound of crumbling rocks resonating within the ridgeline recess. He now sat upright, his knees comfortably half curled in front of him. His arms rested atop his legs with loosely dangling hands. He raised an eyebrow as he watched the rest of his party descend the cliff face into the hazard zone floor. He breathed deeply and slowly.

Rasken pushed off the vertical stones and released her grip. A dull thud resounded as she planted her boots in the dirt and sprung up into a standing position. Without so much as a moment's hesitation, she lurched toward Wright. "Status report!" she demanded.

"Intact, if not a little singed," he gestured toward the faint sunburn-like hue that graced his skin between the scrapes and shallow cuts. They clasped hands, wrapping their fingers each around the other's thumb, into a strongly locked grip. Rasken pulled Wright to his feet. He groaned, "Ugh, a bit bruised, too, I guess." He wrapped his free arm around his ribcage reactively. Rasken glanced over her shoulder to Kyo as he reached the ground, who in turn looked up the cable toward his commander.

"Check on, Psilyria Frost!" Jackson hollered down at the group as he finished his descent.

Lazily, Kensy lifted her arm and waved him off, "I'm fine." Taking a mental inventory of her own status, she stared up the sky. Letting her arm flop back down into the dust, Kensy winced involuntarily as her bruised upper arm hit the ground. She lifted her shoulder and arm to inspect the injury. A deep speckled reddish-purple bruise peeked through the fishnet sleeve on her left arm. She let slip an almost annoyed sigh.

He approached her side and held out a hand, "Was it worth it?"

As she lifted her hand, he grasped it firmly and pulled her swiftly to her feet. They breathlessly lingered there for a moment, both soaking in the energy that raced through their touch. Kensy broke the hold first, casting her eyes away in search of the datapad. In one smooth motion, she scooped up the stolen datapad from the dirt beside her landing spot and began turning it over in her hands as she inspected it. With a shrug she admitted, "Won't know 'til we get it back to the ship. I may have fried the casing, but the data core could still be okay."

Jackson scowled. "Well, toss it in your bag of tricks and let's get moving. I'm sure they heard that crash for miles and I don't want to be in the open when *security* comes to check it out," he made a gesture of air-quotes for emphasis, folded his arms across his chest, and scanned the eerily still horizon.

"Hey Commander," Rasken called toward them questioningly. She stood at the edge of the impact site. Her finger pointed down the center of the wrecked ship. Jackson and Kensy approached to follow her gaze, "Looks like it punched through into some kind of subterranean cavern."

Kensy pushed past the others, "Stand back, I'm gonna check it." Everyone eased away from her as she took a firm stance. She closed her eyes and drew small clouds of energy into the palms of her hands. "Heiga!" she shouted as she thrust her hands toward the wreck. The energy rippled outward like a shock wave resonating through the hull and rocks. A faint rumble was audible for a moment, but the wreck did not move. "I'd say she's pretty stable. It didn't shift or groan, and the wave carried straight down. We could probably climb through it."

Jackson grimaced again, "That thing is a deathtrap. If it shifts again...."

She held up a hand to interrupt him, "It's stable, I promise."

"Better than standing here, I say we go for it," Wright piped in from the back of the group.

"Fine," Jackson resigned. Staring down the belly of the beast, he paused, "If we're gonna do this, I'm taking point." Kensy stepped back and waved him past her with a slight bow. He approached the edge of the wreck, testing it with the toe of his boot. Rasken stepped alongside him and lifted a coil of cable from around her body. She passed it over to Jackson along with a ring of hooks and fasteners. He hoisted the coil onto his shoulder and clipped the ring to his belt.

A knot formed in Kensy's throat as she watched him descend into the wreckage. *This is ridiculous*, she chastised herself. *You checked it. It's stable, nothing cried, or crawled out. And he is a very capable man*, she watched his form as he climbed using the floor grating as hand-holds. *This nervousness isn't doing you or him any favors. Get over it.* She tilted her head to each side, stretching it to clear her thoughts. With a deep breath, she followed over the mangled edge of the cargo hatch and began her own descent.

As she passed through the main compartment, she glanced back up. The little bit of external daylight that filtered down through the dense cloud cover felt as if though it was being choked back in this small space. She watched as Kyo, Wright, and Rasken carefully traced her path through the ship. The climb was slower and more treacherous than she had initially suspected. With another deep breath, she focused on the path down. Cautiously, she crouched on the side wall that lead to the cockpit.

Peeking over the edge, she spotted Jackson trying to find a good footing against the front console. He fussed for a minute before turning his gaze back up toward her. "Careful, there's not much to hang onto in that little hallway." He gestured to the narrowed passage between them. Contemplating the best options for a moment, he paused before speaking again. "Try easing yourself down backward. I'll catch your foot and help lower you down." He beckoned toward her, arms raised to catch her.

"Riiiight...," she hesitantly replied. Laying down on her stomach, she slowly shifted, lowering her legs toward the cockpit. The toes of her boots skidded slowly down the wall until they met nothing but air. She wavered. A gentle pressure against her foot stabilized her.

Kyo came down on the cargo hold wall in front of Kensy and clutched her left wrist, "It's alright. Guide yourself." Kensy nodded as she allowed herself to slip over the edge. She felt Jackson wrap an arm around her calves as he brought her down against his own body. He let go of her boots and moved his hand to her waist. Clearing the small hallway, she stretched a hand toward his shoulder. Kyo released her wrist, allowing her to finish her slide into Jackson's grasp. She held fast to his shoulders as he lowered her into the cockpit beside him.

At this unusual orientation, there was little room around them for another. "Give me a sec to figure out how we're getting past this," he hollered back up at the rest of the company. Kensy and Jackson searched about the immediate area. Much of the window paneling was crushed and shattered, but the openings it provided were too sharp and narrow for anyone to climb through.

Kensy spotted a buckle in the framing. "Hey," she held out her upturned arms toward Jackson, "hold on to me, I'm going to try something." He locked arms with her and gave a

247

concerned look. She stepped over the lip of the control console onto the window frame. It groaned under the additional pressure. She glanced at Jackson for a fleeting moment. She drew in a deep breath and stomped with the heavy heel of her boot against the edge of the gap. It shifted but did not give. She stomped again with all her might. It lurched. She continued to slam the sole of her shoe against the unyielding frame time after time. She sighed, "I don't think it's going to—."

Just then, the frame on which she stood buckled. The small side window that had supported her dropped out. She involuntarily shrieked in surprise. Jackson was pulled against the console, fighting to keep his grip on her forearms without being pulled out himself. Her body slammed against the section she had been focusing on dislodging. Her ribs pulsed with pain. She pulled one hand away from Jackson to push against the stubborn pane. As she tried to leverage herself upon it, a hideous squeal of buckling metal filled the air around them. The panel's warped edge sheared apart.

Jackson clamped both hands around Kensy's clasped arm as both she and the window swung precariously over the darkness of the cavern. Futilely, her left hand flailed for a hold. With one final snap, the window plummeted toward the unseen ground. Amid her struggle, she registered the sound of sundered metal and glass like sheeting. She stopped struggling. As her eyes turned toward Jackson, the wheels of her mind turned. He fought to pull her back up. Kyo began to scramble down behind the commander.

Jackson's eyes met Kensy's. She was calm, almost confident, and the flickers of energy danced through her irises, "Let go."

"I'm not letting you fall!" he shouted at her.

She gave him a gentle smile and spoke softly, "Trust me." He could feel the tingle of energy through his skin as he held her clasp. He looked at his hands, then back into her eyes. In that moment, everything seemed to slow as he breathlessly watched himself open his grasp. She fell away from him with a whisper, their eyes locked for that last second, "Ivanigis."

A brilliant burst of light blinded everyone. The energy formed and hardened into a thick armor over her whole body. The black tendril wings erupted from her mark of the void, spreading in every direction. They pierced the walls and pulled taught as she landed, crouched with head down and arms spread, in the center of the chamber.

The glow of her armor and wings illuminated the room. Her landing had blasted the ground around her free from debris, leaving only stone and tightly packed dirt. She gracefully rose to her full height. Her eyes scanned the room for movement before she directed her glittering gaze back to the wreckage. She nodded to him that all was okay. He exhaled in relief and shook his head in resignation.

As she watched him turn to the matter of helping the others down safely, Kensy felt herself waiver. She stared at the clasp intently. The swirling energy still coursed through it to maintain her void form. She sensed the oceans of energy at her fingertips and a shadow of weariness lapping at her constitution. Her body was being taxed ever so slightly by these surges of power. *How long can I keep this up?* She flexed her fingers. *I have to pace myself better. Can't afford to fatigue-out here. I won't be any use burnt out.* She clenched her fist in determination. *I will do better! I have to do better!* Slowly, she brought the energy of her form in close. The cavern dimmed around her and her wings dissolved into shadow.

Chapter 37

Onward & Inward

"Look on the bright side, if we ever lose Rasken we can just
follow the trail of bubble gum."
~ Sergeant Kort Shane

A booming moan of creaking metal echoed down upon the group in the cavern. All eyes turned toward the crashed ship as Kyo reached one foot toward the ground. He eased himself off the cable. The groan came again. "We should not linger," Kensy noted as she examined the wreckage.

"I thought you said it was stable," Wright's voice betrayed his nervousness.

She turned her eyes toward him, "That was before my creative departure from the ship. It is entirely possible that we loosened whatever is supporting it on our way through." She watched as his gazed darted about the cavern with every crumble of dirt and gravel.

Jackson approached the center of the room, his rifle at the ready, "Doesn't look like there is anything of value in here. We should get moving." He nodded for the company to follow as he turned toward a large tunnel that snaked away into darkness.

Staring at the ceiling, Kyo absently waved a hand at Kensy, "Umm, Psilyria...." With a loud pop, a crack shot across the rocky canopy. The grinding of stone filled the room with noise and dust. A large boulder dislodged itself, crashing into the path ahead of them.

Instinctively, Kensy shot her wings of psionic energy out to encompass the group. She threw her hands up. The energy that surrounded her body coursed up and off her fingertips as a glittering barrier formed above them.

Rasken quickly surveyed the boulder and turned back toward her commander. "We'll have to find another exit. This one's no good," she shouted at him over the cacophonous sound of the collapsing room.

"Make it fast!" Kensy cried out as she struggled against the weight bearing down on her barrier. She closed her eyes and began chanting under her breath in an ancient and alien tongue.

The ground trembled. Wright stumbled to one side, slamming a portion of the wall with his shoulder. Packed dirt and debris gave way to another cavernous passage. Catching himself on the edge of the newly formed lip he squinted into the darkness. Bellowing as loud as he could, he called to the others, "Over here! Quick!" He frantically waved them toward the hole.

Rasken and Kyo darted toward him as fast as their legs could carry them. Jackson moved up beside Kensy, "Time to go."

She glared up at the ship as the far edge of her barrier began to buckle. "Go!" she grunted under the weight, "I'll be right behind you!" Jackson hesitated. "Go! Now!" she screamed at him.

He hustled toward the opening that Wright had moved into. Jackson stopped in the mouth of the passage and held out a hand toward her, "Kensy, come on!"

Rocks began to punch through her barrier, raining down throughout the chamber. She took a deep breath to gather one last surge of energy, "Raga ami velgihr!" Mustering all the force she could, the barrier was shoved up and away. She released the energy and pivoted into a dash. Nearing the exit, Wright and Jackson each grabbed one of her outstretched wrists. They pulled in unison, tossing her into a forward roll. With an agile leap, Jackson jumped out of the path of the collapse and steered himself into a run, trailing a few feet behind Wright.

Kensy came up out of her tumble as her fellow captain caught up to her. He snatched her hand up and pulled, nearly dragging her off her feet. They ran blindly as the sounds of the collapse faded behind them. Disoriented and exhausted, Kensy stumbled and fell, jerking her hand from Jackson's grasp. The strain of her manifestations had taken its toll. What little she could see spun around her as she tried to push herself up from the dirt. Her lungs burned as she tried to slow the labored breath that filled them.

Voices danced around her, muffled by the haziness of her fatigue. As she rose to her hands and knees, she felt the warmth of Jackson's fingers wrap over her left shoulder. Blindly, she reached out for him, her hand coming to rest on his bicep. Even through his armored jacket, she could feel the strength there. It comforted her as she steadied herself, "I'm okay. I just need a minute...."

He slung his rifle on to his back and used the now free hand to dig into his jacket. Producing a small disc from an inside pocket, he ran his thumb around the outside edge. The small circular form glowed to life. As the lamp gathered in intensity, the cavern came alight. Rasken fussed with her scanner, slamming it against her palm to solve whatever issue she had with it. Kyo glanced over at her incredulously, "You know... that doesn't actually fix anything, Lieutenant."

She shot a glare toward him, "Stow it, Ensign." She sighed. "Looks like we must be getting closer to the source of the jamming. Scanner is on the fritz...," she paused, tapping her nahdvi, "Comms are down too."

"We knew that this was a possibility." Jackson crouched on one knee beside Kensy, "First order is to get some kind of bearing. Scout ahead. Figure out where we are. Then we'll try to narrow in on the jammer while we look for the others." Rasken nodded in acknowledgment. She signaled her underlings to join her and the trio disappeared down the corridor.

As they faded from sight, Jackson turned his attention back toward Kensy. "That was almost ugly back there. You doin' alright?"

Kensy sat back on her knees and took a deep breath, "Yeah." She shook her head to clear it. "I don't know. I'm not tapped out. I can feel an ocean of power at my disposal but perhaps...," her voice trailed off.

He gave her a stern gaze, "Perhaps what?"

"Perhaps it's too much." Their eyes met. The worry in her eyes spoke volumes to him, "I think... I've never...," she let out a frustrated sigh as she fought with the words. "Ever since I touched the veil, the power is beyond anything I could have imagined. But it's also beyond anything I have ever managed to manifest." Her voice softened, "I can feel it wearing on me. *I am the weakness.*" She looked down at her hands.

"That just means you need to take it a little easier," He furrowed his brow, "We're a team. Let us do our part, pull our own weight." He gave her shoulder a gentle squeeze. Kensy cupped her head in her hands for a moment. *He's right. Slow it down. You can do this. They can do this. It's what we trained for.* She pushed her hair back from her face and nodded. "Everything good?" he inquired.

"Yeah, guess I'm just tired. That took a lot out of me." She thumbed back toward the collapsed tunnel behind them. Her gaze drifted back to his face. For a moment she studied him, then very carefully she raised her hand. The soft pad of her thumb slid gently across his cheekbone. He watched her questioningly. She drew her hand back, staring at the fine black dust that she had wiped away. With her other hand she pulled her fingers across her own mouth, collecting the same darkened dust from her own skin, "No more tattoos. I guess we are ourselves again."

He reached up and brushed the rest of her crumbling tattoo away, "I guess so." She blushed and cast her eyes down. Her hands fell to her pants. A thought crept into her mind and she began patting down pockets as she searched her own person. "Something wrong?"

She shook her head and sighed, "I didn't bring a hair tie. I should have known better."

"Here," Jackson passed her the lamp and moved behind her. Meticulously, he began to untangle her hair.

"You have all kinds of talents I am unaware of," Kensy smiled to herself.

Jackson grunted in indifference, "I have a little sister. ... had a nasty habit of getting her hair into tangled messes all the time when we were growing up. So I've had practice." When her hair was sufficiently straightened, he pulled out his handkerchief and bound it securely.

He stepped back and allowed her to check it. Her fingers traced the lines, painting her a picture of her well bundled hair, "Thanks. Feels like it will hold pretty well. Should be good if we get into a firefight down here." He lifted her to her feet.

She brushed the dirt from her clothes as Wright approached the light, "We found something you should probably see for yourselves." The two captains exchanged a quick glance. Jackson reached back over his shoulder with his right hand and gripped the rifle stock that rested there. Firearm at the ready, he nodded to Kensy.

She turned her head back to Wright, "Alright, lead on." No words passed between them as they quietly made the way down the tunnel. The passage narrowed sharply. Wright turned sideways and shuffled further on. Kensy slipped easily through behind him. Jackson struggled to press through with his heavily armored gear, forgoing stealth as the concealed plates ground against the walls.

He thought to grumble about the passage for a brief moment before Kensy's words stirred his attention. "Stars alive," she gasped. The cavern would have been spacious if empty, but clutter filled much of the space. Piles of bones and machine parts sat heaped over themselves. Some of the larger parts protruded from the walls, caked with mud and dust.

Kensy knelt down beside one barren skeleton. She examined the twisted form carefully. Wires curled around and through the bones like spiderwebs. Further up the same pile sat a structure eerily similar to the machines from Bhelnir and Morwhex, save for the partial human form that had been merged into the core of the construct. All the permutations of machines and bodies seemed slightly different as the designs were tweaked and changed. Decades of evolution filled the chamber. "This is insane!" Kensy's mind raced with all of the possible explanations for such a find.

With a soft blue pulsing light, half a dozen small sensors flew overhead toward a central point. They collected inside a spherical casing which plummeted into Rasken's waiting hand. She tucked the orb away and approached Jackson, "Pulled a holographic scan of the room in case we can't make it back to study. I recommend we keep moving for now. That jammer's still up and...." The clatter of pieces sliding off a heap across the room interrupted her.

The company of soldiers snapped their weapons into position, ready and waiting for any incursion. Kensy spied a small silhouette skittering along the far edge of the room. She watched as it paused and dug through more of the debris. Cautiously and quietly, the group closed in on the unknown entity. Kensy dashed up alongside Jackson. He held one arm up to bar her way as he crept toward the creature.

It popped up from the heap, facing away. Everyone paused. It turned a small part over and over in his knobby, thin fingers. Satisfied with his find, the creature wiggled out of the pile and scampered toward an opening in the side wall. A piece of bone beside Kyo shifted. The creature looked back to inspect when he beheld the armored company that had closed on him. With a shrill squeal, he dropped the item and fled into the neighboring room.

Jackson moved to pursue when suddenly Kensy's hand fell over the breach of his gun. She gave him a stern look and stepped past him. Her delicate fingers scooped up the abandoned scrap and slowly she followed. The smaller room was little more than an alcove. More clutter lined the walls, but the center sat one strange heap of fur and metal unmoving. The smaller creature cowered behind the center mass with a frightened whimper.

"Come out now! Your hands where I can see them!" Jackson shouted as he entered the small confined area. Another pained whimper emanated from the creature.

Kensy huffed at him, "For crying out loud, you're going to scare the poor thing to death! Let me handle this."

In a hushed tone, he protested, "You don't know what that thing is capable of or why it's here. It could be dangerous."

Without toning down her voice, she retorted, "He's not. Call it intuition... and put the gun down." Stepping forward, she crouched down. She held out the part. Her voice became soft and welcoming to the tiny alien, "Did you need this? It's okay. My friends aren't too good at meeting new people. You can come out. We just want to talk."

A tiny face peeked around the edge of his hiding spot. The big, beady eyes darted between Kensy and the rest of the ground team as they apprehensively lowered their arms. Slowly, he hobbled toward Kensy's outstretched hand. Very gingerly he lifted the piece, turning it over and over in his long fingers, "Kigh no want badness. Kigh only fiddle-fix Rauk and Gizmo. Kigh just want all go home. Kigh miss home." His common speech was rough as he tried to explain himself.

"Kigh?" Kensy warmly inquired, "Is that your name?"

The small creature chittered nervously, "Kigh'Lehken." He pointed to the hulking mass beside him, "Rauk." Carefully, he set down the part and reached behind to grab a round metallic ball almost too big for his small frame to hold. He sadly rubbed his cheek on it, "Gizmo."

She knelt down, "Kigh, how did you end up here?" Her eyes darted about the room and back to the small figure. At only two feet tall, his stature was akin to that of a small child. His face sloped into a stout muzzle, and his body was covered over by a ragged but padded suit that made his figure seem a little on the portly side. His kangaroo-like feet were bare and beaten up by the rough terrain. Behind him, a long fluffy tail curved out of sight.

Gently, he set the dormant Gizmo aside and turned back to Kensy. "Had home on salvage skiff. Wandered wherever findy-finds good. Nearby Kigh get call for fiddle-fixing, so Rauk and Kigh come to people-rock to see. After landy-fall Kigh ask what need the fiddle-fixing but people-rock-people get angry. They attack Kigh and Rauk." Kigh gestured wildly as he explained his predicament. "They take Kigh's tools and Rauk and Gizmo." He pulled his tail in close and began grooming it, "When Kigh sneaky-sneak in to find Rauk and Gizmo, they no work anymore. People-rock-people hurt them, take their parts and toss-aside." He looked up at the hulking form of Rauk and wrapped his fingers around a tuft of hair on his friend, "Kigh no leave without Rauk...." Kensy could sense the sadness in his broken words, "no leave without Gizmo. And Kigh almost out of time."

"What do you mean?" she asked, confused by his despair. Jackson stepped closer to listen in as he relaxed his stance.

"Rauk save Kigh. Rauk protect Kigh and Gizmo from badness. Rauk is Kigh's friend, only friend." Kigh climbed the hulking Rauk. Hanging his tail over Rauk's back, he hung down and opened a panel just below the collar-bone. Kensy and Jackson approached to investigate. A power read-out flickered faintly with a sickly yellow glow across the worn metal interface. He tapped his thin index finger on it. "If go red, Rauk die. Kigh lose only friend."

Kensy gasped and covered her mouth for a moment, "Stars! He's not a construct. He's alive!" Jackson pulled at Kensy's shoulder, guiding her a few feet away from their new acquaintances.

"I have some concerns about what we're getting ourselves into here." He looked over the alien creatures cautiously.

"We need allies out here," Kensy argued, "We have no idea what we're gonna face on this mission. These two have been in the thick of this for a while. There is no telling what they could have seen or heard that could help us."

"We can't exactly lug them around with us," Jackson scowled at her, "We still have a jammer to shut down and crewmen to find. Not to mention shutting down whatever is going on in this hell-hole of a colony. They are a liability."

Unwavering in her determination, she countered, "I will not leave them to die because it is inconvenient for us. Kigh sounds like he knows what is needed to save his friend. We help him get his friend back on his feet and then no more liability. We only have to gain from this."

Jackson stared at her unflinchingly.

"We save them. It's the right thing to do," she asserted.

Jackson sighed in resignation, "Fine."

Kensy pivoted back toward Kigh and Rauk, "Kigh, do you know what you need to help Rauk?"

"Yes, yes. Kigh know," his head snapped around to search his surroundings. He scampered down Rauk and off onto a heap on the side. Kensy and Jackson watched as he fashioned a writing implement and surface from the assorted parts and pieces at his disposal. His jittery little hands sketched out a rough schematic on the salvaged canvas. He skittered up to Kensy, "They take from Rauk, need stealy back to fix Rauk.

Kigh no can make new one. Kigh tried, no good." He fidgeted in place, "You get? You help Kigh, help Rauk?"

Kensy took the drawing graciously and patted little Kigh between his semi-floppy ears, "We are gonna go stop the badness. And I will keep a special lookout for this. We'll make sure you get what you need to help Rauk." She stood up, "Stay here but be ready. Everything will be okay. We'll be back soon." Hope sparked in the small creature's soft doe-eyed expression as he gazed up into Kensy's soft sea-green eyes.

Chapter 38

Hostile Intentions

"...corrective action has been taken."
~ *Lieutenant Lindsay Rasken*

Silently and swiftly, Reily pushed back from her perch. With a cat-like grace, she scaled the earthen terrain almost noiselessly. As she neared the upper reaches of her climb, she paused to survey the surroundings again, making sure everything remained unaware of her presence. She crested the rise and rolled away from the edge toward her sniper rifle that rested against the cavern wall. Neira and Shane waited patiently nearby.

"It's just the one guy. Looks like he's prepping some kind of interrogation table," she summarized in a hushed tone. "There's a whole row of the tables, all currently empty but not unused. Two base level egress points, looks like they have seen a lot of traffic. Saw a catwalk on the far upper side. Couldn't determine much about it from a distance." She secured her weapon as she spoke, "Oh, and he has one of those black things on the back of his neck. Doesn't seem to help his awareness any. Got within maybe thirty feet and he never so much as flinched in my direction."

"So, do we move in and clear the room or find another path?" Shane posed the options to Reily and Neira.

Neira thought on it for a moment, "You say he looks like he's preparing for something?" Reily nodded in affirmation. "We lay low for a little bit, keep eyes on him, and find out what's going on. If we keep pressing, we could lose the opportunity to get intel on this operation covertly, and I want some answers."

Together, the trio crept back up to the edge and peered over, looking down into the room below. They hunkered down as one of the lower doors swung open. Another guard entered the room. They met alongside the table that now sat almost vertically. "I can't make out what they are saying," Shane whispered. He rolled on to his back and began rifling through his gear for something to resolve the issue.

Reily placed a hand on his arm to still him as the men parted ways. They listened for the door to close and were again left with one guard. Shane shrugged and shifted onto his shoulder to gaze back over the room. The shadows on the opposite side of the cavern stirred, catching Neira's attention. She narrowed her gaze toward the catwalks in an attempt to identify the subtly deviating presence.

She elbowed Reily and pointed to the disturbance. Silently, Reily leveled her rifle at the source of the movement and stared down the scope. She looked up then back through her eye piece to confirm. "What is it?" Neira prodded.

"It's the others," Reily kept a bead on her captains, "They see the guard, but I don't think they have noticed us."

Neira glanced down at the oblivious guard and returned her gaze to the other group. She tilted her head down behind the rise, "Visiri activate. Resume hostile territory navigation mode." At her command, the eye patch flashed to life, then shifted into a more subtle configuration. "Enable sniper sight." She waited as her cybernetic augmentation adjusted. Her distance vision became sharper. First, she trained her gaze on the guard. He seemed too preoccupied to have noticed the discreet flash. Her focus shifted to the far side catwalks. There sat Kensy and Jackson crouched carefully at the entrance to the room. She waited for a moment.

They were visible in such clarity it was as if the room between them had fallen away, eliminating the distance almost entirely. Kensy turned to the side and spoke to those around her for a moment. Jackson nodded in Neira's direction and pointed his rifle at the unaware guard to keep watch. Kensy looked back toward Neira and began tracing faint glowing lines in the air. The power only lingered for a moment before dissipating into nothing. Neira watched carefully.

As Kensy's message concluded, Neira pushed away from the edge. Her hands danced through the air in reply. Kensy watched, her eyes glittering with flecks of violet energy infusing them. Their exchange was interrupted by the harsh slam of a lower door. Jackson spun around, catching Kensy's shoulder and pulling her back into the doorway. He pressed a finger to his lips and glanced back over his shoulder.

Two burly guards dragged in a limp husk between them. The figure was almost entirely obscured by their enormous silhouettes. They spun him around and slammed him into the interrogation table's waiting restraints. As they stepped back Kensy gasped, and looked wide-eyed at Jackson. The battered and broken captive was none other than Daily. His head rolled back, "Aww, come on guys, I thought we were just beginning to get along," Daily coughed and blood dripped over his lips. He smiled weakly.

A familiar and stocky man walked in with a self-important air. He stormed up to the guards and impatiently waited for them to finish securing the prisoner. "Hurry up! Hurry up!" He barked at them. "And get me a status report on the other one!"

One of the guards turned and looked down upon the small greasy man, "Processing and activation are complete."

"Hey, guys, this is all a big misunderstanding. Just let me give the boss a call and we can clear this whole mess up," Daily continued to try to sway his captors.

The mayor sneered at him in response. "I don't know who you people really are, but it doesn't really matter anymore.

Your friends won't make it off this planet alive. The Vagabond wants them and he will get what he wants." With the snap of his fingers, the mayor drew the attention of his guards, "Prepare him for the next phase. And send someone to check on that ruckus in the zone. If they were nosing around up there, I want the bodies!" He hustled from the room in an awkward scurry.

The two who had escorted Daily in moved to the sides of his table. They began cranking it into a horizontal position while the original guard approached a workbench and began to fuss. Kensy glanced at Neira. With a swift hand gesture, the mercenary began to descend toward the unsuspecting jailors ahead of Shane. Jackson looked at Kensy questioningly, "What is she going to do?"

"All she said was stay put," Kensy whispered back as she crept forward for a better view, "but I suspect... she's going to kill them." Jackson and Kensy's eyes locked for a moment before turning back to the scene unfolding below them.

As Neira reached the base of the slope, one of the guards looked up. He opened his mouth to sound the alarm, but only a gurgle came out as a spray of blood covered the man behind him. He wavered and slumped down beside the table. The remaining two turned toward the intruders.

The second towering guard advanced upon Neira, reaching for his sidearm. She broke into a charge. The distance between them disappeared rapidly. She planted her Ausk-Chelkai into the ground, leveraging all her weight upon them. Her body swung between the blades and up into a kick. She planted the heels of her armored boots into the upper torso of the goliath, sending him reeling backward. On the back swing, she landed gracefully and pulled her blades from the packed earth. She gave him a smart glare, daring him to come at her again.

The gun had flown from his grip, but instead of recovering it, he roared in anger. His eyes became hollow and mechanical. Small metal plates ripped through his skin, creating wedge-shaped blades over his arms and fists. He threw a heavy punch toward her. Despite her heavy armor, she swiftly spun under the extension of his arm and planted the forward curve of her left blade into the base of his spine. With a twist she wrenched it ninety degrees and ripped the length of her blade up along his back. As she spun around to face the final remaining hostile, her foe toppled over helplessly.

She slowly strode toward the last man standing. He scrambled at his workstation to complete whatever task he had begun. She tapped gently on his shoulder with her bloodied blade. Like a wild animal striking out, he turned and lurched at her. She stared him down unflinchingly as her fist rose, blade in hand, straight into his throat. The cut was swift and clean. She pulled back and pivoted toward the interrogation table where Daily lay.

Movement at the edge of her vision caused a moment of pause. The small black marks from the guards' necks fluttered and buzzed as they picked themselves up from the corpses. As they unfolded from their positions, tiny metallic wings and legs emerged. The bug like creatures drew long wires from the spines of their victims. Suddenly a series of shots rang through the cavern as Jackson, Shane and Reily each obliterated a bug. Neira gave a nod of thanks to the others and headed to Daily's side.

Shane approached the open door and crouched. He stared down the sights of his rifle while he kept watch for reinforcements. Neira placed the curve of her right-hand blade into the mechanisms of the table, severing the restraints. Daily coughed and pulled away from the bindings, "Nice to see a familiar face. What took so damn long? These people are downright nuts," he jested as he rose from the table. Reily began her descent into the room, keeping an eye on the door opposite Shane.

"Keep it moving, Yappy. We still have a mission to complete," Neira ordered as she turned back toward the direction of the catwalk. She glanced up at Kensy and Jackson with an acknowledging tilt of her head. Daily followed a few steps behind, then stumbled to his hands and knees. A soft but sickening sound rose from his slumped form. Neira reactively pivoted back toward him to render assistance, "What's wrong, Turbo?"

He flailed a hand at her, "No, no. It's fine. Just a little internal disagreement here."

She scowled and turned toward Shane. Kensy kept her eyes on Daily. Something shifted in his manner. She squinted as she tried to place her unease. Daily clambered up the workbench beside him, keeping his head down ever so slightly. His hand found a spiked apparatus in the center of the bench and his fingers wrapped around it as his head turned toward Neira.

There, Kensy beheld the gruesome realization. Blood and fluids drained down his face from his now empty eye sockets. A menacing smile curved over his lips, "Guess I'm just not feeling like myself after everything." Daily rolled one shoulder back in a stretch as he closed in behind Neira. The shift of his jacket revealed a small black shape embedded into his neck. Reactivating her vision infusion, her eyes traced the shape as a piercing shriek escaped her lips.

Daily's fist flew through the air toward his prey. Neira twisted her body sideways and into an arch to avoid the swing. He over-extended and his balance faltered for a moment. Neira planted the front of her blades into the dirt. Her boots clipped his bloodied chin as she cartwheeled away from her assailant. They each took a wary stance, evaluating each other for tactics and weaknesses. With a resonating blast, Daily crumpled to the ground.

Everyone stared bewildered at the source as Rasken pulled her rifle back to her shoulder. Tears flooded down her cheeks despite her stone faced expression. She turned to her captains, "I would like to report the compromised state of one Crewmen

Anthony Daily. Crewman was captured by the enemy and upon recovery was found to be hostile. For the safety of those remaining and the integrity of the mission, corrective action has been taken."

"Understood, Lieutenant," Jackson somberly replied.

Kensy's eyes wandered over the faces of her companions as she processed everything in the stunned silence of the moment. A stray tear escaped down her cheek. Another muffled pop filled the air. Tiny metallic pieces scattered across the ground before the creature could release itself.

Reily stood from her position and walked up to Daily's corpse. She pulled a pair of small metal tags from his body. In their place, she set a small dome shaped device. It projected an opaque force field around the remains. She turned her gaze up to Rasken, "I'll handle the rest, sir. Keep moving. Keep on mission." Rasken's eyes quivered with the weight of her actions. She pivoted sharply. Snapping her gun into position, she pushed onward, leading the group further into the underground maze.

Chapter 39

Malek

"How many bloody corners does this place have?!"
~ *Ensign Ashar Kyo*

Jackson kept his shoulder pressed snugly against the edge of his rocky cover as bullets whizzed by and shattered on the rocks behind him. The faint sizzling of plasma on stone filled the air around him as he swapped his gun's reservoir for a new one. His fingers danced over the gun's holographic interface to adjust his shots.

Rasken backed around the corner across from him and slammed her back into the wall. Her breath was heavy from the adrenaline pulsing through her system. She leaned over, resting her gun and hands across her knees for a moment, "It's no good. There's too many, and I can't get a decent enough view to see what we are dealing with." She wiped sweat from her cheek with the back of her hand and carefully peeked around the edge. Another volley of shots peppered the area. She recoiled, "But *they* certainly have a nice vantage. Lucky those damn bugs don't improve their aim."

"Let me." Kensy knelt down beside Jackson and shook her hands out. She inhaled deeply. Firmly, she pressed both hands to the ground and gathered the violet light beneath her fingers. Closing her eyes, she whispered, "Heiras Heiga." Everyone shuttered as a pulse rippled through the cavern, tracing every crevasse and outcropping. She furrowed her brow as she focused on translating the feedback into a mental map.

She flinched as the rocks beside her cracked from the impact of a shot. Her eyes flew open as she backed up further. Jackson glanced down toward her, "Anything?"

She stood and began waving her hands in the air as she described the layout, "The tunnel continues down about fifty feet, then there is an opening into a larger space. Another ten or fifteen past that there is a fork in the road. Feels like that's where most of them are staked out. That's all I could get." She flexed her fingers to clear the pulse sensation.

Jackson looked back to Rasken and her underlings, "Looks like we're gonna have to push." He clenched his jaw for a moment, "We'll have to rush them. Wait for the reload and close before they can recover." Everyone nodded. The plan was dangerous but thanks to another cave-in the path behind them had collapsed. There was only forward now.

Rasken lit up, "Hey wait!" She rifled through her tactical vest pockets. "Got something." She pulled a small handle from its hiding place and tossed it to Jackson. "Cross had that in her crate of toys. Supposed to be a shield. Some super experimental tech."

"And you were just hoarding it?!" Jackson raised one eyebrow.

Rasken shrugged, "What can I say? I like new toys." She unwrapped a chunk of bubble gum and popped it in her mouth with a grin.

Stowing his rifle, Jackson examined the shield device for a moment. It was heavier than he had anticipated. He slipped it over his left hand and activated it. A series of metal bands sprung from the device, expanding in all directions until it formed a full body riot shield of plasma, titanium webbing, and tiny scales. He smirked, feeling the hum of the shield in his grip. He nodded in acceptance. With his right hand, he reached down to his thigh and pulled away what appeared to be a metallic box on a hand grip. Automatically, it began to unfold. The metal plates and pins shifted, fastening into new configurations until the sword's full form could be seen.

Rasken smiled and popped a bubble, "Captains first!" She primed her rifle. Glancing at Wright and Kyo she barked orders between slaps of her gum, "Alright, slackers, let's give 'em some cover fire." Both men readied themselves and nodded in compliance.

Jackson glanced down to Kensy again. She collected a brilliant light between her hands, shaping it into her longsword. With a flick of her wrist, the excess energy scattered away, leaving only the crisp, clean psiblade form. "Ready when you are."

Jackson hunched down slightly as he pushed into the oncoming fire. He braced for the barrage. As the rounds impacted, the empty casings rained down upon the ground. The plasma of each shot melded into the shield, fortifying it further. The additional weight, however minor, was still noticeable. He held fast, moving one step at a time down the corridor. Kensy followed behind with her right shoulder toward him and her clasp pulsing with a faint purple light.

Rasken moved across the hall and held her rifle steady as she aimed past Jackson's shield. Swiftly, Kyo darted down the hall behind Jackson and Kensy. He crouched behind a jutting face of stone and began returning gunfire to the enthralled soldiers firing upon them. Wright sprinted up behind his captains a pulse grenade in hand. Seeing an opening, he lobbed it across the ground, rolling between the feet of one enemy.

Jackson pulled the shield down close to himself, and Kensy as the grenade detonated. A flash illuminated the hall for a brief second. The shock wave that followed rumbled the earthen cavern and disoriented the attackers. Dirt shifted and sprinkled sporadically from the ceiling. Jackson rushed forward, slamming one man with the face of the shield. The foe screamed in pain as the searing plasma burnt his flesh.

269

Another slipped past the shield's edge in an attempt to advance on the others. Reactively, Jackson brought his sword in a sweeping arc over his head. As he swung down, his grip changed, plunging the tip into the man's exposed back. He jerked the sword free, raising it to block a bayonet headed for his chest. Continuing his motion, he brought the blade in under his assailant's arm and slashed across the man's rib cage. Pivoting back to his left, he slammed another foot soldier to the ground.

Out of the corner of his eye, Jackson spied another enemy moving in for the flank. He cursed under his breath. Unable to block in time, he braced for the hit. The would-be assassin stumbled and fell at his feet as Kensy drew back from her lightning fast strike. Scrambling for a better position to surround the two captains, the remaining enthralled soldiers fell to Rasken and Kyo's covering fire.

Everyone paused. Watching. Waiting. "I think we're clear for now." Kensy finally spoke up. Momentarily, she glanced into the room that splintered off beside them. Before she could return to her thought her attention was redirected. As she released her psiblade's form into a fine purple mist, she took a few jogging steps into the room. The others followed behind. Wright and Kyo took up watch at the doorway as their superiors converged in the center. "Bingo," Kensy dug into her pockets and pulled forth the salvaged canvas. She held it out in front of her.

The room was lined with workbenches and various manufacturing equipment. At the center of it all sat a partial construct of some kind. The intent behind its design was impossible to determine, but within the metallic skeleton stat the very piece that Kigh had sketched out for her.

She grabbed at a large wrench and began bashing the surrounding pieces apart. Jackson retracted his shield and sword as he stepped forward. Securing them to his sides, he freed his hands. He wrapped his fingers around the broken

270

scrap and pulled, allowing Rasken access to the desired component. "That's all well and good, but it could take us hours to fight our way back to them," he grimaced.

"I'll go," Wright volunteered, easing back from the doorway.

Rasken glared at him, "You're injured."

"A few bruised ribs...," Wright popped a small syringe from his gear and stabbed it into his own leg. "...that are now taken care of." His lieutenant unwaveringly scrutinized him. "I can move faster and quieter alone. With the scans we've taken down here, I can find a new path back without drawing attention, deliver the part, and catch up." He looked among the officers. "I am the best stealth operative on this team. You can't afford for me *not* to go."

Rasken handed him the piece and a spare cartridge for his gun, "Fine. But you get your ass back to the group asap. When we evac you had better be there or I will kick your ass." He snapped to attention and saluted her. He nodded to the others and swept out of the room back the direction they had come with a surprising silence. "I swear...," Rasken began.

Kensy placed a hand on Rasken and Jackson to silence them. Her eyes darted back and forth as she processed the sounds that were creeping into her ears. *What?* Jackson mouthed toward her without a sound. Cautiously, she turned her head to look behind them. The sounds slowly gained in intensity until they reached an audible level. Everyone looked around nervously as the cavern began to crumble. "We have to go now!" she shouted over the ruckus.

Jackson snatched the shield from his side and deployed it just behind Kensy. A hail of rocks clattered against it. His knuckles turned white as he held the heavy shield steady. "We need a direction," he called out to her. Kyo's footing faltered as the ground beneath him shifted. He tumbled backward. Rasken swooped in, jerking him back to his feet.

A searing red light began to pulse through the cracks that formed throughout the floor and rear wall of the workshop. Kensy's fingers instinctively reached for Jackson's jacket. She gave a quick tug as she stepped into a sprint. Deftly, she sidestepped a falling chunk of stone. She gave a fleeting glance back as Rasken and Kyo fell in behind Jackson. Her mind raced. She hadn't gotten a good enough visual of the cavern to know the best way to go. *Use your instincts! They're usually right on*, she coached herself.

She could feel the shaking of the cavern in every pulse-pounding step. There was no sense of time anymore, only the current moment that seized her every breath. She pushed through the pelting rain of dirt and rocks. Her boots thudded against the ground in a rhythm much like her quickening heartbeat. A dull grinding noise met her ears as she felt the sting of debris grating against her skin. She had slipped on the turn. Jackson knelt down, shielding her. The ground was looser here. Her eyes scanned the area as she pushed herself up from the gravel.

Kyo and Rasken took up a protective stance flanking the captains. Slowly, the rumble subsided, leaving the squad in silence. Breaths slowed and apprehension crept in as they soaked in the stillness. "We need to get out of here," Kensy whispered toward Jackson. "This place is death." He stared at her expression. If there was fear in her, he could not see it. She looked at the cavern around them with a solemn concern, her mind churning over the possibilities before them. She scowled, "There is a presence here. Something touched psionically but clouded. I can feel it."

"Where?" he inquired.

"It's chokingly strong, oppressive," she shook her head, "It is almost overwhelming. Pinpointing it is like trying to pick out a single scent in a perfumery. There's just too much to nail it down." She sat back and gazed up into his eyes. "I could tell you more if we got closer, but...," she hesitated, "I'm not prepared for... this. Whatever it is... is bad."

He processed her words carefully. Standing tall, his shield folding back into itself, he addressed the group, "Our priorities have just gotten a little shake up. Any recon we do from here on in is incidental only. Mission one is now shutting down the source of the jamming and evacuating our people." Everyone acknowledged with a nod. "Now...."

A small burst of debris filled the hallway beside them. Neira leaned through the newly formed hole, "Are you going to join the party or just stand there and make speeches?"

Jackson narrowed his glare in her direction. Rasken approached the opening cautiously and glanced in, "Where are my people?" She stepped through the opening, bringing her gun up as she scanned the area.

"Back topside by now, looking for a good exfiltration point." Neira reached in and wrapped her hand around Kensy's thumb. Kensy did the same, creating a firmly locked grip. Neira pulled, hoisting her friend over the uneven terrain of the opening. She turned away from the hole, "They took the remains with them." Rasken nodded. Neira scanned the group as Kyo and Jackson emerged. "You seem to be missing one as well," she uttered, noting Wright's absence.

"He's running an errand," Kensy responded as she took in the enormity of the cavern. Distant noises filled the air with a harsh ambiance. The walls vanished into darkness beyond the outcropping on which they stood. A low warm glow made the edge faintly visible to the keen eye. Carefully, Kensy neared the edge and peeked over. Her eyes went wide. Sprawled over the top of a furiously bubbling lava flow hundreds of feet below sat a massive structure. Its spidery limbs reached into the walls, suspending its intimidating silhouette in every direction.

Rasken also leaned over to survey the chasm. She shook her head and took several steps away from the precipice, "That is a long way down." Silently, the shadows above them shifted. Watching. Waiting. Rasken glanced to Neira, "Don't tell me—."

"...that's the source of the jamming. Yeah, as far as I can tell, it is." Neira crouched down beside the containment canister to double check it. "I was just formulating a plan on how to take it down when I got a blip on my scanners." She thumbed toward the opening she had blasted.

Jackson stormed up to her, "Did you even think about it before you blew any potential chance we had at stealth?"

With a swift grace, Neira snapped to her feet to face him, "It was a risk; but so is this whole damn mission. I did what I had to so *you* wouldn't be lost running around these tunnels like a rat in a burning building."

"Enough—!" Kensy pivoted back to end their bickering when the shadow caught her eye. From above, the darkened figure dropped. The ground shook with the force of his impact. Kensy stumbled as the rocks shifted ever so slightly under her. The soft and slowly crumbling edge was too close for comfort. She lifted her head to see the rest of her company reeling from the concussion. There, in the center of the outcropping, stood a familiar figure. Even at full stature, his form was warped, his eyes hollow, and grotesque metallic plates protruded from his sundered flesh. Her brow furrowed as his name passed over her lips, "Malek."

She inched forward, all too aware of her precarious position. His empty eyes fixated on her, even as the rest of the company began to circle. The intensity in the air became palpable. At the base of his neck, the same black mechanical construct that had manipulated Daily could be seen embedded within the skin. Kensy held her palms out toward him as if to hold him at bay, "Whatever they have done to you, we can figure this out. We can find a way to fix it." As she pleaded with Malek, her eyes darted to Jackson. Slowly, he tried to curve around Malek's right flank.

As he spoke, the voice that poured forth was not his own. It spoke in discordant mechanical tones, "What I have done is show this man to his rightful place. He will be preserved with the others." Malek lifted his chin and stepped in Kensy's direction. "As will you all in time." He snapped his hands upward. Suddenly, the ground and walls erupted around the company. Neira let out a pained grunt as she and Kyo were pulled backward against the jagged walls. Rasken and Jackson thrashed against the metal tendrils that wrapped around their arms, legs, and torsos, dragging them down to their knees.

Kensy watched in stunned silence. Before she could mount a reaction, her friends and subordinates were restrained by slithering mechanical chords wrapping over their bodies. She flexed her fingers, gathering a crackling black energy through them. The mutated Malek spoke up again, "Now that the distraction is dealt with, we can talk."

She inched further from the edge toward Jackson, "Somehow, I doubt you want to talk." Her movement was slow and subtle as she gauged her opponent.

He looked down toward her hands. "Fascinating. You must be the one from Bhelnir. The one who stood against me."

"I don't know who you think you are, but I will always oppose those who would inflict senseless harm," She traced possible avenues of attack in her mind, calculating power bleed off and areas of effect for her various abilities. *The positioning's all wrong. If I miscalculate, I could get one of the others caught in the attack. I can't risk the friendly fire.* She bit at her lower lip. *All I have is my psiblade. It will have to do.*

He shook his head dismissively, "I had hoped that an individual of such talent would learn and evolve into... more. But it seems that such a progression is not within the scope of potential outcomes. On Bhelnir, you surrounded yourself with those of lesser power, which resulted in their deaths. And what are you doing now? Repeating the scenario." He turned his attention to Jackson. With the slightest of hand gestures, another mechanical chord crawled up his captive's body. It coiled around the commander's neck and tightened. "Should he die like the others? Do you wish that badly to see everything end?"

"No!" Kensy reactively shouted. She shifted backward on her heels. Her hands fell still. The power she had gathered crackled and fizzled out. Her eyes danced across the faces of her companions, tears collecting in her eyelashes. "We fought because you would have killed us all anyway. You *did* kill them!" She shouted at her adversary.

Malek's attention turned back to her, "No. I would have preserved them. What I offer is transcendence." He circled her. "You brought those children death as you will to all of these people." He leaned in to whisper in her ear, "But perhaps that is not the way it has to be. Perhaps we can reach an arrangement...."

"Kick his fucking ass," Neira grunted furiously. The tendrils wrapped further gagging and silencing the hostages. Jackson writhed against his restraints, attempting to gain better positioning with his hands. The hilt and shield handle were so close. If he could only activate one or both of them.

"Tell you what, if you allow me to study your fascinating abilities, I will not submit your friends for processing today. We will depart this system peacefully, without further conflict. Resist and I will honor your history. They will die horrifically here before you, just as your compatriots did on Bhelnir."

Tears steamed down her cheeks. *I can't allow anyone else to die because of me. If I can buy them enough time, they could regroup.* She cast her eyes down. "Fine."

Chapter 40

Bonds

"Handle with care."
~ Nordux Crystal handling instructions

Jackson fought against his bindings as he kept his eyes on Kensy and Malek. He had promised that she would not relive the events of Bhelnir and now, before him, the source of that horror dug at those memories again. The monstrosity possessing Malek drew close to her, his breath feeding false promises into her ears. A fury began to build inside the commander. This was unacceptable. Tears collected in her eyes and her lips sealed her surrender, "Fine." She turned her face away, "I will do as you ask if they are freed unharmed."

The rage coursed through his body. He wrenched sharply at the mechanical tentacles that bound him. It was enough. His hands grasped the sword hilt and shield handle. He deployed them instantly. Shards of metal and sprays of plasma erupted from his position as he broke free. Staring down the hostile Malek, Jackson ran the flat of his blade up against his neck and ripped. The sword sheered through the chords wrapped around his throat and mouth. Unwavering in his determination, he cast aside what remained of the broken tendrils.

Malek slowly turned to face him with a look of amusement, "Hmm. Perhaps you are worth a sliver more consideration." Malek pulled away from Kensy, allowing her to slip past him. Wide-eyed, she beheld Jackson's liberation. She had never before seen the fire that raged in his eyes now. Snapping her clasp hand downward, the psiblade longsword appeared. She drew her sidearm from her thigh holster, keeping her gaze trained on Jackson for confirmation. He remained focused on the enemy at hand. Malek looked between the two with his grotesquely hollowed out eyes, "Well, this should be most educational, at the very least. I have already learned much from this vessel. He excelled at martial combat. Shall we see how useful his skills are?"

Malek unfurled his embrace toward Jackson and Kensy. The flesh on the insides of his forearms peeled open and dozens of small plates curled outward. They locked into one another until broad black blades had formed from each hand. He smiled malevolently. Rasken gasped and gurgled from behind Kensy. She glanced over her shoulder as the chords tightened around the lieutenant. The same desperate utterance echoed from Kyo and Neira. She spun around, striking at the ground where the chords originated with the sheering force of her psiblade. Loosened by the strike, Rasken ripped away her bindings and drew in a deep gasp.

Malek lunged toward Kensy's exposed back. With lightning speed, Jackson intervened. He pivoted, thrusting his sword between Malek and Kensy, steering the strike off to one side. The tips of their blades dug into the dirt. Jackson hooked the blade with his and turned his opponent with a wide overhead arc. As the back of Malek's shoulder was pulled forward by the swing, Jackson slammed the shield into his torso. The plasma sizzled against his skin, but he remained unfazed.

Rasken sprung forward to assist Kyo, but the tendrils grasped at her ankles, tripping her. Kensy leapt over her and thrust her psiblade into the wall with all of her force behind it. It pierced into a cluster of tendrils just above Kyo's shoulder with a crackle of energy. Kensy focused her power in to the blade. The tendrils shuttered and ceased moving. He freed one hand and tugged at the wrappings on his neck. "Go," he rasped.

Kensy pulled her blade and glanced to Neira, who remained motionless. "Neira!" Kensy screamed. The mercenary had been curled sideways against the broken wall, her back toward the others. Kensy fired a grazing shot at her friend, sundering a handful of chords that bound her left arm. In a shower of sparks, the mechanical coils fell free, so too did Neira's arm. It dangled limply at her side. In a moment of panic, Kensy broke into a run. As she reached Neira, with tears in her eyes, she tossed her gun aside. She retracted the form of her psiblade into a dagger-like shape and began tearing at the cables with it. "Neira, Neira!" she called, pleaded, and cried. *Stars, no! You can't leave me! Please, Neira! Please!*

Malek's cackling laughter did not reach Kensy's ears in her fit of panic. He stepped out of the shield slam and cocked his head sideways as he examined the group. "Seems that I have managed to reduce the best of you to nothing. What chance do the rest of you have?"

Jackson narrowed his glare as he interceded, "Either you don't have access to all of that man's memories or you need to look harder." Taking to a defensive position with the shield forward, he prodded at his enemy, "Take a look at his training. He might be good, but I'm better."

The monstrosity's face became expressionless and flat. With the scraping of her psiblade against the stone, Neira's body fell against Kensy and her Ausk-Chelkai clattered to the ground. She released the knife into a cloud of purple-ish fog and cradled her friend. Kensy reached up to Neira's jugular to check for a pulse. As she did her fingers passed over the armored metal collar that wrapped around the mercenary's neck. There was a flash of light from beneath it. She froze. The caress of wind passed over Neira's lips as she breathed in deeply. Kensy shuttered with relief.

Malek spun toward Jackson, unleashing a flurry of blows against the shield. Jackson pushed back with all of his strength. Their blades clashed against one-another, the metallic surfaces of the blades reflecting the low light of the cavern. The sounds of the duel echoed through the company as Rasken and Kyo freed themselves from the remaining active tendrils. Kensy stared down at Neira, lost in her own thoughts. The clash continued through the seemingly endless moments.

Seeing an opening, Jackson drew back with labored breath. He examined his opponent again as he steeled himself for further melee. Malek moved without fatigue or concern for injury. Blood coated his grotesquely modified body. What little could be seen of his dark olive skin was washed out to an ashen tone. "You're not wearing down yet, are you, Commander?" he snidely questioned. Without hesitation, Malek lunged forward with his right shoulder.

Jackson brought up the shield to receive the blow, but the assailant had counted on this. He rolled against the sizzling face of the plasma matrix to the left. As he cleared the shield, his blow followed. He brought the right arm blade in for a stab at Jackson's back. The commander took a step back toward Malek with his right foot, causing the blade to graze his rib cage instead. Dropping the sword and shield to the ground he clutched at the razor sharp plates of Malek's arm. Using the remaining momentum of the blow and leveraging his attacker's body against his own, he threw the monstrosity toward the edge of the precipice.

Jackson fell to one knee and clutched at his side with his bloodied hands. His heart pounded in his ears. His breath burned in his lungs. He drew in a deep breath and grasped his weapons once again. Jackson hawked a glob of blood and spit from his mouth, "Don't count me out just yet." The thinned layer of plasma on the face of his shield flickered. With the slide of his thumb, he adjusted the settings. The form of the shield shrunk down, condensing the remaining material into the more manageable heater configuration.

Suddenly, from above, a hulking figure dropped onto the battlefield between Jackson and Malek. Jackson instinctively stepped back. "It's all right. He's with us." A voice called from behind. Everyone looked to see Wright descend quietly, a cocky smile across his face, and clinging to his back, a small creature with a bundle of salvaged parts and pieces.

Kensy looked up from her stupor at the commotion. Neira stirred. "If that's a friend, tell him to kick the metal jackass off the cliff and let's be done with this place." She groaned and tried to sit up.

All eyes turned back toward the large, imposing form of Rauk. Malek charged forward for another attack. The ground around Rauk erupted in another volley of mechanical tendrils. As they tried to lash themselves around his hulking form, he ripped them from their anchors. Sparks and shrapnel flew. He opened his hand and swiped toward Malek. Unable to escape the massive grip, Malek was knocked aside. He scrambled back to his feet when the booming voice of Rauk rolled forth, "I've had about enough of you and your machines!" he huffed heavily.

"I will harvest your parts and leave you to rot, you filthy abomination," Malek hissed at him.

"You tried. And failed." Rauk stretched his neck and arms, readying himself for confrontation.

Neira touched Kensy's leg, "End it." She narrowed her gaze in Malek's direction.

Kensy nodded, "I know." She stood. Her footfalls echoed softly as she walked up beside Rauk. "Thank you." She placed a hand on his enormous arm and stepped in front of him. Her attention turned back to Malek. Her head down, she approached him, "You would take everything from us without pause. You steal and destroy. No more." With sorrowful but dried eyes, she looked up at him, "I'm sorry." Instantaneously, she threw her palms forward and released a torrent of energy into his form. His body cascaded backward off the precipice. At the edge of her hearing, a single word reached her in his voice: *thanks*. With a furrowed brow, she watched him fall. Did she imagine it? His body was dashed against the structure in the chasm below and limply rolled off into the bubbling lava.

Everything began to rumble. Several places in the walls cracked with a furious red glow emanating from within. Neira clipped her blades to her back and stumbled toward the containment canister that laid discarded against the wall of the cavern. She fussed with the controls, "Something tells me the neighbors are getting ready to move out. We should do the same!" She shouted over the ruckus.

"What are you doing?" Rasken yelled back.

Neira managed to dislodge the center of the container. Rising to her feet, she discarded the pieces of the core's safety shell one-by-one. She walked to the edge. "Leaving a little parting gift," and with that, she cast the Nordux Crystal into the air. It cascaded down hundreds of feet on to the structure. As it struck the outer hull, the air rippled with the shock wave of the blast. The area around it became clouded with shrapnel and debris. A broken message crackled over the team's communicators, "...-alling Strike Tea-... anyone copy? Re-... Scythe calling...."

Neira threw up one hand and pointed at the rear wall, "Everyone hug to rock face!" She placed her other hand on her nahdvi and tilted her head down, "Bryden, tell me you're getting this."

"We hear you," his voice snapped back through the static.

"Can you get a lock on my position?" She glanced toward the others as they clustered against the wall alongside their new alien friends.

"Roger that. Registering you about 65 feet below the surface. Reading multiple life signs in your vicinity," he relayed.

"The ceiling it pretty high in here, which should mean minimal ground cover between us. Now listen, there is a hostile structure just past my position. Scythe should have some decent ordinance on board. I want you to use everything you have to bring this cavern down on them. Then fly down and get us off this rock! You hear me?" She glanced down at the damage she had done with the crystal. Tiny black dots skittered over it as the construct appeared to begin repairing itself. The dots spread up the crumbling walls. "And make it fast!"

"Target acquired. Clear the area." The red glow within the walls intensified as the rocks began to rain into the lava below. Neira sprinted toward Kensy. The chamber echoed a thunderous storm of explosions. The light of a ghastly green sunset burst forth from above. Everyone cowered against the side as the tails of another missile volley became visible. They pelted the opening wider, showering everything below in rock and heavily packed dirt. The transport snaked in through the opening and up against the shelf.

The loading door dropped as the tail of the transport swung toward the group. Shane leaned out with one hand extended, the other securely grasping a cargo net. He waved everyone forward. Neira glanced toward the left as they sprinted for their ride. Her scanner fluttered with information as the black dots crested the far lip. "Hurry it up!" she called out in a rasping yell.

One by one, they leapt toward the door as Shane hoisted them inward. He looked questioningly at the lumbering alien form of Rauk. As Wright leapt forward, he pulled close to Shane and hollered over the noise, "Chill, he's a friend."

Shane looked at him skeptically, "Whatever you say...."

Rauk leapt onto the transport, Kigh and his scrap curled inside his arms. It bobbed under the weight. He slumped down and pushed in toward the center of the vehicle. Neira brought up the rear, springing into the air as the now identifiable army

283

of black mechanical spiders skittered toward her. Even as her jump fell short, Shane caught her. His fingers clutched her right arm just above the bracer near the elbow. She wrapped her fingers around his forearm as he pulled her on to the hatch. Hastily, he shouted back over his shoulder, "Go!" Their knuckles whitened as they fought to maintain the grip. The engines fired a quick burst, blasting the nearby machines away as it propelled the vessel forward. With Shane's help, Neira clamored into the safety of the hold as the rear door closed.

Jackson leaned over the co-pilot's seat, "Get us back to the ship!"

Daniel's eyes remained on the sky in front of them. "You don't know the half of it...." He reached over and pressed a large button on the center array of controls. "Decontamination protocols engaged," he announced as a pulse of light passed through the sealed shuttle. They crested past the last outcropping of rock, and the horizon opened up before them. Kensy gasped. Showers of light and shock waves cascaded through the air. Dozens of ships exchanged fire within the upper reaches of the atmosphere. Daniel glanced down at his console, "Oh, you have got to be kidding me!" The entirety of the Cruxias Hazard Zone erupted. Red light poured around the silhouette of the colossal structure as it lifted toward the sky, surrounded by a swarm of smaller flying constructs. "Belt in as best you can, people! This could get a little... harrowing."

Daniel's hands danced over the controls as he navigated the barrage of flak that littered the air between them and the DeCadejra's hangar. "Scythe coming in hot. Alpha on board." The transport shuttered. "Reily!" He hollered toward the back. Deftly, she slipped past her captain into the co-pilot's seat. "I'm getting sick of these jerks rockin' the boat. Clear us a path."

She smirked, "My pleasure." The gunnery controls lit up under her hands.

"Gabel, sir, you and Psilyria Frost might want to ready yourselves. We're gonna be coming in hot and you're gonna be needed on the bridge asap." Daniel pulled Scythe sharply to the left as one of the salvage ships pitched toward the ground in a hail of smoke and flame. Jackson gave him a quick pat on the shoulder. Gently, Jackson pressed a hand against the small of Kensy's back to urge her toward the exit. Together, they maneuvered through the crowded interior, steeling themselves for the next stage of the battle that lay ahead.

Chapter 41

What We Leave Behind

*"Sometimes the most heartfelt expressions are
little more than a gesture."*
~ Lieutenant Daniel Bryden

The sound of the captains' boots thundered against the floor of the deck, marking each stride on their run toward the bridge. "Deploying Strategic Operations command console. Be advised the path to the bridgehead will be altered." Kensy glanced upward as if to look at Maggie's disembodied voice. Without pause, Jackson and Kensy veered around opposite sides of the forward elevator housing. Immediately, she understood.

In the center of the Strategic Operations Center walkway rose an impressive-looking podium of controls and displays. The path gradually expanded to either side to accommodate the console. As she neared it, Kensy leapt into the air. Narrowly clearing it, she tucked to a roll and rose back to her feet, maintaining her stride. Jackson skidded to a stop as the podium reached its full height. A holographic representation of the battle space encompassed him.

"Ivanigis!" Kensy shouted as she passed through the corridor to the bridgehead. The glittering purple energy of her power erupted from her body. She dove into the waiting beam. The light wrapped around her, instantly connecting her to the ship. She spun weightlessly as she waved her arms in swirling motions, "Ivanigis ahri." Her ethereal armor rippled and expanded in all directions. Effortlessly, it coursed over the hull, creating an additional layer of protection woven through the ship's shields.

"We've got bad news incoming!" Morgan called over comms. Kensy glanced down toward the surface as the alien ship broke free of the last vestiges of its terrestrial bonds. A furious red glow flowed from the outer edges of the construct toward the center and up into a series of sharp spires. The pulse rocketed off the tips into a singular spiraling ray. "All hands brace for impact!" Morgan danced the DeCadejra to the side. The concussive force of the blast echoed through the decks. "Not to rush you guys, but we could really use a plan right about now."

"Button it, Threaux," Jackson snapped back. "Point defense on the swarm ships. Aim for power cells. Let's clear the air, people!" He surveyed the data streaming through the console's interface.

"Sir, we have two hostiles remaining from the approach group and another two ships have entered the fray from orbit. We have orbital defenses pounding the entire area and the unidentified entity from the planet, intentions unknown," one of the nearby crew relayed in summary.

"It intends to kill us, soldier. Give me a status report on our heavy hitters: missiles, cannons, beams." His hands sifted through the overlays, organizing the streams of feedback into a more coherent layout. Everywhere he looked, more fragments of information flooded in.

Another crewman spoke up, "Looks like the swarm ships are trying to penetrate the shields."

"I've got it." Kensy blinked slowly as she focused on her tether to the ship. Her eyes began to glow with a soft violet light. Her fingers carefully manipulated the psionic streams that surrounded her. She grasped the unseen force and jerked it inward. Lightning sprung forth. It funneled through the beam and out over the smooth exterior plating. The crackling serpents of electricity struck at the swarm ships that fought against the shields, explosively rupturing them.

She pushed her hands out once again, sweeping them to the sides and up again as if to conduct the symphony of her powers. "Volgihr," she whispered. The barrier extended into a stormy tide. It swept across the sky, fading gradually. The remaining swarm ships and nearby orbital platforms dropped into the lower atmosphere before shattering on the stony landscape below. Lights on-board the closest of the pirate ships flickered as it tried to climb away from the blast. The engines sputtered, sending it careening into another vessel.

Jackson raised an eyebrow as he watched the two ships sink toward the planet. He smirked momentarily before turning his attention to the alien monstrosity. He zoomed his display in on it, assigning targeting parameters, "All weapons lock on Primary Target. Fire at will." Hundreds of panels opened up across the hull in unison. Projectiles streamed from the ports, pelting the Vagabond ship with a hail of fire and explosions.

Jackson zoomed in on his scans of the primary enemy vessel again. His eyes searched the structure. "No way ...." he muttered under his breath. He selected the area of interest and forwarded the information to Neira's nahdvi. "Looks like your little stunt isn't even slowing them down. The damage is almost completely repaired." He began entering the updated targeting points for the crew.

Her voice called back over the channel, "Whatever repairs they are making won't be as strong as the original framework. Pound that spot, and you'll see better weapons penetration at the very least."

"Yeah, yeah, already on it," he cast his hands to the sides, sending the data out to the surrounding consoles.

Before he could continue his banter with her, Morgan's voice rang out over the ship-wide comm, "Enemy ship charging main weapon. All hands, brace for impact!" Morgan pulled hard on the control gyros directing the ship upward, behind the bow of another oncoming pirate vessel. The red beam from the alien ship sheered through the pirates' hull and slammed into the shields of the DeCadejra. The ship rocked sharply, tousling crewmen and unsecured equipment throughout. Kensy's form curled up slightly as she let out a muffled cry from the air being knocked out of her. Morgan glanced up toward her pained expression, "Um, Commander...."

Jackson looked toward the bridgehead questioningly. "All stations continue firing!" He shouted over the operations center. He shifted around the side of the console and began down the hall. Kensy lifted her head and narrowed her eyes at the silhouette of the enemy ship looming before her. Flames wreathed her vision for a moment as the interceding vessel erupted into a hail of scrap metal. Slowly she uncurled her body, opening her arms, and tilting her head back. She closed her eyes. The ambient energy began to ripple and shift. Jackson paused. He looked around, catching the barely visible flickers in the air around him. He glanced toward Kensy. Before he knew it, he was in a full run up the corridor.

Kensy pulled the energy inward. It flared around her in brilliant prominences. The words, "Yhir Nu'hai," spilled from her lips. She brought her focus back to the enemy. Her blazing eyes fell upon the target as it launched another beam in her direction. She swung her clasped hand forward, directing the arcs of energy at her foe. Her strike wrenched the face of the enemy ship downward, sending the beam slicing toward the open and crumbling cavern below.

She fought to maintain her concentration through the strain. Her power faltered, and she felt herself begin to fall backward. Suddenly, she felt her perspective forcefully shifted from ship to bridge. Futilely, she tried to catch herself stumbling onto the walkway in front of Jackson. His hands slipped under her shoulders as he dove to catch her. Battling her fatigue, she struggled to sit up.

A warning lit up the screen beside Morgan. "Really!?!" He exclaimed in frustration.

"Report, Threaux!" Jackson shouted at him.

Morgan shifted his eyes back to the primary interface, one hand skittering across the hard boards, "Enemy ship took direct hit. It caused the beam weapon to fire into the planet." Morgan scanned the feeds, "Looks like they are adjusting course."

Kensy clutched onto Jackson's arms as she pulled herself to her feet, "I can finish them off. I just need one more good shot." She extended her hand toward the beam. Jackson tugged her back into his hold. She looked up at him confused, "I have to stop them from hurting anyone else! Let go of me!"

He scowled at her, "You won't help anyone by going back into that beam." He glanced past her, "Threaux—."

"Enemy preparing for jump." Morgan frantically examined the battle space, "But we have bigger problems.... The planet is destabilizing. Rapidly."

Jackson kept one arm wrapped across the front of Kensy's shoulders as he barred her from the beam, "Get us out of here!" he yelled down at his pilot.

"Where?" Morgan deftly swung the ship around a geyser of lava as it ruptured the surface violently. A blast of stone and gas launched into the sky, sundering a ship approaching from the aft. The very air trembled with the gathering pressure and heat.

"Anywhere but here! Now, Threaux!" Jackson ordered. Morgan pointed the fore of ship toward the stars and slammed the gyros ahead as hard as he could. In a flash of light the ship leapt into the vastness of space and away from the deteriorating world of Rosealleon. The plasma of the virtual controls burned against his palms for a moment. He released them and the ship decelerated gently, gliding through the blackness.

Morgan placed both hands on his head and breathed a deep sigh of relief. He spun his chair around toward his captains, "So, I take it you had to kick the hornet's nest and then shit went sideways." He leaned against one arm of his chair, one eyebrow cocked in anticipation of a response.

Kensy slumped against Jackson, her eyes cast downward as she stared off into nothingness, "All those people... lost. Gone forever."

Jackson relaxed his hold, "From what we saw down there, I think they were lost a long time ago. There was nothing we could do for them. The best we could do is let them rest free of those machines. And we gave them that." Silently, Kensy glanced at him with pleading eyes. "Yeah, I know. Doesn't make for much of a victory," Jackson stood, letting Kensy rest where she sat. "Threaux, find out where we are. And bring the ship down to yellow alert for now. Until we know more, we are gonna sit tight." He glanced down toward Kensy, "You should go get some rest. It has been a long enough day."

She huffed in defeat, "I'm too tired to argue." He helped her to her feet. She wavered for a moment as she got her bearings. She hesitated, catching a glimpse of the weariness in his eyes.

"Something wrong?" he inquired as he noticed her trepidation.

She shook her head, "Just a little wobbly. Mind walking me part way?"

Daniel sauntered out of the corridor. "Crisis averted for now. I can handle things here. Why don't you two make a pit-stop by medical before retiring for the night?" He pointed down toward Morgan, "You too, Threaux. Consider this shift change. Go get some rest."

Morgan sprang out of his seat and jogged up the stairs, "Don't have to tell me twice!"

Daniel rolled his eyes and sauntered down toward the pilot's seat. Jackson shrugged, "First officer's orders, I suppose." Kensy cracked a fatigued smile and leaned against Jackson for stability. "But seriously, are you okay? Seemed like... maybe you were taking some of those hits."

Kensy took a mental inventory of herself for the first time, "I don't think I'm hurt. But I could feel it. Like the ship was an extension of myself. It's hard to explain." She straightened her posture, letting go of him, "When I'm in the beam, it's like I *am* the ship."

"Whatever happened back there, those were some pretty wicked fireworks." He shot a careful glance down toward her as they walked. Her steps were uneven and staggered.

She looked down at her hands, "I did what I had to. I only wish I could have done more."

He stuffed his hands in his pockets, "That kind of thinking is what gets you into trouble. I thought you were gonna take it a little easier after our last little talk."

Kensy rubbed at her bruised shoulder and looked away, "Yeah, well... old habits."

He raised his chin, "Guess then the rest of us are just gonna have to step up our game." She blinked, a bit taken aback by his phrasing. She looked up at him as he confidently strode forward. He spoke the words as if it was no more difficult than that. Casually, she turned her gaze aside. A faint flutter filled her chest as her mind churned through the feelings of reassurance, uncertainty, and curiosity.

As they entered the operations center, all was quiet save for the soft hums and chirps of the consoles. Jackson and Kensy glanced over the standing crew. Men and women stood in silent respect for a moment. With respectful nods, they slowly sat back down and returned to work. Jackson nodded back. Kensy watched, confused by the exchange. With the command console retracted, the two captains proceeded straight toward the elevator. The doors closed behind them.

Jackson broke the stillness, "New ship, new mission, new command, and we survived our first major battle." He paused, "They were saying *thank you.*"

Kensy wobbled the toe of her right boot against the floor, "We didn't *all* survive, did we?" Her thoughts drifted to Malek and Daily. "We all walked into that mess and we didn't all walk out. And *I*.... We couldn't even bring Malek back. I pitched him off that ledge like it was the only option." She bit at her lip.

"That place back there... it was a battlefield. You did what you had to. We all did. That *thing*... that wasn't Malek anymore." Jackson placed a firm hand on her shoulder.

Her lip quivered as she thought on his words, "Maybe you're right. But it doesn't make them any less gone. Everywhere I go...," she looked down at the ground. "Funny thing. I could almost swear when I sent him flying that I heard him say something... thanks."

Softly, he responded, "I believe it." Kensy looked up as he continued, "From what I knew of the man, he would have wanted someone to end it if he couldn't. He was a fighter. He knew the risks. We all do. The men and women of this ship are here because they each have something in their lives worth fighting for. Loved ones. Dreams. Hopes. Duty. Every path led to this mission for one reason or another. The best we can do is to keep going. Every breath taken between now and the end of our lives is a victory as long as we keep moving forward."

"Well, then...," she turned her eyes to meet his and gave a gentle nod.

Chapter 42

Restless

"Not sure if I should be worried or jealous, the captains are taking a late night walk together...."
~ Crewman J. Kakigori

Kensy stumbled through the darkness. The terrain below her feet was rugged and treacherous. Her eyes turned upward, drawn by a single beam of light as it pierced the abyss before her. It fell upon a haggard form. The figure's arms were bound across a high metallic bar that stretched into nothingness. The head hung down, her ebony locks falling over her in sickly glistening clumps. A dark viscous liquid poured over her shape from elsewhere. It soaked into her tattered Psicorp uniform and dripped from her bare feet. Kensy's eyes widened as she beheld the broken visage of Elle.

A sickly yellow light rose from below, illuminating the ground around Kensy's patent leather boots. Little by little, the jagged floor took shape. The lines of scattered bones and hollow skulls became visible. Kensy stumbled again as her eyes searched for a way out. She could feel her heartbeat rising in her ears as it beat more and more furiously. The sound of skittering metallic legs echoed from the darkness. Her eyes darted from side to side, trying to pinpoint the source of the sound.

Slowly, an inky black shadow crept over her from behind. The grotesque razor points were all too familiar. Reactively, she brought her psionic blade into form as she spun around, catching one of its sharp, spidery arms in an attempt to stab down at her. Her blade hummed under the pressure of holding her attacker at bay only inches above her head. Sparks showered down upon her vibrant plum uniform top. She heard the whine of the drill-like heads as several mechanical tentacles emerged from the monstrosity before her. She thrust her sword in an arc, tossing aside the piercing arm.

She began backing up as the arms stabbed toward her again and again. She parried the blows as flashes of energy burst from the points of contact. Dust and bone chips were cast into the air with the spin of each drill head as they narrowly missed her lithe form and crashed into the osseous ground. Kensy had precious little time to think as she defended against her colossal foe. The echoes of aberrant chittering surrounded her again. The sound encroached upon her, but the source was still unseen. Again, her heartbeat intensified.

Feeling cornered, she stopped. The towering form of her attacker reared back with all of its arms for one massive strike against her. She closed her eyes and clasped her sword hilt in front of her face with the blade pointed down. Under her breath, she recited an ancient prayer in a language that had not crossed her lips in many years. The creature began to descend upon her, as if in slow motion. The fog of power poured from her lips as the prayer continued. It gathered upon the length of the blade like faerie dust, glittering and brilliant.

Without opening her eyes, she plunged the blade into the ground. Everything started to shake with a gathering intensity until the very ground beneath her began to crumble and peel away. The final word of prayer crossed her lips and her eyes opened. A pulse of energy traveled down her sword. As it hit the ground, a shock wave rippled out from her, pushing her enemies away.

Kneeling, she swiveled her body away from the colossus. She wrenched the sword out of the ground, using her own body as a fulcrum. A razor sharp wall of purplish light emanated from the gash in the blackened surface and rose up, sundering the creature completely. Her blade arced over her body and slammed into the ground. The light trailed behind it and faded as it broke against the darkness like a dashed wave.

Everything slowly faded as she knelt in place, catching her breath. She was left in stillness on a glassy black surface. Hesitantly, she turned her gaze upward again. There in the darkness still hung Elle, drenched and tattered. A voice emanated from her that was foreign and cold, "This data will be analyzed and integrated...."

Suddenly, Kensy looked down at her hands. A warmth and pressure seized them, whisking her out of darkness. Her breath felt pressed from her lungs. She gasped and sprung upright in her bed. She stared down at her clenched fists, disoriented. Two strong, familiar hands enveloped them. She glanced up at Jackson's stern gaze.

She turned her head. There in the doorway stood Daniel, hand still on the dampening control. Kensy glanced between them, "Uh, what—."

"...was that all about?" Jackson interjected.

Kensy sighed, "Just another bad dream." She exhaled and leaned forward, resting her forehead against his hands. She relaxed. He drew away one of his hands and used it to smooth her hair down gently. Jackson subtly nodded for Daniel to leave. With a quiet acknowledgment, he turned and departed, leaving the pair alone in the stillness of the room. Kensy lifted her head slightly, "What did I do this time?"

Jackson placed his free hand down on the bed beside her, "Maggie notified us that your pulse was too high and that her attempts to wake you were unsuccessful. Then, as we were about to enter your room, there was a burst that shook the whole deck." Kensy pulled up her knees and buried her face in her arms. "No damage, it just shook the furniture," he reassured her. She grumbled into her arms. Jackson raised an eyebrow, "What was that? I don't speak mumble."

She glanced up at him incredulously, "I said, why can't I let the dead rest?"

"Another dream about your friend?" he inquired.

She shook her head in affirmation and let her legs slide back under the wrinkled covers. "I don't get it. It's almost like she's trying to tell me something. But...."

All of the sudden Jackson became very aware of his proximity to her. He had sat down beside her to wake her, but now it felt so close. His right arm arced over her legs and rested on the comforter to hold him up. Her strawberry blonde hair cascaded past her shoulders, curling gently against her satin nightgown. He stared at her lips for a moment. He took a slow and carefully measured breath, "But?"

Kensy shook her head. Her eyes scoured the stars that danced outside the overhead window. She dropped her gaze, "I don't know. What I saw this time was... different. She looked broken. And when she finally did speak, the voice was not her own." She shrugged. They sat in the quiet for a moment, each contemplating what to say next. Kensy bit at her lower lip pensively, "You know, I don't think I'm gonna be able to sleep for a little bit. I might go for a walk." He nodded and folded his hands together over his knees. "You want to come with me?" she cautiously asked. "We might not get mugged this time."

He fought the urge to smile, "Yeah, sure. I could do that. Just give me a minute to throw something different on."

For the first time, she realized that he sat before her in nothing more than his pajama pants. Her face flushed red as her attention was drawn to his tan, muscular chest and arms. She stammered as she tried to gather her thoughts, "Uh–Of course." She gave a nervous half laugh.

"I'll meet you in the foyer," he cracked a discrete smile as he rose from her bed and headed for the door. Kensy nodded as she watched him go. The door slid shut. She exhaled in relief, planting her hands on her face. "Aaah!" Combing her fingers through her hair, she chastised herself, "You are ridiculous!" She leapt out of bed and headed for her closet. Pushing the door aside, she began sifting through her wardrobe. "We might not get mugged this time...." She derided herself in a mocking tone, drew the pieces of an outfit from their resting places, and began to change. "Really? You had to revisit that one?"

She took a deep breath as she finished dressing. Glancing to the side mirror, she inspected herself. Her loose-fitting peridot shirt had always been a favorite. Complimented by a pair of straight-legged khaki pants and strappy sandals, she was comfortable, but perhaps a bit overdressed for a simple walk. She scoffed at herself and closed the closet.

Kensy smoothed the front of her shirt down and took a deep breath before stepping out of the room. Her eyes darted toward Jackson's door as it slid open. He stepped out in dark jeans, a plain gray long-sleeved shirt with the cuffs pushed up, and casual hiking boots. At the right side of his belt sat the palm-sized clip of metal and leather that she had taken note of before. She tucked a stray lock of hair behind her ear, "Mind if I ask?" She pointed to the clip, "You almost always wear it but it's not a part of the uniform...."

Jackson ran his hand over it, "It was my older brother's a long time ago. Now it's just a memento." Jackson leaned against the side of the elevator housing as they waited. "What about you? Have any little fragments of the past that you carry around?"

Kensy shook her head, "Nah. Just scars and memories. They weigh enough."

"I hear that," the lift door slid open and allowed them entry. "Well, where to?"

Kensy contemplated for a moment, "Maggie, are our new friends awake?"

"Yes, they are getting settled into a lab space on one of the central decks until accommodations can be made. Would you like to proceed to their location?" Maggie's mechanical voice answered.

"Sounds like a fabulous idea," Kensy glanced to Jackson.

He shrugged, "I'm just along for the walk."

The lights passed by as the elevator descended to the appropriate floor. Kensy clasped her hands behind her back and leaned against the wall, "Do you still have reservations about them?"

"It doesn't matter. They are here now. We'll see where things go from here." He crossed his arms. "If you recall, it took me a bit to warm up to you, too. It's nothing personal. I'd just rather be careful than regretful."

Kensy tilted head to the side for a moment, "That's fair enough." The doors opened. Leisurely, they strolled out into the halls. Following Maggie's directions, they meandered toward the lab. As Kensy raised a hand to knock, the doors opened. There, floating in the center of the threshold, a spherical robot flitted about as it examined the approaching captains. An iris like aperture adjusted back and forth with a subtle whine. A voice from farther in the room chirped at the construct. It turned and flew toward the sound.

Kensy and Jackson stepped forward warily. Rauk turned his head toward the movement, "Ah, come in." He rose to his feet and meticulously began to unplug a number of chords and cables from his left arm. Beside him on a small ladder stood Kigh chittering away at the small robot. The two captains glanced around at the chaotically ordered room. Crates, parts, and pieces littered the entire area. Rauk lumbered forward, reaching out with one massive hand to shift one of the larger piles aside, "Please, come in."

Kensy ran her fingers over the edge of a nearby box, "Did we have all of this stored in here? We can get it moved...." She glanced toward Jackson as she spoke.

Rauk waved her off, "Oh, it's fine. Some of the crates were shuffled, but we'll get it cleaned up. Kigh likes to organize.

Then we'll see what we can do to be of service to you." Jackson shot him a questioning glance. Rauk shifted toward the back wall again and slumped down in his spot, "Before, I did not have the opportunity to thank you for your aid. If you need anything of us, just ask."

"I am just glad you made it out of that place. No one deserves that." Kensy smiled sheepishly. "I must admit, I was unsure of what to expect when we ran across your small friend in that cavern. I have never encountered one of your people before."

Rauk nodded in amusement, "You perhaps expected my intellect to be inversely proportional to my size." He let out a hearty laugh, "Most do regardless of species. A perception I have used to my own advantage many times before. There is no harm done. You helped, that is what matters." Carefully he began plugging the cables back into his arm. "I am zog. We originally came from the planet Kedag, a very long ways away. Kigh is a malckiev from somewhere past... Nosdan, no Rasktir." Kigh scurried back and forth, organizing the debris while they talked. Rauk raised one finger and pointed at the hovering ball that trailed behind his companion, "And that is Gizmo, he came from Kigh's imagination."

Kensy snickered. She cleared her throat, "Well, let me formally introduce myself, I am Psilyria Kensy Frost. And this...," she held out one hand toward Jackson as she hopped up and sat on one of the crates, "is Commander Jackson Gabel. We are the captains of this ship."

Rauk bowed his head in respect, "It is an honor. I am Rauk Draugkgern and you have met Kigh'Lehken."

Jackson leaned his shoulder against one of the taller boxes, "What were you doing out here?"

"Salvage. Humans are known for their propensity to create and abandon when things go wrong. We figured even with the competition, it would be a profitable venture. We'd been working out of a nearby sector for several months. We got a call asking for some engine parts, so we went to check it out." He shook his head. "That whole place just felt wrong. When we brought them the parts and offered to do the repair work for them, they became... weird."

Jackson crossed his arms, "Is that the technical term for it?" Kensy shot him a concerned glare. He shrugged and turned his attention back to their guests.

Rauk smirked at the comment, "In this case, yes." His expression became serious once again. "We went into some kind of mining compound. There were strange machines waiting for us. They seemed to come out of the walls. I unfortunately don't remember much else until I came to in that cave."

Kigh ran up to Jackson and Kensy, "Yes, yes. You help Kigh. Save Rauk. Ship-talky-lady-voice give Kigh tools for to fiddle-fix Gizmo. Kigh, thank you much, much." His big eyes darted between them for a moment before Gizmo's whirling distracted him again. He scampered back to his task, all the while chattering at his robot in his native tongue.

"They took many pieces from my augments but you recovered the last of my core components and for that, I am grateful. Once Kigh has my other systems repaired, I will be at your service. I owe you a debt which I *will* repay."

Jackson furrowed his brow, "How do you intend to do that?"

"I know how to dismantle and repair a decent range of techs. And I suspect that if you are investigating the source of Rosealleon's apparent infestation, you will face many battles ahead. I will fight for you to see such an enemy felled." Rauk stared back at him with an honest intensity. "My strength will be yours."

Kensy hopped up from her seat, "First things first. See that you recover." She smiled. "Now if you'll excuse us," she looked to Jackson, "We have a walk to finish." Rauk nodded to them as Kigh peeked out to wave and became buried in a shifting pile of parts. The gentle giant scooped his hand into the pile and lifted his small friend out of the mess.

Jackson shook his head at the duo and pivoted around to follow Kensy from the room, "Where to now?"

"How about—," she tried to turn to face him as she walked ahead. Her heel caught against the floor mid step. Instinctively, he reached out snatching her hand from the air. He pulled her up, keeping her from the fall. The redirected momentum brought their bodies together. There was a catch in her breath as she reeled from the experience. "Thanks," she whispered. Nervous giggles bubbled out of her, "Evidently I need different shoes."

He stepped back and looked down at her sandals. "Probably a good idea," he replied. A soft, genuine smile crept across his face. Her gentle laugh resonated through him. "Come on. You can plot a new course while you change your shoes."

Chapter 43

Pieces

*"The Illusive was so aptly named that the truth of her
existence has eluded historians for decades."*
~ Aepexian Historian J. Zeratech

Kensy leaned forward over the war room table, staring down at the warped hull plate she had retrieved from the Rosealleon crash site. The Illusive. The name alone conjured a thousand questions. Legends had spawned from the rumors of its existence. Ghost stories swirled through settlements and outposts of the mysterious ship's activities. And the truth of it all sat before her now. On either side of the metal placard, the holographic interface of the table encased the black box and datapad of the ship's log files. The data streamed across a curtain of virtual screens as she zoned out.

With a soft whoosh, the doors to the war room opened. Jackson strode in leisurely, his uniform in perfect order. "You're up early." He paused, "You did get some sleep after our walk, right?!"

She pushed back from the table as he circled toward her, "Some. Turns out having wicked nightmares about dead friends is a little unsettling, even after late night strolls through an alien ship with good company and a few laughs." She crossed her arms and smirked at him with tired eyes.

"Everything okay?" he gently pried.

Her eyelids fluttered wearily as she looked back toward the collection on the table before her, "It was just a restless night."

With one deep, intentionally slow breath, she placed her right hand on her hip and thrummed her nails against the table with the other hand. "Something is nagging at me. The source of all this chaos...," she stopped for a moment to collect her thoughts, "That slimy little mayor mentioned a, title? The Vagabond. And then when we faced down Malek, he spoke as if there was a secondary consciousness controlling him. He mentioned me standing against him on Bhelnir. I've been trying to piece together who or what it is, but I don't think we have enough pieces yet."

Jackson rested both palms against the edge of the table, "How so? Lay it out for me." The doors whooshed again. Daniel and Allen quietly stepped into the darkened room amidst the captains' conversation.

"Well," Kensy searched for her starting point, "First, this." She tapped the air over the items on the table with an open hand. "The Illusive was a smuggling ship that was in service starting June of 547 according to the plate and everything I could track down. It was operational for almost exactly one-hundred years until it responded to a pickup call at a station, here." She called up a holographic astrogation chart over the center table. "Now this is where things get weird."

"Mystery smuggling ship operates for a hundred years before things get weird? That's a pretty good run." Daniel noted.

"Logs state that it docks with the station for about an hour. Then undocks, departs, and is entered as 'no contact' in the main ledger." Her fingers busily danced over the table controls as she spoke.

Allen rubbed his chin thoughtfully, "Could have been a small pickup, or a person, that they wanted to keep off the books."

Kensy tipped her head to the side, "Maybe, but three days later...." She hit a small icon beside her hand. In place of the astrogation chart, a window popped up. Everyone redirected their attention to the screams that emanated from the visual log playing before them. Pieces of the images flickered in and out, fragmenting as the computer tried to reconcile the data. Bloodied fingers reached toward the camera desperately. A harsh mechanical chord rang out, and the feed ended. "I believe everyone on that ship perished, and that was their final moments. I think they picked up more than they bargained for on that station."

"So they got hijacked?" Jackson asked.

"Not exactly. The computer wasn't accessed again until I downloaded these files. But two days after that last log, the black box registered a terminal descent into atmosphere. The ship crashed on Rosealleon June 647."

"Any chance someone could have walked away? We didn't find any bodies, or parts, that I can recall." Jackson stood up straight and folded his arms.

"Not with my understanding of physics. But whatever killed the crew of the Illusive made it to Rosealleon. Missing person cases filed after that jump up dramatically until 662 when more than a hundred-and-fifty people vanished in six months. Rosealleon then blamed the Terra Ascension Core for the mining incident that supposedly caused mass hallucinations. The resulting investigation incited panic in the population, and they seceded from the Ascension."

Jackson began to sway in place as he followed the pieces in his mind, "Okay. So how do we get to Vagabond? *What* do you think Vagabond is? And what pieces aren't fitting?"

She tilted her head down, "I can't figure out what exactly the Illusive could have encountered on that station that...," she began counting out her points on her fingers, "boarded their ship without them knowing, wiped them out without showing itself in the visual log, managed to survive the crash on Rosealleon, and then bided its time for fifteen years before turning an entire colony into a bunch of mindless thugs."

Daniel put up a hand as he processed the information, "It might not have been all at once. The missing persons could have been whoever it was recovering and recruiting. When he had enough to influence the whole, he cleared the board of outside influences."

Allen nodded in agreement, "After that, the colony would be a great place to set up production facilities without drawing attention. I managed a glimpse of Lieutenant Rasken's scans of that chamber you found our new friends in. Looked like they had been experimenting for some time, trying to perfect the tech. Probably the same place that made the machines that attacked Bhelnir and Morwhex Four."

"I was afraid of that." Kensy shook her head, "I don't think they have it down yet. The control is still imperfect. Back on Rosealleon during our initial recon, Neira and I were being followed, so I tried to seduce the guard—."

"What?!" Jackson blurted out. The three men stared at her with various looks of surprise.

Kensy waved the shock away, "Neira's idea... to lure him into an alley where she could incapacitate him. Beside the point. No amount of seducing would have worked if he was just an automaton." She continued, "Then even after they... changed Daily and Malek, both retained little *bits* of who they were." She waved a finger toward the back of her neck, "Those little bug bots seemed to be the key to making everyone into thralls."

"Thralls," Daniel nodded, "that's a good name for them."

"So on Bhelnir, I fight machines built most likely on Rosealleon. We get to Rosealleon and hear the mayor say, 'The Vagabond wants them and he will get what he wants.' to Daily. So he isn't the one in charge, this Vagabond figure is. Malek attacks us the same way the colonists reported being attacked over fifty years ago, with metal coils coming out of the walls, almost killing Neira...." she choked on the words as they formed in her throat.

"Not almost. Did." A voice called from a side door in a raspy tone. Neira slowly meandered toward the group, rubbing the side of her bruised neck. She held up one finger to halt any questions or reprimands, "Lazarus Collar on my armor. Let's not go there. And, no, I will not go back down to medical to wallow in misery." She looked sternly toward Kensy, "Continue."

Kensy took a deep breath, "Anyway. He talks all about Bhelnir as if he was there, as if he had seen me before. We know, whoever this guy is, that he likes his tech. I also felt a strong psionic presence both on Bhelnir and Rosealleon. But to have orchestrated all of this he would have to be either very old or a group of people spanning generations."

"You think the same person or thing that ended the Illusive's career is the same thing that is now being called the Vagabond?" Jackson questioned.

"Out of curiosity, I looked back at the original message the Illusive received from the station over seventy-two years ago. It's signed V." Kensy slid the transmission file toward him. "I looked for some evidence of a change in behavior that would signify a different controller at the helm, but every place that presence goes, it consumes the people that it comes into contact with. Whoever is behind this seems to have been there from the start."

"Great, more breadcrumbs," Neira groaned.

"I think our best bet is to back trace this thing, find out where it originated, but...," Kensy sighed.

"But...," Jackson gently pried.

"But there is a possibility that whatever overtook the Illusive could still have a presence on the station. I'm spit-balling theories here based on rough data. Just docking with that station could be a danger." She shrugged and leaned back onto the tabletop.

"Alright then. The DeCadejra stays at a safe distance away. We take a small ground team in a shuttle to investigate the station. We go in full evo-suits. Do a drift over, that way there is no direct contact with the ship. We can keep the risk localized and before returning, DeCadejra runs every scan and test in her data banks until we know it is safe to come back." Jackson proposed.

"That seems doable," Daniel affirmed.

"I've already sent the coordinates to Morgan. We should be there in a few hours." Kensy glanced between her collaborators.

"Then it seems we have work to do. I'll go get the evo-suits prepped for use." Allen turned away as he waved to the others.

Daniel followed suit, "And I'll go line up the shuttle."

Neira turned toward Kensy, "Guess I'll go dig up what I can on this crazy station, or Vagabond, or whatever. It'll give me something to do." She grunted as she started to move again.

"Are you okay?" Kensy asked softly.

"Doc fused all the fractures but says the rest will just take time." Neira rolled her eyes, "If I have to stare at those sterile white walls any longer I may throttle someone."

Kensy shook her head, "Just take it easy, please."

"Pot. Kettle. Black." Neira called over her shoulder as she departed the war room.

Kensy smirked and slumped down on a nearby bench. She crossed her legs at the knees. Her patent leather boots glistened in the low light. She ran her right hand down the tails of her plum Psicorp uniform top, smoothing it against the charcoal slacks that tucked into the top of her boots. Jackson sauntered over and sat down beside her. "I don't know what we are walking into here."

Jackson shrugged, "Seems to be the standard. Bhelnir, Morwhex, Pluto, Rosealleon...."

"Yeah, I guess." She leaned her head against his shoulder. "Do you think anyone's left on that station?"

"After seventy-some-odd years? Everyone on-board would be close to a century. Probably a nursing home by now, lots of senile old people running around in walkers," he jested. She giggled at the thought. They sat in the quiet for a long while, just letting the moments tick by.

Kensy lifted her head and sighed heavily. She rose from the bench reluctantly, then felt a gentle tug at her hand. She swiveled her head around as Jackson rose to his feet. "I have a request." She shifted to face him. "Please stay behind on this one." His eyes pleaded with her.

"What? Why?!" Kensy asked in a hushed yell.

"Can you guarantee me that you have completely recovered from Rosealleon? You tapped out in the cavern. You *fell* out of the beam." Kensy cast her eyes away from him as he spoke. "Sit this one out. Just this once. Give yourself that at least. We'll stay in radio contact. You'll be aware of everything that is going on. And if, when, something unexpected does happen, you'll be in command of an entire warship to fix it." He gently squeezed her hand, "Please."

Reluctantly she nodded, "Fine. But just this once!" With that, he patted her on the shoulder and quietly drifted out of the room. She huffed in frustration. Closing her eyes, she began reasoning to herself, *He's right. You know he is. You can't keep flaking out on the team. Rest, recover, and be better next time!*

Chapter 44

Abandoned

"Well this place isn't ominous at all ...."
~ Ensign Ashar Kyo

Kensy paced anxiously across the floor of the bridgehead, her eyes fixed on the virtual windows that filled the forward walls. She watched as the small silhouette of a shuttle neared the eerily still space station that drifted ahead. Trying to ignore his overly fidgety captain, Morgan focused on the readouts that streamed over his hardboard controls. Daniel stood at the top of the stairs, alongside the beam entrance, calmly observing. She glanced up at him, "I'm still not clear on why you aren't piloting the shuttle."

He smiled, "I made sure they're in good hands. And I'm needed here more."

Kensy furrowed her brow and turned back to the windows as Jackson's voice called over the comm, "Alright we are in proximity. Going to head over and see if we can override the airlock controls." Kensy stopped and watched, her every nerve on edge. "Got it. Looks like we're in. No signs of movement so far. Power is off station-wide. Atmospheric readings are minimal. Keeping comms open from here on in." Jackson glanced down at the distressed metallic plates that lined the hall before him. With a flick of his wrist, he turned the control on his sleek environmental suit's belt. Gently, he sunk toward the floor of the station until his boots met with the walkway. "Personal gravity field activated."

Jackson looked back over his shoulder as the rest of his team entered the station behind him. "Let's shed some light on the situation, shall we, people?" Rasken cracked with a smirk. Kyo rolled his eyes and switched on his suit lights. Reily floated past the others before activating her gravity generator. Carefully, she peered through a large observation panel into the office beyond.

"See anything?" Shane asked.

Reily turned around and pointed upward, "Freeze-dried coffee spots on the ceiling. No one has been here for a very long time." She pulled her rifle forward to double check it.

"How do you know it's coffee? Could be anything," Wright strode up beside her.

She lifted an eyebrow as she gave him a fleeting glance, "Empty mug locked down to the desk... Instant Human: Just add coffee. Just guessing they weren't tea drinkers."

"I'm sure the fact that they were coffee drinkers is really gonna to change everything. Now can we find out where these people went? Let's focus on the mission." Jackson moved up toward the first security door. He leaned down to examine the door's mechanisms. With the slightest pressure, the lock's housing shattered, allowing the door to waft freely from its place. "First security door passed. Keep your eyes open, people." He steeled himself and pushed forward, "There are extensive signs of material fatigue in the entry area. Pushing further in." An ominous moan of metal echoed around the company as they proceeded.

One room at a time, they inspected the lay of the space station. Every room and hall seemed much the same: abandoned and cold. They reconvened at the entrance to the administration offices. "I don't get it, Commander, everything was just left. There are personal effects all over the place. If they bailed on this place, I would think it might have been important to take their photos or kids' artwork. Something is definitely wrong with this place." Rasken surmised, a hint of disquiet slipping into her voice.

Reily moved up along one of the walls, and began slowing walking forward her eyes trained toward the ground. "I can't say I disagree...," Jackson glanced toward Reily questioningly, "but we've found no evidence...." He furrowed his brow as he continued to watch her inch down the hallway.

Cautiously Wright shuffled toward her, "Reily? You got something?"

"Yeah...," she absent-mindedly responded, "maybe... something...." Everyone watched in silence. She slowly headed around a corner. Wright trailed a few paces behind. Watching. Waiting. She descended down a short jog of steps and froze. Kneeling down, she zoomed her scanner in. "Commander...," she called out. Slowly, she backed up the stairs again, some small discovery cradled in the palm of her suit glove.

Jackson took a few brisk strides toward her. She spoke up again, "I wasn't totally sure what I was seeing. My scanner is picking up degraded biological traces in the seams." She pointed to where the floor met the wall. "And then there's this." She opened her fingers, revealing two discolored, semi-translucent slivers. "They were embedded in one of the stairs. First signs of a struggle. Someone was either trying to claw their way up the stairs or was being dragged down them."

Jackson inhaled sharply. He turned to the others, "All right. We are heading down to the next level. Stay together. Keep your eyes peeled for more clues. This generation of stations should have a generator room close by. We'll see if we can bring it online, get a bit stronger sensors at our disposal. Move out." The team closed ranks. As they began to maneuver toward the stairs, every footfall was announced with a moan of structural stress.

Morgan slammed the mute button and spun around, "Stop! Just stop!" His agitated stare fired back at Kensy.

"There is nobody home over there. So chill out and stop pacing behind me."

Kensy reactively shrunk back from him, "Sorry." She inhaled deeply, pivoting toward the curving stair that lead to the beam entrance. At the top, she stopped and placed both hands on the railing. She closed her eyes as she fought against the knot in her stomach.

"It's okay," Daniel reassured her.

She turned her head toward him, "I have a really bad feeling about this and my intuition usually doesn't miss the mark. I just can't put my finger on it from here. I should be with them."

"DeCadejra, are you still receiving? We heard something loud then it went silent." Jackson paused and leaned back against the wall for a moment.

Morgan unmuted the comm, "Everything is hunky-dory here, just dropped something on my control panel."

Jackson shook his head in exasperation, "Threaux, try not to spill crap on the controls of the priceless alien warship we've been given. You don't have a large enough paycheck to replace it."

"No promises, boss. They did tell me to make myself at home." Morgan snarkily retorted.

Kensy used her nahdvi to mute them again, "Thank you, Lieutenant."

"I didn't do it for you. You won't write me up for sassing a commanding officer. Gabel would. Without a second thought. Everything is black and white to that guy." He glared at the mute button until the small red light disappeared from it, then turned his attention back to the readouts.

Jackson entered the main corridor with his rifle at the ready as he scanned for any signs of movement. Darkness clung to the walls in stained, streaking hand-prints. He turned his eyes toward a mangled door that hung weightlessly at the entrance of the generator room. Very carefully, he reached out toward it and pulled. It effortlessly glided into the hall in front of him. He guided it free of their path and let it drift.

Wright and Reily slipped past him into the room and began to search. They followed a trail of darkened smears toward the main controls. Wright turned to double check behind them for but a moment when suddenly Reily let slip an abbreviated shriek. Alarm ran down the spine of each and every person. Wright snapped back to the front and exhaled in relief. "We're good. Got a little startled by one of the original denizens."

Jackson moved swiftly toward them as the others fanned out across the room, "You found someone?!"

Wright moved up toward the frozen and withered corpse that lay before them. "Yeah, there's not much to look at, though."

Jackson rounded the corner beside the rattled Reily. "That is freakin' nasty," she muttered as she turned away. Jackson beheld the gruesome sight and subtly nodded in agreement.

"Commander, please talk to us," Kensy politely called to him.

It was good to hear her voice in his ear. Silently, he was thankful that she was safely back on the ship. He crouched down beside the body to inspect it more closely. "Looks like this guy was having a very bad day. Lots of visible trauma on the body. Poor sap was probably bleeding out before he got to this sad state. From the positioning, I would say he dragged himself in to the control and pulled it before the atmosphere and gravity were lost. The body is thoroughly dehydrated and frozen solid, hand still on the kill switch," he surmised for her.

"Guy probably figured he'd take whoever did this to him down with him." Wright hypothesized.

Kensy switched her nahdvi to only broadcast to her fellow captain. "Jack, I don't like this. What if that station is off for a reason?" she whispered to him.

He tilted his head down as he quietly replied, "That's a chance I think we have to take. If there is a possibility to learn something more here...," He glanced up to Wright and nodded. "Trust me."

"Sorry, bud," Wright apologized to the frozen husk. He peeled the hand off the switch, shattering it. Firmly grabbing the bar himself, he slammed the safety forward. The generators sputtered for a few seconds before firing up into a full roar. Energy crackled across long, cold conduits until it found a way to the environmental systems. Lights flickered to life throughout the station.

"Hey, boss. That brought the servers up across the hall. I'm gonna start digging into the mainframe." Reily stated with renewed purpose, "By the way, got another three nasty-ass ice cubes over here."

"Just because Hensley isn't here to do it, I have to ask. Did you girly scream at them, too?" Kyo chimed over the comm to her.

In an unamused, tone Reily flatly replied, "I will kick your ass."

Wright smiled at the exchange, "I have ten on Reily."

Jackson stood back up, "Enough with the comedy. We have a job to do."

"Um, Commander, ...about that...," Rasken nervously beckoned, "I found the rest of the staff." Jackson stepped over the body and headed down the bank of generators toward the lieutenant. She stood at the edge of the room. Beyond her boots, massive limbs of twisted metal curled into the hollowed out center of the station. Dozens of frozen figures decorated the wreckage with various haphazard mechanical components disfiguring each of them. Vacant eyes stared out into nothingness from partially shattered skulls. The light of her scanner orb flashed from her hand. Clutching it tightly, she murmured, "What the hell happened here?"

A blaring alarm sounded at Morgan's side as warnings lit up his screens. Mumbled and mashed together expletives crossed his lips in an almost undiscernable fashion. "Get out of there now!" He yelled over the comm.

Jackson turned away from the hideous display, "Threaux, what is going on?"

"Get out now!" he yelled again, "The generators jump started an old detonation sequence. The station is gonna be dust shortly. And so will everyone else if you don't haul ass out of there." His hands frantically danced over the controls as he brought up every defensive countermeasure he could find.

The station team looked at each other for a brief moment, as if to confirm what they had all heard. Wright glanced down at the lever, "I am going to shut it back off." He grasped it and attempted to wrench it back into the original position. It resisted until... snap! Just above the pivot point, the handle splintered apart. "Damn it! The kill switch broke. I can't shut it off. Maybe we can short out the power junction—."

"No!" Kensy piped up, "If there is enough juice in the system already, with the degradation that place has seen, you could detonate it early or cause a million other problems. Just get out of there!" Kensy looked up toward the beam.

Daniel stepped between her and the entrance point, "No. There is enough at risk right now without you jumping into the fire." Kensy anxiously looked back to the virtual windows and the small shuttle that rested just outside the station. She bit at her lower lip as she counted the seconds. "We all do what we have to," she said under her breath.

Jackson stopped himself at the doorjamb of the adjacent room and shouted, "Reily! Evac, now!"

"Well then...," she gripped the drive she had been fussing with and wrenched. Sparks showered the air between them as the connections ripped free. She darted toward him with the component curled in her arm. Upon reaching the door, she turned her gravity generator off and launched herself down the hall like a shot. She turned her generator back on at the base of the stairs and joined the rest of her team. Their boots thundered against the flooring as they raced toward the entrance they had come through.

Jackson trailed just behind Reily as he urged them through the maze of offices and corridors on the main level. Popping sounds echoed toward them as long dormant pipes became pressurized and ruptured. A bulkhead in their path began to close. Kyo noticed the shift of movement as he ran. His eyes darted about, looking for a solution. Suddenly, he skidded to a stop in front of a nearby office door. He kicked with all his strength, ripping the door off its mountings. It clattered to the ground as the station's gravity re-engaged.

He reached down and stood it up on its side. Dragging it into the hall, he wedged it under the descending bulkhead. The metals screeched against one another in a test of strength. He waved the others through while he braced the opening, "Go, go, go!" Reily reached out her free hand. He firmly grasped it and jerked her past. Beckoning toward Jackson, he called out, "Hurry, Comman—." Without warning, an explosion rocked the hall.

Jackson pushed forward into the cloud of gas that now obscured his vision. A mechanical scream emanated from just ahead as the pressure of the bulkhead shifted the bracing door. Carefully, but swiftly, he found footing through the mass of sundered plating from the broken conduit. Coming upon the opening, he did not see Kyo. He crept past the tenuous support and hunted for his crewman in the fog, "Kyo, talk to me."

A faint groan drew his attention, "Sorry, boss." Jackson knelt down beside him as Kyo coughed blood into his helmet. "Damn, that's not good." Kyo kept one hand clutching tightly to his abdomen as he struggled to sit up.

Jackson looked him over for a moment, "Alright, on your feet, soldier." He pulled Kyo's free arm over his shoulder and hoisted him to his feet. "DeCadejra, we are gonna need medical on standby. Have a suit rupture and internal bleeding." He pushed onward. "Come on. It's just a little bit further."

Kyo coughed again, "Go, Commander, you won't make it dragging me behind."

"If I recall crewman, I don't take orders from you," Jackson wryly remarked. "Now let's move!"

Kensy turned to Daniel, her knuckles white as she gripped the railing. In a hushed tone, she spoke, "They're not going to make it." Daniel looked down at the flashing warnings that lit up the holographic screen to Morgan's left. He nodded an acknowledgment. Pivoting, he briskly walked toward the operations center. Kensy stepped up to the control beam's entrance and glanced past. Her eyes focused on the station, *Please make it back. The crew needs you. I need you.*

As they shuffled toward the airlock, Jackson grabbed a short baton shaped device from the side of his suit's belt. He handed it Kyo, "Let's seal that up." Kyo held it against the rip in his suit for a moment. Dozens of tiny arms reached for the open material. It latched on and pulled the tear closed.

Kyo wearily nodded, "Thanks. Wasn't sure where mine went."

They shuffled up to the airlock and peered through the window. The rest of the station team navigated to the shuttle with the small boosters in their evo-suits. Jackson looked back to Kyo, "This is gonna be rough, but as soon as I let go, hit the thrusters and shoot straight for the transport. I'll be right behind you." Kyo grunted and braced for the push. Jackson hit the airlock control and shoved Kyo out with all his strength.

"I've got him!" Rasken called back as she met with Kyo in the empty space between the shuttle and station.

Jackson pushed off the station and sailed through the darkness. He grabbed the edge of the door and pulled himself in behind Rasken and Kyo. He looked over the personnel on board briefly, "All accounted for. Get us out of here!" He slammed the door shut. Even with the inertial dampeners on the crew staggered as the shuttle rocketed away from the station.

A glittering purple beam of energy fired from the ship before them and struck a point just shy of the station. Jackson's eyes widened as he realized what was happening, *Kensy*. The light began to spread like water over a balloon as it encompassed the station. She coaxed the form closed and fed more power into the manifestation to strengthen it. She closed her eyes as she focused on the psionic structure.

The station erupted. Flames licked outward and immediately died as the last vestiges of oxygen from the station were consumed. The smoke swirled around the debris and shrapnel until finally dispersing into the vacuum of space. Kensy fought to keep the remnants of the station contained as the shuttle escaped. The barrier flashed with the impacts of the colliding fragments.

"DeCadejra to Shuttle, scans are complete. You are cleared to dock. We are setting up medical and decontamination in the fourth hangar bay for you. Come on home," Daniel called to the small vessel. It changed course and banked back toward the ship.

Kensy sighed and released the barrier. "Flight Lieutenant, get us a safe distance away. I don't want anymore surprises." She gracefully descended from the beam, "The bridge is yours." a soft smile curled over her lips in relief.

Morgan lifted his chin, "Yes, ma'am." The shuttle docked and the hangar doors secure, he guided the ship into the dark expanse beyond.

Chapter 45

Paper Trail

"Nothing makes someone more productive than boredom."
~ Ensign Kaitlyn "Kait" Reily

Kensy sat on her lounge reading in the stillness of her quarters. She thumbed through the holographic pages as if were a paper filled book from days long past. Her left leg curled beneath her as she listened to the soft ambient music that filled the room. A knock at the door stirred her from the words in front of her.

"Come in," she called as she deactivated the book and closed its casing. Placing it on her legs, she glanced toward the opening door. Jackson stood there in his dignified captain's uniform. His eyes met hers as he raised his head. She blinked and cast her eyes away. With a subtle wave of her hand, she beckoned him to join her. "It's good to see Doc finally let you out of quarantine." She smiled, "I dare say Morgan will be glad to see a face other than mine. I've just about driven him to distraction."

"Good. He deserves it for all the times he has done the same." Jackson sauntered in and sat at the other end of her lounge. He leaned forward, resting his forearms on his knees.

Kensy snickered, "Somehow, I don't think he considers it fair play." Jackson shrugged heedlessly. She wrapped a finger around her ponytail, twisting and smoothing it over her shoulder. "How is Kyo doing?"

"Good. Doc regenerated a bunch of the damaged tissue so he's at least back in one piece. She has him on light duty though for the next two weeks." He shifted restlessly. "Things been pretty quiet in the rest of the ship?"

Kensy ran her fingertips over the contours of the lounge's armrest, "Yeah. I ordered some rotating down time for the crew. Figured it certainly couldn't hurt. Things were a little tense after Rosealleon and the whole station mess." Kensy blinked slowly, "A few of the crew asked if they could put together a service for Malek and Daily." Her words came out barely above a whisper, "Just glad we didn't have to add any more names."

Jackson turned his head toward her, "Yeah." He quietly studied the sadness in her expression for a moment, "Thank you." She brought her eyes to meet his again. Earnestly he tried to reassure her, "Everyone on that shuttle, myself included, would've been blasted into oblivion if you hadn't put up that barrier. You know," he chuckled, "we wouldn't have been in that mess if I had just listened to you in the first place." Kensy curled her finger in front of her mouth as she tried to smile discreetly. "It's perfectly okay for you to do the whole 'I told you so' bit. I deserve it."

She placed both boots on the floor and stood up from the lounge. Taking a few strides forward, she set her book on the desk beside the door and turned back, "How about we just appreciate that everyone lived to see another day and call it good?"

He leaned against the backrest. "I think that's doable." He watched the elegant shifts in her posture as she stood before him, marveling at her every mannerism and the natural grace that was reflected in the most subtle of her movements.

Butterflies filled her chest as she sensed his gaze upon her. *You're being ridiculous again!* She furrowed her brow, trying to suppress the feeling, "Reily sent up a message a while ago that she had something to show us. Since the quarantine has been lifted, maybe we should go check it out."

Jackson stood up from the lounge, "Sounds like a plan." He stepped between Kensy and the door, pausing as he glanced back toward her. "One more thing before we go...," he drew an uneasy breath, "how are *you* doing? That was a pretty significant display of power."

She smiled softly. Raising her right hand, she manifested a fist-sized wire-frame icosahedron. Her fingers gently coaxed it into a slow spin before she waved it away, "Good as new."

He nodded in approval as his eyes shifted back to her, "Very nice." He gestured toward the door, "Shall we?"

She motioned for him to lead the way, "By all means." They entered the lobby together as Kensy looked upward, "Notify Reily that we will meet her now."

"Message sent." The mechanical voice chimed back, "Message received. Ensign Reily will meet you in the war room to present her findings. Other parties notified: First Officer Bryden, Alpha Squad Leader Rasken, Chief Engineer Petroski. Do you wish for me to notify Graven Commander Cross?" Maggie inquired.

Kensy glanced toward the door adjacent to her own, "No. Let her rest. I will give her the briefing later."

Jackson glanced at Kensy as they boarded the elevator, "Is she still recovering from Rosealleon? I didn't think anything could keep her down for long, not even dieing."

"And you'd be correct. She won't take the time unless she has no other option. So I'm eliminating the option." Kensy crossed her arms in an attempt to shake the memory of holding Neira's motionless body.

"She sounds as stubborn as someone else I know...," he stuffed his hands in his pockets.

She gave him an incredulous glance, "Where do you think I learned it?" They both snickered.

The elevator doors opened again on the Strategic Deck. "After you," he bowed slightly to allow her past. She shook her head and stepped forward, recomposing herself. They proceeded down the hall, giving a wave to Rasken and Allen as they approached from the opposite direction. Together, the four officers entered the war room where Reily and Daniel waited.

Furiously Reily fiddled with the component she had recovered from the station. "Gonna be just a sec...." Allen strode up beside her and examined her work. "I think I can make it interface with the table. I had it working down in the quarantine." She grumbled in frustration, "It's just being difficult now. This tech is old as dirt."

Allen smiled, "May I?" Reily sighed and nodded in acceptance. "You just forgot this connection here." He lifted a stray bundle from the chaos of her set-up. She handed him one of her jury-rigged adapters. Carefully, he fed the broken wires into the receptacle and stood back as the table lit up.

"Thanks." She began sifting through the partially corrupted files until she came upon the logs she was hunting for. "Okay, we know that the last place the Illusive docked was with the station prior to the crash on Rosealleon. But I believe the station was just another casualty of this *thing*. The station was evidently a supply depot. The logs I recovered have hundreds of destinations and points of origin. Needle in a haystack stuff. But something caught my eye...." She opened the file.

With one quick tap she turned around to her audience, "This place," The holographic table opened a registration file for a client colony. "Galliane Prime. For years this place received regular supply drops from the station until three months before the station went offline." She slid one finger across the edge of the table.

The visual log, despite the pixilation and stuttering, began to play. A young man spoke in a relaxed and routine manner,

"Quartermaster's log: XJK486. The colony at Galliane Prime will no longer be receiving supplies from us. Seems that the colonists ran into some trouble. The settlement and dig site were abandoned a few weeks ago. Garr authorized us to recover the last drop plus the shipment we were scheduled to pickup, anyway. He has it stored down in the sub-level for now. Guess they are going to send an investigator at some point. Not a high priority with everything that's going on. Also, remember to update charts for Axys Nine's new coordinates."

Rasken popped her bubblegum loudly, "So they bailed on a colony, that happened a lot back in the day."

Reily shifted through the logs again, "Yeah, but this time... one week later the station begins logging malfunctions in the lower levels. At first it's just small stuff: sensors skipping report intervals, doors that lock or won't open. After a month, they start having major problems: gravity and environment systems fritz out, two workers get killed doing repairs, supply shipments get rerouted. All of the logs after that are too corrupted for me to recover."

"So you are thinking they picked up something nasty from that settlement and it infected the station?" Daniel stared scrutinizingly at the files. "No chance it could have come from elsewhere?"

Reily folded her arms and crossed her ankles as she leaned back on the table, "I have been staring at these files for the last several days to kill the boredom of quarantine. This is the only one that stands out in the time period with what we already know. Most of the rest is everyday junk from the standard work files to personal communications and a small mountain of gossip."

Kensy's eyes trained on the display, "A colony and a dig site. Makes me wonder what they dug up." She glanced to Jackson, the wheels turning in her mind.

"Do we know where this colony is located?" He asked Reily.

She nodded, "Yeah, the logs included coordinates. Should be there in a few days."

"Good work. Looks like we have our next destination. Relay the coordinates to Threaux." Jackson addressed the group.

"On it, sir," Daniel promptly replied.

"Ensign, round up the team. We have preparations to make. I want everyone on top of their game for this." Rasken ordered her subordinate, "Tell Hensley, if he's done gimping around, he's back on board for this one."

Reily deactivated the connection to the table and began scooping up the parts and pieces. Allen stepped to her side once again, "Go on. I'll take care of this. I'd like to take a look at it myself, anyway." She nodded and pivoted toward the door.

Slowly, everyone, save for Jackson, filtered out of the room. He let silence creep into the room again before speaking, "I assume you caught all that." Without so much as a glance toward the auxiliary door, he called to a figure in the shadows. Neira rolled her shoulder against the door frame as she stepped into view. "Do you ever get tired of lurking?" he asked with disdain, clearly echoing through his words.

She sauntered down the shallow steps in his direction, "No." Her voice still rasped slightly as the scars of Rosealleon healed. "Why, Commander? Does it unnerve you?"

He shot her an icy glare, "I'll never understand your obsession with cloak and dagger b.s." He leaned back against the lip of the table and crossed his arms over his chest. "Was there something you wanted or are you just going for the giggles?" he sneered.

Neira slumped down on the adjacent bench, "I want to know what you've gotten. I know she confides in you."

He scowled at her, "I've gotten that you are paranoid."

Neira raised one eyebrow at him incredulously, "You don't expect me to believe all that time you two spend alone is innocent small talk?! I heard about the night before the station. Your long late night *walk.*" She crossed her legs at the knees and leaned forward on them.

Jackson rolled his eyes, "There is nothing going on beyond what is required of us. The only mystery here is your little phantom conspiracy. Kensy has nightmares periodically, which you would know if you *talked* to her. And I can't fault her for that, the crap she's been through." He shook his head.

Neira narrowed her gaze at him. "And you think her out-of-control nightmares have nothing to do with the psionic manifestation I showed you? Or this new enemy that appeared from nowhere and began targeting her?"

"Honestly?" Jackson pushed off the table, "What I think is someone involved in this whole mess on Bhelnir, on Rosealleon, figured out who she is and looked her up. They hacked some files and decided to employ some psychological warfare. The rest is just a person, with a busy body friend, trying to process everything and get through the next day as best she can." He stormed toward the door, "She's your damn friend. You go talk to her!" He took a few long strides away from the room before slowing his pace. *What if she's right? What if there is some crazy psionic thing going on here? Not like there's anything I can do about it.* He shook his head. *This is just crazy talk. There has to be a logical explanation for all of it. Nightmares of dead friends, psi-walking, mind-controlling machines... why couldn't things be boring?* He stuffed his hands in his pockets again and continued down the hall.

Chapter 46

Galliane Prime

"The whole thing between Frost and Gabel is just getting painful to watch."
~ Specialist Nathan Wright

The cargo bay echoed the various sounds of their movement as the ground team readied themselves for the mission ahead. Jackson fastened the last of his tactical vest pockets and holstered his pistol. His hand wrapped around Kensy's sidearm as it rested on the armory bench in front of them. Carefully, he passed it grip first toward her waiting hand. Daniel strode up confidently, "All right, the shuttle and pilot are all set for you."

Jackson clasped his hand and patted his shoulder with the other, "Thanks, Bryden. She's all yours. We'll be in contact. Keep the engines warm." Kensy shot a smile at the two men. "Hopefully this place is as deserted as it's supposed to be."

"Try not to set off any self-destruct sequences while you're at it," Daniel quipped.

Jackson shrugged the jab off, "Yeah, yeah. Try to keep the comedy to a minimum."

"Yes, sir!" Daniel snapped to attention. Kensy quietly giggled as Daniel shot her a wink. He leaned over toward her and whispered, "Keep him out of trouble."

Slinging his rifle over his shoulder, Jackson rolled his eyes and pivoted toward the shuttle. Loudly clapping his hands together, he shouted over the sound of the engines, "Load up!" and briskly strode toward the others.

Kensy whispered back, "I'll do my best." She shrugged and jogged to catch up with Jackson as he stepped into the transport.

"Alpha ready and on-board!" Rasken popped a piece of gum into her mouth. Jackson tapped the pilot on the shoulder and motioned for departure. The doors promptly slid closed as the shuttle lifted out of the docking clamp. Gracefully, they glided into the lower atmosphere. The shuttle danced through the rocky landscape until it finally approached the designated landing zone.

Jagged shale like stone jutted out of the dense shrub covered landscape. One at a time the ground team leapt from the transport onto the outcroppings. Kensy gazed over the scenery as she tried to absorb every detail, "It's quite a view. No wonder they tried to settle here."

Jackson scowled, "Yeah, but no good place for a set down." He glanced back toward the pilot and waved his hand in a circle. The transport lifted back into the air and headed off to scout the nearby region. The commander headed for the front of the pack, "Just ahead is the main settlement. Supposedly, this place has been abandoned for a long time, but as we have seen, that doesn't mean it's safe. Keep your head on a swivel. We are looking for any kind of evidence or data on what happened here. Spread out and stay in contact!" He pulled his rifle to the ready. With a nod, he beckoned Kensy to follow as they traversed the rugged terrain to their destination.

She examined the structures as they neared the colony, "Amazing. It looks like they built over the original structures when they attempted to resettle this place!"

Jackson looked at her quizzically, "*Resettle?*"

Kensy placed her hand in his as he helped her up one of the sharper rises, "When I looked up this place up records said that the last group picked the site because it had shown signs of numerous prior colonization efforts including early spaceflight humans."

"How early are we talking?" he inquired.

Kensy tried to recall the details of her reading as they jumped the last small intervening crevasse leading to the central plateau, "Um, pre-Divergence, maybe. Before solsons or voidir, back when everyone was terran." She ran her fingertips over the outside of the nearest building. Fascination filled her words, "They say that those first humans shot themselves into space with no thought of returning. When they finally happened upon a habitable planet, they landed, and used the very ships that had delivered them as fodder for building a new life."

"You're talking like seven hundred years ago." He grumbled, "I couldn't do it. I hate being stranded."

She glanced toward him, "And yet we've gotten stranded, at least for a little bit, just about everywhere we've gone. Morwhex, Rosealleon...."

He shook his head, "Yeah, exactly." She smiled and ducked into the doorway beside him. Jackson surveyed the surroundings before stepping in behind her.

"Ooh! Communications consoles." She ran her hands over the dust covered panels. The toe of her boot tapped the corner of a drawer that sat slightly ajar. She knelt down beside it and tugged. The metal heaved before surrendering to her pull. She lifted a cumbersome cylinder from its socket and blew a cloud of residue off the housing. "Well, that one's useless. Check around. Maybe there is a power cell around here that isn't completely shot."

Together, they began rummaging through the crates and compartments that filled the room. "Hey, found one," Jackson heaved the fresh cylinder from its resting place. "Are these fusion cells?"

Kensy nodded, "Seems like it. Pretty popular with expeditions cause dormant they'll keep for ages. And when you do activate one...." She rotated the central rings on the device. Suddenly it began to glow intensely, "they put out a crap ton of power." He lowered the cylinder into the receptacle. Instantly, the base came to life. Lights flickered overhead, the computer consoles buzzed, and some distant machinery began to hum benignly.

"We've got juice here. Was that one of you?" Shane called apprehensively over the comm.

"Roger that, plugged in a power cell here," Jackson confirmed. "Notify me if you detect any problems. Otherwise, make the most of the power while we have it." He turned back to Kensy as she fussed with the console in front of her.

"Hmm," she struck at the mechanical controls one at a time until finally eliciting a reaction. A vertical panel beside her lit up with a roughly projected interface. "Well, that did something." She meticulously navigated through the displayed file lists, "Oh! Expedition log. Let's try that."

She clicked on the directory. The image of a brown-haired man in his twenties appeared on the screen, "Our very first expedition log! Cass got us all set up and we've already begun to take a look at the site's many amazing finds. I can already see why the original human colonists must have picked this place. The ruins here are fascinating. She theorizes that it was constructed by a civ that had some way of harnessing raw ambient energy, but we will have to look into that later. First order is determining why the original colony failed. If we can determine that, then we can avoid the same problem."

"I'll see if I can find something a little more recent...," Kensy scrolled through the list of entries, "No way...." She pulled up the title that had drawn her attention.

The man spoke again, "We finally found it!"

A bubbly platinum-haired woman bounced into fame and grasped onto his shoulder, "Did you tell them yet?!"

He smiled and continued, "In our process of analyzing the previous human settlement, we found the Vagabond project.

It's no longer an obscure rumor. We have evidence that it really did exist! The purpose of it is unclear, but the technology is still mind-blowing. Rikes thinks the project may have something to do with the first colony's failure, but...."

"He's just being a jerk because his extinct alien resurgence theory fell apart," the woman interjected, making mocking faces at the camera.

"But in all seriousness, this is where the real work begins. There will be a lot to dive into tomorrow," the young man wrapped up.

Kensy furrowed her brow as she reached the bottom of the list. The young woman appeared on the screen, bleeding and bruised. Her clothes were tattered and streaked with dirt. "I am recording this last message for anyone within broadcast range. We failed the same way as everyone else who has touched this rock before us. Don't come searching for us. Nuke this place from orbit and don't look back. There is no one left." She sobbed quietly, "What we woke up will destroy everything if it isn't stopped. It has been evolving for centuries and we gave it everything it needed to keep going. I'm so sorry." She turned her head to the side in an attempt to compose herself, "It's trying to capture our sentience, to devour what makes us human. Rikes, Howerth... they tried to reason with it. It replied, preservation *must be achieved,* before it turned them on each other. *Nothing* can make it off this world. It is up to you to turn this place to dust." She inhaled deeply, "This is Casstheryn Vysra, Galliane Prime Expedition Coordinator signing off for the last time." The video stuttered to a stop.

Jackson looked at Kensy, "Well, clearly this place was never nuked."

Kensy lifted her hands from the controls and took a step back, staring at the log, "It was never broadcast. She went through all of that and never got the message out." Jackson placed a hand on her shoulder and squeezed it gently. For a moment, glistening drops collected at the corners of her eyes, "They were so excited...."

A tiny shift of movement on the ground beside them caught Jackson's eye. From one of the crates crawled a small Y-shaped creature. Its chitinous shell shimmered like metal. Quickly, he stomped on it. The bug crunched audibly beneath his boot. He stepped back and examined the remains. A gooey smear and a broken shell remained. "Well, I think I know where the Thrall design came from. Seems there is an actual bug that looks like them."

Kensy glanced down at the mess. Jackson shrugged. "Hey boss," a voice called over the comm. "We got bugs. Like the ones on Rosealleon, only—umm—real, with guts and crap." Kensy smiled weakly and shook her head at Hensley's description.

"Yeah, we've seen them too." Jackson replied. "Seems like our enemy spent some time here. Anyone have the means to contain one of these things so we can study it?"

"Already on it. Wright and I are collecting flora and fauna samples as we speak." Rasken assured. The sound of a popping bubble echoed over the communicators.

Jackson grasped Kensy's right hand and spun her toward the door, "Come on. I'm sure there are other things you want to check out. The ship can upload the files for us to dive into later." He gave her a nudge. Kensy nodded and headed for the door. Quickly, Jackson hit the broadcast switch on the main console before following her out. "DeCadejra, I have opened a broadcast link to the local comm center. Upload what you can onto a secure data bank. We'll examine it later."

"Understood Commander," Daniel replied.

Kensy and Jackson strode through the heart of the colony and up the rise beyond. She glanced back to see the rest of Alpha Squad combing through the outer reaches of the settlement. She continued up the steps backward as she examined the path. Coppery colored veins traced through the stonework in flowing lines. She pivoted toward the main dais in awe. A series of pillars and geometric statues encompassed a central archway.

Jackson raised an eyebrow as he ran one hand over the smooth surface of a nearby pillar, "I can see why they thought it might have something to do with energy manipulation. The patterns... they look like your control clasp."

Kensy raised her arm in front of herself. "They do, don't they?" she murmured.

Suddenly, the ground around them began to quake violently. They both grasped onto the pillars to keep from falling. Kensy turned her gaze back toward the colony as the buildings began to crumble. Distant figures scrambled against the jostling terrain to get clear of the collapsing colony. Static blared over their nahdvi. Jackson lurched toward her pillar, shouting over the thunderous rumble, "We're gonna have to make a run for the extraction point." Kensy nodded in acknowledgment.

Slowly, she eased toward the stairs. Placing her feet out in front, she pushed up and began a stumbling run downhill. Jackson followed on her heels, one arm extended toward her, ready to lend aid if needed. The sky above them darkened. Kensy grasped at her chest as a powerful psionic presence pressed down upon her. She stumbled to her knees. Jackson grabbed her shoulders. She looked up at him with wide eyes, "They're coming! I can feel it again."

Like a swarm of locust the black machines of Bhelnir and Morwhex rose up into the air, closing in from all sides. "Evacuate now! Repeat, we have hostile forces engaging from all directions!" He called frantically over the comm. The shuttle swooped into position on the far side of the colony. He watched as the first of the ground crew scrambled aboard. Leaning down, he spoke into Kensy's ear, "We have to keep moving." He pulled her to her feet and again they began to run.

A rain of explosions peppered the area around them as the Subjugators bombarded the landscape. Kensy ducked in close to one of the broken walls and covered her head. She tried to force the oppressive feeling of the psionic presence aside. Jackson skidded into cover beside her. Her eyes darted over their surroundings, "We'll never make it." He covered her with his arm as a hail of rock blasted over them. "We need to go back." She pointed up toward the ruins. "High ground."

"It's too open. We'll get blasted before we can get to the top." He shouted back.

"Well, we can't go in there," she thumbed toward the heart of the colony. "We'll get crushed to death. At least if we run, we have a chance. Those ruins are the only thing I can see that's not falling down around us!" An adjacent building shifted on its foundation and began to twist toward them as it fell.

"Go!" Jackson shoved her abruptly. Pulling his rifle to the ready once again, he began to jog backward, letting loose a spray of shots to either side to cover their retreat.

Like it or not, circumstance had committed them to a path. They darted for the stairs. Kensy pressed her hands into a wedge in front of her as she ran. The sparkle of violet energy coalesced around her fingers. Concentrating on the energy for a moment, she whispered, "Volgihr." She thrust her hands out and apart. Like a tidal wave, the manifestation washed up the steps, forcing the enemies ahead of them off either side with tremendous speed. The wave broke against the dais pillars. They began to resonate softly. The vibrations traveled down the steps and beneath Kensy's feet.

Distracted by the sensation, Kensy barely noticed as one of the Subjugators descended beside her. Narrowly, she dodged to the side. Its long piercing arms screeched against the glassy marbled stone. She brought her clasped fist up to parry the spinning drill heads that followed the strike. Her psiblade sliced through all but one, sundering them. The rogue drill clipped her collarbone as she turned out of the blow.

A faint metallic snap reached her ears, and her hand immediately reached up to her neck. It was gone. Her eyes fell upon the glittering pendant as it careened through the air toward Jackson. It glimmered at the edge of his peripheral vision. He hunkered down for a moment to analyze what he had seen and catch his breath. There, the pendant dangled from one of the steps ahead. Kensy watched it as best she could between repelling attacks. Jackson rose back up and sprayed another volley toward the closing enemies.

Gritting his teeth, he turned and darted for the necklace. For one moment, everything seemed to slow down. Kensy watched his hand close around the trinket as his name streaked off her lips in fear. The intense glow of a beam struck through his vest. He crumpled onto the ground in pain. A warm energy passed over him and the sounds around him faded for a split second.

Kensy raced down the newly cleared steps and hoisted his arm over her shoulders as she dragged him to his feet. "Ivanigis ahri." Her words rolled into the air. Light burst from her entire body and wrapped around the both of them. "Come on, just a few more steps."

The resonation of the steps and pillars became more intense. With a whoosh, unseen energies stirred by Kensy's power coursed up the steps and into the center archway. The confluence of power swirled within the arch. Kensy set Jackson safely in the shadow of one of the statues. He grunted in agony, "Well, that smarts." Instinctively, he clenched his fist tighter. The tangled chain tensed around his fingers, reminding him of the treasure in his grasp. He glanced to his closed hand.

She carefully pried at the vest to assess his wound, "I've never understood that saying."

His eyes fluttered for a second, "It means hopefully whatever stupid thing you just did hurts enough that you will be smart enough not to do it again." He tried to sit up straighter with a wince, "I think I can guarantee it won't happen again." He lifted his rifle and fired through the core of a machine as it crested the dais into his field of view.

"None of that." She scowled at him with a firmness he had not seen before. "You're not bleeding much. It went clean through. Cauterized along the way." She scanned the horizon, her determination renewed. He watched with a fascination as she churned through possibilities in her mind. She stood defiantly, her eyes locked on the portal that formed before them. One step at a time, she walked to the center of the top stair. Her fingers curled around the hilt of the psiblade as it materialized in her hand. "DeCadejra, we are pinned down in the ruins. It's too dangerous for extraction. We are going to retreat through the portal." Kensy slowed her breath and closed her eyes. She clasped the hilt of her sword in both hands as the Subjugators launched toward her. Opening her psionically infused eyes, she plunged the blade into the ground.

Blinding light erupted from all around the pair. Swiftly she swooped under Jackson's gun arm, causing the weapon to clatter against the stone dais from his weakened grasp. She lifted him from his resting space and dragged him into the swirling gateway. The air was forced from their lungs as they felt an intense acceleration hit their bodies. The ground rushed forward abruptly. Kensy staggered to her knees, still clutching Jackson. His head lulled as he fought against unconsciousness.

He lazily rolled away from her on the cold ground. "No, no, no. Don't quit on me now. We have to keep moving," she patted his cheek. He forced his eyes open and nodded weakly. Once again, she hoisted him to his feet, and they took a moment to scan their new surroundings. Dense emerald jungle sprawled over grand granite crags. The portal hummed behind them with an ominous intensity. "Okay, time to go." Holding tightly to each other, they headed into the strange and beautiful alien wilds.

Chapter 47

Gone

*"Whoever said, what you don't know can't hurt you,
evidently wasn't a soldier."*
~ Lieutenant Commander Daniel Bryden

Daniel stood in the center of the Strategic Operations Center, his white knuckles curling over the top edge of the control console. "Sir, enemy forces are swarming the site," one voice called up to him.

"Ground quakes are continuing to level colony structures on the main mesa," another reported.

"Calculating counter interference!" a voice echoed from the far reaches of the room.

Daniel stood tall, "Report on ground team extraction!"

"Sir, Alpha team is accounted for, but the shuttle has taken fire," a young female crewman looked up toward him. "Commander Gabel and Psilyria Frost are not aboard."

"Tell them to get back here. Notify the standby shuttle to prep for immediate launch." He hollered back with an unwavering authority.

Maggie chimed in, "Transmission incoming from Psilyria Frost."

A hush fell over the command center as her voice crackled over the speakers, "DeCade–...pinned down... too dangerous f–...–ing to retreat thr–...."

Daniel turned and shouted over the crew, "Get me a clear line!" A shock wave rippled outward from the ruins. With a jolt, a beam of purple and white energy erupted from the planet's surface. It pierced into the blackness of space, shaking the entire ship as it passed by.

"Stars!" Neira gasped from behind Daniel. The daze of the moment broke and the reports flooded in again. A cacophonous noise rose as everyone began to speak at once. Neira placed a hand on the edge of the console, "Bryden, what was that?"

Furiously Daniel scanned the information streaming in front of him, "I don't know, but it came from the ruins... where Kensy and Jackson are." They exchanged worried glances.

"I no longer detect Psilyria Frost or Commander Gabel on the planet's surface." Maggie reported flatly. The hush fell over the bridge again as the startled crew looked to their commanding officer for guidance.

Daniel tilted his head down and raised his eyebrows as the implications sunk in. Very slowly, he responded, "What did you say?"

"I no longer detect Psilyria Frost or Commander Gabel on the planet's surface." Maggie promptly replied. "Their bio-signs no longer register within the specified proximity."

He swallowed hard at the news, "Are you telling me they have been killed?"

"I cannot reach such a conclusion at this point. While Commander Gabel's life signs were in flux at the moment of detonation, no biological evidence of them remains at the site. They are quite simply not there anymore," the mechanical voice attempted to clarify. An eerie stillness set in around them as everyone waited in quiet anticipation. Daniel and Neira stood in tense contemplation for several long moments.

"Sir," a meek voice broke the silence, "Alpha team has returned."

Daniel pushed back from the console, "I want scans of every inch of that planet. Forward any fragments and morsels of data on that beam directly to me. I want to know what it was and where it went. And tell Alpha to report to the bridge immediately!" Everyone snapped into action, sifting data, and relaying information. He took a carefully measured breath.

Neira leaned forward, tilting her head to look at him with her one good eye, "What are you thinking in there, Bryden?"

"I think we don't know enough about what just happened and Alpha had eyes on the ground." He adjusted the streaming displays on the center console. "I am going to believe that they are out there alive until I see otherwise with my own two eyes."

Neira straightened her posture and crossed her arms over her chest, "Can't argue with that."

Chapter 48

Crystalline Connections

*"Observations of humanity through this
conduit have proven most illuminating.
Perhaps it's time for a little nudge...."*

~ *the Nexus*

A delicate dripping sound rolled through the cool air of the cavern. Abruptly, the scuffle of boots interrupted the stillness as Kensy and Jackson stumbled into the stone sanctuary. The entrance curved sharply into a larger alcove. Warily, she led him toward the rear of the chamber and propped him up against the wall. He grunted involuntarily as he clutched at the wound in his torso. A few distant blasts echoed toward them. Kensy glanced over her shoulder nervously. She helped settle him into a stable resting position and whispered, "Sit tight. I'm going to lead them off. Shouldn't be too hard to lose them in this jungle. I'll be right back."

Jackson clutched her wrist weakly amidst labored breaths. She rose to her feet again, her hand slipping from his grasp. Deftly, she darted back out of the cavern and into the thicket beyond. He watched, helpless to stop her as he drifted from consciousness. Slowly, the sounds of gunfire and explosions faded into the distance. Quiet settled into the cave once again. Shadows passed by the entrance with every muted gasp while minutes turned to hours and the light of day steadily crept toward the alien dusk.

At long last, Kensy's hand planted against the stone as she caught herself. Noiselessly, she snuck back into the mouth of the cave. There she lingered for several long seconds. No rustle followed. She sighed at the relief of not being followed. Her gaze turned to the motionless figure resting against the far wall. "Jack!" She rushed to his side, her hand slipping under his collar. His skin was slightly clammy to the touch, but his pulse and breathing continued.

She looked him over for a moment as her mind weighed how best to help him. Carefully, she unfastened his tactical vest and pulled him against herself, heedfully slipping it from his arms. Setting it aside, she cautiously laid him flat on the cavern floor and began to examine his wound. The black long sleeve shirt he wore glistened with blood.

"Sorry, I had to leave. I couldn't let them find us... find you," she spoke aloud as she lifted the shirt and began to tend to him with the supplies from his vest. "I didn't know it was this bad. Should have known that the portal didn't do you any favors. The force behind it dropped me and I wasn't even hurt." She brushed at a scrape on her cheek with the back of her hand, "Well, not significantly anyway."

Her fingers grasped a tool from his first aid supplies. She inhaled anxiously, "It looks like you have some internal bleeding... I'm sorry, this will probably be really rough." Very slowly, she slipped the shaft of the implement into the wound. "Please sleep through this," she softly prayed. Pressing the contacts on the end, she watched an intense light fill the flesh and fade once again. Gingerly, she withdrew it and wiped it on the edge of his bloodied shirt. "It looks like the seal took. That should hold you over for a little bit." She rolled him slightly to one side to examine the exit point. "You're going to have to take it easy until we get back to the ship."

Meticulously, she cleaned the openings and smoothed bandages over them. After pulling a few more odds and ends from his vest pockets, she rolled it up and tucked it under his head. "Hopefully they get here soon wherever *here* is." She rocked back against the wall, staring at his motionless body that stirred only slightly with the rise and fall of his chest. "I've really gotten us into a mess, haven't I?" She cradled her head in her hands. An electric crackle emanated from beside her. Her eyes shifted toward the glowing creature that stood there, "Nexus?"

"Of course," he stated in a pragmatic tone. Kensy watched as he circled her unconscious companion. "I see you have found yourself in an interesting predicament. What will you do from this point?"

"Well," Kensy inhaled sharply again, "I need to keep an eye on him, make sure his condition doesn't deteriorate. I need to protect us somehow, barrier, wards, something...." Shaking her head, she felt resigned to her frustrations, "I don't know what to do. I know I can't do it all."

"Have you considered forging a link?" Nexus nodded toward Jackson. "With that, you could accelerate his healing psionically and maintain a passive watch while focusing on other... issues."

She scowled at him, "I admit I've thought about it but, ... the last time was a very long time ago and it was a two-way street. Elle was a willing participant, not to mention another psionic. The bond we had...." She closed her eyes for a moment as she recounted drifting through the emptiness of space alongside her best friend, "I don't know if I have a strong enough connection with him."

Nexus cocked his head to the side and smiled strangely, "I think you will surprise yourself. Besides, it's rather chilly in here. If the link works, you could keep the cold at bay with little more than a thought. Could be useful given your limited supplies. It will be dark soon and temperatures will most likely drop further."

"You make it sound like such a simple decision," Kensy conceded. Contemplatively, she rubbed her hands together.

Shifting onto her knees beside him, she studied the lines of his face. With a gentle touch, she reached out and ran the tips of her fingers across his brow, then down the side of his face. "Okay," she whispered. Her head hung in a brief meditation as she quieted her nerves.

Watchfully, she straddled his stationary form, placing her hands flat against the stone adjacent to his shoulders to hold herself aloft. With measured breath, she leaned down and placed her forehead against his. Her eyes closed as she focused on the flow of energies within her own body. She traced the current with her thoughts. Pulling from her core, she directed the current to pass from her into him. She felt as the stream of psionic energy swirled in and around both of them. The violet glow of her power encompassed them completely, synchronizing the rhythms of their bodies. Nexus looked on as an illusionary chain formed between their hearts and faded away. Kensy opened her eyes, allowing the manifestation to subside. "I think it worked," she smiled in relief.

"Of course," Nexus repeated, "Now it is time to attend to other matters." Kensy rose, stepping toward the entrance. She paced in deliberation. "A piece of your mind is now tied to the link. Further dividing your attention could prove dangerous. The powers at your disposal are limitless, but as you have discovered, your biological capacity is not. There is, however, a way to do all those defensive measures you are cogitating on... if you are willing to learn."

She glanced at him curiously, "There is? Absolutely! What would you ask of me? What do I need to do?"

Nexus waved one of his dagger like paws, sending forth a gust that cleared the loose dirt from the area in front of him, "Take a seat." Kensy folded her legs together as she settled into a comfortable position. Nexus aligned himself with her. "Close your eyes. Imagine a vessel. A crystal. See the points and edges that form the structure. Find the pattern. There is a geometry, an order, to it. Now focus on making your power solid, crystalline, just like the vessel. Built the framework. Seal the shell."

Instinctively, Kensy raised her hands, between which wisps of purplish light danced. As Nexus spoke, a shape emerged from the chaos. Little by little, her delicate fingers wove energy and matter together. The last seam knitted together and released a pulse. A violet-black fog filled the vessel. Kensy opened her eyes. She stared in awe at the creation floating before her.

"Congratulations. You have created your very first psi-crystal." He explained, "Now any energy that you funnel into it will charge it like a battery. You can use it to power manifestations. It will maintain them without your continued concentration. However, it cannot repair or embolden a failing construct and, once depleted, any remaining tethers can continue to pull at the energy it is constructed from, destroying it." He tilted his head. "Why don't you try a barrier now?"

Kensy backed away from the floating crystal and stood up. Moving toward the entrance, she waved her clasped arm toward the entry, filling it with a shimmering protective wall. "Good. Now grasp the channel of power that ties you to the barrier. Draw it to the crystal." Kensy grasped the ethereal thread and pulled it to the waiting psionic vessel. As they touched, the thread connected and began funneling the swirling fog into the barrier, freeing her from it. Her eyes widened. "You will need to charge it, but you understand basics."

Kensy smiled, "I would hug you if I could. Thank you, Nexus." She sat down at the crystal once again. Shooting a glance in Jackson's direction, she felt the subtle pounding of his pulse, echoed by her own. *We'll make it through. I promise!* She inhaled deeply, putting her mind to the task of funneling power into the gently bobbing construct. Slowly, the last vestiges of day receded from view, leaving them in a low green glow of evening and the soft violet light of Kensy's manifestations.

Chapter 49
Promise

"Every heartbeat is a promise kept."
~ Commander Jackson Gabel

Jackson fought to open his heavy eyelids. Wearily, he blinked as the stone ceiling above him came into focus. His body was warm but stiff. Slowly, he rolled his head toward the faint light that filtered in through the curved entrance. He breathed deeply, listening to the soft sounds of the midnight shrouded cavern. Water trickled in the distance. A steady breeze danced across the opening, rustling the foliage beyond.

He could hear the delicate hum of energy and his own heartbeat. A strange echo followed each pulse. He placed two fingers on his neck and felt his singular pulse. His brow furrowed as he tried to decipher the sound. Pulling his hand back, he stared at the necklace that dangled against his palm thanks to the web of delicate chain that wove around his fingers. The broken ends hung loosely, swaying gently as he turned his attention from his hand to his surroundings. For the briefest of moments, he caught sight of Kensy sitting across the cave with her legs folded, hands resting upon her knees, and her head tilted down.

An unusual pressure moved across his torso, drawing his attention. There, he beheld an alien creature of indigo and dark violet. Its sharp feline form shifted and flickered as its glowing eyes watched him carefully. Instinctively, Jackson rolled out from under it and scrambled backward only to be reminded of his injuries with sudden jolts of pain. With a grunt, he clamored against the wall in an effort to rise to his feet.

"Fascinating." The creature spoke as it glided to the ground.

"It talks. Of course it talks, I'm hallucinating. Why wouldn't it talk?" He muttered to himself. He looked down for the first time, beholding his own appearance. His boots and pants were ragged and dirty from the battle and subsequent hike. His torso was bare save for the bandages that covered the wounds.

"You are not hallucinating," it tilted its head, "though I admit I did not suspect that the link would allow you perceive me. I am intrigued that such an ability could be transferred between your kind."

He scanned the room quickly, spying his bundled vest that had gotten tousled as he had scrambled away. Draped over a nearby rock, his shirt was laid out perfectly flat. He snatched it up. Quickly, he felt the subtle damp cold of the fabric. Ignoring it, he slipped the shirt over his head and braced for the inevitable chill against his skin, but it did not jar him like he had suspected it would. All the while, he eyed the cat-like creature suspiciously.

Very gradually, he circled the edge of the room toward Kensy. She did not stir. Upon reaching her, he knelt down and touched her shoulder, "Kensy?" Her head swayed slightly as she began to fall over. Reflexively, he caught her and cradled her sleeping body. "Kensy!" he expressed in alarm.

"Now, now. You wouldn't want to wake her." The creature sauntered toward them and settled into a half curled position, his tail wrapping around himself. "She's exhausted. It has been a long night for her between tending to you and setting up protections for the cave."

Jackson stared down at her serene expression. He tucked a finger under a stray hair and brushed it from her face. Relaxing slightly, he shifted toward the wall once again. He sat so that she could rest against him undisturbed. Raising his gaze, he spoke in a hushed tone, "So, if you are not a hallucination, what are you?"

"I am the Nexus, the living embodiment of psionic energy and the conduit through which all the such power flows." He meticulously smoothed his elegantly pointed whiskers with one of his dagger like paws.

Jackson huffed slightly, "And why are you here?"

Nexus raised his chin and straightened his posture, "It was she who first came to me. She crossed the veil, seeking the power to protect. I granted her request."

Jackson looked down at her, "Bhelnir."

Nexus nodded in affirmation, "Through her, I have discovered that humans, despite your youth and fragile bodies, are an interesting and complex race. Through me, and the mark I have granted her, she has access to a depth of power unknown to any others among your kind."

"You mean to tell me that she is the first human you have ever granted the mark of the void to?" the commander looked to the energetic feline skeptically. "There are all kinds of rumors and cases of people trying to 'touch the veil' in our records."

Nexus's eyes narrowed to slits as he gazed off into nothingness, "Those who have reached to the calm beyond the veil in the past have come away broken or scarred by the process. Until she stood before me, I figured it was impossible for your kind, much like an infant trying to capture a flame and getting burned by it instead." He glanced back to the commander, "She is unique even among your kind. In her heart there exist equal parts: sorrow, strength, and hope. They both burden and liberate her. The dichotomy is fascinating.

Wouldn't you agree?" Nexus studied his reaction as he gazed down at her peacefully slumbering visage.

Jackson sighed softly, "What happens now?"

Nexus began to sway his tail hypnotically, "Even as she sleeps there is a link between you, forged by her from the connection that you share. It is what keeps you warm and eases the pain of your injuries. She has done all she can to heal and protect you both. For now, you rest. When you both, wake it will be time to figure out what comes next." Jackson yawned and tried to speak up as the want of sleep crawled over him again. Nexus's tail lazed against the stone floor as his expression shifted into a satisfied smile, "Now that's better."

In the solace of the cavern, the two slept tranquilly, nestled together. Jackson's arms wrapped around her as she curled against him. The hours slipped by uneventfully while Nexus watched over the pair, until at long last, Kensy stirred. She opened her eyes slowly, confusion setting in as she sat upright. Jackson's arm slipped from her shoulder as he raised his head. Her eyes darted about, trying to reconcile the last memories before sleeping with her new situation. She turned toward Jackson as he rubbed the sleep from his eyes and smiled at her, "Hey."

Kensy felt her cheeks flush at the realization that she had slept against him. Turning her head away, she replied, "Hey." She shuffled to her feet, "Feeling better?"

He brought his knees up and rested his forearms against them, "Not gonna be running any marathons yet, but yeah, feeling slightly less like I've been run through." She snickered. Composing herself, she held a hand out toward him and helped him to his feet. He momentarily grabbed her shoulders for stability before straightening his posture. "So, busy night?" Kensy looked to him, confused. "The talking cat thing explained, sorta." He pointed toward Nexus.

A stunned expression filled her face, "You can see him? How is that possible?" She turned to Nexus.

He smiled wryly, "The link seems to have conveyed more than the ability to sense each other."

"Then the echo I'm hearing...," Jackson's gaze fell upon Kensy again as the sound of heartbeats grew ever so slightly louder. Timidly, she reached her fingers toward his chest. At the gentle touch, both heartbeats gained in intensity. She took a deep breath as she withdrew and, once again, it faded into the background. He cleared his throat, "We should... probably, uh, figure out our next plan. What do we have?"

Kensy nodded, welcoming the distraction, "Well, I had to dig into the supplies in your vest to patch you up. There is drinkable water at the back of the cave. I filled your flask already. I did use some of the water to wash the blood out of your shirt. It was pretty bad."

Sincerely, he interjected, "Thanks." They made eye contact for a split second before he averted his gaze. A faint sensation of movement against his palm drew his attention once again to his hand. With a soft expression, he slowly and carefully he began to unwind the tangled necklace. "Kensy...," he lifted the necklace for her to see. His eyes rose to her stunned expression.

She reached out, her fingers slipping behind the pendant to steady it, "I thought it was gone. How did...?" Her brow furrowed as she caught sight of the bloody smears that had dried upon the polished design. "You were hurt because of this. Because you tried to retrieve it...."

He smirked, "What can I say? I'm a cheap bastard, —didn't want to have to buy you a new one." Her expression did not lighten with his jest. He sighed, "All joking aside, it's okay. When we get back to the ship, we'll clean it up, get someone to fix the broken links, and then it will be like new. We can pretend I never dove after it in the middle of a firefight like an idiot." He let it drop into her hands. A moment of awkward silence grew between them. He cleared his throat, "So...." His eyes searched the area for an escape, "What about weapons? What's our status?"

She scuffed the toe of her boot against the ground, "I think we dropped your rifle back on Galliane. My pistol is nearly depleted from taking potshots at the things that followed us through. So pretty much just your pistol is all that's left. Well, and after actually getting some sleep, I should be good to go." She lifted her clasped hand, letting the glittering violet light dance through her fingers.

He reached for his gun among the items that she had pulled from his vest, "Okay, next... do we know where we are?" Methodically, he began checking his weapon.

"I know that we are not on Galliane Prime anymore, but other than that, no." She nervously chuckled, "Looks like I got us stranded again. Sorry."

He paused for a moment, "It's not like there was much of a choice. We're alive. That's what matters." With a grunt, he slipped his tactical vest back on and holstered the gun. Kensy moved to his side, collecting the remaining odds and ends to be returned to his vest pockets. "Besides, if I have to be stranded, at least the company's not bad." His mind caught up to his mouth, *A pickup line? Now, of all times? Really? You really just did that?! To Kensy?! Moron.* He pulled the flask from her hands and tucked away, "Seriously, if I was stuck with Morgan, I might just throttle him." *Nice cover, hopefully she buys it.*

She struggled to suppress a giddy smile; *The company is definitely not bad.* She nodded as he took the last of the supplies from her. When only the necklace remained in her hands, they both paused. He coiled it into a small bundle and slipped it into an interior pocket. Nexus observed them in amusement. "There are a couple points of high ground around us, but I'm not sure how rough the hikes are gonna be. And if those things are still hunting for us, ...getting a signal out could be risky." She paced the cavern floor in thought.

Jackson placed a hand on her arm to stop her, "How about we pick a point and head for it. We go nice and slow, keep a low profile, and listen for incoming signals. The ship is more than likely looking for us by now. If we catch something, we can respond. If not, we keep our heads down and wait." He glanced toward the doorway, "Looks like we still have at least a little bit of night left judging by the low light. Now is as good a time as any to cover some ground."

"Okay," Kensy turned back toward where she had fallen asleep. Her eyes fixed upon a distortion in the air. She cupped her hand around it and swiveled her wrist below it. The distortion faded and the floating crystal became visible to the naked eye. She severed the threads that wove into it and it dropped into her hand. The barrier melted away from the entrance. A number of runic wards flashed, then faded from the ground and walls.

"Release it as you do your psiblade. It will return when you conjure it forth in the same manner." Nexus informed her. He watched her concentrate, and the crystal drifted away into a fine purple fog. "Excellent. It seems you have well enough in hand for now. I will take my leave."

Kensy looked down at him, "Thank you, Nexus, for everything." He bowed to her and vanished from sight.

Jackson stepped around her, "For the record, I am never telling anyone I saw a talking electric cat." He fastened his vest securely, pushing past the twinge of soreness.

Kensy smiled, "It will be our little secret." She flexed her fingers anxiously, "We ready?"

Jackson pulled his pistol, grasping it in both hands, "I'll follow your lead."

Kensy slipped out of the cave ahead of him and began navigating through the dense foliage. Every step was carefully placed, and branches held still while they passed through. A soft light filtered through the canopy and covered the landscape in a green glow. Luminescent ferns and flowers stood scattered among the undergrowth, lighting small pockets from below. Kensy paused to take in her surroundings, *So beautiful. Too bad we had to be here under these circumstances.* She sighed.

He crept up beside her and looked out into the verdant patch before them, "Wha–...."

Her eyes darted about suddenly. She pressed a single finger over her lips. The hum of energy and the twisting of metal reached his ears. Together, they hunkered down and listened. Branches snapped at a flurry of precision shots. Glistening black metal peeked through the trees as the Subjugators advanced through the rugged terrain.

Kensy tapped him on the shoulder. She pointed to him and opened her hand, patting the air. With her other hand, she indicated herself, drawing a half circle outward. He reluctantly nodded and watched her duck noiselessly into the brush. Apprehensively, he breathed deeply, affixing his gaze to the menacing targets.

Silently, she slipped around the enemy forces into a better vantage point. The points of four towering machines advanced between her and Jackson. Slowly, one began to veer toward him. Her jaw tightened as her fingers wrapped around the manifesting psiblade. Swiftly, she launched herself toward the nearest one. Her blade sheered through its stationary wing and cleaved into its tripod like legs. It tumbled to the ground in a mechanical scream. She plunged her sword into its core while turning to face the remaining enemies.

The next one let loose all of its flexible arms, the ends of which opened into razor-sharp claws. They shot at her. Deftly, she danced to the side and parried the tentacles. Hooking them with her blade, she twisted them in on themselves. Several snapped as it writhed against her vibrant psionic sword. It raised up the piercing arms to strike down upon her. Gunfire rang out over them as three white hot rounds burrowed through the core of the construct. Jackson stood defiantly in its faltering shadow.

Without so much as a moment of respite, the other two monstrosities descended upon them furiously. Jackson tucked into a roll past his adversary, rising to his feet behind it. It spun around with all of its appendages extended. The metal coils struck his side and bent around his ribcage, the force of which lifted him from his feet and flung him toward a tree. He grunted at the impact. Using the trunk as a support, he struggled to stay standing. The same white hot plasma flew from his barrel and peppered the machine inert. Winded, he glanced toward Kensy eagerly.

Her psiblade sparked and sizzled through the core of the automaton. She stepped back, wrenching it from the shell of her foe. Jackson exhaled in relief and sunk to the ground, holding his ribcage. He unzipped his vest, pulling his shirt up to inspect the impact site. Kensy released her blade and ran to his side.

His head bobbed as he fought the pain. A sympathetic twinge ran through her from the link. She closed her eyes, tracing the flow of power through his body. It swirled around the internal wound, pulsing with his heartbeat. She glanced toward him as her fingertips delicately peeled the bandage away from his skin, "You're hemorrhaging again and I already used the emergency probe to stop the initial bleeding." She furrowed her brow, "I don't.... We have to...." She rubbed at her forehead as she contemplated the possibilities.

He pushed the bandage back into place and gasped her arm, "It's fine. We have to move. If there are others...."

"You can't move like this!" She looked him in the eyes, "There is something I could try."

He could see the anxiety in her expression. Her unease gnawed at him, "I trust you. Do it."

She cupped her hands over the entrance and exit points. The purple light coalesced against his skin. Focusing, she coaxed it back and forth through his body like a gently rolling wave. She felt the torn tissues knitting themselves closed as the excess blood and rent flesh pushed free. A soothing warmth radiated from her touch. She gingerly lifted the saturated bandages from his skin. "You'll need new ones, but that should help a little, at least until we can get you some real medical attention."

He pulled the rest of the unused bandages from his breast pocket, "That's some touch."

"Easy," she re-covered the wounds and inspected the fresh bruising that emerged down the left side of his torso. "It's only temporary. Another rupture like that and I won't be able to do anything." Water collected at the edges of her downcast eyes.

He leaned toward her distant gaze, "Hey, thank you." He gave her arm an affectionate squeeze, "Now how about you help me up and we keep going? You promised me a view."

She smiled and slipped under his arm. Grabbing his wrist and waist, she lifted him to his feet once again. They headed onward. For hours they trudged ever upward, around bubbling streams and broken crags. Kensy paused to survey the surroundings, "I think we're almost there. Shouldn't be far now." Exhausted, they continued forward, one step at a time.

Loose rocks tumbled down the hill as the solitary pair shuffled up the steep ledge that jutted above from the canopy. They ducked beneath the overhang that protected the majestic bluff. Stepping out into the softly glowing night air, they gazed over the landscape. Exaggerated hills rolled in all directions for miles, coated with dense plumes of lush vegetation. Looming above them, an enormous planet rose over the horizon accented by two pearl like bodies that floated among the stars in the dark green tinted sky.

"Well, I suppose it's not a terrible vacation spot. Nice view, but they really need to work on the hospitality and accommodations," Jackson jested. He winced as pain surged from his wound.

"Let's take a seat." Kensy guided him back under the overhang, easing him down against the rock face. She spoke, slumping down beside him, "The nights here seem to take forever." She stared out at the seemingly unmoving stars. "My sense of time is completely shot." She glanced to him as he passed over the uncapped flask from his vest, "Where do you think we are? Definitely on a moon, but Galliane didn't have any moons." She took a sparing sip and handed it back.

"No idea," he shrugged, "We survived getting shot through a psionic doorway, through space, unprotected, in the midst of a horde of homicidal machines. Stranded, wounded, hungry, tired. This is so far out of my realm of expertise.... Must be a Tuesday." He took a small swig from the flask before tucking it away.

Kensy giggled. The smile dropped from her face as doubts began to nag at her thoughts, "Do you really think they're looking for us? What if they don't find us?"

He looked down at her wringing hands. He reached into her lap and pulled one of her hands to his knee. There he laced his fingers through hers, "They're coming. I promise." He caressed the back of her hand with his thumb. He tilted his head with a smirk, "And then we can give them crap about being late to the party." She smiled at the thought. Slouching onto his shoulder, she let the moments melt away.

As they began to doze, a familiar engine purr descended over them. Kensy was jolted toward alertness as Jackson tensed up. The silhouette of a small ship coasted into view at the edge of the bluff. The side door slid open abruptly. Stepping onto the precipice, Neira raised her chin and placed her hands on the top edge of her plated skirt, "Hope you two aren't getting too comfortable. Slacking time is over." Kensy bolted to her feet and hugged Neira, "Whoa there, Turbo, this is a cliff."

Kensy stepped back, "How did you find us?"

Neira shook her head, "Ask the brain-trust back on the ship. I'm just the escort." Visiri scanned Jackson as he staggered to his feet. Kensy dropped back to aid him. Neira gave him a scrutinizing glare, "Not dead yet? Hmm. Not bad." Kensy helped him into the shuttle.

Neira stepped in behind them and pulled the door shut. Jackson tilted his head back against the seat, "Not for a lack of trying." Neira raised an eyebrow skeptically.

She sauntered up to the co-pilot's seat, "Tell them we've caught a pair of comets and are headed home. Have medical on standby."

Chapter 50

Trust

"I trust that someday you will find your prince."
~ Psionica Ellise Neru, deceased

Light flooded into the rooms as Kensy and Jackson each stared into their private conference screens. Firm but kind, Doctor Tyronis began to wrap up her talk with the recovering captains, "Now, you've both had your injuries treated, but it will take time for your bodies to accept and finish the healing process. Given what you went through, I am willing to let you stay in your respective quarters, but I expect you to use this time to rest. I have given Lieutenant Bryden strict orders that you are to be left undisturbed. And I don't want to either of you roaming around or I will order medical restriction." She tapped a stylus against her desk, "Get some rest. We will talk more tomorrow." The two captains nodded in acknowledgment. She reached forward, disconnecting from the call, leaving Jackson and Kensy with only each other.

Kensy rested her head on her hands and her elbows on the desk, "How are you feeling?"

Jackson stretched slightly, "Sore but otherwise fine. Doc said the regen was easy thanks to that little bit of magic you wove back there." He leaned back in his chair. She blushed at the memory, *I trust you.* He shifted his weight onto one of his chair's armrests, "How are *you* doing?"

She contemplated her response for a moment, "I thought a couple times there that one or both of us weren't going to make it. I'm really happy I was wrong." She bashfully bowed her head, "I don't think I could do this without you. Running a ship, having so many people depend on me...."

"I think you're too hard on yourself. You've never let me down." He could sense her through the walls, their heartbeats still echoing each other softly. He glanced between the source of the sensation and the screen. Did she feel it too? "Get some rest. It's been a long day. You'll feel better in the morning."

She brushed the hair from her face, "You're right." She smiled, "Good night, Jack."

He returned the smile, "Good night, Kensy." The screens turned off leaving each in the silence.

Kensy pushed back from the desk and began to change into her nightgown. Butterflies filled her chest as she glanced toward his room. The hem of the satin gown danced around her legs. She closed her eyes. The residual sensations of the link persisted. She cast it aside. Sitting down on the edge of her bed, she began to brush her hair out.

Jackson stared at her wall for several minutes. Even without seeing, he knew she was walking around the room in her nightly routine. Drawing in a deep breath, he rose from his chair. He tried to force the thoughts of her aside as he peeled his shirt over his head and tossed it toward the lounge. Running his thumb along the waistband of his pajama pants, he subtly shifted them into a more comfortable position. He sauntered toward the bedside when a strange sensation struck him. A knot formed near the center of his chest. He pressed his hand flat against the source of the discomfort, his heart. Looking down, he furrowed his brow as the faint crackle of red electricity sprung forth from his chest and he collapsed on top of the covers.

Kensy looked up at the drifting crystal pillars. Storm clouds crept overhead, illuminating the sky with flashes of lightning. The churlish wind tossed her ponytail about wildly. Sorrowfully, she stared into the abyss as the darkness below the floating marble floor seemed to crawl and claw toward her. A sigh escaped her lips, "Back here again...."

"Kensy?" a voice called from behind. She turned to look at him in his dashing olive and black officer's uniform, "What's going on? Where are we?" Jackson stopped on the stairs, just shy of her. She stared at him, bewildered. Jackson gave her a scrutinizing glance before inspecting the maze of ruins and the view beyond. "What is this place?" Tears welled up in her eyes as she hesitantly reached toward him. Her fingers met with the fibers of his jacket. She gasped, clasping her hand over her mouth. She searched her thoughts for an explanation, *nothing*.

"You're not a mirage. Are you really here?" She asked softly.

He threw his hands in the air, "Where is here?"

A giggled emanated from behind him. He spun around to face an ebony-haired woman with silver eyes smiling up at him. "Ooh, he's cuter in person. I approve." Immediately, Kensy's face flushed red in embarrassment. The woman lightly skipped up the stairs past him in her distinctive plum and charcoal Psicorp uniform. She leaned in and whispered loudly. "So, has he figured it out yet?" Kensy and Jackson stared at her in confusion for a moment. She threw her hands into the air emphatically, "Really?! Glaciers move faster than the two of you!"

"Elle, how—." Kensy started.

Jackson pointed to the woman, "Elle? *The* Elle?!"

A strange pulse rippled out from Elle's body. She struggled to catch her breath, "Damn. We have less time than I thought." She looked toward Kensy with a pain in her eyes, "There's never enough time." Suddenly she lashed out, striking into the center of her friend's chest. Kensy blinked out of sight before Jackson could react. He stared at her in stunned silence. Contending with some unseen force, she clutched at her chest.

Regaining his wits, Jackson's expression melted to determination, "What did you do to her?"

With labored breath Elle stumbled onto the stair, "I've... sent her ...elsewhere. And I will do... the same to you... momentarily. I... have to warn you...." She looked up at him, her very appearance tattering before him, "She's not strong enough yet." She tilted her head and gritted her teeth, trying to still the force that battled against her internally, "The Vagabond... is more than you can imagine." She cried out in agony, "And he is not the only evil. Some shadows persist... even through the light." Fighting to stand tall, her eyes met with his, "You have to promise. *Never* let go. *Ever.* Promise!"

He nodded without understanding, "I swear."

Elle relaxed between arduous and weary gasps. She shuffled up to him, "Find the way out."

Her hand cracked into his sternum and he felt the world shift through him. The air left his lungs as he slammed flat onto his back amidst a darkened forest. He rolled to his side, blinking the disorientation away. With a grunt, he pushed the racking pain from his mind. His hands pressed into the rugged ground as he crawled to his knees, "Kensy? Kensy!" he shouted over the rumbling thunder. He lifted his head and squinted into the stormy woods as the faint sound of his name carried across the wind. "Kensy!"

In the distance, a flash of violet light shot into the air, exploding a falling tree into splinters. He stepped up and pushed into a run. Low branches cut at him as he dodged between trees and grotesquely sprawling undergrowth. More bursts of energy volleyed through the air. His pace quickened. He called out again, only for his voice to be lost against the roiling storm. He could feel the intense echo of her distressed heartbeat rising alongside his own.

Sliding into the clearing behind her, he stopped to catch his breath. Kensy snapped toward him, her glittering hands raised together in preparation for releasing another burst. Her hands trembled and tears stained her face. Dropping the power, she ran to him and threw her arms around him without thinking. He embraced her tightly in return. She whispered, "I thought I was alone again."

"Not anymore," he rubbed her back, staring into the landscape. The ground shattered and fell away as writhing black prominences and red lightning slowly devoured the horizon. He pulled her shoulders away and grasped her hand firmly, "We have to move." She glanced behind. He squeezed her hand tightly, "Time to go." Hand in hand, they broke into a heart-pounding stride through the treacherous wilds.

Searching for some sign or sense of escape, Jackson caught sight of a strange structure past the treeline. He guided them toward it, hoping for a respite from the consuming shadows. An ornate towering archway rose from a large tiered dais. Within two heavy doors sat ajar, backlit by a golden light. The pair dashed through the waiting portal.

Jackson released her hand and swung back to slam the doors closed behind them. The sound resonated around the chamber. He looked down at his hands and uniform, confused. Black gloves tucked into the sleeves of a dapper navy jacket. Champagne colored accents trimmed his cuffs and collar. Finely braided ropes wrapped loosely around his shoulders and a silky sash draped across his body. He looked down at his black matte slacks and shiny boots. From his belt hung a sheathed ceremonial sword.

He turned to Kensy, but words escaped him as he looked upon her. Layers of gossamer pink fabric fell in elegant lines over her lithe figure. Soft strawberry blonde ringlets cascaded down her back. Every movement was highlighted by the shower of glittering jewels that adorned her face and figure. Her arms were unaltered and unarmored by the familiar trappings of her clasp and bracer. She fidgeted anxiously, lost in thought. "No, no, no... this is wrong. This is all wrong."

He grasped her by the shoulders, "No matter what this is. We have to find a way out."

Another tear streamed down her face, "You don't get it. You shouldn't be here. This shouldn't be possible! But you're here and it's my fault!"

"It doesn't matter. Trust me, I will lose my shit about this later. But right now we have to figure out how to get out of *this*." He lifted her chin, "We can worry about how and why after we are safely back on the ship."

She looked at him with a weeping smile, "We *are* on the ship. We're dreaming." She turned out of his grasp, "You're here because of the link I forged between us. I did it to save you, but now it's endangering you." She sniffled, "We have to break the link."

Jackson scowled at her, "And how are we supposed to do that?!"

She pivoted back, and drawing a deep breath, held out her right arm. A jeweled bracelet jangled around her wrist, "Sever the connection." She blinked nervously, her hand trembling, "Cut the clasp and maybe we can stop it."

"Are you out of your mind? I am not cutting your arm off." He shook his head in disbelief. "The clasp isn't even visible in here." He held his sword hilt firmly in its sheath, "No! There has to be another way that doesn't involve harming you."

She pleaded with him, "Please, I don't know what else to do! So far, we are retracing all of my nightmares—in order. I can't go back to the next one! I can't...."

Jackson stood in quiet contemplation for a few long seconds, "If this is a dream... then we change it." He grasped her hand once again with determination. "We find someplace else to go, make our own way." He wiped the tears from her face with his glove, "Do you trust me?"

"I do," she nodded, "I trust you." She blinked as her thoughts wandered, *More than that, I think I love you.* She smiled softly, "I trust you." They both jumped as the door rattled. Tiny shadowy tendrils began to seep hungrily around the edges. Jackson tugged her into a run up the majestic grand staircase leading inward. Extravagantly carved pillars slowly gave way to soaring trees. The ground changed from carefully sculpted stairs to rising earth the farther they climbed.

Light began to flicker through the branches. The ground leveled out for a moment. Stopping to gain their bearings, they exchanged glances. Their clothes had changed once again. Jackson found himself dressed in khaki cargo pants with his plain black dress shirt and leather jacket. Kensy spun around to examine the surroundings, her flowing peridot shirt swirling around her torso. The left sleeve bunched slightly at the top of her bracer while the right side obscured the returned clasp. Her vest hung unzipped over the shirt and her dark pants tucked neatly into her boots.

"Okay, this is different... where do we go now?" She looked at him with pleading eyes.

A confident smirk crossed his face, "I know where we are." He kissed the back of the hand he held. "Come on." He darted up the hill with her in tow. Her eyes lingered on him as they ran, *Ever my shining knight. It could be the link, but I feel so drawn to him. How does he find so much strength to move forward?*

Jackson swept aside a low-hanging branch as he headed for a flicker of metallic sheen that beckoned him onward. Kensy slowed her pace as she beheld the object of their pursuit, causing him to tug at her arm. The silhouette of the Illusive waited patiently, its doors open. Jackson nodded toward the silent ship, "Come on. Let's get out of this nightmare."

Cautiously, she followed him inside. "Jack, how is this going to get us out?" she turned her worried gaze to the ground.

"Hey," he brushed her hair back from her face, "we'll figure it out." He swallowed hard, "When I saw the ship go over the edge of that cliff... I didn't think there was any way you were coming back. But you survived. You found a way. And this ship lead us exactly where we needed to go. That's what I'm counting on." He cradled the back of her head with his fingers and she looked up at him. He breathed deeply, "We'll find a way. We've come this far, let's find where we need to go." He felt the pull in his chest. His heartbeat quickened in time with hers.

Suddenly, the doors slammed shut. He wrapped an arm around her instinctively as the moan of metal echoed around them. Subtly, the ground began to shift and tilt. He pulled her into a corner where the sidewall separated them from the cockpit. Clutching her to his chest, he braced them both for the inevitable impact. Slivers of glass and metal erupted up the small corridor as the ship nosedived into the unknown. Kensy buried her face in his shirt until they finally ground to a stop.

She looked up at him. He smiled through the wince of pain, "What is it with this ship and rough landings?" Gravity now pulled her against him. They remained still for a moment, waiting for another shift or creak. When is did not come, she carefully pushed herself to her knees and crawled off to the side, allowing him to sit up. "If this was real, that would definitely leave a bruise." He shrugged it off, moving to the edge of the small hallway. Backing over the lip, he glanced down. Mindful of his positioning, he released, dropping onto the console below. He beckoned to her, "I'll catch you."

She followed his lead, falling into his arms. He gingerly set her down alongside him and looked at the fractured windows. "Are we really going to do this again?"

He rubbed her arm, "This time," he stepped onto the window frame, guiding her to stand with him, "I'm not letting go." They held each other's hands tightly and locked eyes in that suspended moment, as if nothing else existed. The frame snapped beneath their feet, sending them cascading from the confines of the cockpit.

He gasped sharply as he sat upright. The room was cold and dark, his covers wrinkled under his collapsed weight. He sprung to his feet and ran for the door. It slid out of his way abruptly. His eyes met hers as she staggered back against the frame in relief. She slumped to the ground burying her face in her nightgown covered knees. He exhaled, pressing his back to the foyer wall. *The nightmare is over. We made it. Together.*

Chapter 51

This Moment

*"Courage is not the absence of fear, but rather the ability
to move forward in spite of it."*
~ ancient human proverb

The doctor tucked her brown and silver streaked hair behind her left ear. With a casual stride she exited her office into the main sickbay. Stopping at the end of the beds where Jackson and Kensy sat, she patiently waited for the attending tech to finish changing Jackson's bandages. She tapped her datapad on her leg in contemplation, "It would seem, according to the sensor logs, that neither of you had quite the restful night I had ordered. Would you like to explain what was going on?" She looked between them.

Jackson sat up, slipping his uniform undershirt over his head, "Stress. Guess getting beamed through space and stranded for a few days may have had some lingering... side effects." Carefully, he slipped his arms into the sleeves of his uniform jacket and pulled it up onto his shoulders.

Kensy smiled at him gratefully before solemnly turning to Doc, "I had another episode. I think it may have caused a sympathetic response in the commander because of the powers I used to stabilize him." She glanced down for a moment, "I didn't have the dampeners up high enough, a mistake I won't repeat."

Doc glanced between the two of them skeptically, "All right. No medical restriction this time, but I will be keeping a closer eye on this. If it happens again, I want you both down here for full physical and psychological evaluations." She sighed and walked back to her office.

Jackson clicked his belt as he stood up. He smoothed the wrinkles from sitting and followed Kensy from the room. She looked down at her palm-sized datapad, "Hmm, looks like Daniel is setting up a meeting in the war room. We should probably head up." Her lips curved into a gentle smile, but her eyes channeled other emotions. He saw the sorrow she veiled behind the brave front, *Is it because of Elle? Was there something in the nightmare that I missed? Why does she feel the need to hide it?*

He stuffed his hands in his pockets as they walked toward the elevator. The familiar face of their chief engineer rounded the corner, nearly running them over in his intensely focused state. Allen looked up suddenly, pausing just shy of the pair, "Oh, fantastic! I was hoping I would be able to catch up with you before the meeting." He stepped alongside Kensy, "I hadn't gotten a chance to check in with you lately. How is the stasis device doing? Any problems?" He pointed at her bracer.

She shook her head, "Nope. Checked it this morning, still humming away. There's a little color fluctuation toward the center, but that's kinda been the norm."

He noted down her feedback, "Neira forwarded your device schematics to me. I've been working on something, but there is still a lot of work to be done on it before I would feel comfortable testing it practically." He tucked his notes away, "Let me know if anything changes."

She tipped her head respectfully toward him, "Thank you, Allen. You do more than I could hope to ask for and your insights are greatly appreciated." They reached the waiting elevator. Jackson held out one hand to allow Kensy in first. The two men swept in to the lift on either side of her.

"Aside from the technical, how are you two?" His demeanor turned grim, "I heard things turned pretty ugly down there."

Jackson blinked and sighed in exasperation, "I am going to be answering that question for weeks, aren't I?" He scoffed and glanced down to Kensy, "We're good?" She nodded in agreement as he shrugged, "See? We're good."

Allen leaned toward Kensy, "You know, you two were stranded for about three days. It is perfectly acceptable to take a full day, or three, to recover."

Kensy chuckled and patted his arm, "It's okay. We're fine."

The elevator opened on the appropriate floor and they filed out in the direction of the war room. They quietly proceeded down the hall to the chamber. The main doors whooshed open at their approach. Daniel looked up from the main table with a grin, "Ah, our illustrious leaders' return!" Beside him stood Doctor Micah Hirayama with her straight black hair and olive eyes. Neira and Rasken glanced up from their small talk. Daniel surveyed the room, "I think that's everyone." He looked to Micah, "If you want to begin...."

She tapped her fingers across the tabletop, "Thank you, Lieutenant. After downloading the databanks from Galliane Prime, I had my team dig into the files." She brought up a strange looking schematic, "This is what caught my attention and evidently the attention of the expedition staff. Hundreds of years ago, rumors circulated of an Artificial Intelligence designed to help the early space-flight humans survive the harsh reality of outer-space. Now, most of the rumors considered it a failed pipe dream, an uncompleted fantasy of the tech community. These schematics are for an AI core unlike I have ever seen before.

"It would be capable of consuming a wide variety of environmental and material inputs for the purpose of self-learning. Given that we can write intelligent algorithms, this might not seem like much, but the scale of this thing is mind-blowing. They wanted to create the ultimate protector, something that could evaluate any threat and adapt even if that meant changing itself."

Neira raised one eyebrow, "You are telling me that this *thing,* that has survived all this time, murdering hundreds if not thousands of people, is a computer designed to save us?"

Micah lifted her chin, "And I think it has killed far more than that. Something went wrong in the Vagabond's self-evolution. On Galliane, one scientist theorized that it had wiped out the entire original human population. They were a flourishing people, spread far and wide across the planet, until they all just disappeared."

Kensy furrowed her brow, "Is it possible that they could have traveled off-world like we did? Through one of the archways?"

Allen leaned forward on the edge of the table, "From everything I've gathered on the structure of the arches, they would have had to been activated by a psionic—."

"—which were practically non-existent back then," she cut back in.

Rasken popped a bubble, "So we know where it came from. We know it's freaking old. We know it's a bat-shit-crazy homicidal bucket-of-bolts. But where is it? Back on Galliane?"

Micah shook her head, "I don't think so. I found several references to a station that used to be close by, Axys Nine. It was also mentioned in the logs that Reily recovered. The station was moved away from Galliane, then vanished. I think it moved itself to the station."

Jackson rubbed his forehead, "So we just need to confront a homicidal computer on a long-lost station that could literally be anywhere in the galaxy." He sarcastically derided, "Why didn't you say it would be so easy?" The officers looked around in awkward unease.

Thoughtfully Kensy replied, "Clearly we need to investigate further, but we know our enemy now." Subtly Daniel slid his finger over the intercom control as she spoke earnestly, "When this all began we stumbled in the dark, blind to the nature of the thing that sought to destroy us. We faced fear and loss. We witnessed firsthand the devastation that he leaves in his wake. But we have survived his onslaught. We have found where he began. With the knowledge we now, have just imagine what we can do from here. Don't lose heart. I know it seems like so much is still beyond us, and the road will not be easy, but we will not give up. We will not allow more innocents to fall victim to monsters in the dark. We stand on the edge, unwavering in our determination, stronger together. We will find the Vagabond, and we will end his reign of terror."

Cheers erupted over the nahdvi, startling Kensy as Daniel lifted his finger from the control with a smirk, "I think it's safe to say that we're all with you, captain." Kensy's face flushed red. Politely, she bowed out of the room.

"Really, Bryden?" Jackson shook his head.

Daniel shrugged innocently, "What? It was a good speech."

Neira nodded to him, "Yeah, not bad."

Jackson sighed, "You're both impossible." He departed the room hastily. As the door closed behind him, he looked up, "Maggie, where did she go?"

"The psilyria has gone to the captain's observation deck on the top floor, outside your quarters." The mechanical voice promptly answered.

He quickened his pace to the elevator. "Take me there." He stepped in and pivoted to face the door, "Does she seem upset?" He tapped his heel impatiently against the floor. *She finally felt comfortable enough to take command, and he had to pull something like that. Damn it, Bryden.*

"She displays signs of being flustered; however, there is no indication of distress in her biorhythms," Maggie responded.

The few seconds of transportation were almost painfully slow to him. His heartbeat began to race anxiously. The doors opened into the foyer. Drawing a deep breath to settle his own

371

nerves, he stepped out. Quietly, he sauntered around the short wall that separated the observation deck from the rest of the floor. The decor of the room was refined but comfortable. Couches, chairs, and small tables dotted the perimeter, accented by lush greenery and exotic flowers. A railing ran the length of the forward virtual window. Kensy leaned against it, staring out into the ocean of stars.

He walked up beside her, placing both hands on the rail, "Sorry about that. Bryden can be a real pain when he thinks he's being clever."

She bowed her head, "Did you follow me up here just to apologize for him? It's fine. I just wasn't expecting it." She chuckled, "I probably would have choked if I had intended to give a speech to everyone. So, maybe it was better that way."

He hesitated, "It might not have been the *only* thing I wanted to say...." He cleared his throat, "I... about last night...." *Oh, come on! You sound like a bumbling idiot. Just spit it out already.* "I wanted to ask, is that what the nightmares are always like?" *Dodge the subject, oh yeah. That's gonna get you really far....*

She toyed with her fingernails, "Well, *usually* I'm alone."

"You sounded surprised that I wasn't a mirage...," he stared intently at her expression.

She bit at her lip, "Well, yeah." She let out a deep sigh, "The last time I dreamed about the... palace ...there was an image of a person that led me safely away from Elle and out of the dream. I thought it was you, but when I got closer to him, he disappeared, just like a mirage." She glanced to his chest, avoiding eye-contact.

He straightened his posture as he turned to her. Very gently, he lifted her chin. Their heartbeats raced in tandem. "If you ever need me, even to escape crazy nightmares, just say the word," he brushed her bangs aside, tucking them behind her ear. Her thoughts raced wildly, *Tell him! Tell him how you feel. Tell him you are falling in love with him!*

His hand slipped to the nape of her neck. Measuring every breath, they slowly drew closer together. She rested her hand loosely against his chest as she looked up into his intense bright blue eyes. He caressed his other hand down the back of her arm. Surrendering to the moment, he pulled her tightly against him, pressing his lips against hers. Fluidly, she slid her arms around his body.

Her eyes closed as she submersed herself in the sensation of his kiss. Overwhelmed by emotion, her mind flooded with a surge of fear. Suddenly, she felt herself ripped from his embrace by the crumbling ground. Slowly, she fell into the churning storm below, unable to act. Tears streamed from her eyes involuntarily.

Jackson pulled back from the kiss and wiped the tears away with his thumb, "What's wrong?! Did I do something wrong? Did you not want that?"

She smiled at him sweetly, "It's nothing, just a shadow of my past. I promise, I'll tell you about it someday, but right now, ...I just want to forget and be here with you, in this moment." She threw her arms around his neck and kissed him fiercely. Slowly, the lights dimmed on the deck, leaving them alone under the stars.

The Starchaser Lexicon

POWER WORDS

Heiga (he-gah) – a sensory wavy intended to assess general shape and integrity of a space it is cast into

Heiras Heiga (hear-ass he-gah) – a radar-like sensory wave meant to allow a psionic to determine the details of their environment by creating varied resonance when it encounters obstacles

Ivani raga khiran (ih-van-ee rag-a key-ran) – an ability to bolster the strength of a manifestation such as a barrier

Ivanigis (ih-van-eh-giss) – a manifestation held close to the body, creating an armor-like covering for the psionic

Ivanigis ahri (ih-van-eh-giss are-ee) – extension of the basic personal armor barrier to encompass another individual within extremely close proximity

Raga ami velgihr (rag-a-am-ee-vel-gear) – the growing expansion of a manifestation, often used in conjunction with barriers for the purposes of casting hostiles away from the point of origin (like a tidal wave)

Volgihr (vol-gear) – a pulse released into a thundering shock wave to push back hostile creatures and constructs

Yhir Nu'hai (year new-high) – an attack manifestation in which arcs of energy bombard a target repeatedly

TECHNOLOGY

Comm screen – a console that focuses on the processing of communications and data

Daecellyon (day-cell-ee-on) ore – a power-rich, naturally occurring, metallic compound that when properly refined generates vast sums of energy ideal for applications such as space flight

Diklodemir (die-clow-dem-meer) – a medicinal substance most commonly used to treat internal burns caused by implant ruptures, other uses still under investigation

Evo-suits – a heavily engineered suit of armor focused on providing the wearer with protection from extreme environmental hazards such as, volcanic heat, arctic cold, radiation, or the vacuum of space

Flexiglass – a clear and flexible 2 dimensional material which can be used to display data like a note or image, often used as a more transferable medium between disparate parties

GC-L48 container – a commonly used containment device used in a variety of industries for its incredible durability, superior performance, and portability

Hard boards – the physical, unchanging control panels for starship flight, often augmented by an additional set of holographic overlays and virtual control devices

Holo– (technology) – devices that manipulate light and matter to construct 3 dimensional holographic representations of data, such as a holopad (handheld) or a holotable (immovable display center)

Nahdvi (nod-vee) – a compact communication device that can maintain long range up-links; capable of monitoring and transmitting wearer's vital statistics as well as limited environmental telemetry, can also provide limited emergency assistance in the form of distress signals, synaptic pain control and black box transcription; the device creates a synthetic bio-fusion with the wearer and is telepathically responsive. Biologically fuses to the wearer in order to retain an extremely complex biometric encryption matrix, making the device utterly unaccessible to anyone other than the intended user

Nanite – a nearly microscopic machine, often used in the medical field for tasks such as tissue reconstruction, shrapnel removal and infection neutralization

Neural inhibitor – an external device that attaches to a patient in order to regulate brain activity and prevent damage from energy fluctuations as with psionic burnout and stroke-like events

Stellar Industries CS675 Gravinine (gra-vin-nene) Ultra Bike – widely considered the ultimate for single person, multi-environment transportation, this bike is stylish, fast, and harder to come by than most would prefer, can carry one passenger *if* you feel like sharing; the premier model was equipped with such luxuries as GSX Microflex-plate tires and a self-sustaining clash core power module

Suspension chamber – a vertical tube filled with specialized fluids to aid in medical procedures, a harness system to keep the occupant in a weightless state, and numerous tubes and conduits through which necessary substances are delivered to the occupant during the procedure. Often used for assisting in the injection of plasma-like substances for weaponized implants to prevent damage to the subject

ARSENAL

Ausk-Chelkai (osk shell-kai) – a large paired set of wing-like blades originally created by an alien race, known to be extremely difficult to learn how to wield and even harder to master

Chimera – an experimental biological weapon intended to be able to identify friend from foe and adapt accordingly

Combat exosuit – a heavily engineered suit of armor designed to protect the wearer while providing external assistance to aspects such as perception, reflexes, strength or endurance

Control clasp – a complex maze of nodes and wires that are implanted directly into a psionic's body in order to protect the user, regulate the biological impact of their power draw, and to refine and amplify their latent abilities

Nordux Crystals – a highly volitile crystalline substance, initially designed for demolitions work but widely outlawed after it was determined to be too dangerous to handle and too unpredictable for common use

Psiblade – a manifestation created by a psionic that resembles a blade such as a sword or dagger for the purposes of combat

Psionic (sigh-on-ick) – an individual with a natural ability to filter the background energies of the universe into various different forms according to their will and training, often characterized by a redundant nervous system that seems to be used exclusively for conducting these ambient energies, often

feared and dangerous if not properly trained; also referring to things of a psionic nature i.e. abilities, equipment, or an organization
Psi-walk – (master level manifestation) the psionic projects a representation of themselves, most of the time it can be only be used to observe things within a limited range from another perspective

PEOPLE & ORGANIZATIONS

ESFV Themiscyra (them-ess-key-rah) – a ship of the Terra Ascension Core Navy commanded by Captain Alex Hadarian
Kraydian (cray-dee-an) – a mysterious isolationist race, their clergy are often joked about as the universe's most sober denizens as they cannot tolerate fermented liquids exposed to air in their presence without adverse physical reaction
Legacy Flagship DeCadejra (dee-kade-drah) – a strange and beautiful alien warship at the heart of the Legacy Fleet, from which a great deal of humanity's interstellar ships were reverse engineered
Magthaeleon (mag-thay-lee-on) a.k.a. Maggie – the DeCadejra's advanced complexity engine and tactical assistant
Malckiev (mal-key-v) – a diminutive race of marsupial-esque creatures with a knack for tinkering, often overlooked for their size and broken common speech, they make fiercely loyal friends of those willing to spare the time; from somewhere past Rasktir (rask-tier)
Psilyria (sigh-leer-ee-ah) – (f) or psilyrian (m) a high ranking officer in the Psionic Security Investigation Corp; considered masters of their core power set, they are usually in command of small field tactical or training units
Psionic Security Investigation Corp – a specialized intergalactic military for the training of psionics; the go-to place for individuals who need assistance controlling their abilities; a.k.a. Psicorp

Sol System Defense Force – a branch of the Terra Ascension Core focused on protecting and maintaining the human home star system of Sol

Terra Ascension Core – the cooperative force of the human military between the Sol system and the colonies, often joined by those who wish to venture out to see the wider galaxy or simply to escape their home world or station

The Divergence – the common term for a period of about 100 years of rapid genetic change within the human race that gave rise the subraces of Terran, Solson, and Voidir

> **Solson (sol-sin)** – the heartiest of the human subraces, they developed in harsh higher gravity and high hazard environments; characterized by shorter, stockier physical builds, very thick leathery like skin and darker, ruddier tones in their skin and hair
>
> **Terran** – humans that tend to originate on Earth or earth-like environments, they have extremely varied body types, skin tones, and other physical features
>
> **Voidir (void-ear)** – often revered as the most elegant of the human subraces, they tend to originate in low or zero-gravity environments; their bodies have developed with a lighter and leaner physical structure, their skin has a faint shimmer to it that aids in reflecting of low-grade cosmic radiation; the subrace with the highest instance of psionics

The Graven (grey-ven) – a secretive society of elite intergalactic peacekeepers who enforce a "for the greater good" policy across the expanse of civilized space

The Illusive – a renowned smuggling ship that was in service from June of 547 CS to June 647 CS when it mysteriously vanished, placing its legacy firmly in the realm of urban legends and spacer ghost stories

The Nexus – the living embodiment of psionic energy and the conduit through which all the such power flows, often appears as strange cat-like creature with glowing eyes and a sharp looking body from which energy constantly flows

Zog – a hulking race of ape-like humanoids that specialize in cybernetics and begin augmenting shortly after birth; originally from the planet Kedag (ke-dag)

MISCELLANEOUS

Etra Vas – a card game featuring ten suits with five cards each for a total of 50 cards, the goal of which is to crown your court (lord, lady, and knight) with a matching raiment card or to prevent your opponent from completing their court with the appropriate naught card, played with a selection of cards called the Eternium deck

Icosahedron (ahy-koh-suh-hee-druhn) – a 20-sided polygon

Psilic (sigh-lick) Crest – the emblem of Psicorp

The Veil – the theoretical limit for all psionics, a barrier which if broken could potentially kill the psionic by flooding them with too much energy and thus frying their nervous system

A PASSION FOR STORIES

Since childhood Amanda "Amnie" Young has had a passion for storytelling, coming home from those first days of school with boundless excitement at learning she could make her own sentences. She grew up immersed in tales from books, movies, and eventually video games. With all of these different outlets for creativity and story expression, she often found herself torn between paths. Trying her hand at college majors, including creative writing, theatre, screenwriting, and information technology for multimedia, she tried to find what path would best suit her style of storytelling.

As a teen, and again later as an adult, she was introduced to tabletop role-playing games where she could join in collaborative story telling with friends. Empowered by faith, family, and friends, she began to bring her stories and dreams into being. You can check out more of her creative endeavors at:

Deviant Art   www.deviantart.com/stories-n-dreams

Twitter   @ArtbyAmnie & @Stories_nDreams

Twitch   www.twitch.tv/stories_ndreams

Patreon   www.patreon.com/Stories_nDreams

Kensy's journey will continue in …

THE STARCHASER CHRONICLES
Volume 2

Shadows of the *Past*

AMNIE ◆ YOUNG